THE TEST

Hollin withdrew a clear jewel from the leather pack. It was the size of his palm and cut with many facets. He held out the jewel and spoke in a language Gerin thought was Osirin. *"Iva trestalkiri paran yi dakhal sethu . . ."*

A spark of light flared at the heart of the jewel. At the same instant Gerin felt warmth ignite in his belly. It quickly worked its way outward into his arms and legs and up through his neck, as if he was being submerged in hot water. He felt the warmth in his skull and on his scalp; when it reached his face a faint amber light filled his vision, as if he were looking through a piece of colored glass like those in the windows of the hall. He looked down and saw that the jewel was glowing brilliantly with the same amber light.

Then the light was gone, both in his vision and in the jewel, as suddenly as it had appeared.

"By the Blessed Hand of Venegreh," whispered Hollin. "It is you."

Books by David Forbes

The Osserian Saga

Book One
THE AMBER WIZARD

DAVID FORBES

THE AMBER WIZARD

THE OSSERIAN SAGA • BOOK ONE

An Imprint of HarperCollinsPublishers

This is a work of fiction. Names, characters, places, and incidents are products of the author's imagination or are used fictitiously and are not to be construed as real. Any resemblance to actual events, locales, organizations, or persons, living or dead, is entirely coincidental

EOS
An Imprint of HarperCollins*Publishers*
10 East 53rd Street
New York, New York 10022-5299

Copyright © 2006 by David Forbes
ISBN-13: 978-0-06-082011-4
ISBN-10: 0-06-082011-X
www.eosbooks.com

First Eos paperback printing: April 2006

HarperCollins® and Eos® are trademarks of HarperCollins Publishers Inc.

Printed in the U. S. A.

10 9 8 7 6 5 4 3 2 1

My dad *loved* books. He never read fiction——he was pretty much a history and biography guy——but he would have been incredibly proud to see me in print. This is for you, Dad. I wish you could have seen it.

Contents

THE
AMBER
WIZARD

Sontel Girding Mountains

Arlosan
Uplands

Horon

Kaldas
Highlands

Farad

Brill R.

Ferondril R.

The Long Sea

Url-Azgish
(ruins)

Heart River

Soharel River

Irinil

Graymantle Mountains

Igrin Hills

Pellur

HELCAREA

Kirosi River

Plains
of
Drommon

Neiyes Mt. Kail

Moriteri

Nirovai
Deep

Kalemnon

ELLOHAR

Withered Hills

Avelnur

Serel

Gap of
Ellohar

Redh

Ghesevatas

HUNZAR

Mendan Mountains

DOREL

Rhosa

Mespa

Samaro River

Sun

Tumlaren R.

NEDDAR

Scale in miles

0   100   200   300

Map by David Forbes

OSSERIA

Fourteenth Century
of the Common Age

Uplands of Eithos

Cape Igaz

Hazi

Brendis Bay

Tieren's Fence

MALAGAR

Bay of Tassair

Theril River

Failian River

Lingul

Faranwood

Darron

KERYA

Muros

Maurelian Sea

Roumael River

Hallas Bay

Strait of Sechel

HARLAD

Londros

Cape Veilas

Marcarax

Hanadi

Saros R.

Brindal Haro

Athram

Landwall Mountains

TAGEREA

Tappan R.

Pomman R.

Brangaran

Valesh Peninsula

ARMENOS

THRENDELLEN

Taldos

Turen

Winding R.

Trothmar

Gedsengard Isle

Gulf of Gedsuel

Urkein

Candago R.

Cressan

Naevos

Ailethon

Neldemarien

Almaris

The Seawall

Pelkland Islands

Dian's Stair

Agdenor

KHEDESH

Tan Orech

Edonia

Azren R.

Halir Barellen

Lormenien

Tolthean

Istameth

Khedesh's March

Haranwaith

Orech R.

Indis R.

Orleth

Prologue

Prince Teluko threw back the flap of his tent and surveyed the remnants of his brother's once mighty army. A cold drizzle fell over the hills from low gray clouds. He wore no helmet or hood. Rain soaked his hair and pattered against the steel of his armor. He looked over his shoulder in the direction of Tanshe-Arat, the Home-in-Exile where his wife and daughter awaited his return. But he knew he would never see their faces or the beauty of his city again in this life.

Teluko closed his eyes and listened to the sounds of the army around him: weary men speaking in hushed tones, the quiet whickering of the horses, the creak of wagons moving across wet earth. His anger drained out of him, replaced by an overwhelming sadness. They would be obliterated by their enemy. They had already suffered two crushing defeats that had killed more than half of their men. The coming battle would be the last.

He heard steps behind him. Teluko opened his eyes and turned to face Suvendis, his chief war priest. "My prince, we should speak," said Suvendis. He regarded Teluko from beneath the crimson hood of his robe, pulled down low over his blue skullcap. He gripped the witchwood staff at his side with fingers so gnarled they seemed carved of wood themselves. His expression was stoic as usual, unflinching, but

Teluko knew him better than anyone save Suvendis's companion priests, and the prince could tell the older man was troubled. *And who would not be troubled in times like these?*

Teluko nodded and followed Suvendis into the priests' tent.

A servant hurried to Teluko as soon as he entered and offered a cup of wine. The prince took the cup and drained half of it, then dropped down into a small folding chair beside the long plank table, its scarred surface covered with maps and candles, where his other priests stood waiting. Teluko drank more of the wine, then held out his nearly empty cup. At once another servant appeared and refilled it.

The priests all regarded him with the same guarded expression Suvendis had worn. Teluko could sense their concern and worry. *They consider themselves to be more than the rest of our people, different and somehow better—and in some ways they are—but when faced with the annihilation of our race, they feel the same fear as we do.* They all bowed and took their places across from him.

The prince took another sip of wine. "Suvendis said we should speak."

"We need to plan for the morrow, my prince," said Hodentu, the youngest. "The Atalari will arrive by mid-afternoon. Most likely they'll deploy their front lines to the north and south in an attempt to contain our flanks."

"And what do you suggest?" asked Teluko. "There's nothing but open land behind these hills. If we don't stand here, then where? At the very foot of our homes?"

"My prince, we must do *something*," said Hodentu, his voice tinged with urgency and frustration.

"My brother lies near death," Teluko said. "His own priests have refused to let me see him. This is where he commanded us to come before he collapsed on the field. I have no authority to change that unless he dies or commands me to take control of our forces. There's nothing else to be done."

"The king's wound was a grievous one," said Odalend, his deep voice rumbling from the shadows of his hood like the grinding of boulders. He was a huge man, tall and broad and thick; his neck was nearly as big around as one of Teluko's thighs. "It has been five days since he was struck. I fear he may be dead and that his priests are holding that from us to keep the army from complete despair."

"My brother is not dead," said Teluko. "I would have felt his death. The bond between us is deep, deeper than even the closeness of twins."

"The king's priests have been working strange magic whose purpose I cannot fathom," said Suvendis. "When I was refused entry to the king's tent, I sensed powerful forces within. I don't know their purpose, and Nanjelkir told me nothing."

The name of Asankaru's chief war priest set Teluko's teeth on edge. Nanjelkir had refused Teluko entry to his brother's tent earlier, saying it was the command of the king that he receive no visitors.

"It's not fair," said Gythero, second in authority after Suvendis. "We have the right in this!"

"That doesn't matter," said Suvendis. "Might is all that is important, and might is the one thing we do not have this day."

"Fairness and rightness had never been part of our dealings with the Atalari," said Teluko. Their histories told that the Atalari had always hated and feared them. They could not understand why the People of Theros chose to live underground, and believed all manner of sinister motives for that choice, even after the reasons were explained to them. *Our eyes and skin do not love the sun's light or its heat,* Teluko thought. *We are better suited to the cool caverns beneath the mountains, and see best by the light of our lamps.* When they walked aboveground, it was in twilight and darkness. Why was that so difficult to understand?

When the Atalari discovered that Teluko's people could know their thoughts with a touch of the flesh, their initial distrust blossomed into fear and hatred. No matter that this power made learning the language of the Atalari simple, so that the two peoples could better understand one another. It was a power the Atalari did not have, something they had never before encountered, and it shook the confidence of their Shining Nation and filled them with dismay.

After a time there was open war between them. The People of Theros were driven from the North, out of the lands claimed by the Atalari, and created their Home-in-Exile.

The tent flap was thrown back and a figure entered unannounced, his hood pulled low to conceal his face.

"The king has awakened and summons his younger brother," said Tageluron, another of Asankaru's war priests.

"Lower your hood and bow to the prince!" demanded Suvendis. "It is your place to show respect, Tageluron!"

Slowly, the other war priest lowered his hood and inclined his head at Teluko.

The prince rose. "Tell my brother I'll be along soon. I haven't finished conferring with my priests."

"The king has commanded—"

Teluko raised his hand, but did not look at Tageluron. "I've given you my reply, and you *will not* question me. I am not yours to command, though you may think otherwise. Now leave us. We have important matters to discuss that do not concern you." He turned his back to Tageluron and took his seat.

Tageluron did not move. He was about to speak again when Teluko said, "If you do not leave *at once,* I'll have you whipped for disobedience. I am still a prince of our people, and you will obey me or be punished!"

His brother's war priest lingered a moment longer, then left the tent without another word.

"They grow arrogant beyond measure," said Suvendis.

"They follow my brother's lead." Teluko finished his wine and placed the empty cup on the table.

There was little more to say. The army was encamped on the eastern edge of the Beltharos, a wooded, hilly country that stretched all the way to the great cliff into which Tanshe-Arat had been delved. This is where they would make their stand when their enemy came. There would be no further retreat.

Suvendis and Gythero accompanied the prince to his brother's tent. It was the largest in the army and the only one dyed scarlet, with gold and silver patterns worked into the fabric. Framing the tent flap were two tall pylons of black belku wood carved with incantations of protection and words of blessing taken from the tablets of Theros himself, the Lord Father who first united the Nine Clans and made them a true people.

The rain had stopped. Gray tendrils of mist drifted above the ground and curled over the tops of the hills like specters of the dead.

After he was announced, Teluko went to his brother and knelt. "I'm glad you have recovered, my king."

Asankaru, propped up on a narrow bed near a glowing brazier beneath one of the three tent poles, gestured for his brother to stand. "Leave us," he said to the war priests and servants. "My brother and I must speak alone."

Teluko rose and looked at his brother steadily, the first time he had seen him in days. The king looked surprisingly hale. His wound was terrible: an Atalari spear had been driven completely through his upper chest, just below his collarbone. Teluko had not seen his brother fall—he and his legions had been furiously trying to keep their lines from breaking beneath the sheer weight of the Atalari onslaught— but when the hail and lightning abruptly stopped, he knew at once that something had happened to the king. Invigorated, the Atalari surged forward and hacked their way through their forward lines, splitting the army in two. The call for a retreat to these hills had come moments later, the final order given by Asankaru before he fell unconscious.

His wound was heavily bandaged in white linen that bound his left arm across his chest. Though thinner and with a fringe of beard along his jaw, the king's face was lively and full of color. His eyes, the same deep silver as his brother's, glinted beneath his dark brows. "You look well, my king."

"I have my priests to thank. If not for them I would have died."

"Suvendis felt strange energies here while your priests tended to your wound, but he didn't recognize the power they used. Is this some new thing they've devised? They would not speak to Suvendis, but if you—"

"I've no desire to speak of priestly powers," Asankaru said. "It matters not how they healed me; what matters is that I am healed and prepared to lead our people once again. But I've lost precious time. I summoned you so that you could tell me your plans for our victory against the Atalari."

"*Victory?* There are no plans for *victory,* Asankaru! All we can hope to do is hurt them enough before we're destroyed so that they won't take this war to our homes and slaughter our wives and our children!" A blinding rage rose in him. "How *dare* you speak of victory! It's your arrogance that has brought us to the very edge of ruin!"

The king's right hand clenched into a trembling fist. "Throw down your weapon and flee if you must, but the battle is not yet over, and I'll hear no more of defeat!"

"You may not wish to hear of defeat, but that is what we face. What you've brought us to. You thought your powers as a Storm King would swing the balance in our favor even against a mightier foe, but you were wrong. I *told* you this would happen, I *told* you my visions showed me this plan of yours was doomed to fail, but you wouldn't listen. Three times I dreamed of this doom. Three! Never before have I had three visions, but still you wouldn't heed me. Your faith has always been in *your* powers, *your* strength, but this time they are not enough. I know because I've seen it. Deny it all you want, but when the Atalari destroy us, it will be on your head."

Asankaru, his teeth clenched, said, "I could have you executed for what you just said."

"It matters little. If you don't, the Atalari soon will. But if you have me killed, it's because you're too weak to hear the truth. Certainly your sniveling war priests won't tell it to you." Teluko shook his head, his mouth suddenly dry. "If Father were alive, he would have never let you go to war."

"That's a lie! He's the one who told me that one day we would grow strong enough to reclaim what the Atalari had taken from us."

"I remember his words, Asankaru, and they were not spoken in earnest. He was trying to quell your hurt at finding we were not the mightiest people in the world. You were always proud, and his words were meant to soothe, not ignite a fire in you. If he'd known his words would lead to this, he would have bitten off his tongue before speaking them."

"You don't know—"

"No, Asankaru, I *do* know. I remember when you decided to field a great army to attack at the heart of the Atalari. 'They've all but forgotten us,' you said. 'If we strike quickly and kill their Matriarch, their army will crumble and turn inward to defend their borders. We'll be able to return to our lost homes and live in peace.' I thought it unwise but held my tongue. But after my visions I *did* speak out, only to have you accuse me of being craven. You listen to me when my visions suit your needs and ignore me when they do not. You have doomed us all."

"Your visions are not always clear," Asankaru said. "You have been wrong before." Some of the heat had left his voice, but anger still burned in his eyes.

"It's been many years since I was wrong about a vision," Teluko replied. "I am not wrong about this."

"Despite your words, you don't know how this will end," said his brother. "We *will* be victorious. I've not been brought back from the brink of death only to fail now."

"You delude yourself," said Teluko with disgust. He turned to leave, then faced his brother once more. "Perhaps you were right. Perhaps I was craven. If I'd been braver I should have killed you when you refused to listen to me. It would have been a small price to pay to save our people." Then Teluko stormed out of the tent without asking the king's permission.

Suvendis and Gythero hurried to catch up with the prince, whose sudden exit caught them unawares. "My prince, we heard shouting," said Suvendis. "What is the command of the king?"

Teluko's boots sank into the muddy earth as he marched back to his tent. He knew his priests had heard every word spoken, but they did not presume to point out that they had, waiting instead for him to speak.

He marched into his tent and shouted for wine, gulped down the full cup that was handed to him and flung it to the ground. "I knew what would happen, yet I followed him anyway," he murmured. "I am at least as guilty as he is. Perhaps more so, because I knew with absolute certainty how this folly would end, where Asankaru at least has the excuse of his terrible pride."

"My prince, are you all right?" asked Hodentu. "What did the king say to you?"

"Nothing that matters," Teluko said.

It rained again during the night, a heavy downpour that drummed noisily on Teluko's tent. He slept little, and the few dreams he had were dark and troubled. By morning the storm had passed, though dark clouds still hung in the sky, blocking the sun and leeching the color from the world, so that everything seemed sad and gray and dying.

He had heard nothing from Asankaru. He no longer knew what to expect of him. His brother was mad with his hatred of the Atalari; it consumed him like a fever. The prince did not understand it. Asankaru had never even seen an Atalari until he began his doomed campaign. Thousands of years had passed since the People of Theros had been forced from their homes beneath the mountains in the North, half a world away. The story was full of legend and myth, the true accounts lost over the long reach of time.

"My prince, we should pray before the battle begins."

He turned to face Suvendis, then nodded. "I'll pray to my father for guidance. I feel he's near me."

"Of course he's near. Our dead remain with us, to watch and protect us from the Unseen Powers."

"I wish he would appear to Asankaru and tell him what he has done is folly."

"My prince, you know that we cannot see the dead. They are here, but not as—"

Teluko smiled at the priest. "So earnest! Of course I know that. Although it's said the Atalari can sometimes see the spirits of our dead."

Suvendis scowled. "In the old scrolls it's written that the spirits they saw terrified them. They accused us of consorting with demons and other creatures of darkness. Their own beliefs are repugnant, if what's written is true. They believe their dead journey to some distant place where they live in the glory of their gods and wait to be joined by those still living once they die. I do not understand it. Why would they want to leave the world where they had lived?"

"This world is all I want after death. Once I am dead, I will return to Tanshe-Arat and watch and guard my wife and daughter."

"As it should be."

They knelt together, and Teluko prayed.

Father, protect our people in the days to come. I know this army will perish, but guard those we've left behind against our enemies. Asankaru has awakened their terrible might, and I fear in their blinding rage they will not stop until they've killed us all. How he wished for the power of his enemies, that he might speak to his father for just a moment.

He opened his eyes just as the war horns sounded.

The Atalari army would arrive within hours. Teluko wandered among his men, speaking small words of encouragement he hoped sounded sincere. His soldiers were not fools and knew they had little chance of surviving the coming battle, but a commander could not speak of defeat, no matter how certain it was. He did not speak of victory—such a lie was beyond him—but he told his men he believed in their bravery and the courage in their hearts. "We must be strong when the Atalari come," he said.

Asankaru did not leave his tent. The scouts who had sounded the war horns went immediately to the king upon their arrival and remained with him for a long while.

Word reached the prince that the Atalari cavalry had grown to more than three thousand, and that at least three thousand foot soldiers had joined the army since their last battle. Despair filled him when he heard the reports. *They will roll across us like an avalanche,* he thought.

"Have Echareil brought to me," the prince said to a servant. He pulled on his gauntlets and left his tent. A second servant handed the prince his helmet.

He mounted his warhorse and patted the animal's armored neck. "This will be our last ride together, I fear," he whispered.

He trotted toward the front lines on the northern flank. He had positioned two of his legions on low hills that swept upward to the west with a narrow valley between them, choked with brush and small trees. The Atalari would be forced to make a direct assault up the slopes of the hills to reach them. Teluko's archers would inflict heavy casualties, and the lines of entrenched soldiers would be able resist an uphill attack for a long time. But in the end the overwhelming numbers and magic of the Atalari would win the day. The powers of his war priests would not hold against the sorceries of their enemy.

But we will hurt them, thought the prince. *We will make them rue this day for as long as their memory endures.*

His war priests followed him on their black steeds. Neither the priests nor their horses wore armor of any kind. Each held his staff easily in the crook of an arm. They said nothing as they kept pace with the prince. He knew they were slipping into the trances that would ease their ability to call their magic and speak to one another with their thoughts, a power unique to those who underwent the secret rituals of their priesthood.

Some of the soldiers near him were joking. It was good to hear men laugh at a time like this, and the prince smiled.

His priests spread out in a line across the hills and stood completely still, as if time around them had stopped.

He heard men call out and looked to the east. Horsemen raced toward them, sounding their horns. They were Asankaru's scouts, and their appearance meant the Atalari were not far behind.

It did not take long for the Atalari army to appear. A line of armored horsemen formed the van, moving at a quick but steady pace. A low rumble like far-off thunder reached him a few seconds later. Even in the dim light their armor shimmered like rainbows, a sign of their inherent power, a shifting swirl of colors that the prince could not deny was beautiful to behold.

He felt a tightening in his chest. He heard a murmur run through the soldiers around him and saw them point toward the king's tent.

Asankaru had emerged in full armor, surrounded by his war priests. His left arm was no longer bound against him. The king looked at his army and raised his hands. His priests enclosed him in a circle and leaned their staffs toward him, the steel ferrules resting lightly on the sodden grass.

"Proud warriors of the People of Theros, this will be our final battle against our enemy!" His war priests used their powers to carry his voice across the hills so it sounded as if the king stood no more than a few feet away from each man. "There are some that would have you believe this battle cannot be won, that we have already lost. But I tell you that you are better than that! I know your hearts, I know what you are capable of doing! It was I who failed you. I was not strong enough to do what was needed, and I almost perished because of my weakness. But no more! I will not fail you again! Prepare yourselves! Victory is ours!"

He threw back his head and shouted their ancient war cry, *"Ei valros tehu Theros!"*

Teluko realized his brother was mad. There was no victory to be had here. Asankaru could not face what was about to happen. Even with the Atalari army rushing toward them like a flood of death, he continued to believe they could somehow win the day.

Perhaps he said what he did to lift the hearts of these men before they die, Teluko thought. He knew it was something he would never have been able to say. He could not have brought himself to utter such a terrible lie. The words would have choked in his throat. In that regard, Teluko thought his brother was much more suited to be king than he. He could not inspire men; he thought and spoke far too literally to win hearts.

Asankaru threw back his head and unleashed his power as a Storm King, the first born to his people in more than five hundred years.

Teluko saw the power pour up from the earth and through his brother's body. Crackling sparks of energy danced around Asankaru's head like a swirling halo of stars. Even from this distance, Teluko could feel the charge in the air; the hairs on his arms and the back of his neck stood on end. The clouds above his brother thickened and grew darker as he bent them to his will. Wind gusted toward the Atalari army, whose foot soldiers—their spears bristling like a moving forest of steel-crowned trees—were now visible behind the charge of cavalry.

Asankaru's war priests began an incantation. Teluko could sense the power on the hilltop surge to an almost unimaginable level. Their staffs shimmered with dancing blue light.

He heard Suvendis shout to him but could not make out the words, though it sounded like a warning or cry of surprise.

What are they doing? he wondered. He'd never seen anything like this before.

Then a vast amount of energy exploded from Asankaru. The force shook the earth. Echareil staggered and whinnied in fright as he struggled to keep his balance. Around the prince, soldiers toppled or fell to their hands and knees.

What have they done? he wondered. Never before had the war priests been able to augment Asankaru's powers as a Storm King. They were different magics drawn from different sources. What he was seeing should not have been able to happen.

They must have changed him when he was wounded and near death. The strange powers Suvendis had sensed—it was the only explanation. Something that altered him, or them, or both, so that their powers could be used together. He wondered what price his brother had paid for such a transformation.

He looked up and saw the result of this impossible blending of magics. It was as if an inky curtain of night had fallen across the hills. The storm clouds Asankaru had created were as black as pitch and spread across the sky like a growing stain. The dark air took on a greenish cast as lightning flashed within the clouds. The thunderclaps were immediate and deafening. The storm was larger by far than anything Asankaru had ever before created. It awed and frightened Teluko to witness it, and for a moment his heart fluttered with hope that they might indeed conquer their foes.

But I had three visions of our doom! he thought. Was it possible he was wrong, that he had somehow misread the dreams that had haunted him? *Perhaps it is only my own doom I saw, my own death in this place.* He doubted himself, and his powers, for the first time in years.

The magic of the storm continued to build, a charge in the air that rode upon the wind but was not truly of it. Lightning licked down from the clouds and struck the Atalari cavalry, followed by fist-sized balls of hail that smashed their helms and shimmering armor.

The prince looked at his brother and understood the price he was paying for such power. The king himself was little more than a blurry shape within the column of energy that roared up into the sky. The war priests kept their staffs aimed at the king, funneling their own power into his own. But it was too much—it would kill Asankaru if he continued. He simply could not contain it.

Three tornadoes spiraled down from the black clouds. They touched the ground and blasted dirt and debris into the air, then churned their way toward the front lines of the Atalari.

All around the prince the soldiers shouted, *"The Storm King! The Storm King!"*

Teluko whirled his sword above his head and cried, *"Asankaru! For the king!"* Then he spurred Echareil toward battle and wondered—truly wondered, for he no longer trusted his visions—how this day would end.

PART ONE

Power and Life

1

Gerin Atreyano moved with an easy stride across the castle's main practice yard, the toes of his boots kicking up whorls of dust from the bare patches of dirt scattered between clumps of dry brown grass. He carried a wooden sword in his right hand; his left was free. Practice today was with swords alone—shields were not permitted. He wore a leather jerkin under a half-sleeved shirt of chain mail, leaving his lower arms bare. His black, shoulder-length hair was covered by a plain steel helm with flared cheek-guards and an old round dent on the left side, just above the ear.

The heat was stifling, like the hot breath from an oven, but Gerin did his best to ignore it. He focused instead on his opponent. Anything else—the boys and soldiers talking and sparring in other parts of the yard, the clacking sound of wood striking wood, or a grunt as someone took a blow—was a distraction he could not afford.

Gerin scarcely blinked as he circled his younger brother. Therain panted and wiped sweat from his eyes with his free hand. His gaze darted about the yard, shifting from Gerin to the swordmaster and back to the older boy again. "Don't keep looking at me, Therain," said Odnir Helgrim, the swordmaster. With his bull neck, barrel chest, and shaved head, he seemed as solid and immovable as Paladan's Tower, in whose shadow he stood. "I'm not the threat. Concentrate on your brother. I'll wager if you look my way again, Gerin'll make you regret it."

Therain said nothing, but no longer glanced at Helgrim. He made several short thrusts at Gerin's sword, which his brother easily knocked aside since he was taller by several inches and had a longer reach. At twenty-two, Gerin was broad-shouldered but lean, with slender arms and long, agile legs that gave his movements a fluid, graceful flow. He had a narrow nose with an ever-so-slight bump in it at the bridge, and dark blue eyes set above wide cheekbones.

Despite being shorter, Therain weighed nearly as much as Gerin. He was built like the men from his mother's family, solid and strong, like a block of roughly cut stone, his features thick and blunt. He also had his mother's straight black hair and dark, piercing eyes.

"This isn't a mummer's dance," growled Helgrim as the brothers continued to circle one another. "By the gods above, you're supposed to be *fighting*!"

The two had been practicing for more than an hour. They were exhausted, but Helgrim's chiding spurred them into action. Gerin was certain his brother would attack, and he was not disappointed. Therain thrust at Gerin's left side, then pulled back when Gerin moved to parry—Therain then lunged toward his chest. But Gerin anticipated the move and was ready for it. He knocked Therain's sword aside with a vicious upswing, then drove the blunt tip of his weapon into his younger brother's stomach. Therain staggered backward and fell before he could regain his balance, landing hard on his back. He lay panting in the dirt, trying to catch his breath. He held his stomach painfully; it was not the first time he'd been struck there today.

Gerin stood over his brother and shook his head. "That's the second time I've knocked you down," he said. "What's wrong with you today? I think Reshel could give you a good whipping if she had a mind to."

"You're such an idiot," spat Therain.

"Why, because I keep beating you?"

Therain stood up and shoved Gerin hard in the chest, then left the yard, ripping off his mail and throwing it on the ground. When he was gone, the swordmaster folded his arms across his chest and stared at Gerin. Dark hair covered his arms like a pelt; old scars puckered his skin like runic characters. The tattoos on the backs of his hands—a circle within a circle—marked him as a Taeraten of the Naege, the most elite class of fighter in all of Khedesh. "You shouldn't taunt him, my lord."

Gerin wiped sweat from his face. "I was just kidding him a little. But he *was* bad today; even you have to admit that. And he won't learn if he's not pushed."

"I push Therain quite enough," said Helgrim. "He doesn't have the natural ability with a sword that you and your father have, but he's not as bad as you think." He scratched the side of his head, just above his ear. "Though today was an off day, I'll grant you."

"I've seen him practice with some of the guards. He seems pretty good with them."

"He is. It's just you he has trouble with."

"Then maybe he shouldn't fight me anymore. It doesn't seem to be doing either of us any good."

"Aye, we'll see. It's probably a good idea for the two of you to practice with others for a while, at least with swords. Although maybe I should have the two of you practice together with bows. Maybe he can show *you* a thing or two." Helgrim chuckled.

Gerin was not amused. He hated that Therain was better than him with a bow. Much better, actually. It gnawed at him like a bit of rot at the heart of a tree. And if he were to be completely honest, he had to admit that Therain was nearly his equal in battle strategy and tactics. His younger brother could be far too rash for his own good, taking chances that in a real fight would get him or his men needlessly killed, where Gerin was cool and methodical and took only carefully calculated risks. He would not deny, though, that his brother had some gifts in combat planning. Not that he would ever tell him that to his face.

But, by the gods, Gerin could whip him handily with a sword.

He picked up Therain's sword and mail from the ground. "I'm done for the day. It's just too hot to practice."

"Yes, my lord." Odnir spat into the dirt and wandered off toward the other boys.

Gerin carried the two swords and Therain's chain mail from the yard and entered the storeroom in the ground floor of Paladan's Tower. He removed his own mail shirt and jerkin, leaving only a damp, stained linen tunic covering his torso. His hair was matted to his head.

He craned his neck to look up at the spire after he exited the recessed archway that marked the tower's only ground-level entrance. Its dark reddish stone gave the tower a rusty look that contrasted starkly with the whiter color of the castle's curtain wall. He had not been up to the top of the tower for a long time. He shielded his eyes to better see the pinnacle. The original bell housing had been enlarged and the bell removed by Paladin Atreyano two hundred years earlier so he could create an observatory to watch the motion of a red-tailed comet said to be a sign of the ending of the world. The bell was in a storeroom beneath the tower, crated and covered with ages of dust.

Gerin considered climbing the long spiral stair to the observatory—the view was spectacular, perched high above the sharp-edged side of Ireon's Hill over the Kilnathé River—then thought better of it. It was not quite noon, but the heat was already terrible, and he was tired from his practice.

He entered the inner bailey through the Genshel Gate, which opened to a narrow tunnel that passed beneath the inner defensive wall. Arrow loops lined the tunnel walls, and the ceiling contained more than a dozen murder holes.

Marble statues of Vendel and Ulgreth Atreyano flanked the steps that led to the main doors of Blackstone Keep.

Gerin felt a stirring sense of pride when he looked at the faces of his ancestors, the father and son who had taken a minor noble house and forged it into a power of the westlands that had eventually grown into a royal dynasty. *What great men they must have been,* he thought. *Men with vision, and the will to see it done.* He wondered if he would ever have such a bold vision for the future, as well as the strength needed to do whatever it took to make that vision real. Vendel and Ulgreth had been great men, to be sure, but they had also been unrelenting, single-minded of purpose, and at times cruel—necessary and perhaps inevitable, but it took a certain kind of mettle to do what they had done. Several competing noble houses that feuded with them for power had been eradicated at their hands, and the troublemaking Pashti had been mercilessly crushed. *That's why they were great,* he told himself. *Because they had the courage to make the hard decisions.* He wondered if he could make the same decisions himself. He wanted to be great, the greatest Atreyano who ever lived—yearned and lusted for it the way other boys his age lusted after girls—but when was the price simply too high? Was it even possible to know, or was that a question to be sorted out by those who came after to write the histories?

Protect the kingdom, your family, and yourself, his father had once told him. *And not always in that order. Sometimes you must look after yourself first in order to do the same for your family or the realm. And it may be that you will be called upon to sacrifice yourself so that the others may live. Such are the choices that may face you one day when you are king.* He'd never forgotten those words, spoken to him on his thirteenth birthday, when his mother and father had presented him with Glaros, the gleaming and ancient sword of the Atreyano heir, said to have been forged for Ulgreth at the command of his father when Ulgreth had been appointed the first Atreyano duke of Ailethon. Both the words and the sword were equally precious to him.

The recessed doors of the keep were forged of black iron with a golden stag's head raised upon them, the sigil of

House Atreyano. The arch and keystone of the doors had been cut from black rock said to have fallen from a star during the building of the castle, after the razing of the wooden Pashti fort that had once stood upon this hill.

There was no breeze coming through the open windows in his rooms. The curtains hung so still they might have been hammered from lead. He was washing, shirtless, over a standing basin when a Pashti serving girl arrived with water and bread. "Is there anything else you need, my lord?"

"No," he said, splashing water on his face. "This is all."

Gerin was chewing on a soft crust of bread when his father entered. Abran Atreyano had arrived only a few days ago, stopping at Ailethon to see his children on his peregrination through the westlands, visiting lords both great and small. Abran had been king of Khedesh for only six months before deciding to set out on his lengthy journey—his counselors had advised it was far too soon for a new king to be away from the capital for so long, but Abran would not be swayed. Once he made a decision, he rarely gave it thought again, and rarer still changed his mind.

He'd not always been so intractable. King Abran Atreyano was a hard man, often distant and gruff to his children, doling out his affection in carefully calculated doses—save for Reshel, his youngest daughter and favorite—yet he'd taught Gerin a great deal about governing, lessons he'd needed to know when Gerin's grandfather, Bessel Atreyano, had died suddenly, sending Abran to the capital of the kingdom and leaving Gerin as the new Duke of Ailethon. Gerin had been overwhelmed with his new duties—and still felt that way to a large degree—but without his father's sometimes harsh preparations, he would have been completely lost.

Abran had changed when Gerin's mother died of a terrible wasting sickness two years ago. Something in his father had perished with Vanya, and the few soft edges on Abran had become cold and hard. He became even more distant and withdrawn, losing himself for long hours in black, grim moods his family had quickly learned not to interrupt. Gerin wondered if the moods still took him now that he was king, but knew better than to ask.

He waited patiently for his father to speak. Abran was tall, like his eldest son, with brown wavy hair swept back from a high forehead. His trim beard was beginning to show flecks of gray, and the lines around his eyes, which had once shown themselves only when he smiled or laughed, had become permanent engravings in his face. Over the past few years a vertical furrow had appeared between his eyebrows and gradually deepened, as if some invisible force were slowly pressing it inward.

A short dagger with a ruby set in its hilt rested within its black sheath, which dangled from a leather belt. His shirt was made of finely woven linen, deep blue with gold-thread embroidery on the collar and sleeves, and buttons of mother-of-pearl. He stood stiffly and folded his arms across his chest as he looked at his son, much the way Master Helgrim had earlier.

Gerin stood straighter and swallowed his bread. "Hello, Father."

"Hello, Gerin." There was a tightness in his father's voice that Gerin did not like. He looked around the room as if inspecting it for dust. "I was surprised when I found your old rooms empty."

"Matren practically threw me in here. He said the lord of the castle has *always* occupied these rooms and that it was my duty as the new duke to take them." It had seemed vaguely indecent for him to move here and make the rooms his parents had occupied practically his entire life his own. But Matren Swendes, the castellan of Ailethon, had constantly asked when Gerin would like to move from his old rooms, what should remain in the lord's quarters and what should be put in storage, until Gerin finally gave in and commanded that it be done out of sheer exhaustion.

"Let's go to your study. We need to talk."

I'm in trouble, he thought. Though he was now master of this huge castle and all of its holdings, just a few words from his father made him feel like a guilty child again.

Gerin sat in the chair at his writing table while his father poured two cups of water, one of which he handed to his son.

"Therain's upset," said Abran. "You taunt him to embarrass him."

"I was just teasing him a little. He deserved worse. He was really terrible at practice today."

"That doesn't matter. You're the lord of Ailethon now. You need to act the part, which means you don't belittle your brother in public." His tone made it clear that Gerin would be very unwise to argue the point.

"Yes, Father."

"You're too quick to think the worst of your brother. You *do* taunt him in front of his friends; I've seen you do it, so don't bother denying it. Most of the time it's nothing. The gods know that my brothers and I didn't always get along, and still don't. Your mother's death hit him very hard, more so than the rest of you. You cast a long shadow, and it's hard for him to step out of it sometimes. Your mother understood this. She knew how to give him confidence. I wish I had her talent for doing that, but I don't. And now I'm not here to help him.

"Things come very easy to you, Gerin, as they did for me. Swordsmanship, hunting, falconry, even your studies with Master Aslon. Matren says you're doing a fine job as duke, you hardly have to exert yourself to excel. That's why I pushed you harder than everyone else. If I didn't, you would expect *everything* to be easy. I demand that you be the best you can be. You will be king one day, after me, and you must be ready for all manner of hardships and difficult decisions. It was my duty to see that you're prepared, as much as you may not have liked it at times. When you're angry with me because of something I did to you, remember that my father did the same to me, and his father to him. It is a small price to pay for the privilege and power we enjoy."

Gerin did not speak. He knew quite well how much his father had pushed him compared to his brother and sisters. The pressure his father had put on him to do things "perfectly" had been unbearable at times. He remembered vividly the moments when he failed to live up to those expectations—a hunting trip when he missed a spectacularly antlered stag; his father finding him after his very first night out drinking, passed out on the floor just outside his door, his face near a pool of his own vomit; a May Fair joust in which he had been handily defeated by Tomis Belvendur; and too many others to contemplate. The withering sense of disappointment in his father's narrowed eyes, the set line of his mouth, the small shake of his head, were even worse than when he simply yelled at him. The last thing in the world Gerin wanted to do was to disappoint his father. He wanted his father to always be proud of what he'd done, but his father's expectations were so ridiculously high that even when he excelled it seemed merely satisfactory to Abran. What more could he do?

Gerin felt himself growing red at the humiliating memories and tried to push them from his mind. His jaw clenched and he forced himself to relax. His father demanded perfection from *him* and *not* his other children, yet his siblings and even some of his friends saw him as overly confident, even arrogant. Sometimes he thought they were just waiting for him to fail so they could gloat. He bristled. Couldn't they see how hard he worked, and how hard his father had pushed him? Why would they want him to fail?

"He's a better archer than me," volunteered Gerin. "Even Master Helgrim pointed that out."

"Yes, I am aware of that."

Gerin winced at his father's wry tone. "I told Master Helgrim we shouldn't practice together anymore. At least not with swords."

"I agree. There's no point in frustrating both of you. You can practice with Balandrick or other members of the guard. You won't improve if your limits are not tested, and they won't be with Therain. He's not bad with a sword. I've seen him practice with other boys. You just intimidate him, especially with that particular weapon. Though none of this will matter for much longer. One of the reasons I came here was to officially announce that I will be sending Therain to take control of Castle Agdenor and its lands."

"Really? So soon?" Castle Agdenor had been held in escheat by Yurleng Sevreas since Abran's cousin Lesen had died. "Are you sure he's ready?"

"He will do fine, just as you are doing fine. I've already sent word to Count Sevreas of my decision. I've granted him a small holding in Lormenien where he and his family can retire. I will make it clear to him that if he does not go quietly, or leaves behind trouble for Therain, he will find himself on the wrong side of a dungeon door, and quite possibly the headsman's axe."

Abran finished his water and set the cup on the table. "I know how brothers are. I know they fight, sometimes bitterly, but you need to be aware that your actions have repercussions beyond what you might think. Remember that the next time you're about to make some biting comment to your brother, and hold your tongue."

Gerin spent the evening studying philosophy with Master Baelish Aslon. He could have ended his studies upon becoming lord of the castle, but he learned enough of interest from Master Aslon that, at least for the time being, he continued.

The old scholar wore the gray and black mantle and silver wrist bands of his order even in the sweltering heat. What little remained of his white hair was as thin as spider silk and combed straight back along his skull. His left eye had grown milky over the past several years, but his right—a blue so light it seemed transparent—was as lively as ever.

"Our minds, Gerin," said the Master, his voice as raspy as a rusty hinge, "are incapable of perceiving the underlying forms of reality. We must *translate* these basic forms into objects we can see with our eyes and touch with our hands, much as we translate the languages of antiquity. If I were to show you a page of characters in the Hodetten tongue, it would be nothing more than marks on a page to you. You need a key to translate Hodetten into Kelarin so that you can read and understand it. Only then will it have meaning.

"The same is true for reality itself. In its natural state it is meaningless to us. But our *minds* have incredible power." He grinned at the prince, showing yellowed, uneven teeth behind thin pale lips. He tapped at his temple with a forefinger. "*They* are the key we use to translate naked reality into things we can understand, like the chair upon which you sit, or this table."

The Master went on at length about the deductive reasoning Esklaro Vendos Laonn, the founder of his order, used to arrive at the conclusions he set forth in his *Principle of True Forms*. Gerin listened attentively and asked several more questions before the Master finished. Philosophy was the kind of dull, dry material that made him wonder if he shouldn't just call an end to these sessions. He understood that *thinking* about philosophical questions helped exercise the mind, but he felt that many of the questions were meaningless themselves. What did it matter if there were a "true" form of his writing desk? The Master himself said it was impossible to ever see it. What good did it do him to know it was there?

He preferred the Master's teachings on military history and the lives of generals and soldiers. Battle strategy and tactics, castle fortifications, sieges, weapons, the sheer logistical problems in moving large armies—those were the kinds of lessons he enjoyed. And Master Aslon was an able teacher in those areas, which was probably the single most important reason he continued his tutelage. When Gerin had told the old scholar that he would carry on with his studies after becoming duke, Aslon's only condition was that Gerin not dictate the topics. "I must teach as I see fit, with subjects of my choosing."

Gerin glanced out the window and sighed. In fact what he wanted to be doing was drinking a few beers with Balandrick Vaules, his friend and personal guard, and flirting with the bar maids at The Red Vine tavern in Padesh. It was just too hot to think about the true form of reality. It was too hot to think about anything.

"My lord, are you paying attention?" asked the Master.

The prince was jolted back to the matters at hand. "Of course, Master Aslon. You were saying . . . ?" He sighed. War and family history—much less beer and women, he thought sadly—would have to wait for another day.

The next morning, Gerin found his sister Reshel eating breakfast in her sitting room.

"Reshel, can I see you when you're done?"

She looked up at him and smiled. "Certainly." Her blond hair was pulled back from her delicate face by a gold brooch shaped like a gull with outstretched wings. It had been their mother's, and he knew Reshel prized it above almost all of her other possessions. The gull was the sigil of her house, the Tagars of Orlemoré.

Long lashes framed wide blue eyes set above a slender, almost fragile nose. At seventeen, her hips and breasts were just beginning to fill out, but even now it was apparent that her slight frame would never have the full figure of her mother or older sister Claressa. They were as different as he and Therain, and fought almost as much. *I wonder if Father's ever talked to them about their bickering?* Gerin thought.

His sister was a curious and intellectual girl, always listening and absorbing everything she read or heard. That was why he'd come to her now.

"What do you want to talk about?" She took another spoonful of eggs and dabbed at her mouth with a linen napkin.

"The gods. I want to know what you think about them."

She arched an eyebrow at him and straightened in her chair. "That sounds intriguing." She looked at him more closely. "Are you all right?"

"I didn't sleep well last night. I'll be in the library. Will you come when you're finished?"

"Yes. I won't be long."

* * *

Reshel's silk skirts whispered across the tile floor as she crossed the room to the reading table where Gerin was sitting. She sat down across from him, folded her hands and regarded him somberly. "What are you reading?"

"Ekalé Lavaraelios."

She looked surprised. "Why are you reading that? You're usually buried in history books."

"You could look at this as a history book of sorts."

"You know what I mean." She gestured toward the slender volume. "The story of the beginning of the world and the battles of the gods and men is hardly the kind of history you normally read." She folded her hands in her lap. "So why do you want to talk about the gods? Is that what kept you awake last night?"

"They were on my mind, yes." He drummed his fingers on the table. "Do you think the gods involve themselves in the affairs of men? I mean, the old stories say that Telros himself fought on the battlefield when King Iolstath warred with the Threndish, but do you truly think Telros was there? That the chief of our gods would concern himself with such things? Or that when Miendrel sounds Flestos, a war will happen?"

Reshel paused. "I don't know, Gerin. I have no reason to doubt the stories. Why do you ask?"

"I'm trying to understand the gods and their motivations, but so much of it doesn't make sense to me."

"That's why they're the gods. We can't understand them. They're not human, and we can't expect them to behave like us. We don't have the capacity to understand their perspective or their motives."

Just as I can't see the true form of this table, he thought, recalling his lesson from the night before. *Or even your true form.* The idea that Reshel had a true form that was totally foreign and unknowable to him was startling; he had not considered the Master's lesson in regard to people. "Do you think the priests can control the gods with their prayers and sacrifices?"

"Of course not!" She sounded almost offended by the question. "Men don't control the gods."

"But aren't all the rituals of the temple just that? Attempts to make the gods do the bidding of men?"

"No. The priests say the prayers in the hope of moving the gods to grant their wishes. They're said with such exacting care so the gods will hear them. We're a noisy race. The gods don't hear everything. The prayers are a way of getting their attention. Sometimes they grant them and sometimes they don't. I don't think we can ever know why. All we can do is ask."

"Then why are so many of the rituals worded like commands? As if the priests are ordering the gods to grant their prayers? Amnen Petring acts as if he can order trees to fall over."

"That doesn't matter. I don't think the words matter at all, and maybe not even the ritual itself, except in getting the gods to hear it in the first place. It's how the priest *feels* that's most important. It's what's in his heart. I think that's more important than anything. That's probably the real reason the prayers don't work all the time, even when it's the same prayer said by the same priest. It's his intention—and maybe his attitude—that matters most in determining if a prayer is granted. The rituals and words are there to call the attention of the gods and help guide the feelings of whoever is praying, but even if Miendrel hears someone praying that he will wind Flestos doesn't mean the god of war will listen."

Gerin thought about that. It was an interesting idea he hadn't considered.

"So are you going to tell my why you're thinking about the gods?"

He looked at her and smiled. "For now, I'm going to keep it to myself."

"All right." She knew better than to press him when he was reluctant to speak, and he was grateful for that.

"How are you doing with Father here?"

"What do you mean?"

"I mean he was the lord of this place our entire lives. Six months ago you became duke, but now Father returns and it seems like suddenly everything's the way it's always been. Does it seem like your rule here ever existed? That it was nothing more than a dream?"

Gerin smiled and shook his head. His perceptive sister. She and Claressa both could see to the heart of anything, no matter how hidden it might be to those around them. "Yes, it's strange with him back. I feel like a child again. It's too soon since he left. Everyone still thinks of him as the duke, not our king."

She stood and patted him on the arm. "That will all change. One day, when you become king, the same things will be said about you. That you have always seemed the master of Ailethon."

So much had changed in his life recently—his grandfather's death, his father's coronation as king, his own rise to the lordship of Ailethon . . . he hoped things settled down soon, and for a long time.

The previous night, after his lesson with Master Aslon had ended, it was too late to venture to Padesh to drink beer, so he'd returned to his rooms. Besides, Master Aslon's teachings on philosophy had withered any desire he had for carousing.

He hadn't been asleep long when he came suddenly awake. He felt certain there was something else in the room with him. He opened his eyes to mere slits but did not move. From where he lay he had a wide view of the chamber, dimly lit with the cold light of a half-moon spilling through a cross-paned window.

He saw nothing. He sat up and looked around. Perhaps one of the castle cats had managed to sneak into his study. He was about to get up and look for it when the sense of another presence in the room became overwhelming.

"Who's there?" he whispered.

As if in answer, a diffuse yellow glow filled the air. Then something touched him; not physically, but as if an invisible hand had grasped his heart and mind. He felt *power*—raw, unbridled strength that could crush mountains. And he also knew that this power obeyed the will of some unseen and unknown master, and felt the weight of its attention bear down on him. It wanted *him*—for what purpose he did not know—and he felt naked and small next to it.

"What are you?" he managed to say. The diffuse glow flashed suddenly, as bright as the sun. He squeezed his eyes shut against the glare and thought he heard a whispery voice.

"Gerin. Your time is coming."

Then it was gone.

It had been no human spirit. No ghost haunting the old passages of the keep. He was certain of that.

Only something divine could be so powerful.

A god had come to him. He was sure of it. But why? What design did it have for him?

He lay awake for a long while, alone and afraid.

2

Claressa watched her twin brother Therain pace his sitting room from a high-backed chair tucked into a corner near the tall windows that looked out over the walled courtyard in the center of the keep. Her hands were folded in her lap, her nails painted a pale red that matched her dress. Her thick black hair was pulled back from her face with three strategically placed combs; tight curls spiraled down around her ears. Her skin was pale and porcelain smooth, with no blemishes or imperfections of any kind, as if it were the ideal to which all other skin strived to reach. Claressa had a natural beauty that took the breath away from most men who saw her for the first time; they could not stop looking at her. Men desired her, and women envied her. In some ways she had a more commanding presence than her father; if they both stood together in a crowded room, most eyes would be on her.

"So what is it you wanted to tell me?" she asked.

He continued to pace. "Father came to talk to me a little while ago. He said he's going to send me to take over Agdenor soon."

"Therain, that's wonderful!"

He grinned. "I know. I'm excited about it, although another part of me doesn't think I'm ready to be duke of a castle and its holdings." He turned to look at her for the first time since she'd sat down. "Have you ever been to Agdenor?"

"No. Father only took you *boys* when he visited the great Atreyano castles three years ago. You should know that."

Therain ignored her snide remark, which she was certain he did deliberately to annoy her. What was the point in making sharp comments if they didn't provoke a reaction?

"Agdenor's not as big as Ailethon, but it's almost as old," he said. "I'll like it there. I'm sure I will."

She watched him closely as he wandered about the room, not for the first time wondering how children of the same parents could be so different. Gerin was confident and ambitious—sometimes too much so—while Therain was often doubtful and unsure of himself, questioning his decisions. Gerin simply decided and was done with it.

Therain seemed far more capable than he thought himself to be, and she believed in her heart that he would rise to his own once he no longer had to measure the smallest of his achievements against Gerin.

Then there was Reshel, the fragile flower, ready to crack and shatter at the smallest stress. Protected by their father like the most valuable treasure of the realm, the darling of his eye. Sometimes Claressa wondered how her younger sister would ever survive the hardships of the world, even if she was fortunate enough to be shielded from most of them by virtue of being a princess. Claressa had been surprised that their father had not taken her to live with him at Almaris when he'd become king, and had asked him about it one evening. "She's used to Ailethon," he'd said. "She'll marry one day, and I don't want to tear her away from her home any earlier than I have to. It's better for her to be here."

Therain sagged into a chair opposite hers. "At least it will get me away from Gerin. He makes me so *mad* sometimes."

"He makes all of us mad," she replied. "That's what older brothers are for."

Gerin heard a faint knock on his door. A Pashti servant boy named Ialin was standing in the hallway. "My lord, a visitor has arrived who wishes to see you."

"Where is he?" Gerin asked as he followed the boy out of his study.

"He is in the Sunlight Hall with Castellan Swendes, my lord."

"You may go. I know the way."

Ialin bowed his head. "Yes, my lord."

The twin doors to the Sunlight Hall were thrown open, with guards stationed just inside. The hall was a massive rectangular room nestled in the upper floors of the southeastern corner of the keep. Its twenty-foot-high outer walls were pierced with narrow stained-glass windows that ran nearly floor to ceiling, with ornate sconces bolted to the walls between the glass. The lower half of the room was paneled in rosewood; the upper half was bare stone. Heavy beams formed a coffered ceiling, the recessed panels between the beams painted with murals of the Atreyano family past.

Matren and another man Gerin did not recognize were seated at the council table—an enormous rectangle of polished mahogany inlaid with sliver, with matching chairs to seat forty—talking quietly to each other. Beams of light cascaded through the windows and formed pools of glowing color across the yellow marble floor.

Matren stood and bowed his head when he saw Gerin. The castellan was in his fifties, with steely gray hair that fell in loose waves to his shoulders. He had dark eyes and a strong jaw covered with a thick beard. He was skeletally thin; it seemed every vein was visible beneath his dry, wrinkled skin, the faint blue lines like rivers on an old map. He was dressed in loose-fitting trousers and a linen tunic. On his right hand he wore a gold ring set with a triangle of opal, the symbol of his office. He'd been Abran's castellan for twenty-three years, and Bessel's castellan for a decade before that. He knew more about the running of this castle and its holdings than any man alive. Gerin heavily depended on him for advice, and used Matren as his primary counselor.

"My lord," said Matren. He gestured to the man beside him, who had also risen. "You have a visitor."

The man with Matren watched Gerin intently. He was shorter than the prince by half a head. Straight blond hair framed a face that seemed all sharp angles, from cheekbones to narrow nose to the abrupt line of his jaw, like wood that had been hastily planed and chiseled but never finished. His smooth skin was as white as alabaster and his startling green eyes stood out in stark contrast against his pale face.

He wore well-made black leather boots with the tops turned down just below the knees, pale woolen trousers cinched with a wide belt, and a shirt the color of his eyes. A traveling cloak had been draped over the chair next to him, along with a large leather pack.

"My lord, this is Hollin Lotheg," said Matren. "He's from Hethnost, a fortress in the Redhorn Hills."

"Hello," Gerin said, grasping the man's hand. "Welcome to Ailethon."

"Hello, my lord." Hollin glanced about the room. "So you are the master of this place? A large responsibility for one so young."

"I manage. Matren is a valuable asset."

Gerin's father entered the room and paused when he saw the three men at the far end of the table. "What is this?"

"I thought it best to summon you as well, Your Majesty, and Master Aslon, after I heard Hollin's claim and verified it with my own eyes."

Abran crossed the room to them and Hollin was introduced. The king regarded him with thinly veiled suspicion.

"What is this claim of yours?" Gerin asked Hollin.

Hollin looked at him squarely. It seemed to Gerin that in the depths of those eyes he saw the presence of knowledge and wisdom far surpassing that of anyone he had ever known, even Master Aslon. He felt that some power was concealed within Hollin, a hidden splendor lurking just below the surface of his being. *Like Master Aslon's hidden reality,* he thought. The sensation was very strong.

But where did it come from? Why would he sense

something from this stranger that he'd never sensed from anyone else before in his life?

"Hollin is a wizard," said Matren.

Gerin was unsure what to say. "What do you mean, a wizard?"

"It's true, I assure you," said Hollin.

"It is," said Matren. There was an excitement in his voice that Gerin had never heard before. "He showed me his magic."

Abran's suspicion blossomed into open hostility. "I don't know who you are or why you've come, but I don't take kindly to pranks."

"This is no prank, Your Majesty. Please, allow me to prove to you that I am what I say."

Gerin, too, was suspicious, but inclined to let him proceed. "Go ahead," he said before his father could speak. "But I promise you, the penalty will be swift and harsh if we find you're deceiving us."

"This is no deception, my lord."

Master Aslon entered the room and was introduced to Hollin. "He was just about to give us a demonstration of his powers," Gerin said.

"Excellent," said Aslon. "It's been many years since I last spoke with a wizard. Have you come from Hethnost?"

"Yes."

"Please, Master Aslon, hold your questions until he is finished," said Gerin.

Hollin turned to the table and held out his right hand, then began to speak in a language that sounded like Osirin—once the high speech of the nobility of Osseria, which Master Aslon was teaching him—though he spoke too quietly for Gerin to make out any words.

A hazy gray sphere about two feet wide appeared above the table, floating like a wisp of cloud. Gerin drew a sharp breath and saw his father's eyes widen in surprise. Matren was smiling like a child at his first Selhouin's Day feast. Aslon, too, looked delighted.

Hollin twisted his hand, and the sphere flattened into a vertical disk, like a plate standing on edge. He said another sharp word that Gerin did not understand—it sounded like *kaifa,* the Osirin word for *open,* but he could not be sure—and clenched his hand into a fist.

Where the vertical disk had been, there was now what looked to be a hole in the air. Through the opening floating above the table, Gerin could see the storeroom next to the Sunlight Hall, as if the wall between them had somehow been removed.

"This is a Farseeing," said Hollin. "It allows a wizard to see into the distance for several miles before its power fades. Right now we are looking through that wall at the room next to this one. But if I command it"—he pushed his arm outward, as if flinging something away from him—"we can see much farther."

When Hollin gestured, the view through the Farseeing changed with dizzying speed, rushing forward so quickly that Gerin could not see the locations passing by. When the view stopped, they were "in" the outer bailey of the castle, near the practice yard. Several men moved into view, walking very close to the apparent location of the Farseeing, but they did not take note of it.

"Can those men see us?" asked Abran.

"No. That end of a Farseeing is invisible. They could walk through it without any idea that it is there."

He lowered his hand and the Farseeing vanished. "Does that suffice as proof that I am indeed a wizard, or do you need another display?"

"That suffices," said Gerin. He was stunned by what he'd just seen. What a useful device that could be in battle!

"Impressive," said Abran. "I will grant that you are what you say you are."

"Which brings me to my next question," said Gerin. "Why are you here? Did you somehow know the king would be visiting Ailethon?"

"I did not come to see the king, my lord. I came to see you."

"Me? Why?"

"To see if you too are a wizard."

"To see if I'm a wizard," he repeated. The words sounded ridiculous in his mouth. He expected the wizard to start laughing, but Hollin's face remained somber. "What makes you think I am?"

"When I'm finished, I'll explain." He withdrew a clear jewel from the leather pack. It was the size of his palm and cut with many facets. It did not look particularly valuable, and appeared to be glass, though it gleamed more brightly than he thought ordinary glass would have.

"What is that?"

"This is a *methlenel*," he said. "It's the means by which I'll determine whether you're a wizard."

"Ah, the Ritual of Discovery," said Master Aslon. "I was tested when I was a boy by a wizard whose name escapes me. Alas, but I had no talent for magic."

"So you're familiar with what he's going to do?" asked the king.

"Yes, Your Majesty. I experienced it myself. It is as he says: a test to determine if one is or is not a wizard."

"All right. I will allow it. But if any harms come to him . . ."

"The ritual is benign, Your Majesty," said the wizard. "It cannot hurt the prince."

Gerin was annoyed that his father had decided for him, but he did not make an argument of it. "Is there anything I have to do?"

"No. This will only take a few moments. Then we'll know."

Hollin held out the jewel and spoke again in Osirin. *"Iya trestalkiri paran yi dakhal sethu . . ."*

Gerin was startled when a spark of light flared to life at the heart of the jewel. At the same instant he felt a warmth ignite in his belly. It quickly worked its way outward into his arms and legs and up through his neck, as if he were being submerged in hot water. He felt the warmth in his skull and on his scalp; when it reached his face, a faint amber light filled his vision, as if he were looking through a piece of colored glass like those in the windows of the hall. He looked down and saw that the jewel was glowing brilliantly with the same amber light.

Then the light was gone, both in his vision and the jewel, as suddenly as it had appeared.

"By the Blessed Hand of Venegreh, it is you," whispered Hollin. His hands shook and he closed his eyes as if in silent prayer. When he opened them, he regarded Gerin with a mixture of awe and reverence, like a devout believer gazing at a religious icon or holy relic.

What is going on here? Gerin wondered. *Why is he looking at me that way?*

Hollin returned the jewel to the pack. "We have much to talk about."

Gerin sat down. His legs felt weak. "I'd like some answers myself."

"You shall have them. I scarcely know where to begin."

He still regarded Gerin as if he were a figure of legend brought suddenly to life. It unnerved Gerin enough that he blurted out, "Why are you looking at me that way?"

Hollin laughed and wiped a hand across his face. "I offer my apologies, Prince Gerin. I did not mean to make you uncomfortable. Though I have studied prophecies and Foretellings for many years, I have never before been present when one of such importance had been proved true. It's shaken me more than I would have thought, and you'll probably find it disturbing when you fully understand why I'm here and what you are. Or rather, what you can *become*. This is a day unlike any other. You have within you the power to become the greatest of any wizard who ever lived save one."

"That's ridiculous!" said Gerin. "I've never even *seen* magic until now. Not real magic. Just sleight-of-hand tricks from traveling magicians at the fairs." He wondered if Hollin's glowing jewel were merely a more sophisticated version of the same trickery.

But then what about the Farseeing, and the warmth I felt? he asked himself. *How could he make that power, or whatever it was, move through me, if not with magic?*

"My lord, I do not know what to say," said Matren.

"It is obvious, my good man," said Aslon. "Lord Gerin is indeed a wizard, though I too would know what has brought Hollin specifically to him."

"Could I also be a wizard?" asked the king.

"It is possible, Your Majesty, but not likely. I can test you now, if you like."

Abran did not hesitate. "Yes, go ahead."

Hollin once more took the jewel from his pack—a *methlenel*, Gerin remembered; an Osirin word that meant "truth's light"—and spoke the words to the spell, this time directing his power toward Abran.

The jewel showed no light dancing in its heart. "I'm sorry, Your Majesty, but you are not a wizard."

Abran's jaw clenched and his cheeks reddened. He took a step away from the wizard and nodded his head once. "Very well. I am not a wizard." He gestured for them all to sit at the table. "But your test showed that Gerin *is* a wizard. That's the meaning of that light we saw?"

"The Ritual of Discovery allows us to find those who may *become* wizards. Your son is now no more a wizard than you. But he has great potential. Wizardry is something one is born with, but it cannot be used without help. This test identifies those who have the natural talent. The color of the *methlenel* indicates how powerful a wizard you will be."

"And Gerin's power?" asked Abran. "I saw an amber color in the jewel."

The near-religious fervor—a kind of eager, hungry ecstasy that made Gerin exceedingly uncomfortable—returned to Hollin's eyes. "Amber is the most powerful of all. As I said, there has only been one other wizard with an amber flame, and he has been dead for centuries. He was thought to be an aberration, a rekindling of powers much closer to what our ancestors must have possessed before their long decline; a unique event, never to be repeated. Yet here you are. A second amber wizard. You have within you the potential to become one of the most powerful wizards in history.

You will be able to do things *unimaginable* to others with lesser power. It will change your life forever, in many, many ways."

Gerin still could not believe what he was hearing. It was as if Hollin were speaking about someone else. It did not seem possible that he could be a wizard of *any* kind, let alone one of the most powerful.

Yet here was a wizard saying exactly that. He could see no reason for Hollin to lie, no reason for the man to convince him of something that could so readily be disproved. For now, at least, he would believe what Hollin said, no matter how hard it was to accept.

The idea of actually *using* magic was exhilarating; the ability to make wishes, cast spells—or whatever wizards called whatever it was they did—and have those wishes actually happen was almost too good to be believed. Would he be able to turn lead into gold, or transform himself into a wolf or bird, like the wizards from stories? Part of him could not wait to find out.

Yet, at the same time, the idea of being *the most powerful wizard of all* was a grave and sobering one. He was not easily intimidated—he was, after all, a prince who would one day become king of Khedesh. But a vast set of expectations seemed to be enmeshed in the very idea of an amber wizard, expectations he knew nothing about. He'd known his entire life he would become king, and felt prepared, but this wizardry had all just come crashing onto his shoulders. *I don't understand the first thing about magic,* he thought.

"Who was the first amber wizard?" Master Aslon asked.

"Naragenth ul-Darhel. I am sure you know that name. He was once the king of Khedesh."

Naragenth. Gerin had indeed heard of him. The fabled king during the Wars of Unification, when Helca the Conqueror had brought the nations of Osseria to heel and created his empire. Naragenth had perished in battle and the capital city of Almaris had fallen to Helca soon after. It was said that Naragenth had been a sorcerer-king, able to perceive the minds of his enemies and spirit himself from place to place unseen and unheard, but Gerin had always thought those were just stories and legends.

"Yes, I do know who he is. Are you saying that . . . I'm a descendant of Naragenth?"

Hollin arched an eyebrow. "It's possible. Naragenth was believed to have died childless, but records from that time are sparse, and a child of the king would have been hidden to keep him safe from Helca's armies. The fact that you both are from the same kingdom and of royal lineage speaks to more than simple coincidence."

Gerin was silent, absorbing everything Hollin had said. "But that still doesn't explain how you came to *me*. You said you were seeking out me specifically, not my brother or sisters or father."

"You're right, Gerin. I did seek you out. Prophecy led me to you. There are many prophecies in the vaults of Hethnost. Some considered to be so dangerous they have been sealed behind powerful closing spells for centuries. There are other prophecies spread across Osseria, lying forgotten in the libraries and archives of cities where wizards once lived. We spend much of our time searching for these lost treasures— not only prophecies, but artifacts of magic and books of lore and history.

"One such prophecy was discovered fifteen years ago, in the royal archive of Brindal Haro, sealed in a reliquary that had long been forgotten. It was the private writings of a wizard named Bainora Estreg, who was gifted with the power of Foretelling. She shunned other wizards and lived in seclusion, using her powers sparingly for the benefit of the nobles, who in exchange provided her with a manor house and servants to meet her needs. It's not known how her writings found their way to the royal archive, but thank the gods they were not destroyed, or we never would have found you.

"Her writings were studied for many years before we even

learned they were prophecies. Bainora had many dreams, and the manner in which she wrote them down was confusing and difficult to understand. It was only after several events she described came to pass that we realized she had indeed been a seeress.

"She wrote that a second amber wizard would be born in the year 1285, a firstborn son in the house of the Golden Stag. Of course, she wrote only in cryptic references, and many of the things that she wrote we still don't understand, but the scholars who studied her felt certain that her references were to an amber wizard. They reached this conclusion only a few months ago. I was at Almaris when I learned that the sigil of your family is a golden stag on a field of blue. After that it did not take me long to learn that you were the Atreyano born in 1285.

"Of course, your father could also have been the wizard, or your brother or sisters—the scholars were least certain about the date. But you are the one."

Gerin said nothing. Though he was familiar with prophecies—the holy books of Telros and the other gods all contained prophecies of some sort or another—the idea that he was the *subject* of one troubled him as much as the fervor Hollin had shown. How could his choices be his own if they'd been seen long before he was born?

"Did this Estreg woman write anything else about my . . . future?"

"Prophecies can be dangerous things, Gerin, even under the best of circumstances. The one concerning the birth of a second amber wizard was in some ways less so than most, because we were only interested in finding you. If our search for you had failed—if either we'd misunderstood the prophecy or if the prophecy itself were wrong—then we'd lost nothing. We hadn't based our lives or wealth on the outcome of this prophecy. If you had died before I found you, Bainora's prophecy would still be correct; it's silent on whether the amber wizard is actually discovered and trained. But to us it would appear one of many failed prophecies. Armies have marched to war under the banner of prophecy. Cities and sometimes entire nations have fallen because of them. That's why they must be approached with the greatest of caution."

"So you're saying that even if the prophecy did say anything about my later life, you wouldn't reveal it to me."

"If her writings did touch upon such matters, what would you do if I told you? What if it said that you would marry and prosper and have many children and become a wise king? Would that change you or how you would live your life? Or what if it said something terrible would happen, that sorrow after sorrow would befall you? Would you do everything you could to avoid that fate? And what if everything you did to avoid it only made it more certain that the things you sought to avoid would come to pass?"

"All right, I understand. I won't ask again about prophecies. What happens now?"

"I wish to train you. I will go so far as to say I demand it. A power this great should not go unrealized." The wizard's expression grew somber. "I'll tell you now that if you choose to walk this path, your life will change forever. *You* will change in many ways. Your power will be Awakened, and then you'll spend many years studying as a Novitiate."

"What do you gain from this?" asked Abran. "You simply spend years training him, then walk away?" The tinge of suspicion had crept back into his voice. *He's disappointed that he's not a wizard,* Gerin thought.

"The race of wizards is dying, Your Majesty." Hollin's voice was cold and hard, like frozen steel. In it, Gerin heard the first hint of the great orator Hollin might be when he chose, one whose voice could be used as decisively—and dangerously—as any weapon. "There are no wizards on your court, or in any of the cities of your country, though it was not always so. Wizards were once common in Osseria, the trusted counselors of kings and queens. But we have faded, and the world has moved on. I do not blame you for being distrustful. We are not as accepted as we once were. We've withdrawn too much from the affairs of our neighbors, a policy with which I disagree but am powerless to change.

"What I *can* do is train the amber wizard. A mighty power not only among wizards, but a man who will one day be king of a powerful southland nation. I feel this convergence of wizard and king will become something greater than the sum of its parts. I say this not with any knowledge gleaned from prophecy or Foretelling, but simply the voice in my heart. Something new and great will emerge if you allow me to do this in the manner I see fit."

He paused and looked at them both. "That is what I want. To see that Gerin is brought to his full potential, if it is possible for me to do so. And if I cannot, then at least give him the ability to carry on past the point where my own skills fail, and to point him toward further greatness. But I *will* be a part of it, in some way either small or large. That will be my contribution to the legacy of my people—to see that Gerin achieves greatness for our kind before we vanish utterly from the earth."

"What if what you want differs from what he is required to do as king?" asked Abran. "What if his duties of king and wizard are at odds? What then?"

Hollin shook his head. "I do not care what he does as king of Khedesh. How he rules, or who he wars with, or makes peace with, is of no concern to me. *My* desire is make him a great wizard. *Your* duty, King Abran, is to teach Gerin to be a great king after you. And *your* responsibility, Gerin, is to be both a great king *and* a great wizard. It will be much for you to bear, but from what little I've seen, I feel you are up to the task."

"Do you feel he speaks truly?" the king asked Aslon.

"Oh, yes, Your Majesty."

"We should confirm his story with the rulers of Hethnost," said Matren. "I'll dispatch a messenger at once to see if he has the authority he claims."

"I will agree to this, *conditionally*," said Abran. "But if I sense that there is an agenda here harmful to either my family or Khedesh, I will stop it at once. Am I understood?"

"Yes, perfectly, Your Majesty," Hollin replied. "But you have nothing to worry about."

"See that I don't."

Gerin gave his father a quick glance of annoyance. *He has no right to speak for me. I'm the lord of Ailethon now, and I will do as I see fit in my own house.* His father and Hollin were speaking as if he no longer mattered as a person, but was more important as an idea, or a game piece to be moved across a board toward the ideal intersection of wizard and king.

He considered their words. *More responsibility on my shoulders, more expectations to live up to.* But he did not voice such misgivings aloud. There was no point. Because, despite the fear he'd felt when told that he could become the most powerful wizard who ever lived, in the deepest, most secret places of his heart he was as eager for it as they were. He wanted to be as good as they both expected him to be. No, he wanted to be better than that, to shock and surprise them with his abilities, to far surpass whatever they thought he should do. It was frightening, and would not be easy; but he would see it done.

"Years of study," Gerin said with a hint of distaste.

"Don't fret. You will have quite a long life. Like the Atalari of old, whose descendant you are, we live longer than the ordinary mortals around us. We don't live as long as our ancestors did, and in many ways our powers are different from theirs, but our lives are long nonetheless.

"I know that more life sounds fantastic, something all men dream of but never achieve. You *will* achieve it should you become a wizard, but I'll warn you now that your long life can be as much a curse as a blessing. It can't be shared with anyone. There are no spells to lengthen the lives of those around us, which means all those you love—your brothers and sisters, your wife when you marry, your children, and their children—will grow old and die while you remain much as you are today. It's a painful thing to endure."

Gerin looked hard at the wizard. "How old are you?"

"Two hundred and seventeen. I'll live perhaps another thirty or forty years. You see, the strength of a wizard can be gauged by the color of his flame. My flame is golden. Most of the wizards of Hethnost have golden flames.

"Below gold is crimson, and below that white. Above gold is green, then blue, and finally amber. There have been no blue wizards in Osseria for hundreds of years, and there are only three green wizards now at Hethnost. 'The stronger the flame the longer the life,' is an old saying among wizards." Hollin smiled. "You will live a *very* long time."

"Why now?" Gerin asked. "I mean, why would the most powerful kind of wizard appear now, when it seems that wizards are fading from the world?"

Hollin shrugged. "Who can say? Why does the face of a man suddenly reappear decades later on one of his descendants? Wizardry is a trait passed along like any other, the way you and your father are of similar build and height. Some traits skip generations before returning. Some disappear forever. I cannot say why an amber wizard should appear now, what confluence of bloodlines brought this about. All that matters is that you are here now."

Gerin thought about what Hollin had said about a long life and felt overwhelmed with the thought of what seemed the next best thing to immortality. His mind turned to the future, of what he would do with such great power and long life. He thought of the secret dream of his heart—to be the greatest Atreyano who ever lived—a dream he'd never spoken aloud to anyone for fear of ridicule and derision. He'd never known *how* he would accomplish such a thing, which was another reason he'd remained silent, but now . . . it seemed the keys to his dream had been delivered to him unforeseen.

"What's your training like?"

"Are you agreeing to become a wizard?"

"Yes, of course. I'd be a fool to turn you away."

Hollin grinned. "Good. There's much to be learned as a

Novitiate. You must first become fluent in Osirin, the language of wizards and magic."

"I already know some of that. Master Aslon's been teaching us."

"He's been a most proficient pupil," said the Master.

"He said it was once the language of the noble classes in Osseria."

"It was, and before that it was the language of the Atalari. It's good that you know it. It will make your training much easier."

"When can we begin?"

"First we must return to Hethnost. Once there—"

"That's impossible," said Gerin. His father's mouth was open to object, as was Matren's, but they allowed Gerin to speak. "I'm a prince and heir to the throne. I can't be absent from the country for so long. I have duties and obligations to Ailethon and the kingdom that must be met. I can't go to Hethnost. You'll have to come here. There's no other way, no matter what you're offering."

Hollin frowned, then sighed and nodded. "I understand your position as a prince is unique. I am the Warden of Apprentices at Hethnost and have duties of my own that must be met. I wish to be the one to train you, however. It is not something I will assign to another." He folded his arms and drew a deep breath. "I agree to your condition, but will make one of my own. You must come to Hethnost to have your powers Awakened. It's not right that the amber wizard should have his magic brought to life anywhere other than the ancestral home of our people. You will be gone no longer than a few months. After that I will return here to train you."

"That's acceptable." Gerin looked toward his father, who gave him a slight nod. "Will you test my brother and sisters?"

"If they wish. But it's doubtful that they're wizards. It's unheard of for more than one member of a family to have the potential these days. We are a fading people. Once we were mighty, but our blood has long been mingled with those who have no magic of their own, to our detriment. We find only a few new wizards each year now, where once there were hundreds."

"We'll have dinner tonight with my other children," said Abran. He faced his son. "Do you think you can hold your tongue until then? I think it would be best if we tell them all at once."

"I'll say nothing."

"Do you have any more questions?" asked the wizard.

Gerin had many, but his head was already swimming. "None right now."

"Until tonight, then," said his father.

His father, sisters, and Matren were already in the private dining hall near Gerin's chambers when Gerin entered. Hollin had not yet arrived.

"What's this all about?" asked Therain as he came into the room. "Are you finally going to marry off Claressa? Did you find a family desperate enough to take her?"

"At least I'll *be* married someday," she said. "Father, don't lifelong bachelors usually become priests or monks? Shouldn't Therain be joining Uncle Bennjan at the Temple soon?"

"All right, enough," said their father. "Try to show *some* manners, please."

Master Aslon and Hollin arrived together. When they were all seated, Gerin introduced Hollin and told them he was a wizard from Hethnost. Hollin explained the prophecy and what the Ritual of Discovery had revealed.

"I'll say it again," said Hollin when he'd finished. "Prince Gerin has the potential to become one of the most powerful wizards in history. This truly is a momentous event."

"I can't *believe* you think you're a wizard," said Claressa. "I've never heard anything so ridiculous in my life."

"I'm *not* a wizard," said Gerin. "If you would listen better, Hollin said I can be trained to *become* one, not that I *am* one."

"There's something going on here, some hidden scheme, and I'm going to find out what it is!" said Claressa. She pointed a rigid finger at Hollin. "You won't get away with this!"

"He has proved his powers to us," said the king. "Master Aslon underwent the same ritual himself when he was a boy, and Matren will verify his story with the wizards of Hethnost. If there *is* a scheme, we will find it, but I do not believe there is."

Gerin put a hand on his sister's arm, but she shrugged him off and rose from the table. "You're all fools," she said, then left the room, flinging open the door so hard that it crashed into the wall. A servant in the hallway was caught by surprise and had to leap aside to get out of her way.

"Please accept my apologies for my daughter's outburst," said Abran. He looked furious. Gerin knew he would be having strong words with her later. His father was not one to be embarrassed in front of guests.

"Yes, that was terribly rude, even for her," said Reshel, scowling at the door.

"Think nothing of it," he said.

"My congratulations, brother," said Therain, raising his glass. "I wonder what great bit of fortune will fall into your lap next?"

They all raised their glasses and drank.

Reshel stopped outside the door but hesitated before knocking. The dinner with Hollin had ended over an hour earlier. She'd gone to her rooms but had been unable to think about anything except Hollin's tale. The light from the lamp she carried trembled in her shaking hand. Gods above, she was nervous!

She took a deep breath and knocked. She could not believe how hard her heart was pounding. She was so nervous she had trouble catching her breath.

The door opened. Hollin smiled when he saw her. "Reshel. Please, come in."

"Hello." Her voice was barely a whisper. It felt as if a hand were tightening around her neck. She coughed to try to clear her throat.

"May I get you some water?"

She nodded and looked about the room.

"What can I do for you?"

"I . . . I'd like to find out if I'm a wizard. I know you said it was doubtful, but . . ." There. She'd said it.

"Your request isn't ridiculous at all. I'll be happy to perform the ritual for you. Therain was already here."

"He was? Is he a wizard?"

"Sadly, no. And I'll tell you now, it's unlikely that you're a wizard, despite Gerin's potential."

He retrieved something from his belongings. "Is that the jewel you told us about at dinner?" she asked. "The *methlenel*?"

"Yes. Are you ready?"

"I think so. Is there anything I have to do?"

"No."

"Will it hurt?" She hated herself for asking, but couldn't help it.

He smiled and shook his head. "Not at all."

He began speaking his spell. She clutched her hands together and held her breath.

Golden light appeared suddenly at the heart of the jewel, as if some mystical eye had just opened. Reshel felt a strange sensation, a warmth moving through her, working its way from the core of her body outward. When it reached her head she saw a faint glow in her vision, a deep gold color like sunlight on a summer morning.

The *methlenel* went dark. "By the Hand of Venegreh! You *do* have the potential to become a wizard, Reshel. One with a golden flame, similar in power to my own."

"Are you sure?"

"Yes. You can become a wizard."

"Will you train me?"

"Of course. I'd be honored."

"Thank you, Hollin, thank you!" She leaned forward and kissed his cheek. "I can't wait to tell Gerin! He'll fall over from the shock!"

3

Still buoyant from her discovery, Reshel ran through the halls of the keep, wondering where Gerin might be.

She passed an open door that led onto a narrow terrace that overlooked the western side of the castle. There was a woman outside, standing in the darkness at the parapet with a hooded lamp on the tiles at her feet.

Reshel stepped forward and saw that it was Claressa. Her sister, standing with her arms folded across her chest, glanced at her before looking off toward the dark horizon. Her face was stern and angry.

"Go away," she said. "I want to be alone."

Reshel grew angry herself. "I don't care what you want. You were *terribly* rude to Hollin. Father's furious, and he's going to make you sorry for what you did when he finds you. Sometimes I'm ashamed to be related to you. Are you so blind you couldn't see he was telling us the truth?"

Claressa spun to face her sister, and even in the darkness Reshel could see the tears on her face. The sight startled Reshel, who had rarely seen her sister cry. "Of course I believe him! I'm not blind. You're the one who can't see. You're too busy worshipping Gerin to understand." She wiped her cheeks. "Our perfect brother now has *everything*. It's not enough that he's the crown prince of the kingdom, that he's good at everything he tries, now we find out that he's a wizard! And not just *any* wizard, if Hollin is right, but one of the most powerful who has ever lived. And oh, by the way, wizards live for hundreds of years. You can be so *stupid* sometimes! Gerin has everything anyone could ever want, and I'm *jealous*!" She folded her arms again and turned away. "Father's a little jealous, too. Did you see the look on his face when that wizard explained how long Gerin would live?"

Reshel was unsure what to say. This was the first time she could recall ever hearing Claressa voice her true feelings. She felt awkward, as if she had overheard something not meant for her.

"You're right, I didn't understand. But I'm *happy* for him. I'm not jealous." She wondered if it were true about their father.

"Good for you. Now go away."

"Claressa, I just met with Hollin. I asked him to perform the test to see if I was a wizard. And guess what? I *am*! It's true! I'm not as powerful as Gerin, but I'm still a wizard. You should see him and have him test you. Maybe the trait is unusually strong in our family. Therain went to him before I did. He's not a wizard, and neither was Father, but that doesn't mean you won't be."

Claressa looked at her suspiciously. "You can't be serious."

"I am. Go ask Hollin if you don't believe me—he's going to train Gerin and me together. You really should talk to him. You don't have anything to lose, and it's better than feeling sorry for yourself and being petty toward Gerin." She turned and left the terrace without waiting for Claressa to reply.

Late the next night, Reshel visited Hollin again. "I'm not disturbing you, am I?"

"Not at all." He offered her a chair.

"I have a question for you. I've been thinking about it a lot. You told us that we'd live for hundreds of years but that we can't change anyone around us. There are no spells we can work on nonwizards . . . what is that word you used?"

"Gendalos," said Hollin. "It's an Osirin word that means 'short-lived,' though there is a somewhat disparaging connotation to it. It was not a name given in friendship."

"So when I marry, my husband will grow old while I remain young. And so will my children. It seems that would be very hard for everyone, and only get worse as time passes."

"You're very observant. Men and women far older than you have ignored the warnings about what such a long life will truly mean to them, to their eventual sorrow. They see only that they will live a very long life and are blind to the consequences. It *is* a very hard thing to endure."

"That's what I want to ask you. It seems to me that this is something you've experienced yourself. That you've endured the pain of marriage to a nonwizard, a Gendalos." The word sounded strange on her tongue. "I'd like you to tell me about it. If you don't mind, that is."

He sat back in his chair. A distant look came over his face, as if his gaze had turned inward to sort through memories long untouched.

"I'll tell you of my first marriage," he said, focusing once again on Reshel. "I hope you'll glean at least a small understanding from it of what you will face.

"I was seventeen when a wizard visited my village to perform the Ritual of Discovery on anyone willing to submit to it. I learned I could become a wizard. My father was a wool merchant, and I'd planned to follow him into that trade, but this changed everything.

"I was betrothed to a woman named Katara Habel. After much discussion among our families, it was decided that she would accompany me to Hethnost while I was trained. It's a fairly common practice, and though she was understandably nervous, she agreed. We were married before I left my village, and were gone for five years.

"I won't bother you with the story of my training. You'll find out about that soon enough for yourself. We were happy at Hethnost, and Katara bore three children while we were there. But I knew her heart was still in Melu Tanis, and so I decided that after my training was finished we'd go back so our children could meet their families and live among them.

"The village was thrilled to have a wizard, and I was heaped with honors. I'll admit that at the time I was proud and vain, full of myself and my new powers, eager to show them off for the wonder and benefit of all.

"For some reason the birth of our fourth child changed everything. It suddenly made real all of the things I'd been told in Hethnost, that I would one day be unable to bear living among the Gendalos because of what I was.

"I began to search for a way to change a Gendalos to a wizard regardless of what the *methlenel* revealed. I devised spells and created objects of power. I even journeyed to Hethnost to consult the wizards there and scour the library for anything that might help me. I knew that others had made the attempt to change Gendalos into wizards, driven by the same fears that compelled me. I gathered all their records, copied what I needed, and returned to my village. The failures of all the other wizards who'd tried didn't daunt me. I *had* to succeed. The thought of watching my children die haunted me.

"A year passed, then two, then a third, but I was no closer to finding a way to make Katara or my children wizards than on the day I'd begun. Everything I tried had failed. I was ill, hadn't eaten or slept well for months, and at last Katara put an end to it.

"She told that I didn't need to do this, that nothing would change what they were. She said that I'd been blessed with my life but that I had to accept that she and my children could never share in that. They had the courage to accept the way they were. I needed to find the courage to stop.

"In time Katara grew old. Her black hair turned gray and brittle, her straight back became stooped. Her skin, which had once been smooth and soft, became dry and wrinkled.

"But I remained unchanged. I looked no different at seventy-three than I had when my powers had been Awakened. I was wracked with guilt, fearing she would come to resent me for my agelessness. If she ever did envy me—and at times she must have—she never showed it, and never stopped loving me as she always had.

"She was seventy-six when she finally died. I held her as she passed, her hair against my chin as I cradled her head in my neck, rocking her gently. I thought I would die myself when I felt her take her last breath.

"My seven children were with me. They were all grown but had gathered in the house, knowing their mother's life was coming to an end. We comforted each other, but our grief was still heavy and difficult to bear.

"My three sons and I dug a grave behind the house near an oak tree Katara and I had planted when we first returned to the village from Hethnost. My father and mother were buried nearby, their graves marked with two simple stones that were once white but had become gray and worn. Wizards are not buried, but I vowed then to forsake those traditions and join her there after my own death. She had not been a wizard, and burial was the way of the people of our village, and buried she would be. And someday so shall I.

"I left a few months after her death. I no longer belonged there. I'd moved beyond the ability to have normal contact with almost everyone because of my seemingly endless youth, and there were villagers who resented me and coveted what I had. My children still loved me, and my grandchildren and great-grandchildren, but in time even that would change if I remained.

"I gathered my family in my home to say good-bye before I returned to Hethnost. I told them I loved them all and would miss them with all my heart.

"My youngest daughter, Josenda, asked if I would ever return. I told her I wasn't certain.

"I did return once, almost sixty years later. My descendents had grown so vast it amazed me. None of my great-great-grandchildren knew who I was, and I chose not to reveal myself to them. I visited Katara's grave—the oak tree had grown to a magnificent size—and the graves of my sons and daughters before leaving. Even though I knew they'd had long and full lives, it was still a terrible and painful thing to see."

He exhaled a long breath. "I know that seems a sad tale—and it *is* sad—but Katara and I also had a lifetime of happiness together. She was an exceptional woman. Other wizards have had husbands and wives who were not so understanding of their long lives and came to grief because of it." He stood. "I've spoken enough for now. If you like, we can talk about this another time."

Reshel fought back tears. "Thank you, Hollin. You've given me a lot to think about." She hurried from the room, suddenly sad and afraid. Would a man even *want* to marry her, knowing she would outlive him by generations? She'd always liked Gerin's friend Balandrick; what would he think of this, and of her?

She slipped into her chambers, wondering if this were truly the right choice for her. *It's such a high price to pay,* she thought as she closed her door. She leaned back against the hard wood and let out a long breath. But there was also much to gain, more than most people could ever dream of having. How could she refuse that? She would be a fool to do so, and would regret it the rest of her life.

She felt something within her harden. She straightened, then crossed the room to her window, her arms folded across her abdomen. *My father did not raise me to fear hardship, or to slink away because I might meet with sorrow or pain. No, I will not refuse. I will be trained as a wizard.*

4

"**Y**ou're not serious," said Balandrick Vaules after Gerin had finished telling him about Hollin. "You're going to be a *wizard*? And Reshel, too?"

"I'm completely serious." The two young men were riding in the Halbern Hills to the west of the castle, beyond the town of Padesh. It was said that the Bright Folk who had lived in these lands ages before the Pashti came and frightened them away now dwelled beneath these and other hills, and beneath the deep and silent lakes of the westlands, and in the dark forest of Haranwaith to the south. Gerin had never seen one of the Bright Folk, and did not know if they truly existed outside of legend. But it was fun to think about them, and when he was younger, he and Therain and Balandrick had come here to look for the hidden doors in the hills that would lead to their great halls and secret treasures.

Gerin glanced into the trees on the left and right of the narrow switchback path that cut up the side of Twin Oaks Hill, wondering if any of the Bright Folk were hidden there, mindful of their secret doors and treasures, watching them pass.

Balandrick was riding just behind him. "How long is this training going to take?"

"Years." Gerin ducked under some low-hanging branches on the trail, then straightened.

Balandrick groaned and brushed a curl of blond hair from

his eyes. "Years. Ugh. But it's a small price to pay, I guess."

"I'm certainly not going to turn it down. But you're right, it's a long time to wait."

"So you get to be king *and* a wizard. I'll never even be Earl of Carengil. It's not fair."

"That's what Claressa thinks."

"Did she ever see Hollin to find out if she's a wizard?"

"Not yet. Hollin offered to go see her. He thought she might be shy about asking."

Balandrick snorted. "Claressa? Shy?"

"That's what I told him. I said he should just wait for her to come to him. If she was in one of her snits when he tried to see her, she might tear one of his arms off before he could stop her, wizard or not."

They reached the top of the hill and dismounted to let their horses rest, unbuckling bows and quivers from their saddles. Gerin wore an unbuttoned leather vest over a loose tunic, lightly woven brown pants, and brown riding boots. He pulled a padded gauntlet over his left forearm, slipped the quiver across his back, and wandered toward the two huge oaks that graced the hill's summit.

Balandrick followed, also carrying his bow and quiver. He was three years older than Gerin and slightly taller than the young prince he was charged to protect, broad-chested and thickly muscled from his training with the other members of the castle guard. He had brown eyes and darkened skin from working and training in the sun, and kept a trim beard along his jaw that was so light that from a distance it was sometimes difficult to see. His upper right arm was banded with tattoos of his family's sigil, the castle guard company symbol, and several other markings he'd gotten with friends.

Balandrick was the youngest of the four sons of Earl Herenne Vaules of Carengil. Five years ago the earl had arranged with Prince Abran for his youngest son to become Gerin's guard as part of his vassal obligations. Gerin and Balandrick had quickly become friends. Balandrick had once considered joining the Taeratens of the Naege—Helgrim had told him he'd make an excellent swordmaster—but he'd told Gerin he felt inclined to remain at Ailethon. When Gerin became duke, he named Balandrick as the captain of the household guard.

They could see Padesh behind them, with Ailethon just barely visible in the heat-haze above the walled town, seeming to float like an apparition in the sky. There was traffic on the roads to Tilgad and Marren's Ferry, walkers and horsemen and wagons going to and from the markets, all stirring up a cloud of brown dust from the dry dirt roadbed. The sunlit waters of the Kilnathé River sparkled like a silver thread as it meandered down from the north. Beyond the castle they could see the dark stain of the Ashlynne Woods on the horizon, a dense tangle of trees where the two often hunted, just to the east of the river.

"It's strange enough thinking of you as a wizard," said Balandrick. "But Reshel . . ." He shook his head.

"I'm wondering if she'll be able to handle the training," said Gerin as he nocked his first arrow and sighted along the shaft. He released the string with a dull thrumming sound. The arrow sank into the bark of the left oak tree fifty feet away, near the spot he was aiming for but not close enough for him to be pleased.

"Really?" Balandrick sighted and fired. His arrow struck about six inches to the left of Gerin's.

"You know how Reshel is. She's like a piece of porcelain. I've gathered that this training is going to be hard. I'm not sure she's up to it." Gerin fired again, and this time the arrow splintered the side of the trunk, far from his intended target. "Shayphim take me, that was terrible."

"I think Reshel might surprise you. I think she's stronger than everyone thinks."

Gerin shrugged. "We'll see."

Balandrick's second shot struck very close to his first. "Why are we practicing with bows, anyway? You like swords better."

"Because I've been reminded several times recently that

Therain is more proficient with a bow than me, and I'll be *damned* if I'm going to let him be better than me at anything."

Balandrick laughed. "You've got a lot of work to do then. Because he's *very* good with a bow, and you're . . . well . . ." He gestured toward the tree, where Gerin's third arrow landed near the roots.

They practiced for an hour, then drank some water and sat down with their backs against the trees. Gerin looked up at the sky and squinted; there were no clouds, only a wall of bright white haze.

"So what are you going to do when you become king?" asked Balandrick.

Gerin was quiet a long while before he spoke. "I don't know, Balan. Whatever I have to. I'll collect the taxes and repair the roads and guard the borders and settle disputes and everything else a king does. But I don't have any plans for something grand of my own, like commanding some great castle to be built or anything like that. I wish I did." Now that he'd started talking, he found it difficult to stop. He'd kept so much of this buried that at times he felt ready to burst with the slowly building pressure. Now that Hollin had laid before him perhaps the means of achieving his secret dream, he felt he could at last speak of it aloud. "I was thinking that my magic might allow me to surpass even Vendel and Ulgreth Atreyano, but doing what? They took an unimportant noble house that was nothing and created a line of kings. *And* put the Pashti in their place once and for all. My grandfather dealt with the invasions of the Pelklanders, and my father helped him achieve victory when he was younger than I am now. What's left for me to do, even if I am a wizard? Just living a long time won't be much of an achievement."

"You have plenty of time before you have to worry about this. Besides, I think that greatness gets thrust upon a king. It doesn't seem like it's plotted out in advance too often. Your grandfather didn't plan for the Pelklanders to harry the coast, he just dealt with the problem after it happened. You'll have enough to worry about without looking for new problems to fix in order to make yourself great. Besides, planning your legacy or how you'll fit into history doesn't seem to me to be the best way to live your life."

Gerin could not decide if Balan was right, and if he was right, whether that was good or bad. If greatness was something that couldn't be planned, then there was no guarantee he would ever achieve it, wizardry or not.

He suddenly remembered the godlike presence that had visited him in his rooms. Despite the heat, a chill danced across his flesh. What did it want with him? *Your time is coming*—what did that mean? He'd read in the library about men who'd been chosen by the gods to accomplish some task, and none of them had come to good ends. *I will not be a puppet!* he thought angrily. *I will not be used and then discarded.* But despite his assertion, he was frightened to the core of his being. If a god had chosen him, what could he do? How could he defy the divine?

He said nothing of this to Balandrick. His confession to his friend only went so far.

They sat in silence for a while, then gathered their horses and headed for the castle.

They were on the trail leading away from the foot of the hill when they heard riders behind them. A small dense wood blocked their view of the trail, but the riders were coming quickly.

"That's a lot of horses by the sound of it," said Balandrick. "And they're coming fast."

The riders appeared seconds later in the narrow opening between the dense knot of trees, twenty riding two abreast. All of them were armed with short, broad-bladed swords that hung from their belts, and most also carried spears and several knives of varying lengths. About half had bows slung across their backs and quivers lashed to their saddles.

One of the riders was different from the rest. He had no armor or sword; instead, he wore several layers of rough brown leather and carried a long wooden staff with a plume of peacock feathers tied to its upper ferrule. Bands of silver wound about his bare forearms like metal snakes, and his arms were heavily tattooed. His long hair was tied in braids of varying length and thickness. A silver necklace with a number of strange medallions hung low on his chest.

The riders drew up suddenly when they saw the two young men ahead of them. When the man with the staff saw Gerin, his eyes went wide. He threw back his head and let out a shriek that made Gerin's blood chill. Then he pointed at the prince with his crooked staff and shouted in heavily accented Kelarin, "We have found the god-summoner! Our quest is achieved! Take him alive! Do not harm him!"

The riders surged forward. The man with the staff stared at Gerin.

Neddari! thought the prince. Neddar was a country along the southwestern border of Khedesh. The two nations were not at war, but neither were they exactly at peace. The Neddari were a loose organization of clans without centralized rule. They considered any foreigner an enemy, but rarely ventured beyond their own lands, leaving their neighbors for the most part alone and unmolested.

This particular group was a long way from home. *What in the name of the gods are they doing here?*

"Run, my lord! There are too many to fight!" Balandrick drew his bow and quickly nocked an arrow, letting it fly at the man with the staff. A Neddari soldier raised a small round shield and blocked the shaft, which splintered against the steel.

Gerin wheeled his horse Ranno about and spurred him to a gallop. Cursing, Balandrick followed close behind.

They galloped over a wooden bridge that crossed a shallow creek. Gerin tried to remember how far it was to the Padesh Road—a mile maybe, then another three miles to the town itself? *Can we outrun them for that long?*

He glanced over his shoulder. The larger Neddari chargers were gaining on them fast. They had no hope of beating them to town. Balandrick looked back and swore again, realizing the same thing.

They rounded a sharp turn in the trail. The woods thinned
as the hills drew farther apart, giving them a wider view of
the shallow valley through which they galloped. There was
no one else in sight, no help of any kind.

Gerin leaned closer to Ranno's neck and tried to push a
little more speed from the gelding, willing it to go as fast as
possible. His heart raced as Ranno's hooves pounded into
the earth.

They reached a sudden drop-off in the ground. Gerin was
ready for it, but Balandrick, looking back, was not prepared
when his horse Vegos jumped down the slope. He came off
the saddle at an odd angle and his right foot slipped out
of its stirrup. His body slammed down hard on the left side
of the horse, which shied suddenly, its head thrashing about
in terror.

Balandrick lost his grip on the reins and flew away from
Vegos in a tumble. He hit the ground with a loud grunt, then
rolled and slammed hard against a small tree.

"Balan!"

Gerin continued on, torn between turning to help his
friend and fleeing the Neddari. Balandrick's horse was galloping off the trail. Gerin knew there was no chance of him
recovering it.

Mighty Telros, watch over me, he thought as he pulled up
hard on his reins and turned Ranno around. What he was doing was foolish and reckless, but he would not leave his
friend behind.

Balandrick groaned and sat up, holding his shoulder. He
drew his hunting knife—both his sword and bow were on his
still-galloping horse—and stood up just as the first Neddari
reached him.

Balandrick lunged upward with the knife, his teeth bared
in a snarl, trying to slash across the man's waist below his
leather jerkin, but the Neddari brushed the cut aside easily
with his shield. Then he was gone, galloping past Balandrick
in a blur. The Neddari behind the first drew his sword and
swung it viciously at Balandrick's head.

Balandrick held up his own knife at the last moment to block the stroke while he pumped his legs backward in a frantic attempt to get clear of the horses before he was trampled. His knife turned but did not completely deflect the blow, and the flat of the Neddari's sword hit Balandrick along the side of his head with a hard metallic clang. Balandrick fell back, senseless, the knife tumbling from his hand.

"Leave him!" shouted the man with the staff. "It is the other we need!"

Gerin cursed and dragged Ranno around yet again. There was no way to reach Balandrick now. The only thing left to do was escape.

What in the name of the gods do they want with me? he thought as he spurred Ranno on. *Do they know that I'm a prince? But how did they recognize me? And how did they find me?*

He'd only ridden another fifty or sixty yards when the two Neddari drew up on either side of him. Gerin shouted and drew Glaros. These foreign bastards would not take him!

The Neddari on his left moved closer, and Gerin slashed at him with his sword. The tip sliced through the man's shoulder; a spray of blood shot into the air. Gerin veered Ranno to the left, even closer to the wounded man, and rammed the point of Glaros through his throat. Dark blood jetted from the man's mouth; his arms went slack and the life drained from his eyes. Gerin drew the weapon back before it was dragged away as the man toppled from his saddle.

He turned in the saddle and slashed at the man on the other side. But the Neddari blocked Gerin's stroke with his small shield, forcing Gerin's right arm up above his shoulder. With Gerin's side exposed, the Neddari rammed the heel of his spear into his ribs.

The air exploded from Gerin's lungs. He forced his blade down around the Neddari's shield and desperately tried to draw a breath. He brought his sword back to strike again—

A coil of rope fell across his torso and cinched tight so

quickly it nearly pulled him from his horse. His arms were pressed against his sides. The edge of his weapon gashed his leg, and he felt blood run from his thigh down into his boot.

Another rope fell over him and tightened. He shouted in rage and fought against his bonds, but the ropes were thick and coarse and he had no way to move them. He tried to bend his wrist back so he could drag his blade across the ropes, but the Neddari with the spear saw what he was doing and laughed—a harsh, guttural noise full of contempt—then pulled the sword from his hand and dropped it to the ground. Gripping Ranno's reins, he slowed the horse to a halt.

Gerin stared into the man's eyes, refusing to be cowed. If they were going to kill him, he would not flinch from his death. He pushed his arms outward against the ropes, straining with all his might, his side still burning; but he could not free himself.

The Neddari surrounded him in a tight circle. The man with the staff grinned wickedly, revealing long yellow teeth, some of which had been filed to sharp points. Gerin could see tattoos on his face that looked like mystical symbols of some kind.

"What do you want with me?" said Gerin.

The man gestured with his staff to the two Neddari holding the ropes. Immediately Gerin was yanked from Ranno, landing hard on his left side. He grunted and rolled onto his back, determined to see whatever fate they were preparing for him. Two Neddari held his shoulders and two more knelt on his legs, completely immobilizing him.

The man with the staff dismounted and knelt by Gerin. He gripped Gerin's jaw and turned his head to the left and right, as if inspecting a cut of meat. The mad grin was still on his face; his breath was sour, and there was a strange odor mingled with it that reminded the prince of some of the medicinal potions kept by Master Aslon in his work chambers. Gerin saw that the whites of his eyes were tinged with yellow and red; his pupils were tiny black dots.

"You are the god-summoner," said the man, his accent so

thick it took Gerin a moment to understand him. *Yoo er ta ghode-soomahner.* "I saw you in a vision. The Slain God's power waxes full, but He is not yet strong enough to return through the Door of Night. You will open it for Him. I have seen it."

"I have no idea what you're talking—"

The man clamped his hand painfully across Gerin's mouth. "I have *seen* it. I saw that you would be here, at this spot, on this day, and though I did not know this place, I knew my vision would guide me." He looked up at the surrounding hills with awe in his eyes. "And so I am here, as are you. My vision did not fail me, and you will not fail me. I have seen what you will do, but the future is fickle and ever-changing, like the mood of a woman. I must do everything in my power to make certain that what I have seen will come to pass."

He reached down to his belt and withdrew a small leather pouch stoppered with a waxed cap. He broke the seal and poured a small amount of grayish powder onto his palm. For some reason it reminded Gerin of bone dust.

The man inhaled sharply, then blew the powder in Gerin's face.

Gerin drew a breath before he could stop himself. The dust entered his nostrils and throat. He coughed and spluttered and tried to spit it out, but some was already in his lungs and some he'd already swallowed. *Poison! They're poisoning me!*

The man placed his fingers across Gerin's face and spoke in a language the prince did not understand.

"Iqui pak'haro ninjog va'nol quathak . . ."

Gerin began to tremble uncontrollably, his jaw clenched so tightly he thought his teeth would shatter.

A fire ignited in his skull. He tried to scream but could not open his mouth. Blood gushed from his nostrils and ears, and the hot stench of copper filled the air. Gerin forced his eyes to remain open, staring into the face of the man who was killing him.

His vision began to blur, shimmering as the fire in his skull dwindled, the man's face becoming little more than a dark globe filling his vision—a globe shot through with yellow-red eyes that seemed to glow with an inner light of their own.

"Your will is mine now, summoner. The God's return is now all but assured. The vision will come to pass. You will not fail me."

Gerin's jaw unlocked and he gasped for air, tasting the blood that had run from his nose. The seizure stopped and he felt himself begin to lose consciousness. The man with the staff had risen and was climbing back onto his horse.

"The quest is achieved," he said to his men. "We will go home to await the God's Return."

Gerin blacked out as the horses thundered past him.

"My lord, wake up! Wake up!"

Gerin felt a hand gripping his face and for a second feared the man with the staff had returned. His eyes flew open and he saw Balandrick kneeling over him. *Why aren't I dead?*

"Balan, the Neddari, where—"

"Gone. Rode off to the south by the look of their trail. Can you sit up? I want to get these ropes off you."

Gerin nodded but was not so sure. His head ached unbearably. Balandrick put his arms beneath Gerin's shoulders and gently pulled him upright. Gerin groaned and thought he might pass out again, throw up, or both.

"Just hold still," said Balandrick. "Keep your eyes closed."

Gerin nodded, not trusting himself to speak. He felt the ropes loosen and then disappear as Balandrick pulled them off over his head. Needlelike prickles of pain blossomed up and down his arms now that the pressure on them had been removed.

"It looks like they worked you over pretty good, my lord. Is your nose broken?"

"They didn't . . . didn't hit me . . ."

"Did you hurt yourself in the fall from your horse? Your

nose was bleeding pretty good, judging by the blood all over you." Gerin felt Balandrick turn his head. "Your ears, too. And there's a slash on your leg."

The prince finally managed to open his eyes. Balandrick had a dark bruise along his right eye and a nasty cut across his forehead, but other than that seemed unhurt.

"No, it wasn't the fall. The Neddari with the staff blew some kind of powder into my face. I breathed it before I could help myself. That's why I'm bleeding."

"Poison. *Damn* them. We have to get you back to Master Aslon—"

Gerin shook his head. "It wasn't poison."

"Then what was it? Why did they do this to you?"

"I don't know. Help me get to my feet. I need some water." He could still feel the grit of the Neddari's dust on his teeth. He spat, but his mouth was too dry to do much good.

He stood wobbly, his thigh throbbing from the wound, and looked around.

The Neddari were nowhere to be seen. He could see the path they'd made to the south where the high grass had been trampled.

Gerin whistled several times for Ranno, as did Balandrick for Vegos. Neither horse appeared.

"We might as well start walking," said Gerin.

"I need to bandage your leg first. Sit down."

Gerin did as he was told, too weak and light-headed to argue. Balandrick cut several strips of cloth from his tunic and bound them around his thigh. The prince winced as his friend pulled the strips hard and knotted them tightly.

Balandrick stood and helped Gerin to his feet.

"You might want this back." Balandrick bent down and lifted Glaros from the grass. There was dried blood along the blade. "I'm surprised they left this. I found it when I was walking over to you."

"Me, too. I'm surprised about this whole thing." The sword's sheath was still on Ranno. He held up the blade, inspecting the blood, then lowered it to his side and began to walk. His thigh pulsed with a rhythmic pain and his side ached where he'd been hit with the spear; the rest of his body felt loose and wobbly from the dust-induced seizure, but he did his best to ignore his pains and keep moving.

They'd not gone far when they heard the sound of more horsemen behind them. Gerin felt a sudden, sickening dread in the pit of his stomach. Balandrick's face blazed with hatred as he wheeled around, knife in hand, wondering who they would have to face now.

They were shocked to see a company of Khedeshian soldiers riding hard toward them, their helms and breastplates gleaming brightly in the afternoon sun. Gerin counted forty men before he realized that the standard they carried was the emblem of Calad-Ethil, a spear and scythe crossed beneath a tower, all in gold, set against a blue field.

"They're far from home," murmured Balandrick as he noticed the standard. "That's a Southland banner. I'll bet they can give us some answers about the Neddari."

He stepped forward and raised his arms. "Halt in the name of Prince Gerin Atreyano! Halt in the name of the prince!"

The soldiers stopped and formed a line before the two young men. "The prince, you say?" said the captain, marked by the red plume upon his helm and the blue diagonal slash painted across his breastplate.

"Prince Gerin Atreyano. I am his guard, Balandrick Vaules. The prince has just been attacked by Neddari."

The captain drew a hissing breath. "We've been chasing those bastards for days, but they ride light and fast and we've been unable to catch them." He got down from his horse and looked at Gerin, then bowed his head and saluted.

"Their business here is apparently done," said Gerin. He spat again in a futile attempt to get the taste of blood out of his mouth.

The captain raised an eyebrow. "And how do you know that, my lord?"

"First, some water."

"Yes, my lord." The captain turned to one of his men and

snapped his fingers. The soldier handed him a water skin and a rag. Gerin drank deeply, then soaked the rag and wiped the blood from his face and ears.

"Captain, what is your name?"

The man removed his helm and placed it under his arm. His graying hair was tied at the back of his neck with a band of soft cloth. "Teray Melfistan from Calad-Ethil, my lord." He scratched at the ragged growth of beard along his jaw with his gloved hand.

"And you say you've been following these Neddari for days?"

"Yes, my lord. Since we first got word that they'd crossed into our lands. Begging your pardon, my lord, but you said they attacked you?"

"Yes. Me, specifically. They ignored Balandrick."

The captain whistled and shook his head. "That's just not something the Neddari do, my lord. Leave those they attack alive, I mean. You should be dead. Or taken with them as a slave."

"Do you know why they came here?" asked Balandrick.

"No. Could be any number of reasons, but we've never before had a party of Neddari ride so deeply into Khedesh. I don't understand it."

"They said they were finished here and were going home." Gerin pointed along the trail the Neddari had made.

Captain Melfistan turned to his men. "Andros! Take the company and chase them down. I don't want them to leave Khedesh alive. Jurin, Tomos, and Varnil, you're with me. We'll escort the prince back to his home."

The Khedeshians rode hard along the Neddari's trail and disappeared between the hills. Melfistan put his helm back on and swung onto his horse. Gerin and Balandrick were helped up onto the saddles of two of the other men, where they would ride double.

"I'll let you lead the way, my lord," said Melfistan. "I've no idea where we need to go from here."

"Just follow this trail for now," said Gerin. "When we come

around this next hill you'll see the town of Padesh ahead, and beyond that will be Ailethon, my castle."

"Would you mind telling me what happened, my lord?" asked the captain. "I'd like to understand what this attack was all about."

"Not at all. I have some questions for you myself." He described the attack and the words of the man with the staff as best as he could remember them.

"Do you have any idea what it means?" he said when he was done. "What was that man? And what is a 'god-summoner'?"

"The man with the staff is a *kamichi*," said the captain. "It's their word for a wise man or sorcerer. As for what 'god-summoner' means, I don't have any idea about that. Nor who their Slain God is. I do know the *kamichi* have visions and sometimes go on quests because of them, but this is the strangest one I've ever heard of. I'm sorry, my lord. I can make no sense of it."

It troubled Gerin deeply that he'd been singled out as the object of a Neddari sorcerer's spirit quest. Was it somehow connected to his becoming a wizard? It seemed an odd coincidence that this happened so soon after the visit from Hollin.

Still, who is the Slain God? And how in the name of Telros am I supposed to bring him back?

They found Ranno and Vegos wandering a field near Padesh. By the time they reached the gate in the ivy-covered wall around the town, Gerin was beyond exhausted. Night had almost fallen. The watchman stared with open wonder at the bloody prince riding with unknown Khedeshian soldiers carrying southland banners.

It was fully dark when he arrived at the castle. Gerin left Balandrick and the soldiers near the stables and marched wearily to the keep, where he commanded a servant to bring Hollin to him at once.

Gerin had removed his shirt and was washing at the basin when Hollin arrived. The wizard's eyes went wide when he saw Gerin's injuries. There was a deep purple bruise along his right side where the Neddari spear had hit him, and the length of his right leg was crusted with dried blood.

"What happened to you? Are you all right?"

"I've had an interesting day, Hollin. I was attacked by a Neddari sorcerer."

"Indeed," said Hollin. "Tell me what happened."

"That's why I asked you here."

"I will heal your wounds for you if you'll permit me. But we should wait until we're done speaking. The magic will tire you—and me as well—and send you into a deep sleep."

"Of course I'll permit it. My ribs and leg are killing me."

"Does your father know of this?"

"Not yet. I'll tell him in the morning. There's nothing to be done now anyway."

He told Hollin the story, becoming both angry and afraid as he described the dust blown into his face, and asked him if he knew what the *kamichi* had done to him.

Hollin scowled. "The Neddari do not welcome outsiders, so there is little we know of them. They do not allow wizards into their country to perform the Ritual of Discovery. I've heard of the *kamichi* but know almost nothing of their powers. It's said they have spirit-guides of some kind that send them on quests or show them glimpses of the future, which is apparently what happened today. But I can shed no light on who their Slain God is or what involvement you might have with it."

"Could it have something to do with me becoming a wizard?"

"Who can say? But first I want to see if I can determine what he did to you. Relax. This will feel strange but won't hurt."

Gerin inhaled and tried to calm himself. Hollin stood and extended his hand toward the prince. He barked a single word, *"Parnathos,"* then muttered something too low for Gerin to hear.

Gerin's body went cold, as if he'd been dropped into a tub of cool water. His skin shivered and prickled; a moment later he began to shake.

Hollin's expression darkened. He spoke another command and clenched his hand into a fist.

Gerin felt a contraction through the center of his body, a sudden spasm of his muscles and limbs that left him gasping. He felt something alien there, something *other* at the core of his being, like a splinter driven deep beneath the flesh.

Hollin stopped and relaxed, though the dark expression did not leave his face. The coldness and sense of tightening left the prince at once.

"What did you find?" asked Gerin, panting for breath.

"The Neddari has indeed placed a spell of some kind upon you, but I can neither fathom its purpose nor remove it. It is too different from our magic. I do not believe it is active at the moment. It seems to be slumbering deep within you, waiting for a command or trigger to release it."

"You mean there's nothing you can do about it?"

"At the moment, no. But when we go to Hethnost, I will consult with the Warden of Healing. He is more adept at these matters than I."

Gerin slumped into the chair, horrified at the idea that there was a Neddari spell hidden within his body. *And he said my will was his. What if he can somehow control me from afar? Is that his intent? To make me his slave?*

He voiced his fear to Hollin.

"It does not appear to be a compulsion," said the wizard. "They are dangerous, difficult spells, and usually damage those who are to be compelled. You show none of the signs of one under such power. I don't know what his words meant, but I don't believe they mean you have become, or will become, his puppet."

"I wish I were as sure of that as you." Gerin started to lean back, then straightened suddenly as he remembered the divine entity that had appeared in his rooms. "Hollin, there's something else. I don't know if it's related to what happened today or not.

"A few days ago, I sensed something divine in my room." He waved his hands about, grasping for the words to adequately describe the event. "It was a . . . *presence* of some kind; not a person, nothing physical, but it was undeniably real. I could sense that it was huge, powerful. There was a light, and I heard a voice call my name and then say, 'Your time is coming.' I could feel it touch me in some way I can't really describe because I don't understand it myself. But it wanted *me* for something, I'm sure of that." His shoulders slumped. "Then you arrive and tell me I'm going to be a wizard, and now the Neddari hunt me down and tell me I'm going to be a god-summoner, only no one knows what that is. This can't just be coincidence."

Hollin listened intently, saying nothing, though his frown deepened as Gerin spoke. "Perhaps. This is indeed troubling. It is rarely good when a divine power involves itself in the affairs of men. It may be that your power as a wizard—the power you *will* have—has somehow drawn the attention of the divine. It gave you no clue as to *which* god it might be?"

Gerin shook his head. "Nothing."

"Knowing which deity might help us better understand its intentions toward you. But without that, there is little we can do except be vigilant in case it returns. You must tell me *at once* if this presence appears to you again."

"I will. Though I hope it leaves me alone."

"That would be for the best, but if it truly was a divine being, then the likelihood of that is remote. Once they have decided upon something, they rarely change their minds."

Gerin wanted to crawl under his bed and hide. He did not want the attention of a god upon him. He twisted in his chair and winced when sharp pain raced through his side.

Too much was happening at once. The divine presence, his wizardry, and now the Neddari attack. He felt as if his world had been thrown out of balance, that the ground beneath his feet could no longer be trusted to remain solid and true. His stomach knotted with anxiety.

"We've spoken enough for now," said Hollin. "You need to rest and heal your injuries. Lie down on your bed."

Gerin did so and watched as Hollin again held out his

hand and spoke the words of a spell. The prince recognized some of the Osirin words and phrases—*I command, rejuvenation, body,* and *spirit*—but then Hollin's voice dropped to an unintelligible whisper.

A warmth flooded through him, not unlike the sensation of the Ritual of Discovery, flowing outward from the center of his being toward his extremities. But this time he did not see an amber glow in his vision; instead, the warmth pooled around the wound in his leg, the bruise on his ribs, and the damage within his nose and ears, focusing energy on mending the injuries it found.

Exhaustion settled over him so completely he could not hold open his eyes. He felt himself sliding into unconsciousness.

"Sleep now," said Hollin. His voice sounded far away. "We'll speak more of this later."

Gerin heard the door to his chamber open and close, and then was lost in a deep sleep.

5

He awoke very late in the morning. He rubbed his sticky eyes and sat up slowly. Memories of the day before rushed back all at once. He looked at the cut on his leg and was stunned to see that it was now little more than a red welt; it appeared to have been healing for at least a week rather than a single night. The bruise on his side was a small splotch of yellow skin with a faint purplish center, and was no longer tender to the touch. His ears and nose also seemed fine.

Grinning, he got out of bed and poured himself a cup of water from the ewer on the basin.

His grin faded when he remembered the Neddari attack and Hollin's confirmation that some spell had been planted in him that could not be removed. He rubbed his hand across his chest, as if there were some way he could feel or sense the alien power within him and perhaps yank it out.

But he felt nothing. He felt fine.

But I'm not fine, he thought. *That Neddari came to me for a purpose. There's something he means me to do, and he went to great lengths to ensure I do it. But I won't. Whatever it is, I will not do it.*

Gerin's father visited him a little while later. "You know why I'm here." Abran's stare was so intense that Gerin could not meet it.

"You heard about the Neddari."

Abran slowly paced the sitting room. "I've heard that you turned about to rescue Balandrick after he'd fallen even though it put you in greater danger. Captain Melfistan said you told him that's what happened, and Balandrick himself confirmed it."

"Yes, Father, I did. I know it was a foolish decision, that my personal safety as a prince should be paramount to all other concerns, but—"

Abran had raised his hand to silence his son. "I can see you think I'm going to yell at you for risking your life to save your friend. That your life is far too important to jeopardize for something as foolish as sentiment. Which is true. But I'm not going to do that. What you did was commendable. It was *brave*. You made a difficult choice in the face of a vicious enemy. That kind of bravery will serve you well when you become king. Certainly Balandrick will never forget it." He stopped pacing. "I've also heard the Neddari seemed to have sought you out specifically and did something to you. I find this most troubling."

"So do I." Gerin recounted his conversation with Hollin from the night before. He left out the visitation of the divine presence in his rooms. He was not yet prepared to speak of that to anyone other than Hollin.

"So this Neddari sorcerer has placed a spell on you that cannot be removed." Gerin could see his father's anger seething, which made him glad he'd said nothing about the divine presence. It probably would have pushed his father's fury over the edge. "Is this in any way connected to you learning that you're a wizard?"

"I asked Hollin that same question. He could not say."

"I'm having doubts about your wizardry. If this is the kind of problems such powers will attract—"

"Father, we have no idea if it's related or not. I see no reason to question my training until we learn more."

"I've been thinking a great deal about this wizard business. I fear it may cause more problems than it's worth. I can already hear the objections from the nobles. They'll complain that you are under the improper influence of a foreign power, that you'll be little more than their puppet. They'll say that will allow the wizards who control you to take utter control of Khedesh."

"That's ridiculous! I will *not* be a puppet of the wizards or anyone else!"

"I did not say you would be, I said that's what the other nobles will claim. And it is not an easy thing to disprove."

"Then they'll just have to learn to live with it."

"Gerin, it may be best for everyone if you simply forget this wizard business."

He could scarcely believe what his father had just said. His arguments about the nobles were paltry at best; they would always find something to complain about, probing for weaknesses from the crown that they could turn to their advantage. That was an immutable fact, a cornerstone of the governance of the kingdom: the king ruled, and the nobles complained.

His father held his gaze for a long moment, then looked away. And in that instant Gerin realized his father's true motivations.

He was jealous. Of the power and life that had come to his son and not to him.

His father would never say such a thing, of course, and it was possible he did not even realize it himself. Yet Gerin was certain that jealousy was the secret reason for his objections and this attempt to get him to give up his wizardry. There had always been a bit of competition between father and son—it was one of the reasons Gerin worked as hard as he did to excel, to prove himself to his father.

But this was something where his father had no hope of competing, where Gerin, simply by being what he was (or what he would become), would eclipse his father in an almost unimaginable way.

"I'm going to be trained by Hollin. There's no point in discussing it further. The nobles will just have to accept it. Nothing violates the kingdom's laws, and since there has already *been* a king who was a wizard, there is also precedent. You are my king and my father, but you must also accept that *I* am now the lord of Ailethon, and if I choose to do this, I will, with or without your permission."

He waited, his heart hammering in his chest, wondering how his father would react. To his surprise, his father sighed. *He knows I'm right,* thought Gerin. *That's why he's not arguing. He knows there's nothing else he can say.*

"Perhaps. For you, at least. But Reshel . . . I don't know, Gerin. I've not been comfortable since she told me she also has the potential to become a wizard. My first thought was to refuse her permission, but I knew she would not take it well. But where she is concerned, my heart is filled with doubt and misgiving."

"Let her at least make the attempt. From what Hollin's told me, the training can be very hard. It may be that she will not complete it anyway."

"I think she's stronger than you give her credit for," said Abran, echoing Balandrick's sentiment. He wondered what they saw in his sister that he did not. "But I will not refuse her. Not yet, at any rate. Unless we learn something definitive about this Neddari attack that makes me change my mind." He pointed his finger at his son and shook it for emphasis. "I do, however, expect you to watch out for her and keep her safe. See that she does not run afoul of any trouble because of her wizardry. I'm serious about this, Gerin. I will hold you accountable if she does."

"Of course, Father. I always do. *Claressa's* the one I'm tempted to toss from the walls from time to time."

Gerin held a feast in the castle's Great Audience Hall to commemorate his father's departure to continue his peregrination through the westlands. The hall itself stood next to the keep, connected by a covered walkway and several underground passages for the movement of servants and their wares. Its peaked roof was covered in gray slate tiles, with the banners of House Atreyano flying from the four corners.

The inside of the hall was completely open, the high ceiling supported by red-veined marble pillars, eight on each side. The windows in the long side walls were narrow and tall, similar in shape to those of the Sunlight Hall but without the ornate coloring of the glass. One end of the hall was elevated three steps above the main floor and contained the head table for Abran, his family, and important vassals and guests. The main floor, tiled in gray and white granite squares, was filled with long trestle tables and benches for the seating of lesser lords and their retainers.

A band of minstrels played and sang in one corner; jugglers and tumblers performed in a space left open between the dais and the lower tables. Servants hurried about the room carrying plates of roast pork smothered in a cream sauce with chunks of potatoes and red beets, or flagons of beer and wine to replenish empty cups.

Hollin, seated at the head table, was the subject of much discussion.

"Prince Gerin and Princess Reshel are *both* wizards?" said Earl Devram Belormi after hearing Hollin recount his story. "Incredible." Gerin listened carefully for any discontented mutterings about "foreign influences" upon the monarchy, but he heard nothing.

After the meal was finished, some of the tables were cleared and pushed aside for dancing. Gerin danced with Baya Almorand and Tamren Dolring. Baya was a skinny little thing with a pretty enough face, but Tamren had his complete attention the moment he laid eyes on her. In the year since she'd been to the castle she had changed from a gangly girl into a stunningly beautiful young woman. All the young men at the feast were vying for a dance with her. Gerin worked his way to her, forced himself in front of Tomis Gantrel, and asked if she would like to dance.

She smiled and held out her hand. "I'd be honored, my lord."

They spun about the floor for what seemed an eternity.

Several other young men tried to cut in on them, but Tamren said she was Prince Gerin's for the evening.

He caught a glimpse of Reshel dancing with Balan, the two of them laughing and talking like old friends seeing each other after a long separation. He'd sensed a subtle shift in their relationship since the Neddari attack. Reshel had been terribly impressed that Balan tried to unseat a mounted Neddari warrior with merely a hunting knife. It didn't matter that he'd failed; the fact that he tried to protect her brother was enough to make her grin and blush with admiration. She'd had a crush on him since his arrival at the castle, but that seemed to be changing into something a little more romantic and adult.

He looked for Claressa and at first did not see her, then spied her near the head table with seven or eight young men lined up around her, each vying shamelessly for her attention while she feigned disinterest, taking her time deciding which one she would dance with first, *if* she bothered to dance at all. Therain was whirling about the floor with a pretty redhead Gerin did not recognize. *He actually picked a good-looking one. Maybe there's hope for him after all.*

A little while later Tamren's large breasts brushed against his arm three times, the last time lingering for a moment while she gave him a particularly satisfied grin. He was certain she was doing it on purpose. He could not take his eyes from the generous amount of décolletage her blouse revealed. As the dance ended, she bent low so he could see even more of her breasts, nearly down to her nipples. She looked up at him and laughed, then straightened and leaned close to his cheek. There was a thin sheen of perspiration on her face.

"I know what you're looking at," she whispered. "If we go someplace where we can be alone, you can do more than look."

He knew he was expected to stay longer, but the thought of time alone with Tamren was too much for him to resist. He found his father, who was still seated at the head table, and said he was going out to get some air. His father glanced toward Tamren and gave his son a knowing look. "Enjoy your air," he said, then took another gulp of wine.

He and Tamren made their way from the noisy hall and back into the keep itself, then climbed a twisting flight of stairs toward Gerin's chambers.

She held his hand as they rushed up the steps with her in the lead. Giggling, she placed his hand on her bottom, and he made a soft, delighted moan.

They reached a dark hallway. She spun around and draped her arms around his neck, then kissed him hard on the mouth. "Where should we go?" she asked.

"We can go to my rooms," he said, the blood pounding in his head. He kissed her back, nibbling at her lower lip. "But Tamren, we can't make a child." He had to be blunt—he was in such a state that he had no hope of thinking with subtlety. Her father, Owin Dolring, was lord of a minor house that offered no value in a union with a family as powerful as the Atreyanos. Gerin would one day marry the daughter of a major house—according to his father, it would most likely be Mora Oltheri or Pranis Maundell. He often struggled with the idea that his father would decide whom he would marry. While part of him understood the political necessity of strategic alliances for the royal family, another part chafed at the loss of control over such an important aspect of his life. *He* wanted to pick the woman he would wed. Many noblemen simply took mistresses to keep them happy, but Gerin did not want to do that. It seemed an admission of defeat, that their marriages were failures they were unable or unwilling to fix. And Gerin, above all else, did not like to fail.

"I don't want to *marry* you, Gerin," she said, smiling. "I just want to bed you. I like tall, strong men. And don't worry—my mother's a witching woman. I have everything I need."

He squeezed her hand and took her upstairs.

Toward morning, Gerin slipped from his rooms to wander the halls. A rosy predawn light seeped into the corridors.

Tamren was asleep on the bed, her arms curled around a goose-down pillow. He'd returned to the hall after their love-making to say good-night to the lords and his father, leaving Tamren in his rooms. She was still awake when he got back, and they'd made love a second time before falling asleep.

He turned a corner and saw Claressa closing her door behind her. She wore a simple white nightdress with a shawl draped over her shoulders that accentuated her imposing height. Her unbound hair framed her narrow face and neck, and still held the tight curls she'd had done for the banquet. She saw him and paused, smiling radiantly.

He stopped and felt a sudden tightening in his chest; for a moment he was certain he was looking at his mother's spirit, so much did his sister resemble her.

"Did I frighten you?" she asked, breaking the spell that had come over him. "You should see the look on your face."

"No, but for a moment I thought you were . . . Mother."

Her smile widened—the smile that was so much like their mother's it made his heart ache—as if he had paid her an unexpected compliment. *I suppose I have,* he thought. "I feel like her sometimes. I was thinking about her just a little while ago, you know. Maybe she *was* with me just now, and you sensed a part of that."

"I'd like to think that's true."

"Then believe it. There's no reason not to. Is Tamren still in your bed?"

Gerin felt his face flush. "Why are you asking me that? Why should I know where she is?"

"Oh, please, Gerin, half the hall paused to watch you two sneak out."

"Did Reshel see us leave?"

She laughed again, a rich, throaty sound that was nearly identical to their mother's. "Yes, she watched you go with a look of complete distaste on her delicate little face, like she'd swallowed a lump of cooking grease. Balandrick tried to cover for you, but I don't think she believed whatever excuse he came up with."

He frowned.

Claressa said, "Oh, don't worry about our dear little sister. I think she was more jealous of Tamren's breasts than anything. Even *I'm* a bit jealous of them."

He scarcely knew what to say. "Sometimes you are downright wicked."

"I suppose. But at least I slept alone last night."

6

After their father's departure, Gerin and Reshel began training with Hollin. The wizard had dispatched a message to Hethnost informing the Archmage that the amber wizard had been discovered and describing the terms of his agreement with the Atreyanos for their training. Gerin would not be ready to leave for Hethnost for at least a month—the oathtaking of his vassals would occur in a few weeks, and he could not leave before then—but Hollin told them he could begin teaching them before their powers were Awakened.

"You won't be able to perform spells, of course," he said, "but I will tell you more about how magic works and teach you the words of some of the more basic incantations. Give you a taste of the more rigorous training to follow."

They sat in the study in the chambers Hollin had been granted in Blackstone Keep, around a small square-topped table upon which sat a magefire lamp. The soft glow from the small crystal sphere fascinated Gerin. The lamp had a rosewood pedestal and slender silver bands holding the crystal in place, but surprisingly gave off no heat.

"Osirin is a language of power," said Hollin. "All spells are written in it, and all wizards speak it. It shapes the magic that flows through a wizard's body the way a hammer shapes heated metal into whatever form the blacksmith desires.

Osirin forces unformed magic to become magefire"—he gestured to the lamp—"or a Farseeing or a Glamour, or to heal the wounds of a body. By memorizing the more common spells, you'll be able, after a time, to create them at will with a thought or simple gesture, without having to speak the incantation. The *paru'enthred*—the 'inner eye' that allows magic to flow through you—will recognize what you want, much the same way your body remembers complicated sword moves or the fingerings of a musical instrument that you've repeatedly practiced. You perform them without thought. Indeed, after you have practiced for a time, thinking about the movements can actually hinder what you are doing."

"So performing spells becomes second nature," said Gerin.

"Yes. Exactly. You will spend the majority of your years of training learning and practicing spells—hundreds of them—and the theories behind them, so that in time, if you wish, you can create spells of your own."

"I would think that most of the necessary spells have already been made by now," said Gerin.

Hollin shrugged. "Perhaps. But you never know what the future may bring. And as an amber wizard, you may create opportunities of your own."

"How exactly will Gerin be stronger than me?" asked Reshel. "Other than the color, what makes an amber wizard different?"

Hollin steepled his fingers and absently tapped them together. "It is largely a matter of degree," he said. "But first let me explain about the color of your flame, since I don't believe you have ever seen mine.

"The *paru'enthred* that shapes your magic is what determines your strength. I've already said it is like a hammer that molds and forms your spells. But more powerful wizards can also allow larger quantities of magic to flow through them— the 'conduit' through which magic moves, for want of a better word, grows increasingly larger, which enables them to perform spells that are beyond the ability of other wizards. Lesser wizards simply cannot allow enough magic within them to make the spell work. Attempting to perform very difficult spells can burn out their powers forever." Reshel looked taken aback. "Yes," he said in answer to her unspoken question, "that is indeed a possibility. Wizards have destroyed their own powers attempting spells beyond their strength. It is a terrible thing. The *paru'enthred* shatters beyond all chance of repair. If that does not kill the wizard outright, he will usually not live long after. The shock and sense of loss are too great. There are limits to everything, even for an amber wizard.

"But I'm getting ahead of myself. The *paru'enthred* is also like a piece of colored glass—one of the windows in the Sunlight Hall in your keep, for instance. It colors the magic as it passes through you. The Osirin word for this is *yavas,* which means 'taint' or 'stain.'

"When I create the Spell of Discovery that flows through the *methlenel,* I do not use enough magic to cause my flame to appear. The magic is contained and flows completely within me. But if I were to use more magic—well, this will be easier if I show you."

He rose from the chair and stood rigidly straight, like a soldier at attention about to be inspected by his lieutenant. His face became a blank mask, completely devoid of emotion or expression. Gerin had never seen such a sudden, startling transformation, and he found it disturbing.

Without warning, golden fire erupted from Hollin's body, exploding outward in a harsh burst of illumination. Gerin jumped up and knocked his chair backward, where it clattered to the rug-covered floor; Reshel screamed and threw up her hands, a look of shock and horror on her face. "Hollin!" she cried, rising to her feet.

She took a step toward him, but Gerin put a hand on her arm and held her back. "Wait," he said. "He's all right."

The fire that engulfed Hollin was not the same kind of fire as when wood was burned. It moved like normal fire, licking upward in flashing tendrils that evaporated and re-formed almost faster than the eye could see. But it seemed to have a different consistency, somehow thicker and more whole, as if it were something semisolid that merely imitated the fluid movements of true flame. There was no smoke or heat, and Hollin was neither consumed nor burned by the engulfing magic. It was brightest where his skin was bare, as if his clothing impeded its outward flow from his body.

He made a single motion with his hand and the flame ceased.

Reshel sat back hard in her chair, breathing heavily. Gerin picked up his chair and eased himself into it, his eyes locked onto the wizard's face, which had regained its former animation.

"I'm sorry if I startled you," Hollin said, sitting down as well. "What you saw was an outpouring of magic, a *hronu,* as it is called in Osirin. There are two ways for a wizard's aura to appear: the first is what I just showed you. I did not create a spell, I simply opened the *paru'enthred* and allowed the largest amount of magic I can safely contain flow through me. Because it is unshaped, it pours out of my body in its raw state. It does not harm me or my clothing, as you saw, because it is not true fire.

"The second way for auras to appear is if a wizard draws more magic than is necessary to complete a spell. The required amount of magic will be used to shape and control the spell; the rest will be dissipated through his body as an aura.

"Which brings me back to your original question, Reshel. What exactly does it mean to say that Gerin will be stronger than you?"

"You've already answered some of that. You said a stronger wizard has a larger conduit in his body for magic. He'll be able to perform spells that no one else could attempt because they require too much strength."

Hollin nodded, pleased. "Yes, and a more powerful wizard will have more *stamina* than a lesser one, meaning he can perform spells for longer periods of time without exhausting his strength or risking *taglosé,* or 'blindness,' which is what the destruction of the *paru'enthred* is called."

"Can wizards combine their powers?" asked Gerin. "I would think that several wizards working together could overcome a more powerful one through sheer force of numbers."

"A very good question. The answer is both yes and no. For instance, let's say that for whatever reason ten golden wizards wished to place a Binding spell on you after your powers have been Awakened. A single spell by one of them could not hope to contain you even if they caught you unawares; you would be able to dissolve it easily.

"But neither could ten golden wizards create a *single* Binding spell with their combined powers. There is no way for their magic to be joined in such a manner. What they *can* do is each create the most powerful Binding spell they can and hope that the overlapping of all of them is enough to contain you, at least for a time. You would be able to undo the spells one by one, but that would take time and weaken you as you fought so many. There are spells designed to be worked by more than one wizard, and some that could be started by one wizard and finished by another, but that is not a summing of their powers."

"How do you know if you've used too much of your strength?" asked Reshel.

"It's difficult to explain, but you will know. You'll feel a kind of exhaustion begin to take hold, similar to when you exert yourself physically and come to the end of your endurance. When you're fully a wizard you will recognize it. You will feel it and you will have to stop, or your powers will be burned from you. No one is exempt from this, not even an amber wizard."

"I've been meaning to ask you this," said Reshel. "What happened to wizards? I mean, if you read the old stories and histories, it seemed they were everywhere. You said to me once that they—we—are a failing race, but never explained what you meant by that."

Hollin folded his hands and sat very still. In the light of the magefire lamp he seemed almost a statue, his white skin as smooth and hard as marble.

"Many long ages of the world ago, a race of beings named the Atalari came to these lands from the far west, beyond the Barrier Mountains. No one knows why they came, or what their homelands were like. There are no original accounts left of those earliest days, only veiled legends and shadowy myths; rumors and whispers and little more. The oldest accounts we have suggest this migration occurred at least thirteen thousand years ago, when the world was very different from what it is now.

"They came in several waves, separated into loose tribes that settled into the northern parts of Osseria. The name 'Osseria' itself is thought to be derived from an archaic Osirin word, 'Akhalosserë,' the Land of Eternal Light, which Emunial, the leader of the first tribe to arrive here, gave to these lands when they made their first settlement.

"At some point a single leader rose among them and unified the tribes under what was called the Shining Nation. Her name is also recorded as Emunial, though it's not clear if this is the same one who named Akhalosserë. Most believe they are one in the same, though there is no proof of this. She was the First Matriarch of what eventually became an unparalleled civilization."

"So the Atalari were wizards?" asked Reshel.

"No. Not as we are today. Little is known about them for sure, but their powers, as far as can be determined, were very different from our own. The magic of the Atalari was more innate than ours. They did not cast spells or weave enchantments. Their powers were as natural to them as breathing is to us. Unlike wizards, they did not need to have their magic Awakened; it was part of them from birth, though it's thought that their powers did not fully ripen until they became young adults."

"Then what happened?" asked Gerin. "You've said they were the ancestors of wizards, but also that their powers were far different from ours. How can that be?"

"The magic of wizards is descended from the Atalari of old, but it is so different and diluted as to be nearly something else entirely. I don't know that an Atalari walking the world today would even recognize us as kin."

"How did that happen?" Reshel leaned forward, her elbows on her knees, entranced by Hollin's tale. Gerin could see her concentrating on every word, every gesture. *I'll wager when we're done here she runs back to her rooms to write all of this down before she forgets.*

"First you must understand that the Atalari were alone in Osseria for a very long time," said Hollin. "But at some point other peoples entered their lands, men and women who looked similar to them but who had no magic of their own."

"The Gendalos," said Reshel.

"Yes. The Gendalos."

Gerin was confused. "Sorry, I don't know that word."

"It means 'short-lived,'" said Hollin. "It was a term given by the Atalari to those who had no magic. The Atalari were repulsed by what they considered an inferior race and shunned the newcomers, who were awed and cowed by the power of the Atalari. The two peoples remained separate, with the Gendalos retreating from the Atalari lands and spreading into the southlands and coasts.

"Then something happened that changed the very face of the world. A single Atalarin mad with hatred for his own people waged a terrible war against the nation. He used a device of power called the Commanding Stone—whether he created it or whether it was some naturally occurring magic he perverted to his cause is not known—which gave him absolute mastery of beasts called *nahalreng,* what are remembered in our tongue as dragons."

"Dragons?" asked Reshel. "I thought they were just legends. You mean they were real?"

"Oh, yes, very real. They are gone now, but when they first swept down across the nation, they caused unimaginable destruction. Even the mighty Atalari were nearly powerless to stop them.

"That was the beginning of the Doomwar, the great conflict

that brought the Atalari nation to its end. The dragonlord and his creatures ravaged the nation and destroyed its great capital, Vacarandi, said to be the most beautiful city that has ever graced the world. The Gendalos kingdoms were attacked and burned, their people slain or scattered. The Matriarch and Royal Family were hunted down and killed, but a remnant of Atalari warriors and high priests devised a weapon that would end the threat of the dragonlord forever. They drew their enemy into a final battle where they unleashed this terrible power. Nothing is known of it except a name whispered in fear and wonder: the Unmaking. No one survived that last battle of the Doomwar—the Atalari, the dragonlord, and all of the *nahalreng* perished.

"The Last Battle of the Doomwar ended the Age of the Atalari. A thousand-year-long Dark Age followed in which the few survivors of the Atalari and Gendalos struggled to rebuild what had been lost, but the devastation of the Doomwar was so great that the two races nearly perished. Both famine and pestilence swept across the continent. The old prohibitions against the mingling of the peoples were forgotten, and both Atalari and Gendalos joined together simply to survive. And slowly a new civilization emerged from the ashes of the old.

"During the Dawn Age the powers of the Atalari began to diminish, a result of the mingling of their blood with the blood of the Gendalos. A few tried to separate the peoples again once this was discovered, but too much time had passed and they now considered each other kin and would not be sundered. And so the final doom of the Atalari was set.

"In later years the powers of the Atalari had to be Awakened with spells newly wrought for the task. Demos Thelar was the great mind who devised the magic of the Awakening and the Ritual of Discovery, which both of you have seen firsthand. Slowly the powers of the Atalari changed into the magic of wizards, as we came to be called. And yes, Reshel, we grew for a time and flourished across all the emerging kingdoms of Osseria and were a people to be reckoned with;

we were kings and the counselors of kings, and power was ours to give and to take. But all of that has dwindled as our blood fails, the potent strain of the Atalari drowning in the lesser blood of the Gendalos, who in that way at least proved mightier in the end. Fewer and fewer wizards are discovered each year, and I fear the day is not far off when wizards will walk the world no more."

"Another sad story," said Reshel. "It seems all of the stories of wizards are sad."

"As are many of the stories of any race, or any family, or any country. Sadness and tragedy are parts of the fabric of existence; but so are triumph and hope and glory, which are sometimes born from the very ashes of despair and loss. There are many tales of wizards that are glorious indeed—you simply have yet to hear them."

"What about Naragenth?" asked Gerin. "What were his powers like?"

"We know little of the first amber wizard. He lived in a difficult time, just before the birth of the Imperial Age and Helca's great empire. Many records were kept secret by wizards jealous of their power. Helca used wizards but did not trust them, and much of their knowledge was destroyed during his reign and the reigns of the emperors who followed him.

"A few things about Naragenth have survived, though. There is a legend that says he created a staff of power by forcing magic itself to assume and hold a material form. Most wizards believe such a thing is impossible, even for an amber wizard, but there are fervent believers in the staff among those who study such matters, and in the past there have been contentious debates about it.

"But his greatest accomplishment was the Varsae Estrikavis, a library of knowledge assembled at a conclave he convened a few years after becoming king.

"Such a gathering of wizards in that era was unheard of. When an amber wizard was discovered, the wizards of that era were shocked. After his ascension to the throne of

Khedesh, Naragenth contacted the greatest wizards of his age and asked if they would participate in a conclave where they would openly share their wisdom and lore. He proposed that their combined knowledge would be stored in a hidden library called the Varsae Estrikavis. Its contents would be available only to those wizards who answered his summons for the conclave. Naturally there was great interest in such an undertaking, each wizard, perhaps, believing he could leverage the lore of the library for his own personal gain.

"The library was constructed in secret and hidden by Naragenth just before Helca began his wars. The other wizards who had participated in the conclave were not told the secret of its hiding because of the war's outbreak. Many of them were singled out by Helca in the early years of the conflict because of their power and reputations, and were either forced to join his cause or killed outright. Of all of them, only Naragenth himself knew where it could be found. It was a prize Helca was most eager to claim as his own once the rumor of it reached his ears.

"Naragenth's famous death atop the walls of Almaris sealed the fate of the Varsae Estrikavis. No one knew where it was or how it had been hidden. Perhaps the greatest assemblage of magical lore Osseria had seen since the fall of the Atalari nation was lost. The Varsae Sandrova at Hethnost is far larger than Naragenth's library was rumored to have been, but the depth of knowledge the lost library contained probably remains unsurpassed. Or so it's believed."

Something happened to Gerin when Hollin spoke of the library's fate. He was suddenly furious that such a wonder could be forever lost. Blood rushed in his ears; he could sense his heart within his chest clenching like a fist and his face flush with heat. He felt an overwhelming, covetous desire to possess the library for himself, to find it and claim it as his own. The sensation was like a fire burning deep within his heart; a small part of him was dimly aware that this ravenous craving was somehow wrong, that its potency was far beyond anything he should have felt at hearing

Hollin speak of a library lost for centuries. He thought for one fleeting instant that this strange, engulfing, raging greed came not from within him but from somewhere else, like a fever contracted by drinking fetid water or eating spoiled meat.

But then the desire for the library drowned out everything else.

What a feat that would be, he thought. *To find Naragenth's lost library.* Here it was, at last. *This* was the key to greatness he'd been seeking all his life. He would find Naragenth's lost treasure. *I will make my own greatness. Leave nothing to chance. I will find the Varsae Estrikavis if I have to defy the gods themselves to achieve it.*

"Gerin, are you all right?" asked Reshel.

He nodded and said to Hollin, "Has anyone ever searched for it?"

"Oh, yes. Uncounted times. It is without doubt the greatest lost treasure in all of Osseria. Perhaps you'll be the one to find it, Gerin. It may take an amber wizard to find what another amber wizard concealed."

It will be mine, thought Gerin. *No matter the price.*

Far to the south, in the Neddari-border country known as Tikomei Ruwan, a fire burned in a small clearing hemmed by thick, gnarled willows. A young man with a shaved head knelt near an older man lying on his back, his arms folded stiffly across his chest. In his hands the older man held two arm-length rods fashioned from rare *plansa* wood, southern trees with roots so deep they were said to reach to the center of the world. The upper ends of the rods flared outward like thigh bones and were carved with the fierce faces of Lokuras and Panndri, the Twins who Rule the Long Night, spirit masters of the *kamichi*.

The young man, Guso Oletran Faolasar, wore soft lace leggings and a leather vest adorned with bleached animal bones that marked him as a *nirgromu*: one who had taken his first journey into the World That Is Above, the realm of the spirits that was the greatest source of a *kamichi*'s strength.

He threw more *bhosa* grass on the fire and drew several deep breaths as the pungent blue smoke billowed around him, making his head swim with strange thoughts and feelings. An owl hooted in the darkness. *A good omen,* he thought. Owls were harbingers of the spirits.

The man on the ground was Guso's master, Pendrel Yevan Hirgrolei, a *kamichi* Chieftain who had recently returned from a vision-quest into the lands of the unbelievers.

Kamichi Hirgrolei had returned in triumph, the god-summoner found, his vision fulfilled.

The owl hooted again. Guso looked down at his master. He'd been in a vision-trance for hours now. If he did not waken soon—

Kamichi Hirgrolei opened his eyes. He unfolded his arms and sat up, his head wreathed in a crown of blue smoke.

"What did you see?" asked Guso.

"The seed I planted in the god-summoner has taken root," he said. He kissed the carved faces upon the rods and handed them to Guso, who held them with great care—any contact with the earth would sully and destroy the spirit powers contained within the rods. "He has taken his first step upon the path I saw in my vision. His obsession will grow all-consuming. When the time comes, he will do what must be done. The Door of Night will open."

Guso bowed his head, giddy with excitement. "And the Slain God will be freed."

"Yes. It is only a matter of time."

"He will lead us in our war against the unbelievers?"

"My vision did not reach so far into the clouded future, but in my heart that is what I believe. It will come to war. It must. There is no other way."

"Will we wait for the God to return before we act? Would it not show the strength of our faith and our will if we moved now, *before* His return?"

The *kamichi* smiled, a rare sight. "You are in many ways wise beyond your years, Guso. It will be as you say. We will strike early at our enemy."

"Will the Chieftain follow your word? He is stubborn and has no love for our ways."

"We will do it whether he allows it or not. You are right; he will not grant us his own warriors. But we have our own men who will serve us if we ask. They will be enough. We will give the unbelievers a small taste of what awaits them when the Slain God returns to us fully."

The owl hooted for a third time. *A good omen indeed,* thought Guso.

Therain's departure for Castle Agdenor was a less ostentatious leave-taking than his father's had been. He stood in the outer bailey near his escort, a ridiculously large grin on his face. He could not stand still; he walked about, rolled his shoulders to loosen them, clapped his hands and laughed. Gerin thought he might actually explode from nervous energy before he could get onto his horse.

He put his hand on his younger brother's shoulder and squeezed. "Therain, calm down," he said quietly. "You'll be fine."

Therain shook his head. "I know, I'm sorry. I can't tell if I'm excited about going or scared to death. I feel ready to jump out of my skin."

Claressa and Reshel arrived and gave Therain hugs and wished him well. Gerin shook his hand once more, as did Balandrick and Hollin. Therain swung up onto his horse, waved to them one last time, and then rode toward the gate with his escort and wagons behind him.

He'd just vanished through the gate when Gerin caught a flash of sunlight on a guard's breastplate and squeezed his eyes shut against the glare.

When he opened them he saw a vast figure towering over him, a shadow being standing upon the Ossland Plains on the eastern side of the Kilnathé River; the figure's dark head was lost among the clouds, its body and face without feature or marking. Fear clutched at Gerin's heart and he let out a small startled cry.

He blinked, and it was gone.

"Are you all right?" asked Reshel. "All of the color just drained from your face."

Gerin smiled weakly. *It was just a trick of the light,* he thought, trying to push the image of the vast figure from his mind. "I'm fine."

"Shayphim take them to his cauldron for all eternity," said Captain Teray Melfistan under his breath as he and his men galloped down the inner side of a small, bowl-shaped valley toward the burning village. A gust of wind blew choking fumes across their path, dark smoke filled with the acrid smell of burned wood and the deeper, cloying stench of burned flesh. The captain could see some dead livestock near the flames consuming one of the outbuildings, but he knew he was smelling more than just animal meat.

The village was a few hundred yards away. There was so much smoke churning from fires on its outskirts that it was difficult to see anything clearly, but there was certainly fighting of some kind still going on toward the village's center and its far side, where the valley rim was pierced by a flattened tongue of grassland that formed a kind of natural road toward the south. He barked for his men to ride harder—he wanted to get there before the Neddari could escape.

His company had been alerted to the attack by two women on horseback riding frantically with their children. Their husbands had sent them away the moment the Neddari appeared, commanding them to ride for the garrison tower at Veilar Haran. The men had stayed behind to defend their homes. *Probably with pitchforks and axes,* Melfistan thought. *And maybe a few rusty swords if they're lucky.*

"It's the Neddari!" one of the women had shrieked when she saw Melfistan's company appear over a tree-lined rise. "They're attacking Brithkee! Please, hurry!"

He'd left three of his men to escort the women and search the area for any others who'd fled, then rode off in the direction of the village. It wasn't far; two miles, three at the most.

His company charged into a thick curtain of smoke that cut across their path like a roiling wall. His men had all drawn their weapons; he tightened his grip on his sword as the wall of smoke momentarily blinded him.

Then they were out on the other side, into the village proper.

Melfistan took in the scene with darting flashes of his eyes behind his visor—bodies strewn in doorways, mostly villagers, but he felt grimly satisfied to see a few dead Neddari warriors with knives sticking out of them.

"Captain, ahead!" shouted Davin Simmolo, one of his lieutenants, pointing down the narrow lane that cut through the heart of the village.

There was fighting still going on at the far edge of the village, near a small wooden house whose thatch roof was rapidly turning into a flaming torch. The Neddari were all on horseback, about forty in all. He saw three village men— two with pitchforks and one with an honest-to-goodness spear—trying to kill a Neddari who'd been unhorsed. The warrior's left arm was covered in blood and hung limp at his side. He brandished a short sword and was thrusting it toward the closest villager, a large broad-backed fellow who was carrying the spear. *Looks like he knows a little about how to use it, too,* thought Melfistan.

The large villager jumped forward and turned aside the Neddari's sword with the haft of his spear. The Neddari tried to back away but found himself blocked by a knee-high stone wall. He shifted to his right and tried to bring up his sword, but it was too late. With a bellow of hate, the villager drove his spear through the center of the Neddari's laced leather jerkin and out his back. He yanked it free with a savage pull on the haft; the Neddari flopped to the ground in a heap, bent over sharply at the waist like a child's rag doll carelessly dropped in mid-play.

Five of the captain's men veered away from the company

toward Neddari they spied lurking between some homes down side lanes. The Neddari were alone, hurling torches onto roofs and through doorways. The captain had no doubt that they would quickly be dead. *And good riddance to them all.*

Where's the damned kamichi? he wondered. He'd seen no elementals yet, and that worried him. The spirit-creatures that the *kamichis* could summon to this world for brief periods of time were beautiful—they looked like luminous clouds of mist filled with thousands of sparkling pinpricks of light—but they were also extremely deadly, able to burn though flesh and steel in a matter of seconds. There was no defense against them; once one latched onto a man, he would quickly be dead.

It was possible they'd already used the elementals. Even the strongest *kamichi* could only hold an elemental in this world for a few minutes, and after that could not call one again for hours or days. Perhaps they were fortunate enough to have missed the deadly creatures. Or perhaps there was no *kamichi* in this raiding party.

"Protect those men!" shouted Melfistan to his two flanking riders. Through curling plumes of smoke he could see the Neddari formation preparing to ride out of the village. *Bloody cowards!* thought the captain. *Turning tail when proper soldiers show up to fight.* He caught a glimpse of the distinctive leather clothing and peacock-plumed staff of a *kamichi* lurking at the center of the group, his head turned to watch the approach of the Khedeshian company.

"Take them!" he bellowed. "Don't let the bastards get away!"

Neddari archers nocked and unleashed their arrows. Melfistan flinched at the breathy *whoosh* of air as one narrowly missed his head. Two of his men successfully deflected the arrows with their shields, but three others were hit. One was dead, thrown from his horse with a shaft in his throat. The other two were wounded and were able to remain mounted, though they fell behind the rest of the company, no longer able to fight.

His own mounted archers were about to fire at the Neddari when six drogasaars stepped into their path.

Melfistan swore loudly. In the past two raids, the Neddari had not used any of the quick, vicious creatures who lived in the wooded uplands of Neddar. Drogasaars were not man-smart—they did not make tools or clothing of their own—but they could be taught to speak, and had a certain feral cunning that, along with their incredible speed and ability to leap, made them extremely dangerous, especially when they'd been given weapons, as these six had.

Drogasaars ranged between five and six feet in height, with a vaguely bat-shaped head seated between rounded, forward-hunched shoulders. Their squat, powerful bodies were covered in coarse fur; there was a brush of longer, stiffer hair on the males that formed a crest running from the tops of their heads to the middle of their backs. Their legs were thick and strong and could propel them to astonishing speeds.

The six blocking their way crouched, their leg muscles tightening like steel bands, ready to spring at the Khedeshi-ans charging toward them. They'd been given unadorned breastplates by the Neddari, as well as scimitars that they carried in both hands; they spun the weapons with a loose, elegant motion, the tips of the blades tracing circles in the air that caught reflected firelight at the tops of the arcs.

The largest of the drogasaars opened its fang-filled mouth and bellowed, its crest-ridge of hair flaring into a broad V-shape. Its companions followed its lead and also roared, the mingled sound rising for an instant above the noise of the many fires around them.

Melfistan's archers shot at the drogasaars instead of the Neddari, who were riding at a full gallop along the grassy lane that led out of Brithkee. *They're going to get away if we can't get past these things quickly,* he thought.

Even as the Khedeshian archers were releasing their arrows, the drogasaars launched themselves into battle. They were strong enough to cover at least fifteen feet with a single leap, and they jumped in wildly different directions. Only one arrow came near its mark, but the drogasaar was able to knock it down with a lightning-quick flick of its scimitar.

They hit the ground and leaped again instantly, kicking up chunks of dirt beneath their feet, roaring once more as they hurled through the air, their blades stretched out before them.

Their leaps carried them directly into the forward lines of the Khedeshians.

One of the drogasaars came down between the captain and Harlon Yorl, its long arms reaching out in an attempt to decapitate both men at once. With a shout, Melfistan heaved his blade up and knocked the scimitar aside with a resounding clang.

The drogasaar's leap had brought it a little closer to Harlon; it shifted suddenly after Melfistan deflected its cut and swung its blade around into the flank of Harlon's horse. The animal screamed as the weapon sliced through skin and muscle and tendon; its rear legs folded up as suddenly as a bird's that had just taken flight. It crashed to the ground and tumbled toward the drogasaar, whose clinging weight was pulling the dying animal off balance. Harlon was trying furiously to get his blade into his attacker, but the thing was too close, one arm wrapped around Harlon's shoulders while the other continued to dig its weapon into the horse's flesh.

The drogasaar leaped away from the horse, but Harlon was not so lucky. His leg was pinned beneath his mount's crushing bulk. He screamed as its weight snapped his thigh bone cleanly in two.

His scream ended abruptly when the drogasaar cut off his head with a whistling swing of its scimitar.

All of this had taken place in a matter of seconds. Melfistan was still turning his horse to come to Harlon's aid when the soldier had been decapitated. The drogasaar roared and raised its scimitars, then turned to face Melfistan, who was bearing down upon it, screaming with rage.

The creature tried to cut through his horse's front legs, but the captain had expected that. Just as he saw it about to swing, he pulled up hard on his reins; his horse, Meilak, reared, and the drogasaar's scimitars cut through empty air.

Before it could strike again, Melfistan brought Meilak's hooves down on the creature's chest, smashing it to the ground and crushing its ribs. The drogasaar's arms fell against the grass and released its weapons.

For good measure he leaned over and drove the tip of his sword through the creature's mouth.

"Gah, damned bloody things," he said as he pulled his blade free.

Five of his men were dead and four more wounded before the last of the drogasaars were killed. There was no point in chasing the Neddari now, though Melfistan sent men after them anyway because he was a stubborn bastard and would not concede defeat. Besides, it was always possible that some terrifically bad luck would befall the Neddari and allow his men to overtake them. But he was not counting on it.

The broad-backed man with the spear approached the captain as he dismounted. The villager's face was twisted with blood lust.

"Why are they doing this?" he asked.

"I was hoping you might be able to tell me," Melfistan replied, watching as his men gathered their dead in preparation for burial. The Neddari and drogasaars would be thrown into a pile outside of town and burned. "This is the third attack in as many weeks. They've never done this before; not in my lifetime."

The large man twisted his grip on his spear. His eyes shone brightly in a face smeared with soot and blood. "They said nothing to us. They just came and killed and burned."

"I heard 'em say something," said another man. He looked like a scarecrow next to the larger one, a scrawny skeleton with a bit of skin stretched over the top of it. "When they was killin' my brother Elren. I heard one of the bastards say, 'The Slain God will return.' "

The captain grimaced. The *kamichi* who had captured Prince Gerin had mentioned a Slain God. *This is the work of the* kamichi *then, and not the clan Chieftain,* he thought. *And it has something to do with the spirit-quest that brought them to Prince Gerin.* But what was the purpose? What were they trying to achieve?

"Does that mean something to you?" asked the skinny villager.

"No," Melfistan replied. "I've heard that name, but don't know what it means." Behind them, Brithkee continued to burn.

7

Over the next few weeks Gerin spent as much time as he could with Reshel and Hollin, learning Osirin and memorizing the more basic spells. They could not as yet actually work any of the spells—that would have to wait until after their powers were Awakened at Hethnost—but Hollin wanted them to be prepared to practice them soon after the Ritual of Awakening. They learned the incantations for creating magefire, both within a lamp and as a floating spark when no lamp was available to contain the flame; for Seeings, which would allow them to view harm to a body or pierce veils of illusions; for Farseeings, to send their gaze many miles into the distance; for a dozen different healing spells to remedy various degrees of injuries; for Closings, to lock doors or seal windows; and for Warding, Barrier, Binding, and Illusion spells to confound an enemy. They would not learn more powerful magic for several years, until they'd become proficient with simpler spells and comfortable with their powers.

Hollin warned them that the more powerful the spell, the greater the cost to the wizard. "A wizard can exhaust his powers the same as a soldier may exhaust his ability to fight. If that happens, you will be unable to use your powers until you recover your strength. And remember that it's possible to exert yourself to the point of destroying your ability to use magic. You must be cautious of the amount of magic you use, and always try to use no more power than is necessary for the task at hand."

As evening was falling, Gerin and Balandrick were walking through the Grove of Telros, a walled, crescent-shaped plot of trees and shrubs that curved gently around the southeastern side of the keep, when they spied Claressa speaking with a slender, slope-shouldered noble named Avres Telameiden. The reaffirmation of Gerin's vassals was to take place in a few days, and some had already arrived. Avres was the son of Count Resvan and his wife Tarla, both of whom were embarrassingly eager to marry their son into the royal family.

Avres had just presented Claressa with a bouquet of yellow roses, having no doubt been encouraged by his parents to do so. Gerin and Balandrick saw them from the shadows of a free-standing colonnade as she graciously accepted the flowers, then sent poor Avres away with a gentle admonishment that she preferred pink lilies.

"You're a cruel woman," said Gerin, emerging from the colonnade after Avren had gone. "It's like watching a cat toy with a mouse that has no idea what's happening to it. We can't possibly be related. Mother and Father must have pulled you out of a well as an infant—where you no doubt deserved to be—and taken pity on you."

She smiled at him over the roses. "It's so much *fun* to play with them! I'm certain Father already has some dashing young man from a powerful family picked out to be my husband, so these pathetic souls are just wasting their time wooing me with their silly gifts. They seem to think I'm some fragile creature who will swoon at the first compliment I hear."

" 'Fragile creature' you most certainly are not. A lioness perhaps. Or that female spider that kills its mate. Or maybe a snake—"

"You'd best watch yourself, or I'll tell all the daughters of your vassals about that time you got your head stuck in a knot in a tree because Therain dared you to. You were stung by some bees before they finally pulled you out, if I'm not mistaken. One right on the end of your nose. I can still remember how it swelled and turned a marvelously bright shade of red.

"Ah, that's not a game you want to play with me," said Gerin. "Father and I talked when he was here, and I know who he intends for you to marry, even if it won't be for some time yet, so if you say *anything* unflattering about me, I unfortunately would be forced to write to this poor unsuspecting young man and tell him a few unsavory stories about my dear, darling younger sister. And I don't mean Reshel."

"Father did *not* tell you! He wouldn't!"

"He most certainly did. If I were you I wouldn't get my hopes up about someone *dashing,* or even *handsome*. On his best days he just might rise to the level of *homely,* if all the stars are properly aligned and his pimples have calmed. I doubt there's anything to be done about his breath, though. Or the hair on his back."

She wheeled on Balandrick. "Is that true? Did my father really tell him anything?"

Balan did his best to keep a straight face. "I wouldn't know, my lady. If the king had a conversation with your brother about your intended, I certainly wasn't present, so I can't comment on any pimples he may have, or lack thereof."

Claressa stormed off.

"Oh, that was cruel of you," said Balandrick. "Enjoyable, but cruel."

"Take that as a lesson to stay on my good side. I wonder if I could get my father to send a letter telling her that she was marrying the most pathetic, ghastly wretch in the kingdom?"

"I think even your father's too afraid of Claressa to risk that."

Gerin turned to respond and saw a flash of light, like the sun reflecting off a piece of glass. But there was no glass where he was looking—there was, in fact, no sunlight at all in the shadowed corner of the courtyard.

Frowning, he looked up to see the vast shadow figure appear

once again, as tall as a mountain, dominating his entire field of vision. Its heel could obliterate Ireon's Hill, little more than an ant mound compared to the apparition's enormity.

This time he could see points of silver light where its eyes should have been, like flickering stars that had awakened in its otherwise featureless face.

The apparition's head was bent toward the earth and seemed to be searching for something. *It's looking for me,* thought Gerin. Panic seized him. *It wants me for something.*

Then its gaze locked on his tiny form. Gerin could sense the triumph that surged through it, its eyes flashing like twin fires that had been stoked.

It reached for him with a gargantuan hand, its fingers dwarfing the castle. Gerin cried out and stumbled backward, trying to flee. He tripped and fell, landing hard on his back. "Get away!"

The immense hand was almost upon him. He lashed out at it, trying to keep it at bay—

And then it was gone.

"Gerin, by the gods, what's wrong?" asked Balandrick, kneeling by his side. "What were you shouting at?"

He looked at his friend, dumbfounded. "You mean you didn't see it?"

"See what?" Balan said. "What's happening to you? What did you see?"

Gerin slowly got to his feet. He was glad no one else had seen him. They would think he was losing his mind. *And what if I am?* he wondered. "I don't know. I saw a huge shape. I saw it once before, but I thought it was just a trick of the light when I was tired. But not this time. It was there, I know it was."

Balan's expression darkened with concern. "I didn't see anything."

"I don't know how to explain it." He shuddered and folded his arms. "I need to speak to Hollin."

Was this the divine presence that had appeared in his rooms? Was it now showing itself to him openly? Or did this have something to do with the spell the Neddari had placed in him?

"Are you sure you're all right?"

Gerin felt once again that his life was spinning out of his control. Things were happening that he did not understand, events caused by powerful, unseen forces acting on him with agendas of their own. He clenched his teeth together. *Leave me alone!* he thought. *Whatever you are, just stay away from me. I want no part of you, and I will not help you! Do you understand? I will not do your bidding!*

"Gerin, are you all right?" Balan repeated.

He shook his head slowly, feeling helpless and afraid. "No, I don't think I am."

Hollin was deeply troubled by Gerin's story. He paced about his sitting room, his expression drawn down into a deep scowl. "You should have told me about this when you saw it the first time."

"I thought it was just my imagination," Gerin said unconvincingly. *And I was afraid,* he thought. *I didn't want it to be real.* But he could not deny it any longer. "Could this be part of the Neddari spell?" He still felt shaky and unsettled. He was afraid to even look at the sky. "Is it somehow manifesting itself as this shadowy figure? Or is this the divine presence I sensed in my room?"

"What divine presence?" asked Reshel. "What are you talking about?"

Gerin realized he had never told her about the visitation. He described the presence that had woken him and spoken his name and the words, *Your time is coming.*

"I feel like I'm being hunted," he said. "Like there's something stalking me, something I can't see or even understand. If it's the Neddari spell, then I can't escape it because it's *inside* me. And if it's something divine . . . well, how do you hide from that?"

Hollin stopped pacing and faced him, his expression stern. "As soon as this oathtaking is over, we leave for Hethnost. I've allowed you more freedom than usual for those in my charge as apprentices, but my tolerance ends now. You need to begin your training so we can Awaken your powers as soon as possible. That way you'll have *some* means of learning what is happening to you if it occurs again and I'm not present, or of fighting back if that is the only alternative."

He looked at both of them in turn. "You are the children of a king, but when you train with me, *my* will and *my* word are absolute. You need to understand this, because I will brook no argument from you when you are under my care. You must obey my commands the same as you would expect your own to be followed.

"Tomorrow we begin. I will expect the both of you to be here by the eight o'clock bells."

"We'll be here," said Gerin.

Out in the hallway, Gerin stopped Reshel with a gentle hand on her shoulder. "How are things between you and Balan?"

Alarm flashed in her eyes. "What do you mean? What are you talking about?"

"I've seen you two together. I know you've become close."

"Why don't you ask him?" She was angry, her face red, her mouth and eyes drawn tight.

"Because I asked *you*. Why are you so mad about this?"

"Are you going to punish him for it?"

"No, of course not. Why would you think such a thing?"

"He's the captain of *your* personal guard. You'd be within your rights to punish him, or order him to stop seeing me."

"Well, I'm not going to do that. It's your business, not mine. By the gods, Reshel, I asked a simple question, that's all."

She calmed a little, but still regarded him warily. "Things are fine. Yes, we're close. More than that I'm not willing to say."

"All right. I won't press you. I was just curious."

"I hope we figure out whatever is happening to you," she said. "Before it gets any worse."

"So do I." He watched her walk away, glad she could not see how afraid he was.

Near midnight, Gerin shuddered in his sleep. He moaned softly, a low, whimpering sound of fear and terror at the vision haunting his slumbering mind.

In his dream he stood upon a patch of dead earth beneath a starless sky. The darkness was nearly absolute, but he could just make out the murky shapes of bleached bones all around him, skulls and spines and ribs of men piled so thickly together on the desiccated soil that they formed mounds taller than he. A cold wind blew across the bones, whipping his loose-fitting clothes, and he shivered in the darkness.

A faint light appeared some distance in front of him. It took the shape of a doorway floating in the air, a rectangle of faint red illumination, like the glow of molten iron, angry and hot. The wind blew harder and colder, and there was a foul stench of carrion upon it. He tried to step closer to the door but found he could not move, as if his mind had detached itself in some way from his body.

"I have found you at last. You are the one who will open the Door of Night." The voice thundered from the doorway so loud that Gerin flinched and covered his ears. "You will release me from my bondage so that I may carry out my vengeance."

Gerin felt a terrible sense of dread. "Who are you? What do you want?"

"I am Asankaru, the Storm King," it said. "Even now the Door of Night weakens so that I can touch you through the barrier that separates the worlds. I have drawn the knowledge of your uncouth speech from your mind so that we may speak. The time draws near. I can feel it. You will open the Door and set me free. Do not fail me."

The vast apparition towered over Gerin like a mountain, its silvery eyes focused on him with such intensity that he threw up his hands and cried out in terror, "Leave me alone!"

As if in reply, the wind gusted with enough strength to lift Gerin off of his feet and hurl him backward through the air. Just as he was about to crash into a mound of broken, splintered bones, the dream ended. He rolled over in his bed, still asleep, drenched with sweat, his heart pounding. He opened his eyes for a moment, not truly awake, and realized that he'd experienced no ordinary dream. There had been a sense of truth about it, a strong feeling that it was somehow real. *It actually happened to me. That creature spoke to me.* He needed to ask Hollin about it, to find out if the wizard could tell him what was happening to him, and why.

But before he could get out of bed, his eyes fluttered closed and he fell back into a deep sleep. When he awoke in the morning he'd completely forgotten the dream, though he was troubled by a lingering sense of dread that he could not explain and that left him irritable and afraid. When he spoke to Hollin that morning he sensed there was something he wanted to tell the wizard, something important that hovered just beyond the periphery of his memory; but he could not remember what it was, and soon the memory of the dream had slipped completely away.

The evening after Gerin saw the apparition in the Grove of Telros, Hollin found Claressa waiting outside his door in the keep. He was surprised to see her. She rarely spoke to him; they exchanged meaningless pleasantries when they saw one another, nothing more. It was apparent she was waiting for him, probably for some time.

"May I speak to you for a moment?" There was an edge of nervousness in her voice, a tightness she failed to hide.

"Certainly, Claressa. Please, come in." Hollin was not fond of Claressa. He disliked her haughty and arrogant manner and the way she belittled Reshel. Nevertheless, he would be pleasant.

Claressa stood stiffly, her hands clasped in front of her. "I wanted to apologize for my behavior at dinner when you first came here," she said. "I had no right to say the things I said.

I know it was awhile ago, but I felt it better to apologize late than never at all."

"Thank you. It means a great deal to me to know that I'm no longer the enemy." He sensed she wanted to ask him something but was not certain how. He decided to make it easy for her. "I know it was hard to hear such a thing about your brother, and must have been doubly so when you learned Reshel also has the potential to become a wizard. Some families are like that. The old blood runs strong in them."

"Is that really true? Are there really whole families who are wizards?"

"It has happened, though not for some time. The last family where every member of one generation was a wizard occurred long before I was born. For even a brother and sister to be wizards is now a rare thing."

"Do you think . . . is it possible that I'm a wizard?"

"I'll be honest with you, Claressa. It's very unlikely. But we'll never know unless I perform the Ritual of Discovery on you."

She hesitated. "All right. In a way, I don't want to know, but I think never knowing would be worse. And I don't want it said that any Atreyano feared to learn the truth of a thing."

He retrieved the *methlenel,* spoke the words to the spell and felt the magic leap into her, seeking her *paru'enthred* to gauge its strength and reveal it to him by turning the color of her flame.

The crystal remained dark.

"I'm sorry," he said. "You're not a wizard."

Claressa let out a deep breath and smiled. "I'm glad, truly. If you'd said I could become a wizard, I don't know if I would have accepted or not, but I think I would not. But I needed to know." She paced across the floor, her silk skirts brushing softly against the wool rug. "Don't misunderstand; I mean no insult. The gods know the idea of having such power and long life is appealing, and when you told us about Gerin, I admit I was filled with envy. But it also frightens me because it can't be shared with anyone. I'll be married one day, and I can't imagine what it would do to my husband to grow old and die while I remained young. How could he not come to hate me for my life?"

He felt certain she was lying to herself to mask her disappointment; no one ever refused to become a wizard if they had the potential. *Still, if that makes the news easier for her to bear, who am I to contradict her?*

The time came at last for the vassals of Ailethon to reaffirm their Oath of Fealty to Gerin as their new duke. Gerin had never enjoyed the thought of all the political maneuvering that would accompany the event, and found himself loathing the idea as the day neared. Despite all he had learned, he felt as if he grasped less than a tenth of what he needed to know to command the castle properly. *It will all come in time,* he told himself. *Father and Grandfather felt no differently when they became lords here.* But late at night after an exhausting day, he found it difficult to believe his own words.

The vassal lords began to bicker almost before they set foot within the inner bailey. He dealt with as many of the problems as he could, asking for Matren's advice only when he truly had no idea what to do to appease a lord or resolve a dispute.

"You've done well, my lord," said Matren the night before the oathtaking. "The lords have been deliberately difficult in order to test you. I've heard that even the most intractable ones are impressed."

Gerin cocked an eyebrow at the older man. "Really? Your spies heard that?"

"Lord Porrien himself told his lieutenant you were 'a tough bastard like his father.' It was said in a most admiring way."

Gerin felt himself grinning. *It appears I'm doing something right.*

The oathtaking occurred in the Great Audience Hall. Gerin spoke to the assembled vassals of their responsibilities to House Atreyano and lauded them for their faithful service in the past. When he was finished, the lords approached the dais in order of station, knelt before the prince, swore their fealty to Gerin and pledged their lives and the lives of their men in service to him. The old priest Amnen Petring blessed each man with a censer of incense. Before long a bluish haze had enveloped the front of the room. The incense gave Gerin a terrible headache and tickled the back of his throat, and he had to fight hard not to cough.

The celebration afterward lasted a long time, with his vassals congratulating him on his ascension to the lordship of Ailethon. There was some talk of his wizardry and many questions for Hollin.

Much later, after the celebration ended and the lords had made their way back to their chambers, Gerin returned to his own rooms. He'd dismissed Balandrick for the night. Balan had spent most of the feast dancing with Reshel or otherwise keeping close to her side. *Maybe I should make him* her *personal guard,* he thought wearily. Not that he begrudged them what little time they spent together. Reshel's studies with Hollin, and Balan's own duties and responsibilities to him and the castle guard, often kept them apart. He wondered where their relationship would end. Was it conceivable that his father would allow Reshel to marry Balan? Was that, in truth, even what they wanted?

He was nearing his rooms when he heard a shuffling noise behind him. He turned to see a man emerge from a pitch-black alcove he'd just passed. The man muttered, "Forgive me, my lord," then lunged at Gerin with a long, gleaming knife.

8

Gerin propelled himself backward. Had he been a second slower, the knife would have sunk into his abdomen just below his breastbone. He nearly dropped the lamp he was carrying but managed to close his fingers around its handle just before it slipped from his hands, knowing he might be able to use it as a crude shield to deflect the blade, or as a blunt, bludgeoning weapon, since he had no knife or sword of his own with him. He shook his head to clear it but was only partially successful; he'd drunk far too much wine and was far too tired to fight well. He took several more steps back and looked at his attacker.

The man was dressed in filthy rags that covered a nearly skeletal frame. Tufts of matted gray hair stuck out from the fringe of his head in every direction. He was old, Gerin realized: at least fifty. Strangely enough, there was no indignation or rage about the man, no anger directed at him for some perceived wrong he'd done, nor was there the grim efficiency of a hired assassin—who most certainly would not have apologized before trying to stab him—only a kind of sad resignation that Gerin found baffling.

"Please, my lord, I must," the man pleaded, holding the knife toward him. "It's the only way. I have to do this." He slashed again at Gerin's torso, a clumsy roundhouse swing that Gerin easily deflected despite his sluggishness and fatigue.

The sound of the blade striking the steel resounded through the hall, and the flame in the lamp flickered.

This man is no fighter. Gerin could see that his attacker had little skill in hand-to-hand combat. It was simple for him to anticipate where he would strike next, jabbing with the blade toward his heart. Again Gerin knocked the knife away with the lamp.

"Please! If I don't do this everyone will die!" The man tightened his grip on the knife's long handle and drew his arm back. He moved closer, clearly believing Gerin would try to run.

But instead of fleeing, Gerin rushed forward. Before the man could react with his knife, Gerin moved inside his reach and gripped his wrist, using all of his strength to bend it backward so the knife was pointed away from him. With his other hand he smashed the lamp against the man's face, shattering the glass and setting fire to the attacker's hair. The man screamed and dropped to his knees. Blood ran down his face in sudden violent streams from several deep cuts in his scalp and forehead. Gerin twisted his wrist until he heard bones snap—the man screamed again and dropped the knife. Gerin slammed his head against the wall, which made a dull cracking noise against the stone. His screams stopped and he toppled to the floor, unconscious. Gerin picked up the knife and smacked out the man's burning hair; he did not want him to die before he could be questioned.

It was very dark in the corridor. With his lamp extinguished, the only illumination came from a glimmer of moonlight slanting through a windowed alcove a short distance away. *Gods above me, my head hurts.* He rubbed his temple in a vain attempt to halt the painful throbbing in his skull.

He was about to shout for help when soldiers carrying lanterns appeared at the end of the hallway. "Come here!" Gerin shouted. "I've been attacked!"

The men rushed to his side. "Take this man to the dungeon. Be sure that he doesn't die before he can be questioned. Wake Master Aslon to look after his wounds.

"Seal off the castle. All gates are to be closed and locked. No one is to leave until I give the word. Search the keep for any other assassins. With so many lords gathered, I may not be the only target."

More guards arrived, and Gerin took a lamp from one of the men and held it close to his attacker's face so he could get a clearer look. He did not recognize him.

The castle sprang to life as soldiers spread throughout its bulk, shouting commands, closing gates and postern doors, manning the walls and searching the keep before moving methodically to the outlying buildings and towers.

By morning it appeared the assassin who attacked Gerin was alone. No other intruders were found, and no one else had been harmed.

Gerin waited in the Sunlight Hall, where he was given regular reports as to the progress of the search of the castle and the interrogations taking place in the dungeons. He slept for perhaps two hours at some point during the night, unable to keep his eyes open any longer. Master Aslon and Hollin were commanded to tend to the assassin, who had not yet regained consciousness.

"I healed a crack in the side of his skull," said Hollin after he returned from the dungeons, rousing Gerin from his fitful sleep. "He'll live, but it may be a few hours before he awakens. The guards have orders to notify you as soon as he does."

The man was identified as Stefon Malarik, a vagabond and beggar who was said to have visions of the future that he sometimes shouted out in the market of Padesh or from the edge of the town square. He lived with his aged father on the outskirts of Padesh in a ramshackle single-story house.

Gerin ordered Malarik's father to be brought to the castle at once. The old man—his eyes rheumy with age, and with only a single yellowed tooth remaining in his lower jaw—trembled with uncontrollable fear as he was ushered into the hall.

"Are you aware that your son tried to kill me this past night?"

"My lord, I knew nothin' of this," stammered the elder Malarik. If the guards had not been holding his arms, Gerin thought he would have sagged to the floor. "My son, he's never been right in the head. He has visions and terrible dreams of things to come. Makes him crazy. He can't help hisself. He has to shout out whatever he sees or it's like poison in him. That's what he says, like poison. But he's never hurt no one before, I swear. I don't know why he would do this, I swear."

"He said nothing to you about his reasons for coming to the castle tonight? Nothing at all? Didn't you ask him where he was going when he left?"

"Stefon leaves when he wills, my lord. Doesn't like to sleep because of the dreams he has. They torment him." Tears appeared in the man's milky eyes. "Please, my lord, have mercy on him. He's little more than a child in a man's body. I don't know why he done what he did, and I'm sorry for it, but please don't hurt him. Since his mother and sister passed on, he's all I have in this world."

"Your son attempted to *murder* the heir to the throne," said Matren, "and will be dealt with according to the laws of the kingdom."

A sob burst from the old man. His shoulders began to shake and tears ran down the deep creases in his weathered face.

Gerin put a stop to the questioning and ordered that he be returned to his home. "He knows nothing. There's no point in tormenting him further." By law, Malarik would be put to death for his crime, but Gerin's heart was strangely heavy with the thought. *He tried to kill me. He deserves death.* Still, the sight of the old man's naked sorrow and piteous plea for his son's life would not leave him.

Shortly after dawn Malarik regained consciousness and was brought to the Sunlight Hall, led by Balandrick. His face had been cleaned and bandaged. Heavy manacles encased his wrists and were linked to his ankle irons with thick chains. Guards surrounded him as he shuffled before their table, his shoulders slumped, his head bowed. Balandrick stood to the left of Malarik with a short sword in his hand; he glared at him with a murderous stare that Malarik assiduously avoided, as if to meet Balandrick's gaze would invite a slow and painful death.

He feels guilty for not being there when I was attacked, thought Gerin as he watched Balan. *I wonder if he thinks his relationship with Reshel is jeopardizing his duty as my guard?* Balan had not asked to be dismissed earlier that night; Gerin had done so of his own volition. After all, he felt that he should be safe in his own keep, and this kind of assault was wholly unprecedented. He was glad, though, that his father was not here; he would have been even less forgiving of Balandrick than Balandrick was of himself.

"Why did you try to kill the crown prince?" demanded Matren, pointing an accusing finger at Malarik. The old castellan's face reddened and his voice shook with rage. "Did someone hire you? Were you paid to come here and kill him? Are you a Threndish spy, or an assassin from another noble house?"

Malarik cringed from Matren's words. "No, my lord, no one paid me. I didn't want to hurt the prince, I swear, but I had to, I *had* to. If I didn't, then everyone would die—everyone—it's terrible, terrible . . ." He continued to stare at the floor while he rocked back and forth. His chains clanked against one another as he swayed.

"What do you mean, everyone would die?" asked Gerin.

"Death, my lord. Just as I said. Everyone in all of Osseria will be dead. It's terrible. I been dreamin' about it for a long time now, a long time. Each time the dream's the same. I see the prince"—he gestured toward Gerin with his manacled hands, though he did not lift his gaze from the floor—"atop a cliff, so high it's like he can see the whole world from it. But it's not just a cliff, no; he's in a place of the dead, a boneyard filled with the whispers and curses of those cruelly put to death. There's a wind blowin', a fierce gale that howls with the very voices of Shayphim's Hounds." He was rocking his body more rhythmically as he spoke, losing himself in the telling of the vision that haunted him. "But the prince don't pay no mind to the wind, even though it's blowin' his hair an' whippin' his cloak about.

"The sky goes dark with black, angry clouds that blot out the face of the sun. They're boilin' like water in a kettle and slidin' across the sky so fast it makes me dizzy to look at them. The clouds are so thick and dark it's like night has come, but I can still see the prince 'cause there's a glow around him, a strange light that pushes back the dark. It's like he's on fire but the fire don't hurt him."

Gerin felt the blood rush to his head and the flesh prickle on the back of his neck. *How could he know this?* It sounded like a description of a wizard's aura. *What in the name of the gods has this man seen?* He glanced toward Hollin, and they exchanged a knowing look. Hollin cupped his chin in the curve formed by his forefinger and thumb and frowned deeply, obviously troubled. Matren stood with arms crossed, his eyebrows pinched in smoldering anger. Balandrick, though, looked quickly toward Gerin, his expression questioning and disturbed, and the crown prince knew that his friend had understood the implications of what Malarik had just said.

"Then a figure appears on the cliff with the prince, but he ain't no man; this is a creature of fear, a terrible and mighty king in white armor and eyes that glow a kind of silver, like pools of moonlight sunken into his pale face. Somehow he has the prince in his power, freezes him like a statue, and the king moves closer and slides his fingers into the prince's face, right into his skin like they was the fingers of a ghost, while the prince struggles, but it's no use, he can't escape." Malarik grew more agitated, his head shaking back and forth, his eyes squeezed shut, plainly frightened. "The king takes somethin' from the prince, I don't know what it is, but I think he steals his spirit, or destroys it, because then the king steps *into* the prince's body like it was just clothes he could wear. There's this awful rumble, like the earth itself is groanin' in pain and horror of what's about to happen.

A wind blows from the cliff, a dark and terrible gale that doesn't stop, it only grows stronger, as if the gods themselves had made it in anger and unleashed it upon the world. When it touches the prince—he's alone now, the ghost king has vanished into him and there's no sign of him left except for tiny pinpricks of silvery light in the prince's eyes—he falls to the earth, dead. The wind is strong, oh so strong, and it picks me up and carries me upon its breath. It blows across Khedesh, and everythin' it touches dies. Birds fall from the sky, trees wither, grass turns black, sheep and cows and deer and all manner of beasts perish in the black wind; I see Padesh, and as the wind rolls across it, everyone in its walls falls down dead. And the wind keeps blowin', growin' stronger and stronger, sweepin' across towns and cities, over mountains and across rivers and plains and forests and lakes, until all of Osseria is gone."

Malarik let out a deep sigh. His eyes were still closed tight; he was shaking, his entire body wracked with violent tremors as if he were freezing. Gerin wondered if he were having a vision right now, describing for them what he was experiencing at that moment in his mind.

The ghost king with the silvery eyes, thought Gerin. A tremor of fear shivered across his flesh. It sounded like the vast apparition he'd seen. *But who or what is it? And what does it want with me?*

When Malarik spoke again, his voice was very quiet. The passion of his vision had left him. "Prince Gerin, if he lives, will cause everyone in Osseria to die."

"That's ridiculous!" said Matren. "The ramblings of a madman." He turned to Gerin. "My lord, please, trouble yourself no further with this. He's earned death for his attack on your person. Have Balandrick behead him and spike his head upon the walls. There's nothing more to learn from him."

Gerin held up his hand for Matren to be still, then addressed Malarik. "So you attacked me to prevent this vision from coming to pass?"

Malarik's trembling subsided and he looked up at them for the first time with an expression of relief, reinforcing Gerin's thought that he had just experienced his vision in this very room, or had remembered it so vividly that it might as well have been recurring. Then he lowered his gaze once more and nodded.

"My lord, sometimes I dream of strange images that to look at them don't make no sense; but I can understand what they mean. I don't know how to explain how I know these things, I just *do,* I know them in my heart. It's the way it's always been. Sometimes I don't understand them, but most of the time I can see through to the *heart* of the dreams and know the true meanin' of what I see. But this dream was very clear, maybe the most clear I've ever had." He lowered his eyes and his voice dropped to a whisper. "I just couldn't bear the thought of my pa and all those people dyin'."

"I need to examine him," said Hollin. "He may indeed have some power of prophecy that I can detect."

"By all means, go ahead."

Hollin drew several deep breaths to calm himself, then folded his hands together and spoke an Osirin incantation too softly for Gerin to understand. He stopped behind the chained man and stretched his right hand toward the crown of his head.

There was a subtle motion in the air above Malarik, then a faint golden glow appeared, hovering just above him. Malarik did not notice it. The glow coalesced into a wide, flattened circle of dim light that a moment later began to descend. When it touched Malarik's head, the circle rippled outward from the contact in smooth concentric rings.

Malarik was now aware of the wizard's magic and cringed from it, trying to raise his hands to cover his head and failing because of his chains. He groaned and said, "My lord, what is this?"

"Be silent," said Gerin. "We're trying to determine the truth of what you say."

Still cowering from the descending circle of light that cast a faint pattern of shifting shadows on his face, Malarik nevertheless nodded. The circle changed colors, transforming from gold to a rainbow hue that cascaded out from the disk's center.

The circle reached the floor and dissolved in a radiant shimmer. Hollin straightened and blinked several times, as if coming out of a trance.

"What did you learn?" asked Gerin.

Hollin stepped around Malarik and moved closer to Gerin. Matren and Balandrick joined them. "There *are* prophetic powers in him. I don't doubt that he has indeed seen the future at times in dreams and visions, just as he's described. But that says nothing about his dream concerning *you*, Gerin. I have no way of knowing if that particular dream is a prophetic one or something conjured from his mind like any dream you or I might have."

"So you're saying it's possible he's telling the truth, but we have no way of knowing for sure."

"Yes. I'm certain he *believes* he's telling the truth and that is why he acted as he did, but that's all I can say."

"My lord," said Matren, "it doesn't matter what this man believes. An attempt was made on your life, a prince of noble blood and heir to the throne. He should be executed and his head placed upon the wall as a lesson to anyone who would harm a member of the royal household. That is the law. If your father were here—"

"But my father's not here," said Gerin. He faced the guards. "Return him to the dungeons. See that he's not harmed. I may wish to speak with him more."

"My lord, please—"

"Matren, enough. My decision is made."

The castellan swallowed whatever he was going to say, but clearly was not happy about it. "Yes, my lord."

"Do you think there's anything else you can learn from him?" Gerin asked the wizard.

"I don't think so. Even if I was with him while he was in the throes of one of his visions, I don't believe I could determine with any real certainty whether he was truly seeing the future, or if he was interpreting it correctly."

Gerin was disappointed with Hollin's answer. He ached to learn the truth of Malarik's vision. Who was this dark king with him in the vision? Was it the apparition he'd seen twice before? Did Malarik's vision finally give him a clue as to what the being wanted—to somehow steal or destroy his spirit? But to what end? And how could it release a death wind to kill every living thing in Osseria? It seemed impossible.

But what if Malarik's vision wasn't as straightforward as it seemed—what it if it were really a symbolic representation of something else? His mind whirled with possibilities. What else could it mean?

He recalled Malarik's description of a wizardlike glow around him. Could that have something to do with his wizardry? When Naragenth lived there were thousands of other wizards who could oppose his vast strength through sheer force of numbers. From what he'd learned from Hollin, the armies of Helca had been commanded by wizards. The battle in which Naragenth was killed was fought not only with knights laying siege to a city but with wizards casting complex spells and counterspells against one another. What must the foot soldiers have thought, he wondered, slogging through the mud, hacking at their enemies with swords and spears while wizards fought a second, invisible battle all around them? How many were killed by spells of war and death without ever knowing who or what was killing them?

But the world now was a very different place. Wizards were largely forgotten, and those who remained kept to themselves for the most part at Hethnost. When his own powers were Awakened, there would be almost no one who could stand against him. Certainly no single wizard.

Was there something an amber wizard could do to cause a disaster like the one seen by Malarik?

A thought came to him. Perhaps he, Gerin, would somehow set in motion a conflict so vast that it spread across all of Osseria, a war so devastating it left all the nations in ruins.

What could I possibly do to start a war? What could I do that would cause all of the nations to take up arms and fight one another and leave so much destruction in its wake?

The answer that came was unexpected, yet terrifyingly plausible. What if war broke out when he, as an amber wizard with vast powers and a span of life that would last centuries, assumed the throne of Khedesh? What if the fear and uncertainty created by a powerful wizard-king was enough to ignite a continent-spanning conflict?

"You're bothered by something," said Hollin. "Something other than the attempt on your life."

Gerin wasted no time in describing what had just occurred to him.

"It's possible that you're right," said the wizard, "but I would say it's not probable. I said to you before, prophecies are *very* dangerous, for precisely this reason. You're making quite a large interpretative leap, and that is all it is—an interpretation of a vision that may or may not even *be* prophetic.

"The best thing you can do is forget about his dream. The future is not set—it's my belief that prophecies see possibilities, and even those that are so likely as to be nearly preordained may be arrived at through a myriad of paths. Trust me and put this from your mind. There is nothing to be done about it, and dwelling on it will only cause you grief."

Gerin clenched his jaw. He wanted *certainty,* but it was clear that was the one thing he would never have.

9

A week after the oathtaking, Hollin told them it was time to depart for Hethnost. "It may be that the Awakening will disrupt or impede the Neddari spell within you. At the very least we can consult with the Warden of Healing to see if he can remove the spell or render it harmless."

Gerin summoned Matren to tell him their plans and make arrangements for his absence. They left shortly after dawn two days later. Matren and Claressa took their leave of them at the Genshel Gate. "A safe journey to you all," said Matren.

"Don't let my vassals bully you while I'm gone," said Gerin. "Especially Lord Russen. He'll steal the linens from the tables the moment you turn your back. If he shows up at the castle, make sure you lock the gates *before* he gets in."

Matren smiled; Lord Russen's petty pilfering was the subject of many jokes. "Yes, my lord. I'll do as you say."

"Please behave yourselves," said Claressa with a playful smirk. "I wouldn't want you to do anything to tarnish the good Atreyano name."

"You're not coming with us, so we don't have to worry about that," said Reshel.

Gerin swung up onto Ranno. Hollin and Reshel were already mounted, as were Balandrick and the dozen soldiers who would provide their escort. Three packhorses waited behind the soldiers, laden with provisions, their tails swishing lazily.

They rode their mounts through the tunnel and along the slender paved lane that cut across the outer bailey, then passed beneath the raised portcullis of the Gate of the Gray Woman, the main entrance to the castle. Reshel had never been able to discover who the Gray Woman was, her image gracing the steel gates, her left arm raised, palm outward, a hood pulled low so that all of her face except her mouth and chin were hidden. Gerin knew it vexed her to no end that she could not find any references to what she considered an interesting and important part of the castle's history despite extensive searches in the library.

They made their way down the westward-curving road on Ireon's Hill, past an old stone retaining wall cut into the side of the hill, overhung with long weeds like lanky green hair. Balandrick looked back toward the massive gate towers, then said to Gerin and Reshel, "Just think. When the two of you enter the castle the next time, you'll be wizards."

"Assuming Gerin doesn't trip getting off his horse and stab himself with his sword," said Reshel.

Gerin rolled his eyes. "Don't make me wish that Claressa is the wizard."

"If you two think you're going to bicker the entire way to Hethnost," Hollin said, "I'm afraid I'll have to demonstrate several silencing spells. And perhaps one or two for producing boils and exceedingly nasty rashes, just to drive the point home."

"Oh, please, do it anyway," said Balandrick. "I'd love to watch. You just know they're going to do something to deserve it, so why wait?"

Hollin arched his eyebrow. "What makes you think you'd be excluded?"

And we're not even off Ireon's Hill yet, thought Gerin. *It's going to be a long journey.*

As they ventured farther from Ailethon, the hills gradually

gave way to flatter country, sweeping grasslands with but a few sparse trees and copses dotting the landscape. They had entered Terokesh, where many Pashti lived in mud-walled hovels or a few small towns, keeping to themselves, rarely venturing to the markets in the larger communities around them.

When Khedesh had first come to these lands he had conquered the barbaric Pashti tribes and civilized them; yet they still rebelled from time to time. Khedesh's beloved knight Nehros had been murdered in his bed by a Pashti servant that he'd welcomed into his household; the day of the murder had been known as the Sorrow of Nehros ever after.

A few years earlier, after a band of Pashti brigands had murdered several families in the westlands, Gerin's father had remarked that he thought it would have been better if Khedesh had simply obliterated the Pashti rather than waste the effort to bring civilization to a people so obviously unworthy of it. Gerin had said nothing, but had never forgotten his father's words. They troubled him, not only because of their ruthlessness—did *all* Pashti really deserve death?—but also for the casual, almost offhanded way his father spoke, as if the subject were of trivial importance.

After days of travel along the Naevos Road they came to the city of Naevos itself, a once-thriving trading center that had been in steady decline since a plague had swept through the Plains of Ghesevaras half a century ago. The old imperial road that had cut across the plains had fallen into disrepair, and in many places had vanished entirely after the communities that had maintained it had been abandoned or eradicated by the plague.

They spent a single night in the city at an inn near the temple district and left early in the morning. A few hundred feet beyond the city's western gate, the stony ridge upon which Naevos had been built fell away sharply in a series of rough, natural terraces that Reshel thought looked like steps that had been shattered with a hammer. The road swerved its way back and forth down the slope in an attempt to maintain a steady descent. At the bottom the road cut westward across the prairie in a line as straight as an arrow-shot.

It was still almost unfathomable that she was going to become a wizard. She, Reshel Atreyano, the last and least of her father's children, would soon be joining the ranks of a mighty people, the final remnants of the great Atalari of old, no matter that they were in their final, waning days.

She'd always admired Gerin for his ability to make friends and be at ease before crowds of people. Claressa shared much of Gerin's strong personality, though both of them would have been horrified to hear such a statement. She thought it was one of the reasons they fought so much, beyond Claressa's general disagreeableness. But both of them were fearless; Reshel could easily imagine her sister single-handedly breaking the arms of anyone who dared to attack her the way Gerin had been assaulted the night of the oathtaking. Not for the first time she felt pity for Claressa's future husband.

Claressa could command the attention of everyone in a room with a nod of her head or flash of her eyes, and Gerin could do the same with his mere presence. Reshel, however, disappeared into the shadows; if people did not know who she was, they would look at her with no more interest than they would a kitchen scullion. Reshel realized her station required her to be outgoing and personable on certain occasions, and she did her best to do so, but she did not love it, and it was only through years of effort that she could act her part.

She had always thought she would merit little more than a paragraph at the most in the history of the Atreyanos. Her grandfather had been loved and respected—and feared, when warranted—by their subjects, as was her father, and she was certain Gerin would be as well when he ascended to the throne. He was certainly popular at Ailethon. Those Therain would rule at Agdenor would, if not adore him, at least respect him and follow where he led. He was smart—much smarter than many gave him credit for—and she believed he would grow into his role. Claressa would be the mother of proud and fierce children who would rise to greatness in some fashion. Of all these things, Reshel was absolutely sure, and the histories written of them would be long and glorious.

She, too, was meant to be married someday to the son of another noble house, though until now she had never given it much thought. But that had changed. Now she wanted to marry Balandrick. Her feelings for him had grown from a girlish crush into passionate desire; just being in his presence made her feel warm and content in a way she'd never experienced before. Neither of them had spoken yet of marriage, but she felt certain he loved her as much as she had grown to love him. What he did not say to her in words she could see in his eyes when he looked at her, feel in his fingers when he held her hand or stroked her face, or taste in the soft caress of his lips against hers. No, she did not doubt his love.

But she also knew he felt conflicted about their relationship while serving as captain of her brother's personal guard, which was why she had not pressed him to be more forthcoming with her—he had to work that out, both in his own heart and with Gerin. But she did not see why he could not be both her husband and Gerin's guard.

Her father was another matter entirely. She had no idea how he would react or what he would think when she finally told him. But that was something she did not yet have to face, and so she thought about it as little as possible.

Before Balandrick, she'd assumed that the account of her life would merit a few sentences in the annals of the royal family. But her wizardry changed everything. What would history say about her now? Would she still be little more than a passing mention, or would her wizardry afford her a history of her own? What would she accomplish with her new-found powers? What legacy would now be hers to create?

Not for the first time she wondered what she would do with her long life. It worried her, though she would never mention her concern to Hollin or Gerin. Sometimes she had dreams where she saw her husband—whose face she could never see clearly, but she knew in her heart it was Balandrick—and children age and wither before her eyes, then blow away like dust. How would she bear it? Would she be forced to leave them, as Hollin had left his family so long ago? Would she spend her final days in Hethnost with others of her own kind, living in the memories of the life and loved ones she had left behind?

Will I be alone in the end, without family or friends? she wondered. She felt haunted by her own future, powerless to change what seemed a path that, while filled with wonder and glory and happiness for many long years, nonetheless would end in sadness and solitude and regret.

The day after leaving Naevos, they came to another road that led away to the north.

"We turn here," said Hollin. In truth it was little more than a faded path, a single rut of bare earth that cut through the tall grass undulating in the afternoon breeze like a slow moving ocean wave.

A few hours later, while passing a large squarish boulder jutting from a gentle hillside covered with wildflowers, a strong gust of wind blew across their path. Gerin slowed Ranno and looked around as the others continued to ride ahead. He strongly sensed that they were being watched. It grew dark then, as if heavy clouds had passed across the face of the sun, though the sky had been clear. In the next moment the air seemed to thicken around him, holding him as immobile as one of the binding spells Hollin had spoken of, and he wondered if he had stumbled into some forgotten wizard's trap. Time itself had slowed to a nearly imperceptible crawl—even his thoughts seemed sluggish and heavy, as if he were sick with fever.

Then he could move freely once more and the sense of slowed time vanished, though the strange darkness remained. He drew a deep breath and rubbed his eyes, trying to clear his head and vision. When he looked up, he was startled to see a man sitting on a small spur of stone shaped vaguely like a seat that jutted from the boulder's edge. He wore finely made trousers of wool, with soft brown boots that reached to his knees. Tucked into the trousers was a linen shirt so brilliantly white that it made Gerin squint; it had lace at the cuffs and collar, and atop it he wore a vest of burgundy velvet with large gold buttons. His straight, black hair fell across his face in a way that made it difficult for Gerin to see his features clearly.

"Who are you?" asked Gerin. His right hand fell onto the hilt of Glaros. The stranger carried no weapon that Gerin could see, but he sensed that this man was both powerful and dangerous.

"I am a messenger, Prince Gerin. My name is not for you to know."

Yet he knows my name. "Have you been following us? I ask again, who are you? What are you doing here? Who sent you?"

"And I will tell you again, my name is not for you or any man to know. I have already said that I come to speak to you. You would be wise to listen."

There was something about his voice that made Gerin want to trust him, to believe whatever he had to say. *Is this man a wizard?* he wondered. *Is he casting a spell on me?* Gerin felt the unseen power in the man grow even stronger, like the rising heat of a flame. But he detected no malice, no threat. What he felt, he realized, was that merely being in the presence of this man was perilous.

"The divine are curious beings, Gerin," he said. "Immortal, powerful, yet fickle in their dealings with the mortal world. Or so it would seem to men. But there are restrictions even on the divine, rules by which they must abide, as inviolable as the law of death for men. A god may find he is powerless to save what he has created even when that creation is threatened with annihilation. He may be unable to reveal all that he would have known, knowledge that would allay much suffering and sorrow, because in the end such revelations would only cause greater suffering."

"Why are you telling me this?" said Gerin. "Who *are* you?"

"Hear me, Gerin." The man stood. He seemed far larger than his physical self, as if Gerin were seeing only a fraction of the immense power contained in his form.

"There are things the Maker would have you know that He cannot yet reveal to you, things of which I am, at least for now, forbidden to speak. But these two things I may tell you: His Adversary is returning, the one who opposed Him at the beginning of all things and was long ago thrown down in darkness and defeat. Even now he is entering the Circle of the World and binding himself to it as his power waxes. You must be vigilant—the Maker cannot strike him without undoing all that He has built. He must act through others who willingly choose to serve Him and His will. And so I have come to you now, to warn you of the coming darkness and ask that you fight for the Maker when that day comes.

"The other thing I would have you know is this: even a prophet may not fully understand what he is shown. Be mindful of what you are told."

There was another gust of wind, another strange sensation of time slowing and his body being frozen in suddenly immovable air. It ended quickly, and Gerin took a shuddering breath. The air around him brightened, and a warm ray of sunlight struck his face, blinding him for a moment. He turned his head away and squeezed his eyes shut. When he looked back, the man was gone.

Only then did he think of his companions. They had halted on the path ahead and were looking back at him with a mixture of curiosity and concern. "Is everything all right?" asked Reshel. "You stopped and wouldn't speak. You just kept staring at that rock."

"You mean you didn't see him?"

She shook her head. "Gerin, there was no one else here."

He jabbed his finger at the outcropping of stone. "There was a man sitting right there!"

"We didn't see anyone," said Balandrick.

Hollin rode back to him and positioned his horse next to

Ranno so they were side by side, his leg nearly touching Gerin's. "Tell me what happened."

Gerin closed his eyes and lowered his head to think. *What had just happened?*

They dismounted, tethered their horses, and sat near the rock. Gerin told Hollin in as much detail as he could about his encounter with the messenger. His hands shook despite his best efforts to make them stop. "Is this the being who visited me at Ailethon?"

Hollin listened intently, saying nothing. Then he stood and worked several spells on Gerin and the rock where he'd seen the mysterious figure. When he was done, the wizard sat down once more, his face drawn and weary. "I don't sense any power here, magical or otherwise, but that does not surprise me. If this is truly a god who has visited you—or a messenger of a god, if he is to be believed—I would not expect to sense anything. Divine power is beyond our ability to see." The wizard frowned and folded his arms. "Tell me again what this man said to you."

Gerin repeated the stranger's words. A thought came to him. "Do you think he was talking about Stefon Malarik when he said, 'Even a prophet may not fully understand what he is shown'? Maybe he was trying to tell me that Stefon's vision was real but that he misunderstood its meaning."

"It's possible, but there may be other explanations we can't yet see. I don't understand his reference to an Adversary. I would not think it refers to Shayphim, who is more a spirit of evil than a true god. And Shayphim is not returning after a long absence."

"That Neddari called Gerin a god-summoner," said Balandrick. "And this messenger said the Adversary isn't yet here. Could these be new gods of some sort, that Gerin is supposed to somehow bring into the world?"

Hollin was quiet for a long while. "I don't know. And I have no idea how Gerin could summon a god. There are no spells that I am aware of that can do such a thing, even for an amber wizard. I'll discuss this with the Warden of the Archives when we reach Hethnost. There's nothing else I can learn here unless this mysterious figure reappears."

"Then let's get going," said Gerin. Once more he felt as if the course of his life were out of his control, that he was at the mercy of vast and unseen powers whose purpose for him he did not yet understand. "The sooner we get there, the better."

Two days later they could see a dark jagged line across the horizon, rising above the grass like a great wall barring their path.

"Those are the Redhorn Hills," said Hollin, "a spur of the Graymantle Mountains that branch off just to the north of the Gap of Ellohar. Hethnost lies among them in the Telir Osáran. It's not far now."

As they journeyed along the northern path, the line upon the horizon began to resolve itself with increasing clarity. The Redhorn Hills were tall and steep, much higher than the hills around Ailethon, with sharp knifelike peaks scattered among more rounded, blunted crowns. The hills were blanketed with dark pine trees and from a distance seemed covered in a green-black fur of moss.

The path followed a fairly straight course for most of its length. Along the way they spied two small towns in the distance, but they passed them early in the morning and decided not to veer off their course or delay their journey to spend the night.

At one point the path bent backward in a wide arc to the west, following the contour of a rugged natural wall of exposed reddish rock twenty feet high that jutted from the ground like the remains of some ancient rampart. At the far end of the crumbling wall the path turned back toward the north.

"Once we reach that bend up ahead, we'll be within sight of Hethnost," said Hollin.

Reshel's face lit with excitement as she spurred her horse forward. "What are we waiting for? Come on, hurry!"

10

Reshel galloped ahead to the turn in the path, then disappeared behind the edge of the rock. Gerin, too, was eager to catch his first glimpse of Hethnost, but felt he should show restraint in front of the soldiers. "How much longer until we get there?" he asked Hollin.

"Soon. It's not far now."

"What are the defenses like?" asked Balandrick.

"Best you survey the place for yourself when we get there, and ask the captain of the Sunrise Guard. Wizards do not concern themselves overmuch with ordinary weapons. For us, it has long been tradition that magic alone suffices to defend our persons, which is why you will never see a wizard with sword or spear or shield."

Gerin gave him a sidelong glance and his hand dropped to the hilt of his weapon. "That will change with me. I'll not give up Glaros, an heirloom of my house, simply because I've become a wizard."

"That is of course for you to decide. As I said, it is a custom, not a law."

"Don't wizards have weapons of magic?" asked Balandrick. "Magic swords and the like?"

"There are many powerful magical weapons at Hethnost, locked away in the armory vaults and elsewhere. And in the past, when wizards were more numerous, they indeed carried spell-enchanted swords and knives. But that is no longer the case, and many of those weapons have been destroyed or lost their potency over the long years."

On the path ahead Reshel was waving anxiously for them to hurry.

"I'm tempted to stop here and take a nap just to drive her crazy," Gerin said.

Balandrick laughed. "I think she'd probably come and drag you by your boot heels. Which, now that I think of it, would be fun to see. I'll give you a half-dera to lie down in the grass. Come on, let's see what she does."

Gerin feigned consideration. "Tempting, but I'm just not up for being dragged by my boots today. It does bad things to the back of my head."

When they reached Reshel, she turned to them with a beaming smile upon her face. "Isn't it wonderful?" She pointed ahead to their destination.

The fortress sat at the far end of an oval valley more than a mile wide and nearly as deep, with an open southern face across which a long wall with many towers had been built. The sides of the hills enclosing the valley were high and sheer; Gerin could see that in several places what had once been gentle inclines intruding into the valley had been cut away to create cliffs whose gray faces stood out starkly against the darker, tree-clad slopes around them. The hills around the fortress were the highest in the region, with deep shadow-filled valleys and rock-walled ravines between them. An enemy would find an approach through the hills difficult at best, and be limited to lightly armored footsoldiers—horses could not gain entrance to the valley from the hills, and no machines of war or siege could be maneuvered through them. The only practical approach was head-on through the valley itself.

The wall across the valley entrance was anchored into the sides of high conical hills whose summits appeared to have been sheared off and flattened. Thick towers of blue-tinted stone, surrounded by circular walls protecting storage buildings and barracks, stood upon each hill. Gerin could see narrow paths spiraling up the hills to the towers from the valley below.

The wizard pointed to the left tower. "That one is called the Mirdan ne'Cuimaras, the Tower of the Clouds, and the one upon the right is Mirdan ne'Keleth, the Tower of Wind."

They rode on in silence for a few minutes. As they neared the massive twin-doored gate that pierced the center of the defensive partition across the valley, Hollin said, "The wall ahead of us is the Hammdras. It's quite an infamous structure. Venegreh, the wizard who commanded that Hethnost be built and was its first Archmage, felt it was unnecessary. It also added considerably to the expense. But Veilos Tirban, the architect who actually designed and built this place, vehemently disagreed and refused to compromise his vision. He felt that walling off the valley was vital to its security."

The gates themselves—colored a deep red and inscribed with arcane symbols painted in black and gold—were open, the portcullis behind them raised into the massive tower above the gate. There were some soldiers atop the Hammdras, peering at them from the battlements, but not as many as Gerin would have expected.

"Is Hethnost fully garrisoned with soldiers?" asked Balandrick, noticing the same lack of manpower.

Hollin shook his head. "Not for many long years, though that is truthfully of little consequence. The hilltop towers are completely unmanned, and have been that way for more than a century. The soldiers themselves are a dwindling holdover from the Imperial Era, when the masters of Hethnost felt a small army of nonwizard soldiers would be prudent to have at their disposal. The construction of Hethnost itself reflects this philosophy. It is protected by layer upon layer of spells to repel magical attacks, but is also designed to defend against a Gendalos siege."

At the southwestern end of the valley was a lake fed by a stream that flowed down from the hills and entered the valley in a waterfall that cascaded down a terracelike rock face. On the northern side of the lake, where the stream flowed into it, the land was wet and marshy, with tall reeds rising from stagnant pools coated with a layer of green slime.

"That is the Tivar Lhasaril, the Lake of Dreaming, fed by the Aisa Néhos, the Red Water," said Hollin. "It's said that when Venegreh first came to this land, he slept by the lake and had a vision of the haven for wizards that he would build."

Gerin now had a much clearer view of Hethnost itself. There was a second wall about a half mile behind the Hammdras—built in a tighter arc than the outer fortification's slight curve—forming nearly a semicircle from its anchor points against the cliff at the rear of the valley. It, too, had battlements and towers, and looked to be the same height as the Hammdras. The bulk of Hethnost lay inside this inner wall.

The fortress had many high towers with tiled conical peaks instead of the flat, open, battlemented roofs Gerin was used to; some of the towers were connected by slender arching walkways of stone with wrought-iron parapets that made him dizzy just to look at. Dozens of buildings of all shapes and sizes lay within the wall.

Twin hills that stretched nearly the entire width of the valley loomed over the rear of the fortress. The front of the hills was a wall of granite four hundred feet high, capped with a dense growth of trees; it was smooth and sheer across its entire face except for a narrow spur in the center that protruded into the valley like a knife blade on edge. The spur was shaped like a tall narrow wedge, thinnest on top and widening only slightly as it descended into the fortress, resembling a long ramp. It extended about a third of the way into Hethnost, dividing the rear area neatly in two. Gerin could see that a narrow road had been built upon the ramplike slope, which Hollin told them was called the Partition Rock. Fountains had been cut into the Partition Rock on both sides of the road, their waters splashing in deep basins of polished stone. The top of the slope was flattened and leveled, and upon it a vast high-ceilinged hall had been built. A line of red columns with gold capitals marched along its face, supporting the forward overhang of the pediment. The building stood alone save for a single white bell tower rising to twice the building's height.

"What is that?" asked Reshel. "That building that over-looks everything."

"That is the Kalabrendis Dhosa," said Hollin. "Where conclaves and other gatherings of wizards are held. It's seldom used anymore, which is our loss. It's a beautiful place, probably the most beautiful in all of Hethnost."

A black and green standard with a golden hand at its heart fluttered atop the forwardmost tower in the fortress. Just below it flew a red and blue flag with a yellow sun rising from the blue into the red. "Those are the banners of Venegreh and Marandra Kelliam, the current Archmage," said Hollin.

"Where is the Varsae Sandrova?" asked Reshel.

"Do you see the large building on the western side with a domed roof? That is the library."

They reached the main gate in the inner wall, a tall arch with heavy imposts inscribed with a blessing by Venegreh for all who entered the home of wizards. The double gates of blue steel were rectangular and deeply recessed, with an elaborate tympanum showing the carved face of a bearded man with flowing hair surrounded by garlands and rosettes.

"Who is that?" asked Balandrick, gesturing to the carving.

"Venegreh himself. It is one of the few likenesses of him that exist. He was not fond of being sculpted or painted."

They passed through the long gate tunnel. Nine men awaited them at the far end, dark silhouettes against the sunlit courtyard behind them. Gerin could see that one of them wore armor and carried a sword. *Definitely not a wizard, then.* Some of the men appeared to be servants or stable hands.

They entered the courtyard, a rectangular plot of grass enclosed by free-standing columns with statues of robed men and women placed between them and a deep-bowled fountain at its center. Gerin looked beyond the yard at the immensity of Hethnost, awed by the sheer size of its buildings and the grandeur of their designs, the elaborate decorations and intricacies of detail.

"What about our belongings?" asked Reshel as she dismounted and handed her horse's reins to one of the stable hands.

"They'll be taken to your rooms, my lady," said a servant as he slung one of their packs over his shoulder.

"Lord Commander, I have brought my charges here for the Awakening," said Hollin to the soldier, a man of middle years with gray hair cropped close to his head. He was of average height, lean but well-muscled. His breastplate was white, with a rayed yellow half-circle representing the sun painted on its center. A bloodred sash appeared to be his mark of rank, Gerin noted, as the few other soldiers he saw upon the wall-walk of the battlements bore no such decoration.

"Greetings, Vesai Hollin," said Lord Commander Taivos Medril of the Sunrise Guard. He bowed his head to the wizard and held his fist against his chest. "Welcome home. It's good to see you."

Seddon Rethazi, the steward of Hethnost, stepped forward and bowed to Hollin. He was a wiry man with a bald, suntanned head and wisps of white hair fringing his scalp that fluttered in the slight breeze like tattered banners. A thick, well-trimmed mustache covered his upper lip like a brush.

"Your chambers should be ready for you, Vesai," said the steward. "I had them cleaned and freshened the moment you were seen on the road."

"And our guests?"

"The rooms for our newest wizards in the Apprentices Hall are already prepared." He regarded Gerin with wonder. He did not have the same rapt expression of awe and devotion that had graced Hollin's face after he'd performed the Ritual of Discovery, but it was close. "So you are the amber wizard. Amazing. It is an honor to meet you." He faced Reshel and smiled in a warm, grandfatherly way. "And the young golden wizard. We've not had brother and sister wizards here in my lifetime. I'm honored to meet you as well." Before either of them could reply, Rethazi turned his gaze toward Balandrick and the soldiers. "I did not know, however, that others would be accompanying you. If you would follow me, good sirs, I will see to your accommodations."

Balandrick stepped closer to Gerin and said in a low voice, "Are you all right going off on your own?"

Gerin laughed. "Of course. Nothing's going to happen here. This isn't some elaborate kidnapping plot."

"I hope not. I've had enough of people attacking you to last me the rest of my life."

"Stop worrying."

Balandrick nodded. "I'll see you later, then." He exchanged a long glance with Reshel before turning away.

"We'll fetch you for dinner," said Hollin. "Perhaps you could speak to the Lord Commander about the defenses of Hethnost."

"I've got some time to show you around a bit," said Medril. "I'll come along if that's fine with you."

"Certainly," said Balandrick.

Hollin said to Gerin and Reshel, "Come, I'll show you to the hall."

They crossed a paved courtyard and then a garden with neatly clipped grass, trimmed hedges, and bubbling fountains in white marble bowls. Wooden benches with legs and arms of wrought iron were placed in areas of shade near the fountains. As they passed one of the benches, Hollin pointed to an old tree growing behind it. The tree had deep creases in its trunk and grew in a strange spiral shape, as if it had slowly twisted as it aged. Its bark was grayish-white, but it was not a birch, and its leaves were long and pointed and had a faint silvery edge. It was unlike any tree Gerin had ever seen.

"This is a *kahladen*," said Hollin. "They've been held sacred by wizards for ages. It's said that a wizard whose name is now long forgotten once angered the gods, and that in their wrath they struck down the wizard's beautiful young wife as punishment, knowing he cherished her life more than his own. He buried her in her white wedding dress and let his tears fall on her grave, singing a song so beautiful and sad that even the gods who had killed her felt remorse at their deed. As the wizard sang, a white tree began to grow from the mound of fresh dirt and continued until it was a great height. But the wizard's grief was too great, and once the tree stopped growing, he sat down against it and died, his song still echoing through the forest grove. Tiny rivulets of water called Wizard's Tears sometimes trickle down their trunks and are believed by some to be a source of powerful love potions."

"Is this the tree from that story?" asked Reshel.

"Oh, no. No one knows where that one grew, if it ever existed outside of legend. This one is more than three hundred years old, though, and was planted by the Archmage Shatani Zahamburrik in memory of his wife Alaria, a mortal woman who lived her life with him here at Hethnost. He resigned his office not long after her death and left Hethnost forever, returning to the village of his birth to live out his days in grief and solitude."

Near what appeared to be a temple was a graveyard with several hundred headstones, many leaning this way and that over ground that had shifted and sunken beneath them. Some were so old that the carved letters on them had all but vanished, erased by ages of wind and rain.

"I thought wizards didn't bury their dead," Gerin said.

"We do not. This is for the Gendalos servants and soldiers who live here with us. This is the oldest of our graveyards, and was filled long ago. There are two others within the walls of Hethnost and one outside, to the northeast."

A sudden wind blew past them, shaking the branches of the old ash tree that stood inside the gate. Reshel said, "Our mother told me once that every wind that blows through a graveyard carries the voices of the dead upon it, and that if we only knew how to listen, we could hear all they have to tell us: all the secrets they carried while they were alive, and what awaits us after death."

Gerin looked at her, surprised and a little shocked. He had never heard their mother say anything of the sort. What other

things had she shared with his brother or sisters that he knew
nothing about? That they should know things about their
mother that he did not disturbed him; even though he knew it
was ridiculous, he nevertheless felt as if he'd suffered some
sort of vague betrayal.

The Apprentices Hall was a plain rectangular building of
beige limestone with four floors lined with narrow cross-
paned windows. The hall was divided equally, one half for
the male apprentices and the other half for the females, with
separate entrances next to one another. Their rooms were the
first ones within the respective entrances. Now, there were
seven other apprentices in the hall, whose powers had been
Awakened nearly a year ago. As the Warden of Apprentices,
Hollin was charged with overseeing their training; but the
possibility of finding an amber wizard was an opportunity
he would not allow to pass him by—he'd been a member of
the group that deciphered Bainora Estreg's cryptic Foretellings concerning Gerin—so he had assigned the training
of the current apprentices to another wizard, Abaru Mezza,
so he could leave Hethnost to search for Gerin.

Gerin's room was small but comfortable, with a narrow
bed, a desk with an oil lamp—since they weren't wizards, he
supposed they wouldn't let them have magefire lamps—a
washbasin, and a small wardrobe for clothes.

There was a brown hooded robe on the bed. Hollin had
told them they would be required to wear the simple accoutrements of an apprentice. No matter their station by birth,
here all apprentices were equal.

Gerin had also been told that apprentices were permitted
no weapons of any kind. He unbuckled Glaros from his belt
and placed the sword and its sheath in the wardrobe. He had
no fear that it would be stolen, and it was close at hand
should the need for it ever arise.

Later, on their way to the dining hall to meet Balandrick,
they passed through a long narrow garden that had been allowed to grow wilder than the rigidly cultivated areas they'd
seen so far. It completely filled the space between two large

buildings, with gated walls of stone at either end. The trees within were old and tall—birch and linden and magnolia, and a great old elm with branches that drooped so low over the wall they had to duck to pass through the black iron gate. A flagstone path wound through the garden, threading its way lazily among the trunks. Wildflowers flourished at the feet of boulders carefully placed to appear as natural formations, and planters of yellow and red roses had been hung from trellises placed near wooden benches.

"Look at that," Reshel whispered. She pointed to a large statue upon a pedestal of gray marble standing near a willow tree. The statue itself was white, though blemished with streaks of dirt and grime. When Gerin saw it, his breath caught in his throat and a deep chill ran up his back.

The statue rose seven feet above the pedestal and depicted a father carrying the limp corpse of his son, one arm beneath the boy's back, the other beneath his knees. The father cradled his son gently, lovingly, a boy of five or six whose head rested against his chest, his eyes closed, his lips slack. The boy's left arm lay across his abdomen; his right hung limply, the fingers relaxed, and Gerin could easily imagine it swaying lifelessly as the father carried him away from the place where he had died—for surely, he thought, that must be what was depicted. The dead child wore a sleeveless tunic and trousers that reached only to mid-thigh; his feet were bare. He had no wound or blight upon him, no visible injury that could have caused his death. Indeed, he could easily have been sleeping except for the expression on his father's face. It was etched with anguish and pain, a sorrow so deep and penetrating it seemed he must collapse at any moment from the crushing weight of his despair. His head was tilted back, looking skyward; his eyes were wide and imploring, and looked so close to spilling tears that Gerin half expected to see water begin to pour down his white cheeks. The father's lips were parted, as if he were attempting to speak but could not find the strength for his voice. His hair was swept back from his face by an unseen wind, which billowed the cloak that fell from his shoulders.

"It's both beautiful and terrible," said Reshel in the same whispery voice.

"This is *Death of a Son*," said Hollin. He, too, spoke softly, and with a reverence in his voice Gerin had not heard from him before. "It is my favorite sculpture in all of Hethnost. Many find it morbid and avoid it, and in some ways it is, but I find it heart-wrenchingly sad and beautiful. It was made by a wizard named Eredhel Anyakul after his own son drowned in one of the cisterns here. He never sculpted again after this was finished, and in fact went mad a few years later and lived out his days in the uppermost room of the Derasdi Tower." He pointed to a solitary square spire near the foot of the ramp that led to the Kalabrendis Dhosa. He looked at the statue and folded his arms. "I've always imagined that the father is about to speak the name of his son, but that his grief is simply too great to overcome."

"It seems to me he is going to ask, 'Why?' " said Reshel. " 'Why was my child taken from me? Who will answer for it?' He's looking to the gods, but his question is met only with silence and a voiceless wind."

"I like that," said the wizard. "I've also thought this was a potent symbol for wizards and our inability to pass our powers and long lives to our children. I think that's why so many of us are troubled by it; it's too sad a reminder of what we can never share."

At the dining hall, Hollin introduced them to some of the wizards, all of whom were eager to meet the new apprentices. Gerin was overwhelmed with the sense that they already regarded him as some kind of majestic figure, as if his destiny had already been established. He wondered if the prophecy about his life were the cause, if these wizards actually did know something about his future that he did not, even though Hollin had said that prophecies were studied only by a select few, and that they were not to divulge what they learned under any circumstances, with severe penalties if they broke the edict. Still, regardless of what they knew or didn't, the intense degree of expectation with which they looked at Gerin left him feeling intimidated and anxious. He was in a situation he did not completely understand and so did not know how he should react. He did his best to ignore them, but it was hard, especially surrounded by so many.

They met Abaru Mezza for the first time, the wizard who would act as interim Warden of Apprentices while Hollin trained Gerin and Reshel at Ailethon.

Mezza was a giant of a man, standing more than a full head taller than Gerin. He was round and fleshy, with thick meaty arms, a doughy face, and an enormous, solid stomach that preceded him like a herald announcing his imminent arrival. He moved about with the palpable weight of one of the black bears that roamed the highland woods of Khedesh's March. If his name had not given away his heritage as an Armenosean— or perhaps a Tagerean—his great size, weathered complexion, thick brow, and broad, flat nose hinted strongly at the peoples of the Valesh Peninsula that lay to the east of the Landwall Mountains. When he spoke for the first time, gripping Gerin's fingers in a knuckle-grinding handshake and loudly expressing how pleased he was to be meeting the future amber wizard, his strong coastal accent erased all doubt.

"I look forward to your Awakening," he said. "Should be quite a spectacle."

Balandrick joined them a little while later, along with Seddon Rethazi. The two were talking like old friends, Balandrick laughing at something the old man was telling him as they passed through the columned entranceway.

"Where are the soldiers?" asked Gerin as Balandrick joined them.

"Eating in a dining hall reserved for the Sunrise Guard. They're fine. Soldiers are soldiers. They were getting drunk and swapping stories when I left." From the flush in his cheeks, the glassy sheen to his eyes, and the way he spoke a little too loudly, it was apparent Balan had not neglected to join his fellow Khedeshians in drinking a few ales of his own.

* * *

The next morning they were summoned to see the Arch-mage, whose apartments were on the top floor of the manor. The young boy knocked twice on the door, then folded his hands and waited. From inside, a woman's voice called out, "Come in!"

The servant boy leading them opened the door and quickly stepped aside for Gerin and Reshel to enter, then closed the door behind them.

They found themselves in a narrow, dimly lit antechamber with large paintings hanging on the side walls. Beyond the antechamber was a large room with windows on either side of a door that led to a balcony. The door was open, and white silk curtains fluttered in the light breeze blowing in from outside.

There was a woman seated at a round table tucked below one of the windows; she rose as they entered and watched them closely as they came to her. Marandra Kelliam was tall, with lustrous black hair curled into tight ringlets, and wore a rose-colored dress decorated with gold thread. The Ammon Ekril, the great diamond that signified her rank as Archmage, sparkled on her forehead, fastened to a circlet of gold twisted into a braid. The Alkaneiros shone on the middle finger of her right hand, the great ruby ring of Demos Thelar, the wizard who had created the *methlenel* and Ritual of Discovery. Hollin had told them that the circlet and ring were the most ancient heirlooms of wizards, both far older than Hethnost. The Ammon Ekril was one of the few remnants of the Atalari nation itself, so old that its origin was lost in the depths of time.

Hollin was seated at the table and stood along with the Archmage. She folded her hands and regarded them silently as they stopped before the table and bowed their heads. Her face was beautiful yet stern, with high cheekbones and a narrow, pointed chin. It was the face of a queen, regal and dignified, of one comfortable with the ways of power.

"Hello, Gerin Atreyano," she said. Her voice was deep and velvety. "So you are the amber wizard I've heard so much about. And future king of a powerful nation." She smiled for the first time, showing large even teeth. "Please, sit. Eat if you're hungry. I doubt you had time to visit the dining hall before coming here." She gestured toward a bowl of apples and a wheel of sharp cheese upon the table. There was also a pewter pitcher of water and several glasses resting upon a small silver tray.

"No, thank you, Archmage," said Gerin, who'd drunk enough ale to leave him with a dull headache that did nothing for his appetite. Reshel also politely declined.

"I offer you my greeting as well, Reshel. We've not had sibling wizards here for a very long time. It's a rare and wondrous thing, and I'm honored to bear witness to it.

"I'm most eager to see your Awakening, Gerin. No living wizard has ever seen such a thing. I expect the display of power will be memorable."

"I was telling the Archmage of your encounters with a divine power, as well as the Neddari spell and the apparition you saw at Almaris," said Hollin.

The Archmage's finely arched eyebrows knitted above her nose. "Yes. Troubling news, but I fear there is little I can do to shed further light on these events. It seems the arrival of an amber wizard has drawn a great deal of attention, not all of it wanted. I will set the Warden of the Archives the task of finding what he can about this Adversary, but my heart tells me he will search in vain."

Gerin's heart fell. He'd wanted to find answers here to what had become the most pressing questions in his life, but that apparently was not to be. At least not yet.

Nearly every waking moment during the next week was spent in Hollin's company in one of the study rooms on the upper floor of the Apprentices Hall. When Gerin was not with Hollin, he was in the Varsae Sandrova studying Osirin vocabulary or grammar, eating a hurried meal in the dining hall, or sleeping.

The other apprentices were with Abaru Mezza in another

of the study rooms. Gerin had met them briefly one night in the dining hall, but from what they said, their training and his would not overlap at all; he did not expect to see much of them during his stay.

A week after their arrival, Gerin said, "Hollin, why haven't our powers been Awakened yet? I thought this kind of training would happen *after* we were wizards."

"I know you're eager, but it won't do any good to Awaken your powers if you can't do anything with them."

"But you've already taught us spells."

"It's true that you learned some of what you need to know, but there's a formal way of speaking spells that I want you to be very comfortable with before we go further, and neither of you are ready yet, though you're making good progress. It's dangerous to Awaken magic in one who is unprepared. Patience. It will not be much longer."

The Varsae Sandrova was the largest building in Hethnost, seven stories of white stone with rows of free-standing columns lining the path to the main doors. Subterranean vaults and chambers lay deep beneath the building where countless relics rested in silence, many protected by powerful spells. Each floor of the library was divided into cozy reading chambers furnished with tables, chairs, and magefire lamps. The rooms often contained books and scrolls of similar topics to ease the research. The smell of leather and old parchment permeating the air reminded Gerin of the scent of knowledge and wisdom.

He was in a fourth-floor room one evening when a grayhaired wizard named Tomir Gaiden knocked lightly on the open door. Tomir was one of the archivists who worked to catalog and index the library's many thousands of books, scrolls, manuscripts, artifacts, diaries, and journals. Along with the other archivists, he taught Gerin and Reshel the indexing system so they could find what they needed without continually asking for help.

"May I come in?" he asked.

"Of course." Gerin gestured to the chair across the table.

Tomir craned his wiry neck so he could see what Gerin was reading. "Ah, an account of Naragenth. I can understand your fascination with him."

"There's so little known about him. Especially his library. The men who created the Varsae Estrikavis were good at keeping their secrets. Too good."

"Yes they were," said the archivist. "The wizards who came to Naragenth's conclave and contributed to his library kept no written accounts of their deeds. It was simply too dangerous with Helca's armies raging across Osseria. I can't even begin to know what they thought after Naragenth was killed in battle. I'm sure they feared the library would fall into Helca's hands and be used against them. I wonder if some of those same wizards who helped create it would rather have seen it destroyed than captured."

"Do you think it *was* destroyed? That it's beyond recovery?"

"I don't know. The royal palace of Naragenth was burned in a fire a few centuries later. If it was somehow part of that structure, then it may indeed be gone."

That was the first Gerin had heard such a thing. He'd assumed that the present palace, the Tirthaig, had been the palace of Naragenth as well.

"Its legend is perhaps greater than the reality of it could ever be," said Tomir. "But that's one of the reasons it's so alluring."

The same covetous fury that had come over him when Hollin had first told him of Naragenth's lost library ignited within him again. He felt an overwhelming obsessive need to find it and claim it as his own. He would do *anything* to have it. His desire was like the craving of a starving man for a single morsel of food.

"I find it intolerable that a place like that should be lost forever," he said with more heat than he'd intended. "If it still exists, there *must* be a way to find it. If only we could know how Naragenth had hidden it—"

A thought struck him, one so startling the hairs on his

arms and neck stood on end. Reshel's words in the graveyard when they first entered Hethnost rang clearly in his mind.

Our mother told me once that every wind that blows through a graveyard carries the voices of the dead upon it, and that if we only knew how to listen, we could hear all they have to tell us: all the secrets they carried while they were alive, and the mystery of what awaits us after death.

"Perhaps," said Tomir, although his tone made it clear that he did not consider it likely. "But many have spent lifetimes searching for it without success."

Gerin, already planning ways to learn if his audacious idea were possible, did not hear a word the archivist said.

11

Gerin found that the kind of knowledge he was seeking was not easy to locate. He had to be careful. No one could know what he was doing. He could not ask any of the archivists for guidance for fear they would ask questions he could not answer. He said nothing to Reshel, though he longed to ask her advice. But the obsessive desire that drove him demanded that this be done in secrecy or not at all.

Each floor of the library contained an index of the materials stored there. But many subterranean levels beneath the library were not as easily accessed as the upper floors, and he spent long hours every night on each floor searching for the catalogs and the indexes to the lower levels. He did not know if the kind of spell he was looking for even existed, but he was not going to give up until he exhausted every possibility.

There were three floors of circular galleries beneath the Varsae Sandrova's gilded dome, with a gathering area at the lowest level, beneath the dome's peak. One night he found himself at the door to a small room off the uppermost gallery. He feared it would be locked or protected by spells, and was surprised when it opened for him. He stepped quickly inside before he could be seen, though at this late hour the library was deserted. It was still possible he had triggered a tocsin spell that was alerting the archivists even now that the room had been entered, but he could not worry about that. All he could do was find what he was looking for and get out as quickly as he could.

The walls of the room were covered with wooden cases arranged according to the Osirin alphabet, containing the indexes for several of the subterranean floors. He'd stumbled upon it almost by accident while searching another catalog room on the first floor, near the huge marble atrium within the library's main doors. He had discovered an old diagram of the gallery levels, and the description written at this room's location jumped off the brittle parchment as if it were inscribed in flames: *Index for belowground levels.* Finally, he could find out what was contained within the subterranean crypts.

He searched through the catalog with trembling hands, fearing discovery at any moment. Every sound, every creak or squeak he heard, made him jump. If only he could—

Then he found it.

The spell *did* exist. He removed the index sheet from its slot in the case and memorized the location written upon it. The sixth sublevel, twenty-first room. He read the description of the spell again, and the items needed to work it: a device called the Horn of Tireon, weirstones, and the spellbook of a group called the Baryashin Order.

Gerin returned the sheet to its place and cracked open the door. He saw no one. Nearly breathless, he slipped from the room and made his way out of the library.

Tomir answered all of Gerin's seemingly innocent questions about the structure of the library and even directed him to several complete maps of the place. He was amazed at just how much lay belowground. There were nine levels of varying size, each containing dozens of crypts, vaults, reliquaries, and storage chambers. There was no direct passage from the ground floor of the Varsae Sandrova to the deepest level; corridors were often twisting and narrow, connected to the levels above and below by several stairways, none of which were continuous. It was truly a maze.

After he acquired the maps of the lower levels, he

meticulously traced out a path that would lead him to his destination. He had never been to the levels belowground and did not know what to expect. He had no idea if the archivists spent much time there or if they were largely forgotten, used as long-term storage vaults for books and artifacts that would not often be required.

Gerin entered the library near midnight, carrying a single lamp to light his way. When he'd first begun his late-night excursions, he'd considered trying to keep his movements secret, but decided it would be best to move in the open so as not to arouse suspicion. He was an apprentice, after all. Studying in the Varsae Sandrova was certainly a believable excuse for being out so late. He would draw more notice if he skulked about like a thief in the shadows.

Once within the library itself, he shuttered the lamp and made his way to the nearest entrance to the lower levels. He did not want to be seen by any of the archivists, though he was fairly certain that most were in bed by this hour. Still, he took no chances and moved as quickly and quietly as he could through the gloom.

He opened the heavy door—its hinges creaked loudly, making him wince—and unshuttered his lamp. He found himself in an arched brick passageway that descended at a steep angle. The dust here was thick; a heavy gray layer had settled upon the tops of the magefire globes set in wall sconces. This entrance was obviously seldom used, though he had not known that when planning his route. His feet left dark prints in the dust on the steps, like the footprints of a ghost.

He reached the first level and turned right. *I'll pass seventeen doors before I reach the next stairway.* His lamp illuminated the dense cobwebs that choked every crevice and niche of the catacombs and sent spiders, rats, and other small creatures scurrying for the safety of whatever black hole they could find. The darkness beyond the short reach of his lamp was absolute. The air was stale and dry, as if filled with the dust of ancient bones.

A quick walk through a curving hallway led him to

another set of stairs, and he became increasingly nervous the farther he descended. What if he became trapped in here, lost amid the branching corridors and inky blackness? Would they even know where to look for him? They could use the clothing back in his room to perform seeking spells, but how long would it take them to find him? He wondered how he would get out if his lamp went dark. Would the rats and spiders swarm over him if the light were not there to drive them back?

Stop it! he told himself as he descended the third set of stairs. The treads here were cracked and uneven. He concentrated on the floor just ahead of him to make sure he stepped soundly.

It seemed an age passed before he finally reached the sixth level. He had paused several times to consult his directions; everything seemed fine. He drew a deep breath and started to his left, looking for the twenty-first room.

Unlike the dry upper levels, here there were shallow pools of fetid water on the uneven floors. The crumbling brick of the walls glistened with wetness and was covered in places with a damp greenish slime. The air smelled of mildew and rot.

Where the room should have been, he found a short passage that branched off at a right angle to the main corridor. The door at its end was forged of black steel and sunken deep into the wall.

Stamped in gold on its face was the Osirin symbol for death.

Gerin looked at the door more closely. The illumination from his lamp barely reached the length of the short passage, as if something in the air were devouring the light, and the door itself was encased in a deep gloom—the death symbol seemed to float murkily in the air like a silent warning to any who would attempt to enter.

He took one step into the passage and stopped. Something pressed against his chest like an invisible hand, trying to push him back into the main corridor. Panic flooded through him, a gut-wrenching fear that made him break out in a sudden sweat. Something was terribly wrong here. He could not breathe. He felt certain that if he took another step forward he would die, his lungs smashed to pulp, his heart crushed within his splintered ribs. *He had to get away!*

He stepped back and the panic left him as abruptly as it had struck. So did the pressure on his chest.

By the holy name of Telros, what just happened? He set the lamp on the floor, afraid that his trembling hands might drop it. He leaned over, bracing his hands on his knees, and tried to catch his breath. His lungs felt like they were being crushed in his chest. But along with the physical pain, there had been an overwhelming fear, a fear so powerful that he could not have taken another step toward the door had Shayphim's Hounds been nipping at his heels.

This place is guarded by magic. That was the only explanation. Such profound fear did not appear and disappear so suddenly. And he had no other way to explain the invisible yet very physical forces at work trying to keep him from the door.

These spells are a kind of lock, he thought as he regained his composure. Disappointment filled him, but so did a grim resolve. He would not be put off so easily. *Every lock has a key.*

Now he had a new goal: to locate the key that would allow him to enter the forbidden chamber. The powerful spells protecting it were probably created specifically for that room. But no matter how powerful, there had to be a way to open them. There had to be a book of spells somewhere that contained the proper incantations. He realized this meant he would not be able to gain entry until his powers were Awakened, but he also could not work the spells contained within until he was a wizard, so the delay meant nothing. He would search for the key spells now so that everything would be in place when the time was ready.

Several times since he'd begun his search he'd paused to reflect on what he was doing. He knew he was deliberately breaking the rules of Hethnost, and that if he were caught he would almost certainly be punished. As a nobleman who was responsible for upholding and enforcing the laws of the king, he knew that rules and laws served a purpose. Breaking them was the purview of criminals and brigands, thieves and outlaws.

Yet he considered himself none of these. He was seeking lost knowledge, nothing more. It was necessary that he break some rules along the way, but no one would be harmed. There would be no theft since he would return everything once he was done with it. No one would even know unless he succeeded. If he failed, he would return everything quietly and never say a word to anyone.

He had wondered if he should ask Hollin or Tomir about the feasibility of his plan, but his greatest fear was that he would be told no almost reflexively by any wizard he asked. He could clearly hear their rejections. *How could this boy who is not even a wizard possibly conceive of a plan to discover the Varsae Estrikavis? Ridiculous!* And no more would be said of it. They would not allow themselves to believe that he'd thought of something never before considered; it was inconceivable. It would be an *embarrassment*. Better to let the library lie forgotten forever than face the possibility that so many wizards over the centuries had overlooked something so obvious.

There was a part of him that also wanted the glory for finding the Varsae Estrikavis. It would be a feat worthy of Vendel and Ulgreth themselves. Let Reshel try to top *that*. He feared that if he told one of the wizards of his plan, they would continue on without him. After all, he could not perform spells yet. If they decided his idea did have merit, he did not think they would wait to test it until his powers had been Awakened. So he pressed on alone.

But he knew those were just excuses, nothing more than flimsy rationalizations. Whenever he felt that he should confess what he was doing—which had been happening more often, his guilt growing like a living thing within him, demanding that he speak out—something deep within his heart said, *No. This must remain secret.* As if a command had been given to him—though he had no idea when, or from whom—that he had no choice but to obey. He felt himself about to declare what he was doing, and the overpowering need to keep it secret froze his limbs and scrambled his thoughts, and after a few seconds he could no longer remember what he'd been about to do. He attempted to write down what he was doing so he could simply hand the paper to Reshel. His guilt was wearing on him, and he knew in some dark part of his mind that he needed to stop himself; but he could not force the tip of his quill to touch the page, and after a sudden dizzy spell could not recall what he'd been about to write. He sat at his small table, trying desperately to remember, gripped by a growing fear and the sense of impending, unstoppable doom.

One evening after dinner, Gerin went to the library to research key spells. He was searching through the large index room on the main floor when Nenyal Fey, another of the archivists, appeared in the doorway.

"Is there something I can help you with?" she asked. Her long straight hair was tucked loosely behind her ears, and a pair of reading spectacles rested comfortably on her nose. She smiled at him in a grandmotherly way and leaned against the door.

"I'm looking into key spells," he said. He decided there was no reason not to seek her help in this matter, especially since she had offered it. He wasn't having much luck on his own. "I guess it's pretty common knowledge by now that I have an interest in Naragenth's Varsae Estrikavis, and I was wondering how he might have secured it. We know he hid it well, so it's reasonable to believe the entrance is protected with closing spells and perhaps some kind of lethal magic. I was wondering how someone gets past these kinds of spells if they don't know exactly what's been set in place. I mean, if you don't know what spells are there, how can you find the proper key? Just keep trying until one works? If we found the Varsae Estrikavis today, would we even be able to get in?"

Nenyal sat down across from him. "All very interesting questions. Closing spells are fine if you're in a hurry or will be around to remove them when necessary, like sealing your bedroom for the night if you feel the need, or something like that. But they aren't as good when you're sealing something for a long time that will be left unattended. Closing spells are rather easy to break or circumvent. If you're nearby when your spell is broken, you'll know it, but if you're separated by a great distance, the perpetrator will most likely gain entry without your knowledge. In those cases you must use something much stronger. The vaults beneath the Varsae Sandrova are a good example of this."

At her words, Gerin grew still. He waited for her to continue, not trusting himself to speak.

His guilt rose hotly in him, and he wanted to tell her what he was planning, to simply confess everything to her and be done with it; but an eerie paralysis fell over him and sealed his mouth, and a moment later the need to confess had been erased from his mind.

"Some vaults have not been entered in centuries, but they're still well protected. Many of the vaults contain dangerous magic, books of forbidden spells or objects imbued with great power, so they are sealed with spells that are not readily undone. Even you, after your powers are Awakened, would have difficulty breaking through them. Brute force alone is not enough to smash them.

"The spells to open the vaults *are* written down and kept near the Warden of the Archives' offices," said Nenyal. "But in the more dangerous vaults there are layers upon layers of spells around them. It would take far too long to undo them all, and too easy to make a mistake if you tried. Many of the spells are linked, so if they're not undone in a specific order, they'll trigger counterspells that will trap or stun the wizard trying to break them. There are no lethal counterspells in the Varsae Sandrova, but you're probably right in your guess about Naragenth's library. There are almost certainly deadly traps guarding it, wherever it may be. It was a much different world."

"If you don't know the proper unlocking spells, or if the closing spells are too tightly linked, then how do you get into the vaults?"

She leaned closer and smiled, staring at him over the rims of her spectacles. "You use an amulet that has all the counterspells already embedded in it." She folded her arms on the tabletop. "Oh, it doesn't have to be an amulet, but most of them are. Some are rings, others are circlets or wrist bands or necklaces. They can take many forms.

"These amulets contain all the counterspells necessary to enter a particular vault. All the wizard has to do is create a flow of magic into the amulet to activate the spells. Then he just opens the door. It's quite ingenious.

"I'm sure Naragenth must have used something similar to protect the Varsae Estrikavis," she went on. "But even if the library is someday found, if the amulets necessary to gain entry aren't also located, it will be *very* difficult to get inside. An interesting question, Gerin."

"How many amulets are here in this library?" he asked.

"Oh, scores at least. They're all indexed to the room they will open. Would you like to see them?"

Gerin nodded. He could not believe his good fortune.

Nenyal led him through a maze of high-ceilinged corridors toward the offices of the archivists, which he had never visited before. He saw only three other wizards, all of whom were carefully copying manuscripts at angled desks in the scriptorium, working beneath the bright glow of magefire lamps hanging from the ceiling. They did not look up as he and Nenyal passed.

She stopped at a round-topped door at the end of the corridor and said, "*Akavá uldei baraitha!*" A faint golden glow washed across the door, almost too faint and too fast for him to see.

Nenyal spoke another command, which brought the magefire lamps within the room to life. The room was filled with jewel-encrusted reliquaries of various shapes and sizes. She opened one made of a dark polished wood, decorated with gold and sapphires. He could see that behind its doors were rows of velvet-lined drawers. Each drawer was labeled with the vault its amulet was keyed to open.

She slid open one of the drawers, removed an amulet, and handed it to him. It was made of gold and inlaid with silver, about the size of his palm, and connected to a thin gold chain. A runic form of Osirin was inscribed around the edge on both sides. The center contained an image of a winged horse; on the other side was a solitary tower and a crescent moon.

"I know you can't sense it yet, but this amulet contains a great deal of magic," she said. "Even without holding it, I can feel power radiating from it. It's quite strong. There are many spells in it."

Gerin glanced across the labels on the open reliquary but did not see the one he was looking for. It did not matter. He knew where to find the key. All he had to do now was wait.

He was resting in his room the next night when Abaru appeared at his door. His hands were folded across his enormous stomach, and he stared down at Gerin with a cold, somber expression.

"Come with me," said the wizard.

Gerin felt a surge of fear. "Where are we going?"

"You'll see soon enough."

As he followed the large man through the darkness, he felt certain he knew the reason for the summons. His activities in the Varsae Sandrova had been discovered and now he was to be punished. He wondered what had given him away, then remembered the footprints in the deep dust leading down to the lower levels of the library. Another wizard must have seen them and wondered who had been there. Or perhaps he had triggered some hidden alarm during his wanderings belowground. Either way, he would learn the answer soon enough.

What will they do to me? he thought. Would they still permit him to become a wizard? He could not imagine they would deny him his powers, but perhaps they would make him wait—most likely for many years—before he could undergo the ritual. His stomach did a queasy flip, and he had to fight not to groan aloud.

When he realized at last where they were going, his heart soared. Abaru was leading him to the Circle of Awakening. He was going to become a wizard tonight.

The circle was an area of marble tiles near the foot of the Partition Rock. Gray and black pillars a dozen feet tall were spaced around the edge of the circle, topped with thick rectangular lintels inscribed with runic Osirin characters. Magefire lamps hung from the lintels, casting long shadows across the ground.

All the wizards of Hethnost waited there, dressed in their ceremonial robes with the golden Hand of Venegreh embroidered over their hearts, watching him in silence as Abaru led him to the center of the circle. Reshel was already there, standing next to Hollin. He could see how excited she was, though she tried hard not to show it. The night air was warm and the moon was bright and low on the horizon, hanging just above the eastern sweep of the hills like a vast cyclopean eye.

"Tonight your life as a Gendalos ends," said the Archmage. The First Siege, High Ministers, and Wardens stood behind her, their hands hidden in the voluminous sleeves of their robes. "Tonight you will become one of us, a member of the proud race of Atalari who have walked the world for ages innumerable."

She turned toward Reshel. "As the younger, you will go first." Reshel nodded. Abaru placed a hand on Gerin's shoulder and gently steered him out of the center of the circle. He then returned to the circle and handed Hollin a jewel.

"This is an *awaenjir*," said Hollin, holding out the jewel. A white light glowed dimly in its heart. "The *awaenjir* is the most sacred of magical objects, the means by which we perpetuate our kind, made by Demos Thelar in ages long past. I will use it to open your body to magic, to Awaken the *paru'enthred* that sleeps within you.

"Do you stand here willingly, knowing that to undergo the Ritual of Awakening is to risk death?"

"I do." Reshel's voice was steady and clear.

All of the wizards in the circle spoke the Osirin words to begin the ritual with one voice that rang out through the night: *"Ayi telthíen ya ostólanar apasis rendelyen."*

Gerin watched, fascinated, as Hollin spoke a spell over the *awaenjir*. The faint white light grew brighter and turned golden; at the same instant, Reshel jerked as if a blade had been slipped between her ribs. She squeezed her eyes shut and grimaced. Her entire body trembled as if in the throes of a seizure.

Gerin startled in surprise and fear for his sister as golden fire burst from her body. It looked the same as the aura that Hollin had shown them in his tent on the way to Almaris; nearly silent, with no smoke or heat, and a different consistency than ordinary flame. This was magic in its raw, unshaped state, he realized, unmolded by either a spell or a wizard's will.

Reshel shook even more violently as her aura raged even higher. She was bent over at the waist, her lips peeled back from her teeth, every muscle and tendon rigid and tightly drawn, quite obviously in a great deal of pain or distress.

He took a step forward reflexively, but Abaru's hand restrained him. "Stay back, Gerin. She'll be fine."

"What if she's not?"

"Then there's nothing any of us can do for her."

He watched as Reshel fought to bring her aura under control. She made a sudden gesture with her hand, and her aura vanished. She relaxed and braced her hands on her knees, drained by the experience; then she raised her head and looked at Gerin with a joyous expression. She drew a deep breath and straightened.

Hollin bowed to her. "Your old life is gone forever, burned away with the Awakening of your magic. Now your new life begins. *Alai tanatha,* Reshel Atreyano. We are honored to have you counted among us."

The Archmage gestured to him. "You are next, Gerin. Step forward."

He entered the circle. Hollin faced him and held out the *awaenjir*. His face betrayed no hint of emotion. "Are you ready?" he asked.

Gerin nodded.

Hollin again asked, "Do you stand here willingly, knowing that to undergo the Ritual of Awakening is to risk death?"

"Yes. I'm ready."

As the wizard began the Awakening spell, Gerin stared at the *awaenjir* as the rest of the world receded into darkness around its dimly glowing heart. Time seemed to slow as he focused on his breathing, slow and deep, then the *awaenjir* exploded with an amber glow, and everything changed.

Gerin felt something swell at the deepest part of his being, a stirring of something tremendously powerful. A strange kind of pressure increased within him, which quickly grew nearly unbearable. He felt it would engulf him, drowning him from within with its furious, boiling power. He began to panic. He fought to remain calm as the force increased in intensity and coursed through his limbs, touching every part of his physical being. He struggled against the power, but it seemed it would overwhelm him. He knew he should not fight it but could not help himself.

I'm going to fail! This is going to kill me! I can't control it!

The pressure continued to build, like the waters of a river battering the dam holding them from their true course. He squeezed his eyes shut and screamed, clenching his fists and holding them to his temples, which pulsed painfully in concert with forces expanding through him. Distantly, he could hear Hollin continuing the words of the spell, as calmly as when he'd begun. Didn't Hollin realize what was happening to him?

Then the pressure broke and amber fire exploded from his body, engulfing him in a conflagration of magic. He felt it surging through his flesh, strengthening it and burning out impurities. He straightened as the pressure ebbed, then opened his eyes and looked at his hands. Amber wizard-fire poured from them as if they were torches, yet he felt no heat and heard no sound.

The fire reached even higher as his body adjusted to its presence and became a better channel for the power flowing through him. It swirled around him like an inverted funnel, the base of the spiral of fire widening as it whirled with increasing speed.

He sensed something that took his breath away: *the fire was alive*. Not in the manner of men, not something he could speak with, but at some level he was just beginning to understand, the flame—or rather, magic itself, of which the wizard-fire was just one of its manifestations—was *aware* of him.

He realized that his senses were greatly enhanced—he could hear the faintest sounds (even above the delicate whoosh of his magical flame), see farther and clearer than he would have dreamed possible. When he touched his robe he felt textures in the fabric he had never even guessed were there. It was as if the world had been created anew for him, transformed into a place bright and clear and alive.

He tried to bring his aura under control. He could sense the *paru'enthred* at the center of his being, a bright lens focusing the living power flowing through him. He knew instinctively how to stop the magic, though he could not have explained it to anyone, any more than he could have explained how he made his arm move. He simply willed it, and the fire vanished.

Awakening his magic had done more than just allow him to finally use spells. He looked down at his hands. His skin had been bleached nearly bone white. A jittery strength filled his muscles—he felt as if could move with the fluid grace of a deer, or leap to the top of the lintels surrounding the circle. He realized that his sight had become as keen as a cat's, and was amazed at how much more he could see in the darkness beyond the circle, as if the night had filled with a mystical light visible only to him, illuminating a world that had been hidden to him just a short time ago.

Reshel's eyes were now a glittering shade of emerald, *Wizard's eyes,* as they had once been called across Osseria. His must be the same.

Hollin bowed to him. "Your old life is gone forever, burned away with the Awakening of your magic. Now your new life begins. *Alai tanatha,* Gerin Atreyano. We are honored to have you counted among us."

Reshel ran to him and threw her arms around his neck. "It's even more wonderful than I imagined!" He could sense the beating of her heart as she pressed close to him. He worried if this heightened awareness of *everything* would drive him mad. Would he even be able to sleep, or would the touch of his sheets and the slightest sound during the night keep him hopelessly distracted?

He did not have any more time to consider this. The wizards pressed around them, offering their congratulations. "Yours was the brightest aura I've ever seen!" said Oren Nesri. "I'm surprised you didn't burn a hole down through the stone!"

The wizards retired to the dining hall, where a feast awaited them. Each taste of food, every swallow of wine, was like something entirely new to them. They had been reborn into the world, and nothing would ever be the same.

12

It was nearly dawn when Gerin finally made it back to his rooms. A short while after falling asleep, he slipped into a dream he'd had before. Once again he stood in the place of bones, a cold, dead land beneath a starless sky.

As before, a faint red light brightened the air some distance in front of him, soon resolving itself into the shape of a door floating in the air. The stench of rotting meat filled his nostrils and made his gorge rise.

"You, Summoner, must open the Door of Night for me."

Gerin staggered and clapped his hands to his ears to protect them from the thundering voice; he imagined that if it had shouted, the power would have shattered his eardrums. "It is you who will release me from my bondage. Hear me! I must be freed to carry out my vengeance. You will open the Door so that I may at last return. The hour of doom approaches. Do not fail me."

The apparition with the silvery eyes appeared above him, a mountain of shadow against the dark sky. It reached down for him once again with a hand the size of a hill, the featureless fingers open and grasping. The hand radiated heat like a forge. It would surely burn him to death in moments—even before it crushed him to a bloody pulp—if he could not get away from it. But it was descending too fast, and he had time only to throw up his hands before the hand fell over him like a cage—

He woke in his bed. The sun was fully risen; bright light seeped between the shutters across his single narrow window.

He realized that he'd had that dream before and forgotten it until now. He'd meant to ask Hollin about it but it slipped his mind. He cursed his forgetfulness, but there was nothing to be done about it now. The dream felt undeniably true, more a vision or premonition than a normal dream of sleep.

He made an effort to remember details of the dream before they slipped away. Had the being who'd spoken told him its name? No, not this time, but he felt fairly certain it had revealed it in the first dream. He tried to remember it, but the earlier dream was too far gone and nothing came to him.

The sight of the apparition reaching for him would not leave his mind. He rose and dressed. It was time to talk with Hollin.

"I sensed it again," said the Archmage to Hollin. "A disturbance of some kind. Like the world around us . . . weakened for an instant, became somehow less real."

They lay in her bed, their bodies entwined beneath several layers of blankets. The headboard of dark wood rose a full yard above the plush pillows and was carved in an intricate geometric pattern of squares; curtains of white silk hung from the ceiling and enclosed the bed in a gauzy, dreamy barrier.

"I didn't feel anything, but then, you're more sensitive to such things than I've ever been," said Hollin. "Besides, the power of the Ammon Ekril enhances your natural talents. It's no wonder you feel things others cannot."

"In case you haven't noticed, I'm not wearing it," she said. She'd been brushing her fingers across his chest when she sensed the disturbance. She pulled her hand away and rolled onto her back.

"That doesn't matter. After having it on nearly every waking moment for decades, its power has become a part of you, even when you're not in direct contact with it."

"That's nonsense. The Ammon Ekril has been examined

by wizards for thousands of years. I've examined it myself.
There is no hidden power within it. It's a piece of the Atalari
nation of old—perhaps the last surviving remnant—and a
symbol of my office, but nothing more. It is *not* a device of
magic."

He grinned in that knowing way that always set her teeth
on edge. It annoyed her no end when he got like this: preten-
tious and self-righteous, certain of himself to the point of
being condescending.

"But our eyes and our magic cannot see everything," he
said. "I tell you there is a mighty power slumbering within
that diamond that seeps into the one who wears it whether he
wills it or not."

"And again I say nonsense."

"I'm only trying to—"

She held up her hand. "Hollin, please. Not another word. I
don't care about what may or may not be within the Ammon
Ekril. At the moment I'm concerned about these disturbances.
Something dark is happening. I've felt this several times now.
At first I thought it was nothing; it was so faint I wasn't even
sure I'd sensed anything. But not now. It's still weak, but it's
growing stronger. We need to uncover what's happening."

"I wonder if it has anything to do with our amber wizard,"
he said as he rose from the bed. "He's like a lodestone at-
tracting all manner of strange and unwanted attention."

"Perhaps. I am still deeply troubled by this Neddari spell
within him, and the divine visitations he's had, if that's indeed what they were. I do not know what to make of them."

"The Warden of Healing examined him thoroughly. The
Neddari spell is still there. It was slumbering when Kirin
saw it, yet he felt that it had recently been active. But he
could not determine its purpose."

"Yes, he told me."

"I read Bainora's Foretellings again but found nothing to
shed any light on these events."

Half an hour later they stood in the offices of Rahmdil
Khazuzili, the Warden of the Archives. He was old even by

the standards of wizards, with a face that was all wrinkles and loose flesh, as if his skin were too large for his skull and had been folded and pinched into the best possible fit. His eyebrows and eyelashes had vanished decades earlier, giving the skin of his face a smooth, waxy look; the thin hair remaining on his head was surprisingly dark for a man so old, and fell in wispy strands to his shoulders. He tapped his fingers together contemplatively as Marandra told him what she'd sensed.

"Intriguing," said Rahmdil. "I felt no disturbances, but that in itself means nothing. We must investigate this further. Come with me." He rose from his chair, a stoop-shouldered figure shaped like a finger bent in mid-curl, and shuffled from the room. Marandra and Hollin followed.

"Do you know what it was?" she asked as they made their way along a wide corridor.

"I do not *know* anything," he said. "But I *suspect* something."

They made their way to the Warden's private library, a domed circular room sealed with powerful closing spells. Marandra had only been here a handful of times in all her long years at Hethnost. The chamber's tall walls were completely covered in shelves crammed full of books, boxes, scrolls, articulated skeletons of small animals, several stuffed birds in various stages of moldering decrepitude, loose parchments, sealed chests, several large oil paintings propped up on the floor since there was no wall space on which to hang them, and pale busts of wizards. There was a rectangular table in the room's center with more books and papers piled upon it, and three magefire lamps placed along its length. A wheeled ladder anchored into a horizontal track that circled the room permitted access to the upper shelves. The room was dry, the air dusty and stale.

Rahmdil clasped his hands together and looked about the chamber, his lips moving silently, as if mouthing the titles to the various volumes his gaze fell upon.

"Ah, there it is." He pointed to one of the higher shelves.

"Hollin, please get that brown leather book with the gold stamp on its spine."

Hollin wheeled the ladder around the room and climbed to the shelf the Warden had indicated. "This book?"

"That's the one. Bring it down here, please."

Whorls of dust puffed from the old, cracked leather when Hollin placed the book on the table, tiny glowing particles swirling like minute insects, illuminated by the soft glow of the lamps.

"What are you showing us?" asked Hollin. "What is this book?"

"Something I read years ago, which the Archmage's story brought to mind." He was bent low over the table, his back nearly forming a hook, as he flipped slowly through the pages. They were old and brittle, and made sharp crinkling noises as he turned them. Marandra could sense the preservation spells that prevented the ink from fading completely and the pages from dissolving to dust. It was written in a language she recognized as Vethki, the speech of the nomadic Vethkarins of the Plains of Drommond.

Rahmdil looked up at her and grinned, an expression that fell somewhere between endearing and ghastly on his drooping, weathered face. "Amazing, isn't it, what the mind will remember with the proper provocation? I would have no memory at all of reading this if someone had simply asked me about it, yet your brief tale of sensing these disturbances is enough for me to dredge up that memory almost instantly." He glanced up at the shelves. "If only we could search through this great library's collection as easily."

"Yes, that's quite fascinating, Rahmdil," Marandra said, "but what *was* it exactly that you read?"

"Yes, please explain," said Hollin. "I can't read a word of this."

Rahmdil turned back to the book and continued to slowly turn pages. "I will let you know when I find it. Don't want to spoil the surprise."

A minute that seemed an eternity later to Marandra,

Rahmdil jabbed his finger at a page of densely written symbols and incantations, much of which was written in an old form of Osirin. *A wizard wrote this part of the book,* she thought.

"Here it is." Rahmdil picked up the book and straightened a little. "Yes, I think this is what we should do."

"Rahmdil, will you *please* tell me what this is all about?"

"Patience, Archmage. We need to get to the truth of the matter. This book hints at what may be causing what you sensed, but to verify it we must do something dangerous. I do not like to speculate; therefore, until I *am* certain, I will remain silent on what I think *may* be happening. Only when we've conclusively proved or disproved my idea will I speak of it." He carried the book to the end of the table and set it down again, then looked about the chamber until his gaze alighted upon a small chest inlaid with mother-of-pearl.

"What is this dangerous thing you spoke of?" she asked as he pulled the small chest from its shelf. Its lid was gray with dust, which he wiped away with the sleeve of his robe. He brought it back to the table and opened it. Resting on its crushed velvet lining were three glass vials of fine powder, separated from one another by narrow ridgelike dividers also lined with velvet. The vials were stoppered with corks and wax. The powder in each vial was a different color: pale yellow, deep red, and black.

"This is *andraleirazi,*" said Rahmdil. "Ground from the bones of kelíaphars and mixed with habbas root and crushed saeril stone. The colors vary depending on the proportions of the mixture."

Hollin scowled. "Dangerous indeed. What do you plan to do with this?"

"To learn the truth of what the Archmage sensed, we must call a sheffain."

Marandra was shocked by his words. Beside her, Hollin tensed and his scowl deepened. "Rahmdil, you go too far," she said. "What can such a creature possibly tell us?"

"Archmage, if what I suspect is true, then a sheffain is the only way to know with certainty."

"There is no other way?"

"None that I know of. If you refuse to do this, I will abide by your decision, but we will be left only with conjecture as to what you felt."

It took her merely a moment to decide. "Have you ever called one before?"

"Twice, Archmage. But I was a much younger man. I would appreciate some help with this calling."

"I will assist you. Proceed."

As the Warden removed the vials from their chest, Marandra recalled what she knew of sheffains. She had never seen one herself; they were not of this world, though it was thought by some that they had once lived in Osseria—or perhaps some other world—in the physical form they assumed when summoned. Others felt this was wrong, that they'd never had a physical existence of any kind. The only thing known for certain about them was that they were—at least now—beings of spirit; there was no way to know if they'd once had bodies of flesh and blood. The sheffains themselves revealed nothing of their past when called, no matter how hard they were pressed. It was said they could not lie, but she wondered how that could be known for sure. Still, there was nothing to be done about it. If this was the only way to uncover what was happening, then this was what they would do.

Rahmdil moved to an open area of the floor, broke the seal on the red vial, and made a circle on the marble tiles about two yards across. He enclosed that circle with a larger one made from the yellow powder, then encircled that ring with the black.

"The Binding Rings of Barados," he said, gesturing to the floor. "Concentric circles of *andraleirazi* that will imprison the sheffain until we are finished. Archmage, you will help me with the calling; it takes a great deal of strength to pull a sheffain into our realm of existence and hold it here, and I do not think I can do such a thing alone anymore. Hollin, stand ready to help us should the need arise, and be ready to fight should disaster strike and it escapes its bonds."

"Are there spells that work better against it than others?" he asked.

"I don't know. No wizard has ever survived when one has escaped."

"You do not instill me with great confidence, Warden."

"If I thought we would fail, I would not be subjecting either of you—or myself—to this. There is danger, yes, but the three of us should be more than sufficient to deal with it."

"I confess I know little about sheffains," said Hollin. "They're demons of some sort, are they not?"

"No. They are not evil creatures. Neither are they benevolent, but that is not the same as evil. They care nothing for us, good or ill, but being called against their will to this world causes them both pain and fear. They naturally lash out at those who imprison them, the same as we would lash out were we to be similarly whisked from this world and interrogated by beings of a wholly different nature from our own."

"Where are they being whisked *from*?"

"They are said to roam the hidden paths believed to connect different worlds in different planes of existence, but nothing is known for sure." He stepped toward the circle and held the book open with one hand. "Archmage, summon magic into yourself and read the spell with me. The first part will create the barriers that will contain the sheffain. The second part will call the creature to us."

"I understand." She was growing anxious and said a silent meditative prayer to calm herself. "You may begin."

"Hollin?"

"I'm prepared as I can be."

"Very well." He pointed to a line of Osirin near the top of the page, next to a symbol resembling a teardrop with a star flaring from its pointed end. "The spell begins here." He began to read. *"Anu ataré'banath iyé othnirstareos kindal yehos . . ."*

Marandra read along, careful to match her inflections to those of the Warden. She felt the spell taking shape, interacting with the innermost circle of *andraleirazi*. The red powder

transformed itself into a solid ring, as if the individual particles had been fused into an unbroken line. The next moment
she felt a sudden release of magic and saw a shimmering
barrier rise up from the ring like a dimly illuminated wave
of heat, a translucent curtain whose upper edge bled away
into the air about ten feet above the floor.

The Warden continued the spell. A similar barrier rose
from the yellow ring of powder, and finally the black. The
relucent, cylindrical barriers rotated slowly on the rings,
with the middle barrier moving in the opposite direction of
the other two.

"Now, Archmage, the final part of the spell, with me: *Esta
menathros tilu zalkari nennpir olo'pharin* . . . "

The spell intensified, drawing a tremendous amount of
magic from her. She found herself impressed with the Warden for having accomplished this feat alone, even as a
younger, stronger man. She was already beginning to tire.

A spark of light appeared in the air in the center of the inner ring. It quickly grew into a vertical slash so bright she
was forced to squint; then, without warning, the slash split
open, like a weakened piece of cloth suddenly torn wide. But
this was no cloth. It was the fabric of reality itself, the very
foundation of the world, opening to some *other* place she
could not name.

And something came through from the other side.

The sheffain slipped through the tear in the world, a blackness darker than black. It floated in the air, its long legs
curled upward, as if it were sitting on an invisible seat. It was
man-shaped, though it would never be mistaken for a man. It
was difficult for Marandra to see it clearly—part of the difficulty was the presence of the barriers and their shimmering,
translucent luminescence, but even if the barriers had not
been present, or had been wholly invisible, she felt she would
not be able to see the sheffain with any kind of precision.
Though it was present in the room in some kind of physical
manifestation, that presence was not fully realized. It was
like a reflection of a reflection half glimpsed in a mirror. Her

eyes could not locate any hard edges to the creature or see any fine details of its form. Its body seemed to be composed of blue-gray particles of some kind—similar to the *andraleirazi* powder, she realized—that had been forced to hold its shape, though only roughly. The sheffain's presence shifted and blurred constantly as the particles moved about within the confines of its bodily form.

What she could see of it was strange and unsettling. Its head was shaped like a flattened triangular wedge, with oval black eyes set on either side. The eyes were the only thing about it that seemed to have any solidity or true substance. There was no nose that she could see, nor any mouth, though it was possible that it was hidden beneath the pointed tip at the front of its head. Its limbs were impossibly thin, like gossamer strands spun from its narrow torso. Its fingers, too, were long and thin, like segmented needles or the legs of some strange, hairless spider. They flexed continuously, as if in agitation, or perhaps contemplation; Marandra could not tell which.

Its hands lashed forward, the needlelike fingers trying to pierce the inner barrier that contained it. The barrier rippled where its fingers penetrated, like slow-moving rings when a stone is dropped into still water, and there was a discharge of blue energy that washed across the barrier's surface for an instant; but the barrier held. It drew its hands back and lashed out again, harder. Marandra felt her magic shudder as the sheffain's power fought to overwhelm her and the Warden, and in that moment she sensed the pain and confusion that enveloped it. She realized that if it broke free it would rend them limb from limb; but the barrier did not falter.

She saw its mouth open, and the chamber filled with a deep, hate-filled hissing noise that made her want to cover her ears until she realized the sound came from within her mind and she was powerless to keep it out. It could shriek until it drove her mad and there was nothing she could do to stop it.

"Kalen'dremmos!" shouted Rahmdil with a power and authority in his voice that she had not heard before. He

stared unblinking at the sheffain, his free hand stretched toward it with his fingers open and rigid. "I have called you here to this world, and only I can release you. Answer my questions and you will be freed."

"Does it understand Kelarin?" asked Hollin.

"No. It is a being of spirit, unfettered by the laws and limitations that bind the flesh. It will know what we are asking by looking into our hearts and minds, and it will answer the same way. It will respond, and we will know what it has said. Our minds will translate its answers into words we can understand, but it is not speech as you and I think of it. I speak aloud for my own benefit, to help focus my thoughts. Now, no more questions until we are done."

A deep thrumming sound boomed in the chamber, like the beating of a vast drum. Marandra heard a second noise above the thrumming, a kind of scratching sound, high-pitched and faint, like metal scraping across glass. A few seconds after the screeching noise began, she heard a voice in her mind, full of sibilants like the hissing of a snake. *Assssk ussss and rele-asssse ussss, mortal.*

"You have knowledge of the many worlds that coexist with our own," said Rahmdil. "We have sensed a disturbance in our world, described to me as a brief weakening of our reality. It has happened several times recently and is growing stronger. What can you tell us of this?"

In reply the sheffain lashed out against its prison. An ear-piercing screech filled the chamber as its fingers punctured the inner barrier. It did not draw back despite the obvious pain the contact with the barrier caused it. It screeched again, throwing its head back as it ripped its fingers sideways along the barrier, against the direction of its slow rotation.

The red barrier shredded like torn paper and vanished.

Marandra staggered and let out a cry of dismay and pain as the power she'd been pouring into the spell was disrupted by the backflow from the barrier's sudden collapse. The Warden remained steadfast, peering hard at the sheffain as if locked into a battle of wills with it.

With the inner barrier gone, the sheffain's body grew in size to fill the now larger space containing it. Marandra took an involuntary step backward as the creature swelled, its wavering form reaching gargantuan proportions. She realized that if it straightened fully, it would be more than fifteen feet tall.

With another screeching cry, it flung its hands into the yellow barrier. But this time, just as the sheffain's fingers touched the shield, Rahmdil released a flood of magic into the barrier. He'd done something to the magic, Marandra realized, tainted it somehow in a way she'd never before seen.

The Warden's power illuminated the barrier with a flash of brilliant light that instantly focused itself upon the sheffain's fingers, then raced up its arms. The creature writhed in agony as yellow arcs of light danced across its body, leaving curling puffs of greasy smoke in their wake. Its nebulous shape became even more blurry and indistinct, as if it were in danger of dissipating completely. It yanked its fingers from the barrier; the Warden halted his strange magic, and the sheffain's body regained its previous consistency.

Without taking his eyes from the creature, Rahmdil said, "The magic I used was warped in such a way to cause it a great deal of pain. I don't think it will try to break free again."

"Thank Venegreh for that," said Hollin.

"You are in my power," said Rahmdil. "Answer me, and you will be set free. Defy me, and you will feel my anger. What I gave you was just a small taste of what I can do. Now, tell me what you know of this disturbance we felt."

The sheffain spread its arms and threw its head forward, letting out a deep roar completely unlike the previous sounds it had made.

Then it fell silent and lowered its arms, folding them across its chest so its spidery hands lay on its shoulders. A strange pulsing sound filled the chamber, and the magefire lamps dimmed and brightened in rhythm to the sound. Marandra felt something move through her thoughts, like a sudden psychic wind that left her momentarily confused.

I can ssssee into your sssslow and decaying mind of meat.

You already know the causssse, mortal. Why have you called me to asssssk ssssomething to which you already know the ansssssswer?

"Because I am not certain, and we require certainty in this matter. You swear you are speaking the truth? That what I believe is happening is correct?"

We do not deccccceive. Liesssss are a weaknesssss of the flessssh. When we sssssspeak, it issssss only the truth. Now releasssse me.

"Is that all?" said Hollin. "Is there nothing else to ask it?"

"No," said Rahmdil. "We are finished here." He snapped the book closed. "*Buruhk ashka'narjéa!* Return to your home."

The vertical black slit widened and flared with white light that engulfed the sheffain. The particles that comprised its material body broke apart like a pile of sand struck by the wind of a hurricane, exploding into a diffuse cloud that was drawn back through the slit as if inhaled by some great breath. The slit then collapsed upon itself, leaving only the spinning barriers and a sudden silence.

"Archmage, you may cease your magic," said Rahmdil. She did as she was asked. He made a gesture with his free hand and the two remaining barriers expanded outward and evaporated. She felt a faint wave of heat against her face as they dissipated into the air. She glanced at the rings upon the floor and saw that they had reverted to powder.

"I will gather the *andraleirazi* later," he said. He placed the book on the table and sank wearily into one of the chairs.

"You'll not get down on your knees to scoop that powder back into the vials," said the Archmage. "I'll send servants to take care of it. You may supervise if you wish." She straightened and folded her arms. "But now you will tell me what I sensed, or gathering up your *andraleirazi* will be the *least* of your worries."

"Of course, of course." He wiped his sweating brow with a trembling hand. "What I suspected, and what the sheffain has confirmed, is that our world, and the world of the dead, are growing closer."

There was a stunned silence in the room as Marandra and Hollin digested what the Warden had just said. "What do you mean, they're growing closer? How? *Why?* And how did you come to suspect this?"

"A moment, please, Archmage," he said. "The calling was more draining than I'd thought it would be." He closed his eyes and folded his hands beneath his chin. It almost seemed he had fallen asleep. Marandra was about to shake his shoulder when his eyes opened and he straightened in his chair.

"This book," he said, tapping his fingers upon the leather-bound volume, "contains the writings of a group of wizards who lived long ago in the Plains of Drommond, in a small city south of the Igrin Hills, long before the founding of Hethnost. It was they who first thought that our world must be one of many, that not only was there a realm of spirits and a realm of the earthly dead, but also true worlds like our own but separated from us. It was they who first encountered sheffains and devised a means of calling them.

"Another of their discoveries was that the worlds of the living and the dead grow closer from time to time, a kind of ebb and flow like the tides of the moon. The wall that separates the world thins for some reason they never determined; neither did they discover the cycle it followed, if it indeed followed any at all.

"What you told me about the disturbance you sensed reminded me of a passage in here that I'd reread several years ago. Your description sounded very similar to what was written about the coming together of the worlds."

"So now we know *what* I am sensing. But if we do not know *why,* or *how* they are growing closer, then what are we to do about it?"

"I'm afraid there is little we can do," said Rahmdil. "It is a phenomenon of nature, like the tides or a summer storm; they are to be endured, but not changed or defied."

"Is there a danger to us?" asked Hollin. "What if they grow *too* close?"

"Who can say? Such a thing has never happened. As to

whether there is a danger, there may be some strange occurrences as the wall between them weakens. Sensitives such as the Archmage may feel the disturbances more keenly, and some may have troubled dreams. There may be unexplained deaths, and sudden madness, though such things were rare the last time this happened, and it was never proved whether they were related to the closeness of the worlds. I think we can do little but watch and wait and hope that, like a summer storm, this passes without leaving much damage in its wake."

13

To his great relief, Gerin discovered that his senses were adapting to their heightened awareness, though he had several nearly sleepless nights while it was happening. There was an owl nesting in one of the trees near the Apprentices Hall, and its hooting was so loud and annoying he considered doing something to it with his magic, like shaking the tree to get it to fly away. He fought the urge, though, deciding it would be better for him to get used to the distractions and learn to ignore them.

"It happens to all wizards," Hollin told them both. "Don't fret about it. Your bodies will adjust."

After the initial furor over their Awakenings had died down and Gerin could move about again in relative anonymity, he decided it was time to obtain the key amulet.

Well after midnight, he crept into the Varsae Sandrova and made his way to the archivists' offices and the room containing the reliquaries. He carried a magefire lamp but had not yet lit it; his sensitive eyes could see well enough in the gloom of the corridors, and he did not want one of the Sunrise Guards or a restless archivist to come investigating an errant light.

There was no one about. He stopped before the door and drew magic into himself. The sensation still thrilled and excited him. It felt as if his very blood transformed into something fiery and potent, overflowing with power and life.

"Akavá uldei baraitha." Strange that they would have such a basic protection on the very room that contained the keys to the most heavily guarded vaults in all of Hethnost.

He paused. It was a basic protection because the wizards never expected one of their own to break into this place. The closing spell was little more than a formality. The protected vaults underground were locked tight because they contained spells and objects of power that could be dangerous to a wizard not strong enough to control them, or so it had been explained to him, and there were devices whose magic could be released even by an unsuspecting Gendalos. But for the most part the wizards implicitly trusted their own kind.

And he was about to violate that trust.

He wondered again if there were some other course he could take, but felt that if he told someone else, even now that his powers had been Awakened, he risked having the magic he needed kept forever from his grasp. And that was a risk he was not willing to take. He felt powerless to stop himself, but a part of him did not want to stop. He *needed* to find the Varsae Estrikavis . . . it was like a fire burning deep within him, a compulsion he could not resist. There was a command within him to find it—and to find it in total secrecy—that he had no choice but to obey. In some dim and remote fashion he was aware that the command had been placed in him from elsewhere, but whenever he tried to ponder this, his mind turned suddenly to something else and forgot the question at hand almost at once.

So he pressed on, his guilt and doubt all but gone. Once inside the windowless room, he lit his lamp and began to methodically search the reliquaries, looking for the key he needed.

As soon as he realized that each reliquary contained the keys for a different floor of the library, he found what he was looking for within minutes.

The key was actually a small sphere formed of thin concentric rings, with each ring positioned at a different angle from the one above and below it and connected to one another by small posts. At the core of the rings was a ball of blue glass. The rings appeared to be made from gold, though they were threaded with strands of a black metal he did not recognize and fine etchings on the bands that he could not read. It was attached to a long chain, but Gerin slipped it into his pocket rather than around his neck. He then extinguished his lamp and left the room, careful to return everything to its proper place.

"Eiya ostran yel gaiadaro," he said, resealing the door with the proper spell.

This time his descent through the subterranean levels of the library was far different. He could sense magic in the air all around him; his skin tingled with the charge. Each door he passed was sealed with closings and other spells strong enough to keep out all but the most powerful wizards, and many of the magical objects contained within each vault leaked power of their own. After centuries of accumulation, the entire subterranean complex was saturated with magic. It was dangerous to be down here, he realized. He could scarcely imagine that he'd been unable to sense the energies in this place the first time he was here.

When he reached the room, he placed the golden sphere around his neck and released his magic into it. The sphere seemed to expand physically, though he knew he was only feeling the spells within it filling with power, absorbing his magic, preparing to unlock the protections around the vault.

He stepped into the short corridor that led to the door.

The outermost ring of the sphere glowed with a sudden blue-white light as the key spell it contained activated itself and nullified the first protection. Recalling his first attempt, he tensed as he waited for the invisible pressure to begin pushing him back.

Nothing happened. He took another step forward.

The next ring of the sphere flashed with a crimson light as it unlocked the second spell. The rings glowed eleven times before he reached the door, some of them more than once. *Whatever's in here is certainly well-protected.*

He did not allow his doubts to resurface. He reached for the black iron handle and opened the door.

It creaked opened with some difficulty. Loose mortar and dust fell on his head as he stepped into the chamber, like the sediments of a long-sealed tomb.

There were no spiderwebs or signs of rodents. The room was dust-covered and the closed air was stale, but other than that it was probably unchanged since the day it had been sealed, however long ago that was.

The vault was small, perhaps five paces deep, and rectangular in shape. The ceiling was a low arch of brick scarcely taller than his head; the floor was rough natural stone. Two long tables were pressed against the walls on either side, with many small niches recessed into the walls above them. Placed upon one table were boxes and reliquaries; the other held mostly books and scrolls. Most of the boxes and reliquaries were marked with gold lettering on their lids or forward sides. There were also strange objects sitting upon the tables whose purposes Gerin did not know. One looked something like a candelabra made of silver, with the tips of each branch flaring outward to form slender claws that gripped spheres of red glass or crystal. Another was a silver cube with intricate designs etched into each of its sides. The designs were not Osirin or any other language he recognized.

He began to search the room, and finally found what he was looking for in one of the wall niches along the back, exactly as the index described it.

From the niche, he removed a large box of black polished wood and a leather-bound book of spells. Within the box lay a golden horn looped once around itself in a circle; the horn's bell bloomed outward like a flower petal. *The Horn of Tireon,* he thought, running a finger lightly along the plain surface of the instrument. Another compartment in the box contained a leather pouch with five blue jewels that the description in the index had labeled weirstones.

This was the means of locating the lost library of Naragenth. He felt giddy as he closed the box and carried it from the chamber. He was so close now that failure was inconceivable.

He did not realize until after he'd left the vault that he had no means of restoring the spells of protection upon it. *Damned bloody fool!* How could he have overlooked something so basic? He supposed he thought the key-amulet would restore the spells once it had passed back through the passageway, but he had not truly considered it. His only hope was that an archivist did not check this room for a very long time. *At least until I find the library,* he thought. *Then it won't matter anymore.*

The following evening Gerin roused himself near midnight, pulled on a light cloak to help hide the box and book he carried, and slipped from his rooms.

He crossed the courtyard at the center of Hethnost, keeping to one of the paths that meandered among the trees. He created an Unseeing as soon as he reached the end of the courtyard, to prevent soldiers of the Sunrise Guard from noticing his movements. If he ran into one of them face-to-face, they would see through the spell—but from a distance the magic made someone looking in his direction fail to notice him, as if he had slipped beneath their threshold of vision. The spell did not work well on wizards, who could pierce it with little difficulty, but at this time of night he was mostly concerned with the Gendalos watchmen.

He came to a postern door in Hethnost's eastern wall, then made his way to a glade on the far side of Maratheon's Hill, the highest peak on the eastern side of the valley. The glade was nestled in a fold of land halfway down the hill's far side, at the juncture of two other hills. *No one will hear or see anything from here,* he thought as he set the box down on the grass.

He'd spent all day reading the spells he would need. The book was filled with incantations of death and black magic. He understood why the wizards had locked it away; much of it was horrific. He'd not read all of it, but many spells called for the sacrifice of a person—so-called blood magic.

Fortunately for him, his spell had no need of death to make it work: it required only the horn and weirstones.

He drew magic into himself and lit the magefire lamp he'd tucked into his pocket so he would have sufficient light by which to read. Then he opened the book and began the incantation.

The Osirin words shaped the magic flowing through him. He could feel the spell moving around and through him, building and shaping its power. A thick mist formed, flowing away from him into the woods. The mist formed eerie shapes that writhed like tortured spirits, and silence fell unnaturally through the woods.

The spell was long and complex. He spoke with exceeding care, glad his Osirin was good enough to allow him to read it without difficulty, though he could feel himself tiring and fought to maintain his concentration as more and more power was drawn from him.

A dim red light with no discernable source lit the glade, as if the mist had transformed into a vapor of blood. Even the small spark of magefire within the lamp had become a tiny crimson star in the heart of the glass.

The spell seemed to take on a life of its own. The words poured from his mouth, and he was not sure he could have stopped even if he had wanted to. He wondered if some sort of compulsion had been imbued into the spell, forcing the speaker to bring the dark magic to completion.

He reached the end of the first part of the spell and fell silent. Magic still flowed through him. He closed the book, then took the four weirstones and placed them on the ground in a square roughly four feet on a side. The stones pulsed with an otherworldly blue-white glow.

The metal of the horn felt warm when he removed it from its case. He looked at it for a long moment. It shimmered as if there were something moving beneath its surface, just beyond the edges of his perception. *I must finish this*.

Holding the horn at the base of its loop, he raised it to his lips and blew a single piercing note.

* * *

Every wizard in Hethnost woke—the magic-tainted sound was like the horrific scream of some dying animal carried to them from the dark woods beyond Maratheon's Hill. Some wizards tasted the coppery sweetness of blood in the back of their throats; others smelled rotting meat or felt an overwhelming sense of death nearby. Soldiers walking the battlements raised their weapons and sent messengers to wake their commanders, their hearts pounding with sudden fear. Dogs howled in the darkness; horses stirred and snorted restlessly in their stables.

Someone was pounding on the Archmage's door as she belted her robe. She shouted, "Coming!" as she pulled on her slippers. On the far side of the bed, Hollin put on a shirt.

She rushed downstairs and opened the door to the manor. Abaru stood outside, his face haggard and weary. "You heard it?" he asked.

"Yes." She stepped out of the way so he could enter. "Very powerful magic."

"Very *black* magic," said Hollin, appearing behind her. "I've never felt anything that chilled my blood so."

"We need to check on our two newest wizards at once," said Marandra. The thought of that scream—and the taint of magic it contained, of violent death and corruption—was like a cold hand on the back of her neck. "One of them is almost certainly behind this."

"And certainly in mortal danger," said Hollin.

Reshel hurried to her brother's rooms. "Gerin, wake up!" she said as she knocked on his door. She turned the knob, but it was locked. "Gerin, please!" *How could he have slept through that?* She'd woken certain there was a spirit of death ready to snuff out her life, lurking in the dark corners of her room. She'd invoked blindingly bright sparks of magefire to push back the darkness and convince herself that nothing was there.

Now, she invoked a charm that would unlock the door, only to find it was sealed with magic. *Why would he use a Closing on his door at night, here in the center of Hethnost?*

"Stand aside, Reshel." She turned and saw the Archmage and Hollin approach. Their severe expressions frightened her almost as much as the strange animal howl that had awakened her.

"What's happened?" she asked. "What's going on? Has something happened to Gerin?"

"We do not yet know what's happened," said the Archmage. "And as to your brother, the question is what has *he* done?"

She stepped around Reshel and placed her hand against the door. She spoke quietly in Osirin, moving her hand across the wood. Reshel heard the lock click.

Gerin was not inside. "We have to find him," said Hollin.

"Reshel, do you have any idea what he might have done?" asked the Archmage. "Now is not the time for family loyalty. You cannot keep his secrets. Do you know what he's doing?"

She shook her head. "I don't know, I swear. He hasn't told me anything."

The Archmage stared at her hard, as if trying to see the truth of her words. Apparently she believed her.

Hollin stepped closer to the Archmage. "The source of the magic we sensed was not within Hethnost. I think it came from the east. We'll need to organize search parties."

Reshel felt panic rise in her like floodwaters. "What's happened to him?" Her voice was shrill, almost a shout. She thought she would cry.

"I don't know," said the Archmage. "But I fear he's done something terrible."

The horn's call sounded, lingered, echoed, faded. A swirling gust of wind tore through the glade. The mist was blown away from Gerin as if he stood at the heart of a cyclone. Then the wind stopped as suddenly as it had appeared, leaving only tattered remnants of the fog drifting among the dark branches.

It seemed then that the world thinned around him, as if the very earth beneath his feet had somehow become as insubstantial as fog. The intense sensation left him shaken and weak.

When he lowered the horn from his lips, the world itself had changed.

His mind reeled when he realized what had happened. The glade itself was different—longer, with jagged knife-edged stones poking from the earth where before there'd been nothing but green grass. The trees were now mostly bare of leaves, as if it were late autumn rather than midsummer. They seemed somehow menacing, tall and misshapen, with sharp grasping branches like dangling hands.

Even the moon itself had changed, the markings on its face altered into something that looked like a snarling beast.

Where in the name of Telros am I? He was filled with a cold terror and dread. Would he be able to return to his world once he was finished? Had he entered the realm of the gods? Was he near Bellon's mansions and the unnumbered dead who dwelled there? Or was he in Shayphim's shadow-realm, with the demon's Hounds even now approaching, ready to rip out his spirit and take it to the Cauldron of Souls where it would be imprisoned for eternity?

When he looked down at the horn in his hand, he nearly screamed.

The beautiful horn of gold was now a hideous thing, formed of splintering yellow bone. Where the bell should have been there was a skull with a gaping mouth showing rows of sharp, cruel teeth, like animal fangs. The eye sockets were crusted with a thick, congealed crust of dried blood. It looked like it was screaming, and he was terrified that it actually *would* begin to shriek with a voice reeking of a corpse. The back of the skull was fused to the curving pipe of the horn, which ended in an obscene mouthpiece shaped like a woman's sex organs. The sight nearly made him vomit.

By all the great gods of heaven, what have I done?

He began to shake. The horn fell from his hand onto the grass. He wanted very badly to return to Hethnost and forget he had ever attempted this. But would the castle even be there in this otherworld he had entered? Even if it were there, who or what would be living in it?

The silence was broken by the distant wails of creatures he did not recognize and could not name. The cries sounded to him like the screams of the damned, the shrieks of those doomed to eternal torment. He hoped they did not come any closer. He had no desire to see what manner of beasts created such awful noises.

There was nothing he could do but continue to trust that the creators of the spell had not intended for its user to be stranded forever in this nameless shadow-realm. He opened the book with a trembling hand and read the next part of the spell.

This was much shorter than the last, and not nearly as difficult. He concentrated very hard, blocking out the horror of the horn. For the most part he succeeded.

The weirstones glowed more brightly now. He closed the book and shouted in a commanding voice, "Naragenth ul-Darhel, amber wizard and king of Khedesh, I command your spirit to appear in this place! Answer my call, Naragenth! My power compels you! The power of the horn compels you! You must obey!"

A mist appeared within the boundary set by the weirstones. Within the mist a shape began to form. It was little more than a shadow at first, but in a few moments a man stood before Gerin. He appeared solid but was faintly luminous, as if an unseen light were shining upon him.

The man was tall, with wavy black hair swept back from a pronounced peak above a high forehead. A trim beard formed a dark narrow line along his jaw. He wore robes of purple and gold and carried a white rod that Gerin recognized as the royal scepter of Khedesh.

It worked! he thought. *I've summoned him from the dead!*

"Naragenth ul-Darhel, I have called you—"

The spectral form interrupted him with an angry shout. *"Asaqa sugrech valaroq gatrenetembros novenye . . ."*

Gerin did not understand his words. He was not speaking Osirin or Kelarin. He realized that the dead king was probably speaking Hodetten, the language of Khedesh before the Wars of Unification and the creation of Helca's empire.

"Naragenth, please, be quiet and I will explain!" he said in Osirin. His command of the language was still far from perfect, but he thought he could say what he needed. He silently thanked Master Aslon and Hollin for their intense instructions.

To his great relief, the spirit fell silent. He stared at Gerin with open hostility. "You are a wizard?" he asked in Osirin. His accent was strange, but Gerin could understand him.

"Yes, I am a wizard. An amber wizard, like you."

Naragenth made a derisive sound and glared at him with skepticism and contempt. "There are no wizards like me. How have you conjured me here? What is this place?"

"We are near a castle called Hethnost, a home of wizards . . ." Gerin paused, unsure of how to continue. *I have to just tell him,* he thought. "You are dead, Naragenth. I know of no other way to say this. You have been dead for eighteen hundred years. I have called you from the grave."

"Impossible!" He tried to step toward Gerin, but the power of the weirstones prevented him. It was as if he were caged in a cell of unbreakable glass. A smoky glow spread beneath his hands as he pressed against the barrier. "What sorcery is this? How have you imprisoned me? I demand that you release me at once!"

"I can't. You are dead, Naragenth. You were killed when Helca sent his army to conquer Almaris. Try to remember!"

"This is treachery!" He thrust his right arm toward Gerin, then stared at his hand in horror when nothing happened. "You are one of Helca's wizards! You've taken my powers from me! Kill me if you will, but I will never surrender the city to you."

"You cannot summon magic because you have no true body. You are a spirit, Naragenth. I have not taken your powers. Please, try to remember! I have risked a great deal to call you. Helca and his empire are dust. I am not one of his generals. I am Gerin Atreyano, the crown prince of Khedesh. You may very well be my ancestor."

Naragenth lowered his arm. "I remember an arrow . . ." he said softly. His hand moved to his throat. "It pierced me here. I remember now. I fell but could not shout. Then nothing but darkness . . ." He looked at Gerin, his anger spent. "You say it has been eighteen hundred years?"

"Yes."

"How have you called me?"

"A forbidden spell that has long been locked away."

"I know of no spell that can call the dead. It must have been devised after . . . after my own death." He regained some of his composure, straightening and assuming a regal air. "Why have you called me? What is it you want?"

"Naragenth, wizards have almost vanished from Osseria. Most who remain have gathered in Hethnost." He gestured toward the location of the fortress, though he wondered once again if it were present in this shadow-realm. "There is a library there, the Varsae Sandrova. It contains spells and devices of power both great and small, like the spell I used to summon you from the grave.

"But your library, the Varsae Estrikavis, has never been found. We know almost nothing of what it contained. By all accounts, it held some of the most powerful magic of your age. That is why I've called you, so that you can tell me where to find it. Wizards have searched for it since the time of your death. Some fear it perished in a fire that destroyed the royal palace of your day, but I do not think so."

"Step closer, Prince Gerin." Naragenth's voice was commanding—the voice of a king at the height of his powers, of a man used to having his words obeyed without question.

Gerin wanted to ask why, but decided to do as he was asked. He moved to the edge of the square formed by the weirstones.

"You ask me for my greatest secret. I believe what you have told me—that I am dead and the world has moved on. But I want you to prove what you say, and show the courage an amber wizard should possess.

"Give me your hand, young wizard. I want to test for myself the truth of your words. You may not be able to break this barrier any more than I; but perhaps flesh will succeed where spirit did not."

Gerin did not hesitate. He could show no fear to this man

if he wanted to learn the secret of the Varsae Estrikavis. He stepped to the edge of the weirstone boundary and thrust his hand through it.

He felt a piercing cold when he crossed the threshold, as if he'd plunged his hand into frigid water, and his flesh seemed drained of color on the other side, as if he were looking at it through smoky glass.

"Ah," said Naragenth. "So this cage is for me alone. It has no power over flesh and blood." He tried to touch Gerin's hand, but Gerin felt only a slight pressure.

Naragenth straightened, and Gerin withdrew his hand. "Will you tell me where you hid your library? Could it have been destroyed when your palace burned?"

"No, young wizard, it could not have been destroyed because it was not in the palace. I am not such a fool as to hide such a treasure within my own house.

"It is a bold thing you have done. You have earned the right to know my secret. The Varsae Estrikavis was hidden where no man could find it, in the Chamber of the Moon."

"Where is the Chamber of the Moon? I've never heard of it, not in all the accounts I've read of your library."

"Of course you have never heard of it. The Chamber of the Moon was a great secret, and one of my greatest creations. *It is not in Osseria*. It can only be reached by—"

Clouds of blackness erupted from the weirstones, enveloping Naragenth. They swirled around him like a vortex, the black tendrils crawling across his spectral form as if they were living things. He raised his arms and cried out once, then vanished beneath the blackness, drawn back to the world of the dead.

"No!" How could this have happened when Gerin was so close to learning what he wanted?

The blackness spun faster, like a whirlwind, filling the enclosure formed by the power of the weirstones. Gerin could sense tremendous amounts of magic within it. He did not know what it was. The book of spells described nothing like it.

A vertical fissure of blinding white light split the blackness, emanating power. He sensed that the fissure was somehow a crack in the very foundation of reality, that it was an opening to another sphere of existence.

I must stop this!

He poured vast amounts of power into the fissure, trying to force it closed. The pressure increased, and he felt something scrape across his skin like hot needles.

Nothing he did worked. The fissure widened. It was so bright he thought it must be visible for miles. *If I was in a world where anyone could see it,* he thought.

The pressure suddenly reversed, and he nearly toppled over. Instead of pushing against him, now the fissure was drawing him in. He fought to retain his footing, but he was powerless to resist. And he was so weakened from his exertions with the spell that he had almost no magical strength left with which to fight it.

The fissure collapsed when he reached the edge of the weir-stones, like a door being slammed shut. The forces pulling him vanished. But a part of his mind was jerked away as well; something in the fissure had connected itself to him, and it was taking that part of him with it.

The pain was unbearable, an agony far worse than anything he had ever known. He screamed and collapsed to the grass. He was faintly aware that his body was convulsing; he felt a froth forming on his lips, but there was nothing he could do. *I'm going to die here,* he thought. *I'm going to die and no one will ever find me because I'm not even in Osseria anymore. What a fool I've been . . .*

In those final moments before the blackness swallowed him, he thought he saw a shape standing over him, a manlike form shrouded in shadow whose face he could not see but whose eyes gleamed with a silver light. He tried to speak, to ask for help, but he could not, and a second later he saw nothing at all.

Far away in Neddar, Pendrel Yevan Hirgrolei came awake in the darkness of his small cell in the House of Hídal, the ancient home of the *kamichi* of his clan. Moonlight shone through the single window cut in the timbered wall and fell across the legs of Guso Oletran Faolasar, who was asleep on his cot on the other side of the room.

Hirgrolei sat up in his bed, his heart soaring. "Guso," he said. "Guso, listen to me."

His *nirgromu* opened his eyes and took a sudden, deep breath. He was fully awake, and turned his head to face Hirgrolei. "Yes, Master? What is it?"

Hirgrolei could scarcely believe what he was about to speak. *It is done at last.* "My vision has been fulfilled," he said. He could not stop from grinning. "The Slain God has returned."

14

"Here he is!" called out Balandrick. "I've found him!"

Gerin lay convulsing on the ground near the edge of a glade, a thin froth of foam on his lips and chin. Balandrick rushed to his side, taking in the scene in an instant: the golden horn upon the ground, the book of spells and weirstones close by, a lamp dangling from a tree limb. *Gods above us, Gerin,* he thought as he knelt beside him, placing his own magefire lamp on the damp grass. *What have you done here?*

He'd been awakened in the middle of the night by a female wizard who asked if he would help them search for Gerin. When he asked what happened, her expression had darkened. "Did you not sense it?"

"Sense what?"

"A little while ago. A feeling of terror, or death."

His blood had chilled. "I had a nightmare. I thought I heard someone screaming, and smelled something cloying, like blood . . . are you saying that has something to do with Gerin?"

"We don't know. But you had no ordinary nightmare. It was a thing of black magic, and the amber wizard is missing. If you want to help him, come with me now."

The Archmage had met them all near the eastern wall,

a group of more than one hundred wizards and soldiers of the Sunrise Guard. "What we felt came from outside of Hethnost, in the area of Maratheon's Hill. We'll break into smaller groups to search for Gerin. Time is of the essence."

Balandrick had clambered up the hills with Abaru and several other wizards and pulled ahead, terrified that they would find Gerin dead; another, final, failure on his part to carry out his sworn duty to protect the crown prince.

And now he was here. He was glad the Archmage had commanded Reshel to remain in the fortress. She would be out of her mind if she saw her brother like this. "Someone, hurry! I've found him!"

Abaru rushed into the glade, followed by the others in their group. He knelt beside Balandrick and touched his fingers to Gerin's temples. "Fool of a boy," he muttered. "We need to stop his convulsions. Hold his shoulders." Balandrick did as he was asked. Abaru spoke a spell, but Gerin's convulsions continued. The wizard cursed, then tried several more spells. Gerin's convulsions calmed a little but did not stop completely. Balandrick wondered how long he could continue like this before dying of exhaustion.

"We need the Warden of Healing," he said. He turned to say something to one of his companions just as six others entered the glade. Among them was Kirin Zaeset, the Warden of Healing, a slight, slender man with a gaunt face and large, hooked nose. The Archmage was with him, the Ammon Ekril glittering on her brow like a star fallen to earth.

Balandrick moved aside so Kirin could get closer to Gerin. He made a circle in the air with his open hand and spoke several words. A shimmering disk of yellow light appeared where his hand had been. He peered at Gerin through it, then made another gesture. The disk vanished.

Kirin grasped both of Gerin's wrists and said, *"Iya trestari nan kanemnénto lokarnos terû akhabrenelaíth!"*

Gerin's convulsions stopped. Balandrick feared that he was dead until he saw the faint rise and fall of his chest.

"We must get him back to Hethnost at once," said Kirin to

the Archmage. "I can do nothing more for him here. I must study what he's done to learn how to treat it."

The Archmage commanded that the horn, book of spells, and weirstones be gathered and returned with them. Hollin bared his teeth when he saw the book. "The work of the Baryashins," he said with loathing. "What in the name of the gods was he trying to do?"

"We must return him to Hethnost quickly or we may never find out," said Kirin.

"Do you know what's wrong with him?" the Archmage asked Kirin. Despite having worked on Gerin through the night and much of the morning, the Warden of Healing had been unable to revive him. She stared down at Gerin in his bed. His skin was waxy and ashen, his hair matted to his head in damp strands. *What possessed you to do such a rash and dangerous thing?*

Reshel, who had refused to leave his side, patted his face with a damp cloth. Balandrick was also in the room, seated in a chair in the corner. He'd slept only a little; his cheeks were stubbled, and there were dark rings under his eyes. Hollin stood next to Kirin, his arms folded, his expression grave.

"I believe he opened a doorway to another plane of existence," said Kirin. "What he was trying to do, I cannot say, but obviously something went wrong with the spell and now a part of his mind is connected with this other realm." He placed his hand on Gerin's head and spoke a complex invocation. As he spoke, a smoky line of yellow light appeared, thin as a spiderweb. It emanated from Gerin's forehead and rose straight into the air before dissipating just shy of the ceiling. Marandra frowned at it.

"That is the connection I discovered," said Kirin. "With much effort, I might add. It was not an easy thing to find." He withdrew his hand, and the line of light vanished. "The doorway between the worlds is still open. I must close it to break the connection."

"Will closing it hurt him?" asked Reshel.

"I can't be sure. I've never encountered anything like this before. His mind may be irreparably harmed. He may die. But he will *surely* die if the doorway is not closed. Even now it's draining the life from him. I've been able to slow it but not stop it. Part of his mind is wandering in this other world even as we speak, like a lost spirit."

"Do you know how to close the doorway?" asked Hollin.

Kirin nodded. "I've looked at the book of spells he was using, and I've examined the horn." He gestured to where the instrument lay on a nearby table.

Such a beautiful thing, the Archmage thought. It was hard to believe it had been created by wizards as loathesome as the Baryashins.

"I can close the door, but to do so, the horn will have to be blown again."

The Archmage scowled. "It's a thing of death and black magic. Is there no other way?"

"None that I'll be able to find before he dies."

"Then we'll have to use the horn," said Reshel. She looked directly at the Archmage. "Please. We can't let him die."

"Kirin, how certain are you of what you'll be doing?"

"The spell is merely the conclusion of what Gerin began. The doorway he opened remains open. The spell will either close it or not, but it would seem to me that leaving a portal open to another plane of existence is far more dangerous. I don't think his death would close it. If he dies before it can be closed, the opening will no longer be anchored to a specific location in our world, and if we cannot find it, we cannot close it. If we don't do this now, we may not have another chance."

"Do what must be done to close the doorway and revive him," said Marandra. "Do whatever you can to save Gerin, but your first duty is to seal the portal." Balandrick turned ashen. Reshel looked stricken, but did not protest. *A strong girl,* thought the Archmage. *Stronger than she first appears.*

"I'll need assistance," Kirin said. "I'm already weary, and this spell is complex. It was meant to be performed by more than one wizard. I will say that Gerin accomplished quite a feat in completing as much as he did. Far more than I could have, or any of us."

"I'll help you," said Hollin.

"Is there anything I can do?" asked Balandrick.

"No. Only magic can help him now."

Kirin opened the spellbook to the proper page, summoned his powers, and began to read. Marandra felt the air in the room chill as he worked through the spell. She folded her arms and watched both Gerin and Kirin.

Hollin, looking over Kirin's shoulder, began to read his part of the spell. His face was wrinkled and pinched. *He must feel filthy participating in such vile magic,* Marandra thought. Hollin's loathing of death magic was even deeper than what most wizards felt—he had told her that he considered it an affront to their heritage that such terrible powers had been created by wizards. He was deeply and personally offended by the blight he felt that dark magic cast upon the legacy of the Atalari. "We are a great people," he'd said. "And though we've fallen far from the pinnacle of the Atalari's Shining Nation, no wizard should *ever* sully themselves with powers of darkness. It is an unspeakable crime."

Which brought her back to the question of what Gerin had been trying to accomplish. Certainly not something as banal as proving that by himself he could perform a complicated spell designed for two wizards.

Kirin finished his part and handed the book to Hollin, who continued to read the incantation. The chill in the room deepened. The air itself seemed to have darkened, as if twilight had suddenly fallen.

Kirin raised the horn to his lips and sounded it.

Marandra winced. What emerged from the horn was nothing that sounded like a horn, even one sounded badly. What she heard was a scream, a wail of agony and horror and unquenchable sorrow; a cry of someone—or something—dying a terrible, painful death. She did not see how the instrument could have possibly produced such a sound.

The others were affected too. Reshel cried out and covered her ears. Balandrick's head jerked, and he squeezed his eyes shut and grimaced. Kirin was so startled he nearly dropped the horn from his fingers. Hollin flinched and stumbled in his reading of the incantation but quickly recovered.

"Prepare yourselves," said Kirin. "I must sound it one more time." He steeled himself, then pressed the horn to his lips and blew it again.

Marandra stood ready to clap her hands over her ears, but this time the sound of the horn was warm and melodious, a thing of beauty that brought to mind triumph and glory.

The room darkened again as the note faded. She felt a tingling on her skin and sensed that its cause was the power of the spell.

Wind gusted through the room, carrying with it the stench of decaying flesh. Gerin screamed. His body went rigid with pain, his back arching so severely that only the top of his head and the heels of his feet touched the bed. A moment later he collapsed and lay still.

We've killed him! thought the Archmage in horror. *The last amber wizard the world will ever see, and we've killed him.*

The wind disappeared; the light in the room brightened and returned to normal.

Reshel was already checking the pulse in her brother's neck as Kirin bent over to examine him. "Does he live?" Marandra asked in a weak voice. She cleared her throat and repeated her question more strongly.

"Yes, he lives," Kirin said. He created a Seeing and examined him further.

"What about the doorway?" asked Hollin. "Is it closed?"

It was a long time before Kirin responded. He sat back wearily. The Seeing evaporated from the air. "I'm not sure," he said, his shoulders slumped. "I cannot detect it directly, but there seems to be traces of power that emanate from the other plane. I don't know if that means the doorway has still not been completely closed or if I'm sensing echoes of its power. I'll have to study the matter further."

"Will he be all right?" asked Reshel.

"I believe so. He's in a normal sleep now. He should awaken when he's rested."

Hollin faced Marandra. "Since he will live, we need to discuss how he is to be punished."

Reshel paled at his words but said nothing. *Yes, a strong girl,* she thought. *She knows when to keep silent. A rare gift among the young, wizard or otherwise.* She would have to keep an eye on this one.

15

Gerin dreamed that the black Hounds of Shayphim chased him through a dark and tangled forest. He tried to run as fast as he could but stumbled over rocks and fallen limbs and the gnarled roots of trees. The baying Hounds drew closer. He tripped again and fell, his hands sliding across the leaf-strewn path. He rolled over just as two black shapes with eyes blazing like red hellfire leaped, their fangs flashing—

He came awake with a gasp of breath. Though dimmed by the curtains drawn across the window, the light in the room made his sensitive eyes squint. His face was slick with sweat. He was famished, but his stomach felt so queasy he doubted whether he could keep any food in it.

"Thank the gods you're awake." Reshel was at his bedside. She wiped his face with a cold cloth. He shivered and let out a deep sigh.

Balandrick was there, too, his cheeks sunken and dark. He looked like he hadn't slept in a week. "How do you feel?"

Gerin tried to swallow, his throat terribly dry. "Water?" he whispered.

She poured him a glass from a pitcher. "Don't gulp it, just take small sips or you'll be sick," she admonished.

He did as he was told, handed the glass back to her and said, "What happened? How did I get here?"

"That's what everyone wants to ask *you*." An edge of anger crept into her voice. "How could you do something so stupid? Do you know how close you came to dying? What were you *doing* out there?"

"How long have I been here?"

"We found you two nights ago. Stop trying to change the subject and answer my question. What were you doing?"

He sighed wearily. "Trying to find the Varsae Estrikavis."

"I hope it was worth it," said Balandrick. "You were almost dead when I found you in that glade."

"How could those horrible spells help you find it?" Reshel asked. "Have you lost your mind? They had to blow that horn *again* to repair the damage you'd done. It's a foul, evil thing, Gerin."

"Foul or not, it gave me the power to call Naragenth's spirit and ask him where he hid the library. That was the whole point." He was getting angry himself. He did not like being lectured by his little sister. The fact that she was right only made it worse.

She looked taken aback by his words. "You mean you actually *spoke* to Naragenth? What did he say? Did he tell you where it is?"

"He said it was in a place called the Chamber of the Moon, and that it wasn't in Osseria. But then something happened and he vanished before he could tell me anything more. I don't know what went wrong. The spell was broken and I guess I blacked out. I really don't remember."

As he lay there, he felt something break and crumble within him; it seemed a barrier in his mind had fallen away. Sudden understanding came upon him, and it shook him to the core of his being. "There's something else," he said quietly. "Reshel, I was . . . *compelled* to do what I did. I don't know how else to explain it. I *knew* that what I was doing was wrong, but I couldn't stop myself. I even wanted to tell you what I was doing, but something stopped me, made me forget before I could say anything. But it's gone now, and I can finally remember." His anger with her disappeared. *In the name of Telros, what have I done?*

"You're not just saying that to try to weasel out of responsibility, are you?"

He shook his head slowly. Tears stung his eyes and he blinked to clear them. He felt overwhelmed with guilt at having so callously betrayed the trust of the wizards. "I swear. Bring Hollin. I want him to examine me to see if he can get to the truth of this."

"I'll get him," said Balandrick. "I'll be back as soon as I can."

Hollin finished the last of the spells and drummed his fingers along his arm. "There is indeed something here, a magic that has recently been active in you. I believe it is the spell placed in you by the Neddari *kamichi* who attacked you near Ailethon. I'll have Kirin verify this, but I do not believe I am wrong. He sensed that its power had been awakened in you but could not determine its purpose."

"So you're saying this Neddari spell compelled Gerin?" asked Balandrick.

"It is a magic different from that of wizards, but it nevertheless has the characteristics of a compulsion. I cannot perceive the detailed workings of the spell, but I can see enough to say that Gerin was probably powerless to resist it."

"But to what end?" asked Reshel. "What was the Neddari trying to accomplish by having him call Naragenth?"

"To that question, I have no answer. I can't see what they could hope to gain by it. I don't even believe they would know of the existence of Naragenth or the Varsae Estrikavis."

"Why couldn't you see that it was a compulsion before?" asked Gerin.

"When I first examined you after the attack, the spell was inactive, and it was different enough from the magic of wizards that neither I nor the Warden of Healing could determine its purpose or remove it. Now, however, its power has been released."

"I should have been stronger," Gerin said in a thin voice. "I should have resisted more. I swore I would not bow to the *kamichi*'s will, yet that's exactly what I did." He felt utterly miserable. He had failed in an enormous, spectacular fashion, and was not certain how to come to grips with the turmoil that gripped him.

"It was a powerful, devious spell," Hollin replied. "The forgetfulness charm in it made it impossible for you to tell anyone what you were doing, no matter how much you might have wanted to. Now, you need to rest." To Reshel and Balandrick, he said, "And I suggest you both get some yourselves. You look dead on your feet. Gerin will be fine. Now off with you. I need to speak to the Archmage about this."

Gerin slept off and on for the rest of the afternoon. Sometime later he awoke to find the Warden of Healing hovering over him, working several spells. "You're lucky to be alive," Kirin said after a while. "You came very close to death."

"I know. Thank you for what you did for me."

"The Neddari compulsion is still in you. It's no longer active, but its power is lingering long after a wizard's compulsion would have vanished."

"Is it done with me? Is there anything else it will compel me to do?"

"No. All of the power I can detect has no active elements left; it is a residue, nothing more. It's done with you."

"Are you sure?"

"As sure as I can be about foreign magic. You are free from it."

"Can you remove what's left?"

Kirin frowned and shook his head. "No, unfortunately I cannot. It is a strange power, beyond my ability to manipulate. It's difficult even to sense, since it springs from a source of magic so different from our own. But it will be gone in a day or two." He opened the door. "Sleep some more if you can."

Gerin did manage to sleep again for several hours. He finally got up after nightfall. Reshel returned with some food for him and fresh clothes. He ate what little he could, then washed himself and dressed. He sat by the window looking out into the night, wondering about the purpose of the compulsion. And, almost despite himself, he wondered what his next step should be in finding the Varsae Estrikavis. He would not give up on his quest, not after coming so close.

The compulsion is done, he told himself. *Whatever it wanted with me is over. But I did learn something I can use to find the Varsae Estrikavis. I would be a fool to give up now, to throw that knowledge away.*

It is not in Osseria. How could that possibly be? Where else could it be? Naragenth had lived in Almaris, a coastal seaport. Had he hidden it on some remote island in the Maurelian Sea? Perhaps that was the answer. The more he thought about it, the more sense it made. If he had created the Chamber of the Moon on some remote island, it would have remained beyond the reach of Helca's armies, where no enemy wizard would have ever found it.

It can only be reached by—So tantalizingly close! A few more seconds and he would have known the answer. Now he had a clue, but nothing certain. *Still, it is more than I had before. More than anyone since Naragenth's death has ever discovered.* He wanted to be proud of that accomplishment, but could not. He had no idea what role he actually played and how much was determined by the Neddari spell. Besides, the accomplishment had come at a terrible price—his betrayal of the wizards. It did not make him feel better to know that it was a direct result of the *kamichi*'s spell.

He could not be proud of what he'd done, but he would still use the knowledge he'd gleaned. What could those last words mean? Was it hidden in such a way that the entrance could only be seen during certain phases of the moon? Was that part of whatever spells protected it and kept it hidden?

He was interrupted by a knock at the door. Two members of

the Sunrise Guard had come to escort him to the Archmage.

They took him to a council room in the manor of the Archmage. The room was wide but shallow, with a row of tall windows set in the wall opposite the door. He faced a dark polished table whose far side was shaped into a gentle curve. The Archmage and High Ministers—the governing powers of Hethnost—were seated behind it. Hollin sat to one side of the table in an expansive, high-backed chair.

There was a single chair facing the council table. The Archmage, seated at the center, gestured for him to sit.

"Gerin, you are here because you have violated the trust of this council. You are accused of entering areas of the Varsae Sandrova forbidden to you, stealing dangerous artifacts of magic, and performing spells whose use has been proscribed for centuries."

He was about to speak, but the Archmage raised her hand. "However, Hollin has told us about the Neddari compulsion placed upon you, which was confirmed by the Warden of Healing. Because of this, you are absolved of any guilt or responsibility in this matter, though we still have many questions for you."

He released a long breath. "Thank you, Archmage." He spoke in a hushed tone, his eyes downcast. "May I ask a question?" She gestured for him to continue. "What *was* that magic I used to call Naragenth? I mean, I know what it did, but under the compulsion I didn't care that it was locked away, or have any interest in it other than using it to find the Varsae Estrikavis. Who created it, and why? The records I looked through gave no explanation for the horn or weirstones."

She folded her hands on the table and collected her thoughts. "It came from the most shameful period in the history of Hethnost. I knew only a little of this story before now, but since we found you unconscious in the hills, I and others have learned as much as we could about the makers of the spell you used.

"The Horn of Tireon was created by a group of wizards

called the Baryashin Order more than fourteen hundred years ago. The order was founded by a wizard named Evain Stirahl, and was dedicated to finding a means to eternal life. It began as a secret society within Hethnost—the Baryashins made a high art of death, using the power of murder to further their goals. They kidnapped peasants from nearby villages and towns, careful to ensure they left no clues that would lead to Hethnost, and sacrificed them to learn more of the mystery of death."

"Death is a powerful event, Gerin," said Hollin. "It releases potent energies greater than normal magical power that can be harnessed by wizards. But using death for such a purpose is forbidden. It is the greatest sin a wizard can commit."

Gerin wondered what he would have done if the spell had called for a sacrifice. Would the compulsion have driven him so far as to make him kill? He closed his eyes and swallowed. It was too terrible for him to contemplate for the simple reason that he could not, with any certainty, say the answer was no.

"The Baryashins killed many," continued the Archmage. "The exact number is not known for certain, but certainly several hundred innocent people died at their hands. Their existence was uncovered after one of their ceremonies of black magic was interrupted. They were forced to kill the wizard who discovered them, a crime they could not hide for long. They fled Hethnost and went into hiding. It took a long time to piece together what had happened, but in their haste to leave they left enough behind that the full magnitude of their crimes could be learned.

"The wizards of Hethnost were shocked and vowed to bring the order to justice. They searched many years for the Baryashins, but it was centuries before they were found. During that time the Baryashins worked to perfect their black arts. The culmination of their work was the horn created by Tireon al-Vashkiril, a ruthless monster who personally murdered more than ninety people. The horn was the fulfillment of their dream of achieving eternal life. It was an abomination of

magic, made with the power of murder and human sacrifices, mostly of children and young female virgins, whose
blood they considered the most potent of all. The purpose of
the horn and weirstones was to weaken the barrier between
life and death so that after their physical body died, the spirit
could remain in this world and possess the body of a living
person.

"They were discovered by wizards of Hethnost before
they could finish their work. The wizards learned of several bodies that had been found in the poorest sections of
Londros. They had been butchered in the fashion of the
Baryashins, something that all wizards of that time were
taught so they could be mindful of signs of the order. Several wizards who were in the city to perform the Ritual of
Discovery learned of the murders and sent word to Hethnost at once. A hundred wizards arrived at Londros and
quickly located the order, sweeping down upon their hiding place—a manor house just outside the city—and taking
them unawares. Most of the order were killed outright. The
remainder committed suicide before they could be taken,
including Tireon himself. Forty-one wizards were dead
when all was done: four from Hethnost, the rest from the order. The wizards took all of the contents from the manor
house—including the Horn of Tireon—then burned it to the
ground.

"The possessions of the Baryashin were returned to Hethnost and studied. They found books of spells, detailed accounts of their rituals and goals, and many magical devices.
The wizards of that day did not believe the Baryashins had
ever completed work on their goal to outlive their own
deaths. They believed they had destroyed the order completely. Their possessions were then locked in the Varsae
Sandrova, where they remained until you opened the vault."

"Why wasn't the horn ever used before?" asked Gerin.
"The spell I used did not call for a sacrifice. And if it wasn't
ever to be used again, why keep it? Why not simply destroy
it?" He hoped he did not sound belligerent in asking these

questions, but he sincerely wanted to know why such magic was permitted to exist if it was indeed as awful as the Archmage and Hollin said.

"The horn was never used because it was not known what would happen when the barrier between life and death was weakened," said the Archmage. "We knew there would be consequences, but we could not predict what they would be. We do not destroy knowledge, even knowledge as black as this. Though some have argued that we should indeed do just that and cleanse the vaults of any other dark magic contained there." She glanced toward Hollin, who clenched his hands into fists. "Something valuable may come from it someday, but not without much study and a deep understanding of the risks of using such things. Your experience is proof of this. You succeeded in calling Naragenth's spirit, but you nearly killed yourself, and opened a doorway that even now may not be completely closed. We may never fully know the consequences of these actions.

"We've also recently discovered that the barrier separating the worlds of the living and the dead is weakening. This has happened before at least once, long ago. The weakening barrier may have something to do with all of this; at the very least, it made your calling of Naragenth easier. But what else may result from this we cannot say.

"Gerin, we ask that you tell us everything you can about the attack by the Neddari *kamichi*. Leave nothing out. We must try to discover the intent of the compulsion. It may be that it was designed to cause some harm to Hethnost that we cannot yet fathom."

Gerin told them everything he could remember. He found that slipping into the mild trance-state that eased the calling of magic helped him recall details he otherwise would have overlooked.

The First Siege, a black-haired, bearded man named Sevaisan Barlaechi, shook his head. "I don't understand how this *kamichi*'s vision of a Slain God has anything to do with you calling the spirit of a dead wizard."

"Perhaps the *kamichi* did indeed see Gerin summon Naragenth in his vision," said Hollin, "but mistook the spirit of the wizard for this Slain God of theirs, some being of Neddari legend."

"That sounds reasonable," said the Archmage. "Yet my heart tells me it is not the answer."

"There's something else," Gerin said. He described the calling of Naragenth and his words about the Chamber of the Moon.

"That is indeed new," said Hollin. "I've never heard that named before." He looked both surprised and pleased.

"Neither have I," said the Archmage. "We'll have the Warden of the Archives begin a search for any references to this Chamber of the Moon. Some good may come from this after all, if the Varsae Estrikavis can at long last be uncovered.

"There is, finally, the matter of your training," she continued. "I know that I agreed to allow Hollin to train you in your own country, but too much has happened since then for me to continue to sanction it. The Neddari compulsion may be over, but there are still powers attempting to influence you to some unknown end. I feel it would be best for your training to occur here, where we can keep a watchful eye on you and intervene should the need arise."

Gerin was shocked. He looked toward Hollin, but it was clear from the stricken look on the wizard's face that the Archmage had not told him of her decision before voicing it.

They don't trust me anymore, he thought. *So now they want to control me.* He did not blame the Archmage; through him, a foreign power had released a potent spell in the heart of the wizards' domain. Of course he could not be trusted. He would have felt the same had the situation been reversed. But it still hurt to hear it in such stark terms.

"I understand your reasons for wanting me to train here rather than at Ailethon," he said, choosing his words carefully. "But that is impossible."

The First Siege glared. "It is not for you to decide what is or is not possible for us."

The Archmage gestured for Sevaisan to calm himself, then regarded Gerin evenly. "That is my will, Gerin. You and Reshel will be trained here. It is too dangerous to allow your training to continue elsewhere."

"Dangerous or not, you need to understand that I will be trained at Ailethon or not at all."

The First Siege slapped the table with his open hand. "How *dare* you—"

"Silence!" said the Archmage. Sevaisan and the other members of the council quieted at once.

Gerin's heart raced. Would they truly try to keep him here against his will? He looked at the stern faces watching him from the other side of the table and realized he was dealing with men and women who were used to absolute authority over every aspect of life here. That their control could have slipped so precipitously within Hethnost itself must have shaken them deeply, far more so than Gerin had first guessed.

"Archmage, please," he said in the sudden silence. "Let me speak."

She paused, and for an instant he thought she was going to refuse, but then she gestured for him to go on.

"I do understand your desire to have me remain here, I truly do. But you must understand that it is impossible. I agreed to come here to have my powers Awakened, but that is all. If you had not permitted my training to occur at Ailethon, I can say with great certainty that I would not be a wizard, now or ever. I am the crown prince, heir to the sapphire throne. I cannot be away from my kingdom for years while I am trained. I have duties to my father and my people that I must uphold."

"It is well and good for you to say you would have refused to become a wizard now, *after* your powers have been Awakened," said the First Siege. "But the fact remains that you *are* a wizard and bound by the authority of the Archmage of Hethnost."

"I submitted to no such authority." He was still scarcely able to believe what he was hearing. It was almost as if he'd become an enemy to them. And the First Siege's words and arrogance only made him angrier. "I swore no oath, nor will I. My loyalty is to my father and the kingdom of Khedesh. I came here because of an agreement with you that I would return home after the Awakening to continue my training. That is not a condition that can be changed after the fact and without my consent."

The First Siege looked ready to strike out at Gerin with his magic, but the Archmage stood and flung out her arms. "Enough!" she shouted. "Sevaisan, you will be silent. You've not helped matters by treating Gerin as if he were a foe instead of our guest and fellow wizard." The First Siege glowered but did not speak again.

The Archmage did a surprising thing—she folded her hands and bowed her head to Gerin. "I offer you my apologies, Gerin. You are right. We made an agreement with you and your father, and we will abide by it. I allowed my concern over the compulsion and the divine power that has taken so much interest in you to cloud my judgment. I hope you will forgive me."

Gerin was still jittery with tension; he struggled to calm himself before he replied. "There is nothing to forgive, Archmage."

"However, I expect Hollin to keep a close watch on you. I've heard the Warden's report that the power of the Neddari compulsion is spent. Still, we would be remiss if we did not remain vigilant for signs of undue influence."

"The compulsion is gone," Kirin said with a trace of annoyance. "Its purpose has been fulfilled. Prince Gerin is free of it."

"I will do as you ask, Archmage," said Hollin.

The High Ministers returned to debating the meaning of the *kamichi*'s words and the purpose of the compulsion, though they reached no definitive conclusions. Gerin was at last dismissed, and walked alone back to his rooms, tired and hungry, filled with a strange sense of dread that the events the *kamichi* had set into motion had scarcely begun.

16

"I'm ready to go home," Gerin said. "I feel like a criminal here, that everyone's looking at me and judging me for what I did."

He, Reshel, and Balandrick were in Gerin's rooms, seated around a small table with a surface of glazed tiles. A platter of bread, cheese, wine, and grapes sat upon the table, mostly untouched.

"I can understand you feeling that way, but that's not what people are thinking," said Reshel. "Mostly they're talking about this Neddari compulsion and wondering about its purpose. It has them worried. It doesn't make sense that the Neddari would be interested in finding the Varsae Estrikavis—it's not like their *kamichis* could use the magic it contains, even if they somehow found it before wizards did. So what was the point of the compulsion? The return of this Slain God? No one here knows anything about a Slain God, and they haven't found any references to it in the Varsae Sandrova. It's all quite a mystery, but no one is *blaming* you for anything."

He had not told her that the Archmage had considered forcing the two of them to remain in Hethnost to continue their training; it was nevertheless another reason he wanted to start for home as quickly as he could. "But I still feel ashamed of what happened. If only I'd known, maybe I could have fought it better than I did."

"Gerin, that's the whole point of a compulsion. You *can't* fight it. You said yourself you wanted to tell me what was happening but the compulsion wouldn't let you. It made you forget."

He realized she was never going to completely understand; he wasn't sure he fully did himself. He knew what she was saying was correct, that there was nothing he could have done to resist the compulsion even had he known he was under its influence—that was the way such spells worked, manipulating the minds of their victims to ensure that the purpose of the spell was achieved. Yet knowing this did not alleviate his sense of personal failure, that he should have been stronger.

"I'm still ready to leave. We did what we came here to do. Our powers have been Awakened. It's time I returned to Ailethon. I have duties there I can't keep ignoring. There's no need for you to rush back now, but I need to go."

She was quiet for a while. "No, I'll go with you. Part of me would like to stay, but part of me misses home."

"We'll leave in two days. I need a bit more time to regain some strength."

"I'll let Hollin know." She rose from the table and said good-bye to them both.

After she'd gone, the two sat in silence for a while, which Gerin finally broke. "I think what bothers me the most is wondering how far I would have gone even without the compulsion." He spoke softly, staring emptily at the table, unwilling to look at Balandrick. "I can't help but wonder how much of that need to find the Varsae Estrikavis was already in me. I wanted to find it so I could leave my mark in history, by succeeding where so many others had failed. Part of me *still* feels that way."

"You say that like it's a bad thing."

"I know that I wouldn't have stolen the spell, or left Hethnost to perform it without telling anyone, without the compulsion." He rubbed his hands together in an absent, anxious way. "But did the *kamichi* just nudge along something that was already there? How much was *me* and how much was *him*?"

"You don't need to torture yourself over this. You just said you wouldn't have lied or snuck around without the compulsion. So you wanted to find this library for personal glory—what's wrong with that? There are a lot less pure motives I can think of for doing something."

"It's hard realizing that another man could make me do the things I did and I couldn't do anything to stop it. It's wrong. It makes me doubt everything about myself."

"I wish I could tell you I had an answer, but I don't. You can't always second-guess yourself, though. Not if you want to be an effective duke and king. You have to be decisive; your father's told you that since you were old enough to understand. My father told me the same thing, and I'll never have a tenth of the responsibilities that you'll have. You just have to find some way past this."

"Easier said than done."

"I know. But if anyone can do it, you can." Balandrick cleared his throat and glanced around the room as if looking for eavesdroppers. "Since we're confessing secrets, I've got one of my own to share with you. But this is strictly between the two of us—not a word to anyone."

Gerin raised his right hand. "Not a word."

Balandrick cleared his throat again and actually blushed. "I've become rather taken with Reshel. I would have never thought in a thousand years that she was my type, but she's changed in the last few months. I don't know what it is exactly. She's stronger, more outgoing and sure of herself. She used to be the next best thing to invisible, but now she has this . . . *presence* that's quite powerful. We've become very close."

Gerin snorted a laugh. "That's hardly a secret, Balan. By the gods, if that's how well you keep all of your secrets, I'll have to make sure to never tell you *anything* important."

Balan looked mystified. "You mean you could tell?"

"Of course! Do you think I'm blind? Besides, Reshel and I already talked."

"You did? What did she say?"

"It wasn't much. Just that you two were growing very fond of one another."

"I guess that wasn't much of a confession if you already knew. Do you think your father knows?"

"Not yet. But you'll have to tell him eventually if you want to continue."

"I know. That part scares me to death. I can't imagine talking to him about this."

"Think of it as an exercise in courage."

"But she's a *princess*." He got a faraway look in his eyes, then lowered his head and smiled. "But then again, a man's got to have his dreams. You have yours of finding the Varsae Estrikavis, and I have mine. No point in shattering either of them while there's still hope for them both, right?"

Gerin grinned and poured two glasses of wine. "I guess I can drink to that."

Much later that night Gerin was on the verge of slipping off to sleep when Hollin appeared at his door. The expression on the wizard's face—an eerie mingling of somber determination and fierceness of purpose—brought him back to complete awareness.

"Is something wrong?" asked Gerin. He sat down on the edge of his bed and watched the wizard intently as he closed the door behind him and entered the room, his boot heels clicking an ominous rhythm on the floor.

Hollin folded himself stiffly into an armless side chair. He placed the magefire lamp he carried on the room's single table, then looked down at his hands, which he held very still along the tops of his thighs. He drew a beep breath, then looked up at Gerin with an intense, unblinking stare.

"I don't want you to be afraid," he said.

Gerin cocked his head to the side. "Afraid of what? I don't understand."

"I know that this incident with the compulsion has twisted your life into knots. I'm certain you're feeling guilty about what you've done, but you have to keep telling yourself that the compulsion drove you to do what you did."

"I had this conversation with Balan a few hours ago. I understand what you're telling me. But I can't make the guilt go away. I feel like I've failed everyone—myself, you, the other wizards, my father."

"I realize that. As I said, *you* are the only one who can overcome your feelings of guilt or failure."

"Then what am I not supposed to be afraid of?"

"Yourself. Your magic. Of doing what you *should* do when the time is right." Hollin leaned forward; the light from the lamp danced in the center of his emerald eyes. "Your destiny. You asked me once why an amber wizard had appeared now, so long after the first, and I did not have an answer for you. I now think you are here *at this time*—when wizards have almost faded from history—to reclaim our lost place as the rulers of Osseria."

"I still don't understand. I'll be king of Khedesh after my father, but that would have happened whether I was a wizard or not."

"I mean something *greater* than that. You have vast powers at your disposal, Gerin—you do not have any conception yet of how strong you are. And unlike Naragenth, who lived in an age where wizards were on every court and controlled armies of their own—wizards who could, to an extent, contain and thwart the will of an amber wizard—there is no one now with the strength to oppose you."

"What about Hethnost?" he said, making an open gesture toward the room and the fortress beyond it. "Are you saying I should defy the wizards here and just do whatever I please?"

"Not at all. It has long been the policy of Hethnost not to interfere with the affairs of other nations. It was felt that setting ourselves upon the thrones of kingdoms would have only created distrust and fear of wizards in the Gendalos, and that in the end they would have turned against us and persecuted us. I have never agreed with this policy—I've long argued that there is a middle road between seizing power and totally abandoning it, but centuries of tradition weigh hard against me, and my pleas have so far fallen on deaf ears.

"But now *you* are here. Not only an amber wizard, but one who will one day rule a powerful southern kingdom. With your magic, you have the potential to be much more than a mere king."

Hollin paused. Gerin considered the wizard's words carefully, trying to grasp their full implication, the vast import they held for his future.

"You're talking about creating an empire."

Hollin emphatically shook his head. "No. An empire is one possibility, but there are certainly other courses you may take. My purpose here is not to lay before you a list of choices—I am here to make sure you are open to the incredible possibilities that lie in your future. I don't want your fear of what has happened with the compulsion to make you doubt yourself. I can all too easily see you wonder if every decision you make from this point forward is in some way influenced by the Neddari spell."

"Balandrick and I talked about that, too. He said I couldn't keep second-guessing myself, that I had to be decisive if I wanted to succeed as a duke and a king."

"That is good advice. There is little I can add to it."

"I'll do what I can to get through this. But right now it seems like the day when I completely trust my own judgment is very far off."

"That is all I or anyone else can ask of you, Gerin: to do your best. I know you doubt yourself, that you doubt your strength and your decisions. But in time you'll put this behind you."

"I hope you're right."

"I have one more thing to say, and then I'll leave you to your rest. I do not intend for you to go through this alone. I am offering myself to you as your counselor and teacher for as long as you will have me."

"But you're already coming back to Ailethon to train us," said Gerin. "Are you saying you'll stay even *after* our training is finished?"

"Yes. I told you I disagree with our policies of no involvement in the kingdoms of Osseria. I do not like our forced isolation, but so far I have endured it because it was the only course I could see. I could have left Hethnost, but that would have changed nothing. It would do me or our kind little good to become a counselor to a Gendalos king. With you, all of that's changed. I desire to take part in the affairs of the world once more, where my leaving here *will* make a difference."

"If you're asking whether or not I'll have you, the answer is yes," said Gerin. He was surprised at how relieved he felt, knowing that Hollin would be with him even after the end of his training. "But what will the other wizards think about it?"

Hollin's smile was tinged with sadness and regret. "I'm not going to tell them. Not yet, at any rate. There are a few other wizards who choose not to live here—there is certainly no law against it, just age-old custom—but they do not have the privileges and access to the knowledge at Hethnost that I enjoy as a Warden. If I tell them now, they may refuse to provide me with the things I need to train you, preferring to send someone else in my stead. I very much want to be the one to train you and help shape the wizard you will become. I don't like doing this, but for now we must be silent. Do not even tell Reshel, at least not until we are back in Ailethon."

"All right. Not a word."

"While I train you I will simply continue as Warden of Apprentices. I will return here from time to time to check on the progress of the others in training and discharge the duties of my office to the best of my abilities. But when your training comes to an end, I will resign my post and remain in Ailethon."

"What about the Archmage?" Since coming here, Gerin had learned that Hollin and the Archmage had been together for many years.

Hollin's smile grew sad. "We have a comfortable relationship, but in many ways it has been dwindling, like a slowly dying fire."

Gerin felt strange hearing Hollin speak of such a private matter; it seemed vaguely inappropriate, as if he were overhearing something not meant for his ears. But he said nothing and listened while Hollin talked quietly.

"I love her more than she loves me; I think I always have. I think she's simply growing tired of me. The fact that she said what she did about your training without consulting with me first is proof of this. So my leaving here will allow for a clean break between us. It will be hard, and I will miss her, but in the end this will be for the best." He rose, picked up his lamp and turned for the door. "Good night, Gerin."

"Good night." The door closed behind the wizard. Gerin lay down in the darkness, his body exhausted but his mind racing, contemplating everything Hollin had said. *You have the potential to be so much more.* But hadn't that gotten him into trouble in the first place? The desire to be the greatest Atreyano of them all? A desire twisted by the compulsion into something dark and sinister, with a still-unknown purpose. *Yes, but Hollin will be with me,* he thought. *To let me know if my decisions seem wrong or influenced by the Neddari spell.* He felt a little safer knowing that Hollin would be there to give him guidance and advice. In the end, perhaps, everything would turn out right after all.

The next morning Gerin stopped by the barracks where his soldiers were housed and told them they would be leaving the following day. A few wizards said hello as he returned to his rooms; he muttered a reply and continued onward, his eyes downcast as his shame burned hotly once again. *It doesn't matter,* he thought. *I can't help it. I need to get away from this place. Once I'm gone I won't be reminded of it all the time.* Or so he fervently hoped.

Hollin would not be returning with them right away. He had to make preparations to bring the books and artifacts he would need to train them, and he wanted to spend some time with the other apprentice wizards he would be leaving in Abaru's care. Those others would be fully trained wizards by the time he finished with Gerin and Reshel at Ailethon, and though he would be returning to Hethnost occasionally, as Warden of Apprentices he owed them some of his undivided attention before he left, since their studies had been eclipsed by the arrival of the amber wizard and the ensuing uproar over the sounding of the horn and news of the Neddari compulsion.

"I will follow you in three or four weeks," he said to Gerin in the dining hall. "I want to make sure I have everything I'll need. I've been having the archivists copy some spellbooks that I can't take because Abaru will need them for the other new wizards, but they aren't done yet." He chewed a crust of bread, which he washed down with a long gulp of beer. "Are you sure you won't reconsider and wait here until I'm ready? It won't be much longer. A month at the latest."

"I'm not going to wait. I'm already itching to be on the road. Another month will feel like an eternity."

"We do not usually let new wizards out of our care."

"You don't usually allow new wizards to be trained somewhere else, either."

"Don't be difficult, Gerin. I am looking out for your best interest. Reshel's, too. You should have someone with you, if only to ensure you don't inadvertently harm yourselves."

Gerin threw up his hands. "Oh, by the gods, Hollin, then come with us now and have the materials sent later. Or send someone else who can return here when you get to Ailethon. There are other solutions than having me wait here another month, which I am *not* going to do."

The skin around Hollin's eyes and mouth tightened a little. *I've made him mad,* thought Gerin. But he didn't care. He was sick of this place, and nothing Hollin could say would make him remain here a moment longer than he intended.

"I see I'm not going to dissuade you. All right. We'll do it your way. I'll come with you and have the things I need sent

later. I'll bring a few books that you can study on the way.
That way the journey will be at least somewhat productive."

He's really going to make me work on the road, thought
Gerin after Hollin had left. But he would be away from here,
and right now that was all that mattered.

On the day they were to leave, Gerin woke early and dressed
in his old clothes. He thought they would make him feel better, but they did not. Even retrieving Glaros from its storage
place did nothing to improve his mood. He felt as if he had
failed in this place, a deeply personal failure from which he
could never quite recover. *I wonder if I'll ever come back here.
Or, if I do, if I'll ever feel comfortable.*

Reshel and Hollin arrived as Gerin was finishing his breakfast. Balandrick stuck his head in the door and told him that
the soldiers were prepared to leave whenever he was ready.

Several wizards stopped by to wish Gerin and Reshel
well, including the Archmage, First Siege, and a few of the
Ministers and Wardens. The Archmage had especially warm
and kind words for Reshel, and laughed and joked with her
for several minutes, which seemed odd to Gerin; the Archmage seemed rather remote and distant to him, not the kind
of woman who would treat Reshel like a long-lost grand-
daughter. She was cooler to him, her good-bye more stiff
and formal. *Reshel must have impressed her.* He wondered if
his failure to resist the compulsion had anything to do with
her attitude, or the heated argument about where he was to
be trained; he felt a sudden pang of jealousy toward his sister, whose stay here had been untainted by scandal or dis-
agreement. But he quickly pushed it aside, knowing it was
unworthy of him as well as unfair.

The soldiers were at the stables when they arrived, their armor gleaming in the morning sun, waiting by their mounts.

Reshel swung up onto her horse. "Are you ready?"

He nodded and mounted Ranno. "Good-bye, Abaru. Good-
bye, Delarra," he said. "Take care of yourselves. I hope we
will meet again someday."

"So do I," said Abaru. "Perhaps we'll come visit you."

"You're always welcome at Ailethon." He kicked his heels into Ranno and started toward the gate.

Several times on the journey back, Gerin found himself amazed at how far he could see into the distance and how much he could discern in the darkness. When he stared at a tree, it seemed he could make out every crack and crevice in the bark, every vein etched into the smallest leaf even if he were yards away. At night the stars were vibrantly bright, and the darkness around their camp seemed filled with a faint luminescence.

True to his word, Hollin had them studying spells and practicing Osirin each night. Gerin had been allowed to bring along several books about Naragenth, which he examined carefully before he went to sleep for references to the Chamber of the Moon. So far he'd found nothing, but he did his best not to be discouraged. *It will probably take years to search through everything in the Varsae Sandrova that might mention the Chamber of the Moon. I have to be patient. I've already learned more about his library than anyone else for the past eighteen hundred years.* Still, it was hard not to be frustrated, especially when Naragenth had been moments from actually telling him the library's location.

Balandrick sat down near Reshel each night and talked to her about her magic or the Atreyano history she wanted to write. She laughed with him and touched his arm or leaned her head against his shoulder; a few times they even held hands in Gerin's view. It was growing serious, and he decided he had better start thinking of it that way as well. After all, Balandrick was the captain of his personal guard and would one day more than likely become commander of all the troops at Ailethon. He was also one of the few friends Gerin had. He would have to carefully consider how a relationship with his sister might affect his decisions concerning Balan. He did not think it would be a problem—not for him, at least, though he could not speak for his father—but it was also not something he could glibly brush aside or ignore.

Early one morning they came across the remains of a recently destroyed homestead. A column of smoke drifting into the blue sky a mile or so from the road had drawn them to investigate.

The main house and barn had been burned—most of the exterior walls still stood, but empty windows stared at them like gouged-out eyes, the stones above them blackened where smoke and fire had billowed upward. Charred timbers protruded from the open tops of the buildings like blackened bones. Some of the timbers were still hot, the cracked wood smoldering with an angry red heat.

The soldiers drew their weapons and spread out across the homestead. Balandrick and two of the men remained with Gerin and Reshel to protect them. Gerin thought it ironic— he and Reshel were far more dangerous than all of the soldiers combined could ever hope to be—but he was certainly not going to interfere with their sworn duty to protect them.

Slaughtered animals, some killed by bowshot and others hacked with knives, littered the fenced yard around the barn. Gerin could see the burned remains of a few unfortunate animals trapped in their stalls when the fire had been set.

They found the family around the back of the main house. A man, his wife, three children, and two hired hands. At least that was their guess as to their identities and relationships. Their hands were tied behind their backs and their throats had been slit. Pools of blood had soaked into the grass beneath the bodies. Apparently they had all been forced to kneel before they were killed. Their skin had turned black and their bodies had swelled as they'd decomposed, bloating with the gases of death; they looked ready to rupture at the slightest touch.

"Who would do such a thing?" Reshel raged as she stared at the bodies. She covered her mouth and nose with a kerchief; the stench of rotting flesh was overpowering and made her eyes water. "These were children, by the gods! Who could do such a thing to *children*?" Tears of helpless anger appeared in her eyes.

"There is nothing a man will not do to others if he feels the need," Gerin said quietly. "Some don't even need a reason. Some are just evil. That's why we have laws to punish them."

"Whoever did this should pay with their lives. This is an abomination!"

He put his hands on her shoulders. "We can't undo what was done here. We can only hope that one day the men who did this will be brought to justice." He looked down at the bloated corpses. "The only thing we can do now is give them a proper burial."

One of the soldiers approached them. "No one else is here, my lord. Whoever did this is gone."

Reshel put her head against Gerin's chest and began to cry.

The soldiers dug graves with shovels they had brought for digging fire pits; it took them most of the day to finish the work, and it was late when the last of the bodies were buried. Reshel stared at the plots of raw earth with haunted eyes. Balandrick put his arm across her shoulders, and she leaned against him for comfort.

"Promise me that if we ever find who did this, you won't let them get away," she said to Gerin. "Promise me you'll punish them."

"I promise. If we find who did this, they'll pay with their lives." He thought about the terror the family must have felt as they were bound and told to kneel, how the mother and father must have pleaded for the lives of their children. His teeth clenched as he wondered who had been killed first. *If we find the men who did this, I will give no thought to killing them. It is what they deserve.*

Two nights later they came across a straggling woods along the northern side of the road. The trees opened into a small glade, where they stopped to make camp.

Gerin slept fitfully, tossing restlessly beneath his blanket. Sometime during the night he fell into a deep sleep, only to be awakened by a hand upon his shoulder. He opened his eyes and in the dim starlight saw Balandrick crouched over him.

"My lord, there are men upon the road," he whispered. "They're armed and coming from the south. They don't appear to be regular soldiers."

Gerin sat up and wiped his eyes. "Do they know we're here?"

Balandrick shook his head. "I don't think so, but they may see where we left the road. The grass is tall and our path might be visible even in the darkness." He glanced up at the nearly full moon.

"How many?"

"They ride close together and it's hard to be certain, but no more than twenty."

The other soldiers were already awake, standing with their weapons drawn. Gerin ordered Arek Gemmos and Bren Thorides, the two archers in their small company, to conceal themselves in the trees on opposite sides of the glade with their bows ready. Then he commanded two others to wake Reshel and take her to the far end of the glade, well out of sight. Hollin stood with him, oddly quiet, watching Gerin as he issued his orders.

Another soldier rushed into the glade from the direction of the road. "My lord, they're coming this way."

It was too late to hide the horses picketed near the trees, and there was no other easy exit from the glade. They would make far too much noise in their haste to escape if they tried to force their way through the dense underbrush beneath the trees. They could not run and could not hide. All they could do was confront them when they entered and hope for the best. *It may be that they're only travelers like ourselves,* he thought. *It could be the caravan of a merchant, traveling with an armed escort.* But a merchant would not be traveling in the dead of night, and there was precious little in these lands that would require an escort of a score of armed men.

"Were there any bowmen among them?"

"I didn't see any, my lord. They looked mostly to be carrying swords."

"Be ready with your weapons," he said as he drew Glaros. Balandrick stood on his right, sword in hand, as still as a statue except for his right arm, which he rolled at the shoulder to loosen the muscles. Gerin did one of the exercises Hollin had taught him to calm his body and felt himself begin to relax. He expected he would be using his magic this night.

In the distance through the trees he saw three torches flare to life. *They don't know we're here.*

The newcomers soon reached the glade. Gerin could hear several of them speaking quietly. He counted seventeen men riding single file down the winding path through the trees.

The first three men in line entered the glade. Gerin cleared his throat and said, "Good evening to you, gentlemen. I trust your journey is going well?"

His reply was the ringing sound of steel as the men drew their swords. They stopped moving—those in the rear did not attempt to move off the path, as Gerin feared they might. Just as well. It made it easier for him to know where all of them were.

"Who's there?" demanded one of the men. He held out his hand to shield his eyes from the light of the torch carried by the man next to him. Gerin could see the man squinting in his direction.

"Just travelers," said Gerin. "We want no trouble from you."

"Well, it's a bit late for *that*," said the man, who could now see Gerin and the men with him. "This is *our* place, and we don't take kindly to anyone trespassin'." He spurred his horse forward a few steps and gestured for his men to move up behind him. As they entered the glade they spread out around their leader. Gerin could see they were all roughly dressed, their clothes worn and tattered and stained from travel. Their weapons had seen better days. The blades were nicked and dull, the scabbards crusted with dirt and rust. *Scavenged blades,* he thought. *Or stolen.*

"I said we want no quarrel," said Gerin. "If you claim this place as your own—though I see no evidence of that—and you don't wish the company of fellow travelers, we'll be on our way."

Gerin saw the man's eyes swing for an instant to the horses picketed in the glade. *He knows there are more of us,* Gerin thought. He drew magic and spoke quietly in Osirin, creating a Warding between himself and the strangers; it was the first time he had ever made one, and he was pleased and relieved when he saw it take shape. Beside him, Hollin nodded once approvingly. The transparent oval disk hovered in the air, rippling lightly like an upright sheet of water, invisible to everyone except Reshel and the wizard. He whispered another command—the disk widened to protect Balandrick as well, forming a wide, curved shield in front of them. The spell was taxing, and he found he had to concentrate hard to keep it from collapsing.

Hollin created his own Warding, the indistinct edge of his barrier nearly touching Gerin's.

"Don't rush forward," Gerin whispered to Balandrick, "or you'll run into a Warding. Just hold your place." Balandrick nodded, never taking his eyes from the strangers.

"The only place you're goin' is to Shayphim," growled the man. He jabbed his sword toward Gerin and shouted, "Take them!"

Gerin heard a thrumming sound from the trees behind him and saw arrows pierce two of the bandits with a wet thud, driving them backward off their horses.

"In the trees, in the trees!" shouted the leader. Before he finished speaking, two more of his men were down; one with a clothyard shaft in the eye, the other hit in the base of his throat. Five or six of the men, obviously not used to such a rapid counterattack from their intended victims, faltered and broke ranks as some of the others tried to turn toward the edges of the glade where the bowmen were hidden, only to smash into their unprepared companions. Three of the horses were knocked on their sides, crushing their riders beneath them. *Very poorly trained,* Gerin observed with a strange sense of detachment brought on by the calming exercise. *If they were trained at all.*

Hollin flicked his fingers left and right; two of the men cried out in fear and surprise as their weapons flew out of their hands. One of them dropped to his knees and made the sign to ward off evil.

Balandrick had stepped in front of Gerin to protect him, ready to cut down anyone who came at them. Looking past him, Gerin moved to the left, then carefully spoke several Osirin words. *No more strength than necessary,* he reminded himself. *I can't afford to wear myself out before this is over.*

He stretched out his arm toward the leader and felt magic leap from his fingers, the spell taking shape as he continued to speak. His Warding trembled as he lost some of his concentration, rippling like a bed linen caught in a strong wind. It was difficult for him to control two spells at once, even more so than the Baryashin spell had been, which surprised him. He gritted his teeth, focused all his attention on the spells, and managed to maintain them both, at least for the moment.

Gerin turned his hand. The man's arms snapped against his sides as the Binding enveloped him in its power. He let out a shout of pain and his eyes went wide as he struggled against the invisible force.

"Call off your men or I'll crush you like an egg," said Gerin. For emphasis he closed his fingers a little and the leader shrieked in pain.

"Back off, back off!" the man shouted. "Stop the attack!" One of his men who was slow to obey fell with an arrow jutting from his chest. Another was run through by one of Gerin's soldiers. The remainder had fallen back toward their leader, eyeing him warily, wondering why he had called them off.

"I've little use for bandits and highwaymen," said Gerin.

"Let go of me!" said the leader. "What kind of deviltry is this?"

"The kind you should be more respectful of."

Hollin had once again clasped his hands behind his back and was standing very still, watching Gerin intently. *Is he judging me?* Gerin wondered. *Seeing how well I use my magic under pressure?*

"What's goin' on here, Felain?" asked one of the men. "Why'd you tell us to stop? And what deviltry are you talkin' about? I don't see no kind of deviltry here."

"I can't move, you blind fool!" said Felain. Foamy blood bubbled at his lips.

"Deviltry or no, there's still more of us than them," said the man. "Once we take those bastards with the bows, the rest'll fall nice and pretty, just like them folk back on that farm."

Reshel screamed behind Gerin, a shout given power by the magic flowing through her. *"Murderers!"* She ran into the glade, flanked by the soldiers who were moving frantically to protect her. A moment later her aura burst to life, cloaking her in golden fire; the soldiers threw up their hands and stepped away from her. Harsh, flickering light filled the glade and some of the bandits cried out in fear.

"How could you do such a thing to children?"

Reshel stretched out her hand and released a blazing shaft of fire that drilled a hole through the chest of the man who had bragged of their crime. He fell from his horse, already dead, greasy black smoke rising from the ruin of his torso.

The other bandits were driven into a frenzy. Some tried to escape the glade. Others rushed Gerin and his men, shouting with their swords raised high above their heads. One man broke his horse's neck when it crashed headlong into the Warding, the man thrown from the saddle and landing hard on the ground. Gerin was surprised that he felt only a gentle shudder through his power when the horse slammed into the spell, a kind of vibration like a plucked harp string; he'd expected to be pushed back from the force of the impact. But the spell apparently did not yield to force the way a normal barrier did, and he remained unmoved.

Balandrick felt his way around the edge of the Warding with the point of his sword and reached the fallen man before he could get up. With one thrust, he put his blade through the man's throat.

Reshel was moving across the glade, golden fire shooting from her hand, killing those who were trying to flee. Some of the lances of fire missed their targets and sliced through tree trunks and branches with a hot, sizzling sound that reminded Gerin of frying bacon. He worried that she would ignite fires that would burn out of control, but her magic lanced through the wood so quickly that it did not have time to catch fire.

Meanwhile, the archers continued to shoot, their arrows whistling through the glade and thudding into flesh with deadly precision. Two slammed into the Wardings and splintered in midair, the broken shafts spinning crazily as they tumbled to the ground. Gerin wondered what the men who could not see the Wardings must be thinking when they saw the arrows suddenly shatter in empty air.

Hollin killed two men with searing threads of unshaped magic that darted from his hand almost too fast for Gerin to see. He had far more skill than Reshel; both lances of fire struck true, piercing the men through their breastbones. Hollin had moved little more than his wrist and eyes—an impressive display of conserving both his magic and the effort needed to use it.

All of this happened in the span of a few breaths. Then Gerin clenched his hand, and the Binding tightened and crushed Felain. His arms shattered and smashed inward. Gerin could hear his ribs and spine snapping. A gout of blood jetted from his mouth, but he was already dead. Gerin released the spell, his hand falling to his side.

Then it was over. All of the bandits were dead. Some of the horses had fled the glade in terror after their riders were killed. Other horses were dead, and several had broken their legs in falls and struggled on the ground in torment. Gerin's men quickly put them down.

Their own horses were thrashing in terror against their pickets, maddened by the battle and the stench of blood. Some of his men moved to calm them. *Thank the gods that they didn't break their pickets or we'd be walking the rest of the way to Naevos,* he thought.

Two of the remaining torches cast a paltry, flickering light across the glade. Reshel's aura had gone out. The two archers emerged from their hiding places among the trees and picked up the torches from the ground before they could start a fire.

One of the soldiers, a thick-limbed man named Ellos Ivraulkin, had a deep gash on his upper arm where a bandit's blade had slipped between the seams in his armor. The rest were unharmed.

Gerin went to Reshel. She was wandering among the dead men, staring at them with her hands clenched at her sides. There was an expression of unspeakable anger on her face, and a fire of rage and hatred in her eyes.

"I know what you're going to tell me," she said. She turned her gaze back toward the dead men. "What I did was reckless and foolish. But these are the men who slit the throats of those women and children." He could see her pulse throbbing angrily in her temples. "You told me if we ever found them, they would pay with their lives. And they have." She looked at him again, her face defiant, challenging him to contradict her.

He was in no mood to argue. "They deserved to die for what they did. And we probably would've had to kill them anyway in order to leave here with our lives. But listen to me, Reshel: you've killed today for the first time. And though they earned their deaths with their murders and threats to us, don't take joy in the killing. It was necessary and just, but it's not something we should ever take pleasure in."

"Killing them does not bring back those who died at their hands. This is justice, nothing more. And I find no joy in it. Only an end to my hatred, but not to my sorrow."

17

The day after the attack, Hollin spoke to Gerin about how he'd fought with magic. "Bindings and Wardings are contradictory spells, which is why you had trouble casting both at once," he said. "One of the things I will teach you is how to know which spells work better with others, and which work at counterpurposes."

"The Binding seemed to do the trick all right," Gerin said defensively.

"And you did well in holding both together for as long as you did. But you were fortunate that the spells did not mingle; if that had happened, they might have disrupted one another, collapsing both with a sudden backflow of magic. You weren't using enough power to have that backflow harm you seriously, but it would probably have stunned you and left you defenseless.

"I'll show you how to recognize the different kinds of magic that spells use. It's one of those things you have to experience to understand. It's a little like cooking and knowing which ingredients work best with others; you can be told a little of what to look for, but mostly it's just doing it and seeing what tastes best."

"You mean spells have flavors?"

"Not as such, no. But there are subtle differences between spells that you'll come to recognize." He stood and stretched.

"Enough of this for now. We're both tired and need to rest."
He turned to go, then paused. "You did well yesterday. Both
as a leader of your men and as a wizard."

Gerin settled down to sleep, a grin on his face, pleased by
the wizard's compliment. *I guess he really was judging me.*

It was nearly dark when they finally reached Ailethon. The
sight made Gerin's heart leap with joy. *Home at last,* he
thought as they rode up Ireon's Hill. He could see lamps within
some of the windows of the keep and could almost believe his
failure at Hethnost was nothing more than a bad dream.

The guards at the gate sent word to Matren that they had
arrived. "Are you well, my lord?" asked one of the men.

"Fine. Just tired."

Matren met them in the entrance hall of the keep. "My lord,
it's good to see you," he said. "How was your stay among the
wizards?"

"It's a long story, Matren," he said. "Right now I'm tired
and would like something to eat. Is there anything that needs
my immediate attention?"

"No, my lord. Things have been quiet in your absence." He
leaned closer and lowered his voice to a whisper. "My lord,
are you . . . I mean to say, have you and Reshel . . . *changed*?"

Gerin managed a smile. "Of course. Can't you tell by my
skin and eyes?"

Matren peered at him closely. "Indeed. Forgive me, the
light in here is dim. You will have to tell me all about it, my
lord."

"And I will. Just let me get something to eat first."

On their way to the dining hall Matren told him that a
gang of cutpurses had wrought havoc at the markets in
Padesh and Marren's Ferry. The constables in the latter town
had finally captured them during a bloody fight in which two
of the cutpurses were killed. The rest had been hanged from
the scaffolding outside the east gate of Padesh, where they'd
remained for a week before being cut down and buried in the
criminals' yard.

One of the soldiers of the keep had lost part of his hand while drunkenly sparring with a real sword instead of a practice blade. "I thought Master Helgrim would cut his other hand off for acting such a fool," Matren said. "He was *furious.*" He described how Helgrim had made the man carry the severed part of his hand for a week, pierced by a barbed hook and hung from his belt, as a reminder of why drinking and weapons did not mix. Gerin laughed so hard at this image that he began to cough. "Oh my, Matren, I needed that."

Reshel and Claressa were already in the hall, seated as far from each other as physically possible. Master Aslon shuffled in while Gerin was taking a seat. Servants were already moving through the room with flagons of wine and water and plates of cheese and hard bread. Gerin drank some wine and began to chew on a piece of crust.

"Well?" said Claressa. "We didn't come here to watch you eat. Tell us what it was like. I can see it's done wonders for your complexions." Reshel glared at her but said nothing.

Gerin described the fortress and their training but made no mention of the Neddari compulsion or his search for forbidden spells. He and Reshel took turns telling them about the Ritual of Awakening and how each of them dealt with the heightened senses that had followed. Reshel made several sparks of magefire dart about the room like crazed fireflies. For a few moments they hovered above the table, then she grinned and bit one of her knuckles, sending them flying precariously close to Claressa's head, who flinched and demanded in an angry voice that she stop. Hollin watched the exchange with a gleam of amusement in his eyes but made no move to intervene.

After the magefire vanished, Claressa huffed and leaned over the table, pointing a rigid finger at Gerin and Reshel in turn. "There's more to your story than what you've told us. You've been dancing around something and giving each other odd looks. What is it? Are you hiding something?"

My formidable sister, thought Gerin. *She misses nothing.*

"You're right," he said. "There's quite a bit more. Do you remember when I was attacked by the Neddari?"

"Yes, my lord," said Matren. "A dark day. We were fortunate indeed that you were not seriously hurt."

"Hollin found a spell that the Neddari had placed inside me, but he didn't know what it was for and he couldn't remove it. At Hethnost we found out its purpose."

Master Aslon's mouth fell open in alarm. "Did it harm you?"

"Not physically, no. But to fully explain this, I first need to tell you about Naragenth and his library." He sketched out the story of the first amber wizard and the Varsae Estrikavis, and how he could not bear the thought that such a fabulous treasure could remain lost forever.

"Reshel said something when we were standing in the graveyard of Hethnost that sparked an idea." Now that he had begun to speak of it, the words poured from him like a flood. He talked for a long time. Reshel and Hollin added a few key points of what happened at Hethnost when Gerin blew the horn, but for the most part he was the one who told the tale.

"So you still have no idea why the Neddari did this, my lord?" asked Matren.

"We know what he *said* to me," said Gerin. "That this would bring about the return of their Slain God. We just don't know what that means."

"It all sounds so fantastic," said Matren. "Like something from a story of old."

"Let's hope things are a little more mundane for a while," said Gerin. "But enough about this. What's done is done. Matren's told me a little of what's happened while we were away. Does anyone else have anything to add?"

They'd received a message from Therain that he'd arrived at Agdenor and was settling in, but other than that, little had occurred in their absence. "The Neddari have been relatively quiet along the border, to everyone's relief," said Matren.

"Let's hope it remains that way." Gerin looked around the table until he met Reshel's gaze.

"Shall I tell them?" she asked.

He knew exactly what she was talking about. "It's entirely up to you."

"Tell us what?" asked Master Aslon.

"That I killed five men on the road home."

"What?" Everyone in the room other than Gerin and Hollin let out the same cry.

"You can't be serious, my lady," said Matren.

"I'm afraid she is," said Gerin.

Reshel told them about finding the bodies and the ambush in the glade. "Something in me went mad when I heard them admit what they'd done. I don't understand that kind of cruelty, and I hope I never will. How could someone be so casual about murder?"

"Your stay with the wizards was more surprising than I could have imagined," said Master Aslon after a time. "Most incredible."

"I'm sure you can understand that we're tired," said Gerin as he rose from the table. "I need some sleep. If you'll excuse me."

Claressa left with him and stopped him in the corridor with a brief tug on his arm. "Is Reshel all right? The thought of her actually *killing* is almost inconceivable. I can only imagine what it's doing to her."

Gerin paused a moment before responding, surprised that Claressa was showing concern for her sister. *Not that she bothered to ask how I am,* he thought. Well, he couldn't expect miracles. "I think she'll be fine. It was hard for her to see the bodies and know what had been done to them. How they'd died. It was hard for all of us. She's upset, of course, but I think she's handling it well. And I don't think she has any qualms or guilt about what she did. She knows those men got exactly what they deserved."

"Who would have thought. Our little sister . . ." She shook her head in amazement.

"Makes you wonder what else she has in store for us, doesn't it?"

Two days later a pigeon arrived in the aviary of the Tirthaig, the vast royal palace of Almaris. Within the hour a messenger from the Master of Birds knocked on Abran's study door and handed the king a small sealed cylinder. Abran looked it over as he returned to his desk. *A message from Gerin,* he thought as he looked at the seal.

Not for the first time, he felt a pang of envy that his son would enjoy power and abilities almost beyond his own understanding. He'd always admired his eldest son's talents— he saw them as a positive reflection of himself, an affirmation of his own strength that he could sire such a worthy child. But the fact that Gerin was a wizard was both perplexing and disturbing. He had no idea how magic would affect his son, or how his powers and long life would be viewed by the other nobles. Or how Reshel's husband—whoever it turned out to be—would react once he found out that she, too, was a wizard. He did not like uncertainties or things beyond his control. It grated on him—he found it almost offensive that he was forever shut out of comprehending, let alone sharing, such wondrous gifts—but there was little to be done about it.

He sighed and looked once more at the sealed message. He knew his son and daughter had left for Hethnost weeks ago to have their powers Awakened, and expected this message to contain news of the event. Which it did, but there was more as well. Abran's eyes widened as he read Gerin's abbreviated account of the compulsion and calling of Naragenth.

> *I know this news is shocking. It was just as shocking to me to discover I could be manipulated in such a way by the Neddari. Yet, what's done is done, and there is no response we can make. As much as I would like to capture the* kamichi *who placed the compulsion in me and punish him for it—as well as interrogate him about his motives—I know there is no practical way to do this. It is something I must live with and try to forget, as Balandrick has wisely advised me. It will not be easy, but it's something I must do.*
>
> *There is one more thing.*

Before he vanished, Naragenth's spirit told me the Varsae Estrikavis was hidden in a place called the Chamber of the Moon. The wizards have never heard of this but are looking for records of it in their own library. I would ask that you begin your own search through the archives of the Tirthaig to see if there is anything there that may shed light on this. As Almaris was Naragenth's capital city, it may be we have knowledge of the Chamber of the Moon hidden in some forgotten storeroom that the wizards do not.

Abran read the letter once more, then summoned a servant. "Yes, Your Majesty?" said the man with a bow.

"Bring the chief archivist to me," he commanded. "I have an important task for him." The servant bowed again and left the room. Abran wondered to what advantage he could maneuver a find of such magnitude. Would it give him leverage with the wizards themselves? Could he request that they quietly help his kingdom in ways yet to be determined, in exchange for access to this lost library? It would be interesting to find out.

But first they had to locate it.

It might also give him leverage with Gerin. In truth, he feared what his son was becoming: a being of power over whom he had no control. If he could somehow use Naragenth's library to bring his son to heel—should that prove necessary—so much the better.

PART TWO

The War Storm

18

Asleep in his chambers in the keep of Agdenor, Therain dreamed.

He stood in a dark place, enveloped in a swirling gray fog. He did not know where he was, whether indoors or out; he saw no walls or floor, no arches or doorways, no grass or trees or landscape of any kind. The mist was the only thing visible, illuminated from some diffuse source deep within its heart, beyond the range of his sight.

He heard a deep drumming noise, the sound of mountains falling into ruin. He wanted to run, but his body would not obey him and he remained rooted in place, unable even to close his eyes when he realized the thunderous noise was caused by the footfalls of something immense coming toward him.

He looked up and saw a vast shadowy figure moving through the mist. It wore a crown upon its head, and its eyes glowed with a pale silvery light. Its face was shrouded by both the mist and darkness. He feared that the mist would lift and his eyes would fall on its dreadful countenance, and that the sight would destroy him in an instant, searing away his flesh and leaving his soul naked before its power. For surely this must be a god that stood before him, this majestic figure of power and dread.

He sensed a terrible malice emanating from it, nearly

overpowering in its intensity, so strong it took the breath from Therain's lungs.

"I am Asankaru, the Storm King," said the figure in a voice so deep that Therain felt as though his bones were in the throes of some inner earthquake. "You are a herald of my coming. I have returned from death so that the truth of the past shall finally be known. Strike down my enemies and you will be rewarded with life beyond this life. Kill them all. That is my command to you. Kill them all."

Therain sensed a hand reaching down toward him, ready to crush him to dust if he disobeyed. He would do anything, *anything,* to please the god that stood before him. He would—

There was a hand on his shoulder, shaking him gently. Therain came awake suddenly.

Terror flooded through him. He shoved the hand from his shoulder and reached for the long knife he'd been keeping by his bed since the murders had started. He felt the cool hilt beneath his fingers and grasped it firmly, its weight and balance comforting in his hand, then swung the blade wildly through the air as he sat up in his bed. He needed to kill, it didn't matter who; all that mattered was that he obey Asankaru.

"My lord, stop!"

Therain saw a man leap away from him, a shuttered lamp in his hand. He recognized the voice, and some of the rage and terror that filled him drained away. He lowered the knife but did not release it. His breathing was labored, his skin covered in a glistening sheen of sweat.

"My lord, please!" The man was Elmen Hiremar, the captain of Therain's personal guard. "You must have been dreaming."

Therain tried to catch his breath. "I'm sorry, Captain. Yes, I had a dream. It was terrible. These damn Heralds of Truth are haunting me even in my sleep." He placed the knife back on the table and wiped his face with his sleeve. "What's happened? Why are you here?"

"We've captured one of the Heralds, my lord. He killed a man, one of our guards, but we got this one alive."

Therain sat up straighter. "Where is he?"

"In the dungeons, my lord."

Therain rose from the bed and began to dress. The fire in the hearth had burned low, its thinning heat retreating against the chill of the room.

He looked past the captain to the window on the far wall. Snow was falling outside, as it had been for most of the day, thick wet flakes already several inches deep on the castle grounds. The first snow of the year had come earlier than was usual in these lands. It would not last, though. It was still too early in the season. The past week had been warm for late December, and in places the grass had still been clinging to green when the snow began to fall. He usually enjoyed the snow, the silence it brought with it, the sense of stillness and peace. But not this night. First his nightmare, and now this news that the Heralds of Truth had murdered again.

Snow was melting on the shoulders of Elmen's heavy cloak. He unshuttered his lamp and placed it on Therain's reading table. The captain's breastplate was visible where his cloak parted down the center; the steel gleamed in the lamplight, as if his heart were shining through his chest, a glowing core of righteousness. "He's been chained to the wall and thoroughly searched for concealed weapons."

"The dead man?"

"Bann Olgraibin, m'lord. A guard of the North Tower. His throat was slit."

"That makes nine dead in the past two weeks alone," said Therain as he pulled on his boots. The captain knew this, of course, but saying it allowed Therain to focus his anger. "Take me to him."

"Yes, m'lord."

Therain followed the captain down from the East Tower, where he kept his study and bedchamber. The dungeons were buried beneath the Thorn, as the keep of Castle Agdenor was named, deep in the bedrock of Henly's Hill. The killer had been placed in a cell away from others, in a section that had not been occupied for many years. The passageways were low and narrow. Captain Hiremar held his lamp high to light their way through the oppressive darkness.

They stopped at a cell with two guards stationed at a door pierced by two narrow slots with shutters that could be drawn back from the outside—one head high for viewing prisoners within, the other near the floor for sliding in food.

"Anything to report?" asked Captain Hiremar.

"No, sir. Been quiet since we put him in here. Hello, m'lord," he said with a nod to Therain.

"Do we know his name or where he came from?"

"One of the men who helped to capture him knew the man, m'lord," said Captain Hiremar. "That's how we found out something was wrong. A night watchman saw him in the North Tower and knew he wasn't supposed to be there. When the watchman confronted him, the man tried to jump him, but the watchman was able to knock him down and hold him until help arrived. It was too late for Olgraibin by then, though."

"His name?" He gestured toward the cell.

"Sedros Esedraen. A cobbler from Rengel. We're not sure yet how he gained entry to the castle or how long he's been here. I sent some men to the town to see if he killed anyone there before he came to the castle."

Therain stared hard at his captain. "He had help from the inside, didn't he?"

The captain frowned. "I can't say for certain, m'lord, but that is one explanation. I hate to think that these murdering Heralds've infiltrated the castle guard, but I can't rule it out. I've already sequestered all the guards of the gates for questioning. If someone on the inside was helping Esedraen, we'll find him."

Therain spoke to one of the guards at the cell. "Open this door. I want a word with the prisoner."

The man unlocked the door with a large key and swung it open on creaking hinges. Captain Hiremar entered first. The lamp cast a weak light about the small cell, its faintness swallowed by the dark brick and crumbling mortar.

Sedros Esedraen was against the wall opposite the door, hanging from manacles bolted into the brick. He appeared to be unconscious, and rivulets of blood trickled down his arms where the manacles had bitten into his wrists. His dark hair was matted to his head with sweat and blood; his clothes were grimy and torn. A long gash on his left thigh had been hastily bandaged to prevent him from bleeding to death.

"Wake him," said Therain to the guard.

"Aye, my lord." The guard gripped Esedraen's hair with his gauntlet and pulled up his head. Esedraen's mouth gaped open; his eyes rolled up into his head. His skin was sallow, and blood had run from a deep cut on his scalp and dried upon his face.

"Wake up, ya stinkin' murderin' bastard," said the guard. He slapped him hard across the face with his other gauntlet. "The lord o' the castle is here t'see ya."

Esedraen groaned and came awake. His eyes rolled around for a few seconds, trying to focus and comprehend where he was. The guard pulled him up by his hair until his feet were solidly under him.

"I know who you are, Sedros Esedraen," said Therain. "I am Prince Therain Atreyano, Duke of Agdenor and Lord and Warden of these lands. You murdered one of my men earlier tonight." Therain took a step closer to the man. "Before you were captured, you shouted that you were a Herald of Truth. Tell me what that means."

Esedraen straightened. To Therain's surprise, the man grinned, exposing teeth slick with dark blood. He spat a thick glob of bloody phlegm onto the floor. The guard slapped him again. His head rocked backward and cracked into the wall.

"Enough," said Therain, holding out his hand. "I don't want him beaten senseless before he answers my questions."

"I care nothing for your rank or title," Esedraen said in a hoarse voice. "They mean nothing to my master. He is coming, Duke of Agdenor. And when he arrives, you will rue the day you were born."

"And who is your master? Let him show himself to me. I fear no vagabond of the wild who fancies himself a king or

lord. If he has courage enough to show himself rather than
send flea-bitten riffraff to commit his senseless murders, he'll
quickly find himself without a head to set his crown upon."

Esedraen barked a short laugh. "You cannot harm the
Storm King. *He is already dead.* Asankaru walks in our
dreams, and soon will walk in yours. He's conquered death.
We who serve him faithfully will be rewarded with eternal
life. He'll raise us from our graves as he himself has risen."

Therain's legs weakened, but he tried to show no outward
sign of his distress. *By the gods, Asankaru the Storm King!
The name spoken to me in my dream.* How was this possible?
How could he have had the same dream as this murderer?
He had not heard that name or title before tonight.

He cleared his throat to cover his surprise as he regained
his composure. "That will be put to the test, Esedraen. Once
you've told us all we need to know, your head will be severed
from your shoulders and staked above the gate of the castle.
We'll see if your Storm King can reclaim you from Bellon's
embrace after that." He turned away from the prisoner.
"Captain, I want to know how he got into the castle and who
helped him. Use any means necessary to get him to talk. If
there are traitors among our men, I'll have them flushed
out." Therain disliked torture, but saw little recourse. He
doubted Esedraen would talk without being compelled.
Whether he truly fears his own death or not doesn't matter,
he thought as he left the cell. *All men can be broken while
they live.* He did not want any more innocent men or women
to die at the hands of these bloodthirsty Heralds, and if that
meant torturing Esedraen, so be it.

"I need to speak to my counselors immediately," said
Therain to Elmen as they made their way from the dungeons. "I have questions that need answers."

"Aye, my lord. I'll have them brought at once."

Therain returned to his study and awaited his counselors.
The snow had stopped falling. The clouds had parted and the
light of the moon shimmered like quicksilver on the waters

of the rivers where the Azren flowed at nearly a right angle into the Samaro. He could just barely make out the Angle far below him, the small triangle of grassy land whose northern and eastern sides were formed from the confluence of the two rivers. The Angle's third boundary ended at the foot of Henly's Hill, whose eastern side swung in a wide arc between the rivers. That face of the hill was a sheer wall of rock and dirt that bristled with thorns, thistles, and patches of briers.

He'd been at Agdenor only a few months, barely enough time to get used to the place, and now this. When the murders first began, he had suspected Count Sevreas, the previous master of Agdenor, of plotting to destabilize his rule. The gods knew he had enough trouble as it was. Sevreas had bribed many of his vassals to keep them quiet about his illegal activities—mostly smuggling, though he was rumored to have been behind several assassinations—and with Sevreas's departure, those payments had stopped. Even if the count were not behind the murders, Therain did not discount the possibility that some disgruntled vassal was seeking revenge. He'd not yet gained the respect of many of his lords, who referred to him behind his back as "the lord whelp." His apparent inability to stop these murders had not helped, either. *I'm sure Gerin doesn't have this problem with his vassals.*

It was soon obvious, however, that these murders were not a conspiracy against him. The killers all left messages that referred to the "Heralds of Truth," though until tonight no one had known what that meant. Three times the killers had been cornered before they could escape, but they had slain themselves rather than be captured, again with cries of being Heralds of Truth.

Did they all have the dream I had? he wondered. *Is that what's driving them to kill?*

His two counselors arrived together. "There's been another murder tonight by the Heralds of Truth," said Therain as they seated themselves at the round table near the fire. "I spoke with the murderer. Right now Captain Hiremar is questioning him. I want your opinions of what he told me." He told them who Esedraen was and the captain's belief that he had help in entering the castle. Then he recounted Esedraen's words about the Storm King.

Velarien Harres, the castellan of the castle, shifted uncomfortably in his seat. "My lord, I . . . this is very strange. I hardly know what to make of it." He tugged at his tunic and ran his hand along his graying beard. A wisp of a man approaching his fiftieth year, Velarien had been a minor member of the household staff under Sevreas. He'd loathed the count's corruption and was one of the men who secretly funneled evidence against the count to Therain's father. When Sevreas had been relocated, along with the previous castellan of Agdenor, Therain rewarded Velarien by promoting him to governor of the castle.

"Out with it, Velarien," said Wilfros Demaru. "You look as if a mouse ran up your leg." A native of Calad-Ethil, Wilfros's broad, flat-nosed face was dark and leathery, with jowly cheeks that sagged into a thick, flabby neck. He was a company captain who had also refused to tolerate the blatant dishonesty of Sevreas's rule. He disobeyed a direct order to murder a town mayor and had been in the dungeons awaiting execution when Therain arrived. Therain had spoken to him personally after hearing the reason for his imprisonment and was so impressed that he created a second counselor position specifically for him. Wilfros was a man who gave his opinion on matters bluntly; he was not one to be bothered attempting to make his speech more palatable to his audience. Despite his rough edges, Therain liked him; Velarien would tell him how things were, not what he thought Therain wanted to hear. He was also surprisingly well-connected and informed, and had confirmed, to Therain's jaw-clenching consternation, that several vassals were calling Therain "the lord whelp."

Velarien looked distressed. "My lord, the past three nights I've dreamed of a . . . figure, a king. They were terrible dreams. Nightmares, really."

"Are you saying *you've* dreamed of the Storm King?" said Wilfros.

"I'm saying no such thing. I really don't know what to make of it."

Therain's skin went cold. "Describe your dream for us."

"There's not much to it, my lord. In my dream I saw a shadowy figure in a gray mist. He was wearing a crown, and his eyes glowed with a silver light, though I couldn't see his face because of the mist. There was a sense that he wanted something from me, but I didn't know what it was. I could feel a terrible hatred coming from him, almost overpowering in its intensity. Then he said, 'I am Asankaru, the Storm King. You are a herald of my coming. I have returned from death so that the truth of the past shall finally be known. Strike down my enemies and you will be rewarded with life beyond this life.' Then he commanded me to kill everyone." He paused, as if unsure whether to continue. "The most frightening part is that while I was listening to him, I *wanted* to kill. I felt as if some terrible injustice had been done to me, and that everyone around me deserved to die for it. The feeling was very strong."

"That's all?"

"Yes, my lord."

"And you say you've had this dream three times? Was it the same each time?"

"Yes, my lord, the same. They did not fade upon my waking, as most of my dreams do."

"I had that exact dream earlier this night. *Exactly* the same."

Wilfros made a snort of derision. "Please, my lord—"

"I'm telling you that I had this very dream. Elmen woke me from it and very nearly ended up with my knife in him for his trouble. I felt an uncontrollable desire to lash out at anyone simply because the Storm King commanded it."

"Then we must assume this Storm King is real," said Velarien. "And that he is driving these Heralds to commit murder in his name."

"Such a thing does not seem possible," Wilfros said.

"I would not have thought so either, but these dreams are no coincidence," Therain replied. "It doesn't matter whether this creature is truly a spirit returned from the dead, as it claims. The only certainty we know is that there's some man or creature who's entering dreams and causing people to kill."

"How could a man enter the dreams of another?" asked Velarien.

"Magic," said Therain. "I can think of no other explanation. I'll send word to my brother in the morning. Perhaps he or the wizard training him can provide some guidance."

"Let us hope for our sake that they can."

"Yes," said Wilfros. "Otherwise I fear we will be left powerless against this enemy."

Therain managed to get a few hours of sleep after his counselors departed. He woke early, weary and still troubled by the revelations of the night, and was buckling his belt when there was a knock at the door. Captain Hiremar waited outside with two other guards. The captain looked both anguished and angry.

"What is it, Captain?" asked Therain. He stepped aside so they could enter. "Has Esedraen said anything useful?"

"Perhaps, my lord. So much of it seems nonsensical, it's difficult to say. But there's another matter I must tell you about. A servant girl was found dead this morning."

"*Another* murder?"

"I'm not sure, my lord. It may be nothing but a coincidence. There was no harm done to the body, no apparent cause of death. She wasn't stabbed or bludgeoned as the others were, and there was no obvious sign of poison. She may have died of natural causes even though she was a young girl. Her body was taken to Master Evernyes for examination."

"Where was she found?"

"In a hallway near the servants' quarters, my lord. It looked as if she just collapsed on the floor. I sent word for Master Evernyes to let you know what he finds as soon as he's finished."

"What did Esedraen say? Did he tell you who his accomplices were?"

"Yes. We have two gate guards in the dungeons being questioned to see if they've recruited others. They did not deny the charge when confronted. They spouted the same nonsense about the Storm King raising them from the dead for their service. We'll know very soon if there are other traitors among the guards." The captain grimaced, as if speaking of such a thing left a foul, bitter taste in his mouth.

"Did he say anything else about the Storm King?" Therain asked.

"He boasted of it, actually. He said the Heralds are growing in strength and that the Storm King would soon be returning."

"Did he say *why* the Storm King wants them to commit murders? They seem senseless and random." In his own dream, Asankaru had commanded him to kill indiscriminately, but he wanted to know if this was said to everyone or if the command varied from person to person.

"I asked him that, my lord. Why he killed Bann and what he was doing in the North Tower. At first he wouldn't explain, but we got it out of him, sure enough. He's got a few less teeth in his head, not that he'll miss them much. He said the Storm King wants us *all* dead, so it doesn't matter who they kill, as long as they kill someone. 'We obey his command so we'll be rewarded,' he said. I asked if the Storm King wanted everyone dead, didn't that mean it wanted him dead as well, and he said he and the other Heralds would pass through the fire of the Storm King's wrath because of their service to him."

"Is that everything?"

"Yes, my lord. Shall we continue to hold him, or do you want him executed now?"

"Hold him a little while longer. I may have more questions for him, and I don't have his confidence that he'll be back from the grave for me to ask later." He pulled on a heavy black surcoat embroidered with silver thorns. "I have some news for you as well, Captain. Come, we'll talk on our way."

"Going where, my lord?"

"To see Master Evernyes. I have some questions for him myself."

The two guards fell in beside them. Therain asked why they were there. "There may be more of those Heralds about," answered the captain. "Random killings or no, they may make an attempt on your life. These men are hand-picked by me and can be trusted. I want them to accompany you wherever you go."

Therain didn't particularly care to be shadowed, but saw the wisdom of it. "Very well, Captain." He then told Elmen about his own dream and that of Castellan Harres. "I have no idea what to make of it. That's why we're going to see the Master."

Terem Evernyes, the Master's son and apprentice, opened the door for them. He was a scrawny, gangly lad of fourteen with freckled cheeks and large crooked teeth.

"We're here to see your father, Terem," said Therain.

"He's working with the dead girl, my lord," said the boy. "He asked not to be disturbed."

"Boy, how dare you refuse entrance to—"

"It's all right, Captain. He's just doing as his father asked." To Terem, he said, "My calling is urgent. We'll have to interrupt him."

Terem lowered his gaze. "Yes, my lord. Follow me." He led them up two flights of stairs to the work chamber. Master Nadjim Evernyes's back was to them. His robes emphasized his prodigious girth, making him look somewhat like a door propped upright in the center of the room. He stood at a table with several flasks of strangely colored liquids scattered across its scarred and gouged surface. The corpse of the servant girl lay on a table near the windows, where the light was brightest. There was a strong smell in the room, but it was not the odor of decay. Therain guessed the smell was coming from whatever fluids were in the flasks.

"Father, the—"

"I asked not to be disturbed, Terem!" bellowed the Master without turning. "What part of that didn't you understand? I'm in the middle of something very important for the duke."

"But Father, the duke is here to see you. That's why I interrupted."

Evernyes whirled about so quickly, Therain thought he might lose his balance and topple over. "My lord, forgive me! The captain told me to send word when I was finished. I did not expect you to come in person."

"I'm not here about the dead girl, Master Evernyes," said Therain. "Though while I am here I will ask if you've found anything about how she died."

"Not yet, my lord. It is strange, very strange. There was no physical harm to her, and all the obvious signs of poison are absent. No blood or strange smells in the mouth, no vomit, discolored skin, bloodshot eyes, or signs of physical pain as the poison performed its corrupting work—nothing. She was a Pashti, and of course they are weak of both body and spirit; yet still, I would not have expected even one of them who seems so healthy to die so young."

Therain had no time for a lecture on the properties of subtle poisons and how to detect them. "I have something else to discuss with you, Master Evernyes." He described the dream of the Storm King and how it had occurred to both himself and Velarien, and apparently to the members of the Heralds of Truth as well. "It seems as if part of what the Heralds of Truth are saying is true: there is a being of some kind—Asankaru, the Storm King, whatever he calls himself—that is projecting himself into the dreams of others. Can you tell me how this might be done, or where we might find such a being?"

The Master looked stricken. He groped for a chair and sat down heavily. "My lord, I've had the very same dream!"

Captain Hiremar drew a hissing breath. "This is madness. A foe who lives in our dreams. How do you fight such a thing?"

"When did you have this dream?"

"Two nights ago, my lord. It was very vivid and I awoke

from it, which is quite rare for me. I felt angry, and wronged, though I did not know why. It was a long time before the feeling passed and I fell back asleep."

"What of the dreams, Master? Is there a way to cause different people to have the same dream? A potion of some kind that can be added to food?" He glanced at the fire crackling in the gray stone hearth. "Or some powder that can be thrown on a flame and so enter the air upon smoke?"

"I know of no way to control dreams, my lord. What you suggest could cause sleep and perhaps strange visions, but I do not know how to make the visions the same to everyone. That would take sorcery, it seems to me."

So it is magic, thought Therain, confirming his thoughts of the night. Elmen was right. This was madness. How was he to fight such a thing? An enemy that could walk in dreams and command others to kill.

"Master Evernyes, continue your work with the girl," he said. "Let me know whatever you find."

Master Evernyes's examination of the servant girl revealed nothing; it was as if her life had simply fled her body between one moment and the next.

A sheep was found dead of no visible cause, and a hawk fell lifeless from the sky into the bailey of the castle. People whispered about a plague, and Therain himself began to fear it as a possibility. He asked Evernyes about it. "If it is a plague, it is unlike any I have ever heard of," the Master said. "Plagues cause extreme sickness before death. There is great pain and many signs of illness, such as discolored skin, fevers, swelling of joints, bleeding from orifices and perhaps the eyes, eruptions of pustules, foul smells, loose bowels, discharge from—"

"All right, Master, I get the idea," said Therain. "Is there any way to tell if these deaths are caused by some new kind of plague?"

"I've already tried to determine that, my lord," he said. "I've found nothing."

These deaths are a mystery, he thought. *Heralds of Truth killing in the name of a creature that appears only in dreams, then strange deaths without cause. What madness will happen next?* He felt that there must be a connection of some kind between the Heralds and these strange deaths, but he could not see it.

Then the connection suddenly became clear. "Master, could these deaths be caused by magic? More people have reported having the dream of the Storm King, which you said might be a form of sorcery. Could that be the answer? Could these strange deaths and the dreams be the work of a sorcerer?"

Evernyes considered it. "I don't know, my lord," he said. "It's possible, certainly, but I am not a practitioner of sorcery and have little knowledge of it. I have no means of either learning the truth of it or countering it."

Therain had not yet had time to send the message to Gerin that he'd planned. This would have to be included in it. *I only hope he or Hollin has an answer for me.*

19

Three days after Therain sent his message to
Reshel, Esedraen was executed. The two guards who
had helped him enter the castle were executed with him and
their heads staked above the castle gate, as Therain had
promised. Mercifully, there had been no more murders committed by the Heralds of Truth, and he hoped their deaths
would act as a deterrent. *If they believe the Storm King will
grant them eternal life, let's see what the other members think
after the heads have been rotting there for a while,* he thought
as he gazed out his study window toward the Angle. He told
Captain Hiremar to make sure no one got near the heads. He
did not want them stolen so the Heralds could claim they'd
been revived.

Toward evening a soldier arrived from the southwest
borderlands with an urgent message for Therain. He was
brought to the council chamber on the third floor of the
Thorn, where Therain and his counselors were gathered.
Forty feet long and half as wide, the table occupying the center of the room was cut in the shape of a stylized thorn tree
with numerous branches snaking off of the main trunk like
immobile cracks of lightning. The table was painted and
thickly lacquered so that its surfaced glistened in lamplight
as if wet; the main sections of the tree had been colored a
brownish-green that reminded Therain of moss. The thorn

needles themselves had been painted a shiny silver that made them look like steel knives. When he'd first come to the room he was surprised to find that the pointed ends of the thorns were sharp. It was a table one sat at with great care.

"My lord, thank you for seeing me," said the soldier as walked the length of the table to where Therain was seated. "I am Davin Simmolo of the Southern Border Guard."

"Please, sit," said Therain. "Tell me your message."

Simmolo placed his helm on the table and sat in one of the high-backed chairs. "My lord, our company is assigned to patrol the southwestern borders of Calad-Ethil, on the border of Neddar. Our captain regularly sends scouts to spy on the Neddari, which we've stepped up since they began their raids some months back."

"Yes. The raids slacked off for a time, then increased again about a month ago, correct?"

"Yes, my lord. We've had a number of skirmishes with them, but so far the raiding parties have been small, usually less than a hundred warriors and a handful of drogasaars thrown in. It's just indiscriminate killing. There seems to be no overarching goal for these raids."

"But now that's changed?"

The lieutenant nodded grimly. "The most recent group of scouts saw an army gathering along their border, near the villages the clans use for their larger celebrations and ceremonies. They counted at least twenty thousand men, and saw signs that more were coming from the west and south."

"That's impossible!" said Wilfros. "The Neddari clans fight each other more than they fight anyone else. They *never* cooperate."

"I'm aware of that, sir. That does not change what they saw."

"I still say this is ridiculous. The Neddari are savages, they kill one another for sport. They're unquestionably skilled with weapons, but they don't create armies. There has never been a true Neddari army in all of their history. It takes too much planning and coordination. They don't have the minds for it."

"We need to determine the truth," said Velarien. "They may very well have seen a large number of Neddari, but that does not mean it was an army, and it certainly does not mean they plan to invade Khedesh, which seems to be the implication of your words."

"My lord, there's more. Our scouts took a Neddari patrol by surprise very near to our lands. There was a skirmish, and all of the Neddari but one were killed. The captain asked him about the gathering of men and its purpose. He said the Slain God had at last returned and that the unbelievers would be swept away by his holy wrath. It was obvious that he considered *us* the unbelievers."

The Slain God that Gerin was supposed to summon, thought Therain. *What in the name of Telros is going on here?*

"Did you learn anything else from the prisoner?" asked Wilfros.

"No. He died soon after from his wounds."

"Did the captain believe him?" asked Therain. "That the Neddari truly intend to invade Khedesh?"

"Yes, my lord. That's why he sent me to you."

"The Neddari *kamichi* who attacked my brother said that Gerin would help their Slain God return. When he was with the wizards at their fortress, a spell the *kamichi* placed upon him forced Gerin to open a doorway to the world of the dead. He was calling a dead wizard to learn the location of a lost library, but the wizards determined he acted as he did because of the Neddari spell. This gathering of Neddari must be related to that, though Shayphim take me if I can see how."

"I wonder if your brother's actions and the Storm King are related as well," said Velarien. "I find it an odd coincidence that this Asankaru appears, claiming to have returned from the dead, just as the Neddari claim a god of theirs has also returned from death."

"A good point," said Therain. "There may very well be a connection. It may be that the Storm King and this alleged Slain God of the Neddari are one and the same."

"The only thing that is certain," said Simmolo, "is that the

Neddari will invade Khedesh. Soon. Please do not doubt this. I would not have been sent if my captain had not been sure."

There was a cold feeling in the pit of Therain's stomach. *Miendrel has sounded Flestos,* he thought. *War will begin here, in my lands.* He was not ready for this. The troubles of running the castle and its holdings were more than enough for him. *Is anyone ever truly ready for war?* he wondered. But the Neddari apparently were, since they were going to start one.

"Lieutenant Simmolo, you are dismissed," said Therain. "Get something to eat and rest while you can. I'll draft a message for you to take to your captain. Be ready to leave on the morrow. I'll send more men with you to help watch the Neddari. If they begin to move, I want to know immediately."

Simmolo bowed his head. "Yes, my lord."

Therain turned to Castellan Harres. "Send one of your men to bring food. We have a long night ahead of us."

Therain wrote a message to Captain Melfistan, granting him authority to do whatever he felt was necessary to protect and defend the realm against the Neddari. He drafted letters to all his vassals, commanding them to ready their soldiers and bring them to Agdenor as soon as they were prepared to march. He wrote another letter to his brother, asking him to call his own liegemen. *I can summon a force of at best seven thousand men,* he wrote to Gerin. *If the Neddari march upon Agdenor, I must be prepared for a lengthy siege. I cannot hope to defeat such a large force upon the field.* His final letter was to his father, telling him of the situation and what steps he was taking in light of the news he'd received.

We'll see what Gerin has to say about all of this. He'll probably think I've lost my mind. He rubbed his eyes and leaned back in his chair. This seemed unreal to him. Was he actually planning for *war* and a siege of his castle? Based on a single report from a lieutenant of the border watch?

That is why those men guard our borders, he reminded himself. *To warn us of just such a thing. To be vigilant so we are not caught by surprise should war find us.*

"What do you think this Slain God of theirs truly is?" he asked his counselors.

"My lord?" asked Velarien. "I'm not sure I understand."

"It's a simple question. What do you think it is? Is it truly a god, or something else?"

"I have no idea what it might be, or what gods the Neddari worship."

"*Something* has happened to unite them as they have never been united before," Therain said. "What could it be? Has a god truly returned to them?"

"What does it matter?" asked Velarien. "The army is gathering. What of the reasons for it? We need only concern ourselves with what they plan to do."

Therain shook his head. "No. We *do* need to know why. It might be the most important thing we can learn. Wilfros, you said the clans are always fighting among themselves and that this kind of unity is unprecedented. So an army that large made up of so many different clans has got to be difficult to hold together. Old grudges and hatreds between the clans are probably simmering just below the surface. Is it safe to say that only the strength of their leader—whoever or whatever he may be—is keeping the army from fragmenting back into a bunch of feuding clans?"

Wilfros nodded. "Yes, my lord. I see. It's reasonable to think so."

"So if we kill the leader, we destroy the army without having to fight it," said Therain. "The clans will revert to their old ways and stop working together. The army will disperse. The clans may even begin fighting one another."

"What if the leader *is* a god?" said Velarien.

Therain frowned. *A god could most certainly walk in dreams,* he thought. A god or sorcerer would also be able to kill and leave no sign of how the death occurred. In his dream, Asankaru said he wanted them all dead. Was that because they were unbelievers? What was it that did they not believe in? The Storm King himself, or something else?

It doesn't matter, he decided. *Whether the Neddari leader*

*is the Storm King or not, whether he is a god or something
else, doesn't change what we have to do. Our best hope is to
kill him before that army marches against us.*

"I'll follow Lieutenant Simmolo," he announced. "You
said we need to know what is going on down there. I intend
to do just that."

Velarien looked aghast. "Yes, my lord, but we did not
mean for you to go in person! Let others go and report back
to you what they find."

"You should not risk yourself—you're needed here," said
Wilfros.

"I'm needed there more. If we are indeed going to try to
kill the leader of this army, I need to be there. If by some
chance the Neddari are *not* going to send this army against
us, then to kill their captain is an act of war on our part. The
decision must be mine alone. I can't leave this to a commander in the field. I need to be there to understand the situation. What if our only window of opportunity closes while
they are waiting for my reply? If there's any chance at all,
we'll need to seize it quickly." He pushed his chair back and
stood. "I'm going to get whatever sleep I can. Velarien,
make the preparations for my departure. I'll wait three days
to see if my brother replies to my message. I'd like to know
what he thinks of all this before I leave. But no more than
three days." He did not worry about how they would kill him
if he were indeed a god or a sorcerer. *One thing at a time,* he
thought. *One thing at a time.*

20

Gerin trudged through the halls of Blackstone Keep, bleary-eyed and miserable. He stopped to sneeze, then continued on his way, rubbing his eyes. His head felt as if it were stuffed with feathers; his nose would not stop dripping and his throat was sore. According to Reshel, there were no spells to treat such a simple ailment. He could use his magic to help him sleep and perhaps numb the pain in his throat a little, but other than that he would simply have to endure the cold like anyone else.

He had enough to worry about already without having a cold to make him miserable on top of it. A cult of murderers had recently appeared in Ailethon and the surrounding lands. So far they had killed six people. The killings were brutal and utterly senseless. The victims had not even been robbed, just stabbed and left for dead.

But they were not the only ones who had died. There were two more—a farrier from Padesh and a chambermaid in the castle—who were found dead of no apparent cause. It might have just been coincidence, but Gerin's instincts told him all the deaths were somehow related. Master Aslon had tested the chambermaid for poisons, and Reshel had used her powers to see if she could learn the cause of death, but to no avail. "There's no harm to her that I can see," Reshel said. "I don't know why she died." She told him how to create the

Seeing spells she had used, and he found what she had: there was no reason for the chambermaid to be dead, nor the farrier from Padesh. They might have died of some natural cause that had escaped their detection, but in his bones Gerin knew something sinister was behind their deaths.

"I wish Hollin were here," Reshel said. They were in her rooms, sipping mulled wine by the fire. "He might be able to shed some light on this. We're just barely beginning to learn the spells that might help us understand what's going on." But the wizard was not expected back from checking on the progress of the apprentices at Hethnost for another two months.

A servant girl stuck her head in the room and asked if they needed anything.

"No, thank you, Nandis," said Reshel.

"All right, my lady. I'm going to take some dishes to the kitchens but will be back in a little while."

"That's fine."

Gerin could see Nandis over Reshel's shoulder, peering at them from the narrow servants' door. He thought she was about to leave the room, but then her eyes rolled up into her head, she made a strange sound and collapsed to the floor. He felt a chill at that same moment, as if an icy wind had blown through the room. Reshel shivered as well and looked suddenly alarmed. Nandis's head smacked into the bare stone at the edge of the rug with a dull thud. Reshel spun around in her chair and let out a little gasp of shock when she saw the servant's crumpled body.

They both rushed to Nandis and knelt by her side. Gerin felt for a pulse in her neck, but he could already tell she was dead.

"By the gods, Gerin, what happened to her?"

"I don't know."

Reshel closed her eyes and drew magic into herself, working the same spells upon Nandis's body that she'd used on the corpse of the chambermaid.

"What do you see?" Gerin asked.

"There's no reason for her to be dead. Even if her collapse

had been a fainting spell, the impact of her head against the floor wasn't enough to kill her."

He thought back to the moment of her death, seeing her eyes roll back into her skull, her shoulders slump and her head loll as her neck went limp. He remembered the sudden icy chill and wondered if that had been the cause of her death, some invisible power that entered the room and cut her down where she stood.

"I felt something just before she collapsed. Something cold."

Her eyes narrowed. "I felt that, too. It wasn't a normal chill. There was something ill about it."

"Could that have been what killed her?"

"I don't know. I don't know anything right now."

"*Something* snuffed the life from her. This is the third un-explained death. There has to be a reason."

They summoned servants to remove the body to Master Aslon's work chamber to see if he could detect a cause of death, though they did not expect him to find anything. The servants had just left when the door banged open and Amnen Petring swept into the room. The old priest's black and silver vestments hung from his thin frame like an ill-fitting burial shroud.

"I just heard that another servant has died." There was a quaver in his voice; Gerin could not tell if it was caused by anger, fear, outrage, or a mingling of all three.

"These deaths are a judgment upon us from Telros," he said. "We have committed some terrible blasphemy, and must find it so we can absolve ourselves in his eyes. Telros has given leave for the god of war to sound Flestos without end, until Velyol overflows with the dead—"

"Father Petring," said Gerin, "thank you for your concern, but I think it is misdirected. This has nothing to do with the gods."

"The Hand of Death touched your servant before your very eyes! *Of course* it was the work of the gods. How can you deny it? Mark my words, Lord Gerin. The anger of the gods is upon us because we have allowed evil in our midst, and the deaths will not stop until the source of the evil is driven out."

"Father Petring, I don't know what killed her or the others, but it was not the gods. Why would they kill someone who is innocent? Or are you claiming that those who died are the ones who committed this unknown blasphemy?"

Petring shook his head violently. "Telros has removed his blessing from us. *He* did not strike down your servant; she died because of the loss of his protection. These deaths are signs to show us what must be done. Twice now Telros has appeared to me in my dreams. He showed himself to me as a crowned figure of dread and fear. He did not use his true name, but I know it was him. He commanded me to strike down his enemies. He has assumed this dark and terrible aspect as a warning to us. I felt death all around him, and great hatred at what we have done to offend him."

Never argue with a priest, Gerin thought. His father had told him that more than once. They had an answer for everything.

"Gerin, I've had that very dream." Reshel scowled at the recollection. "It was terrible."

"You see?" said Petring, pointing a trembling finger at Reshel. "He has visited your own sister. Do not ignore his warning."

"Both of you, slow down. Reshel, describe your dream to me in detail. I need to make sure I understand this."

Reshel's dream was nearly identical to Petring's. "There was something familiar about it, too. It almost came to me there when I was telling you about it, but now it's gone."

"You said this being in the dream referred to itself as the Storm King?"

"Yes."

"That is the name Telros assumed in my dream as well," said the priest. "His intent is clear. He is sending a storm of wrath—"

"Please, be quiet!" snapped Gerin. Petring flinched and glared at Gerin as if he'd uttered a profoundly foul curse.

"The murders that have been occurring throughout the duchy," Gerin said, "were committed by people claiming to follow the commands of someone called the Storm King."

"By the gods!" said Reshel. "Why didn't you tell me this before?"

"It's not widely known. And you're not part of my council, where this was discussed."

"Tell me everything you know."

So far they had been unable to capture any of the killers alive. One, cornered by the constables in Thorn Hill, had slit his own throat rather than let himself be taken. Gerin had been told the cut was so violent that the man nearly decapitated himself. Before killing himself, he'd shouted, "The Storm King is coming! All of you will die!" Then he'd dragged the knife across his neck. Notes has been left with two other victims that said, *We obey the Storm King. Soon all will feel his wrath.*

No one knew who the Storm King was or how he recruited his servants. The man who had been cornered had been a simple farmhand before he'd begun killing.

"What if these murderers are having the same dream?" Gerin asked after detailing the events for his sister. "Could this figure in your dream be real?"

"Of course he is real!" Petring straightened his back and glared at them with haughty indignation. "It is Telros speaking to us through—"

"Father Petring, thank you for coming. I appreciate you sharing your thoughts with us. But my sister and I need to speak alone."

"If you ignore these warnings, you will doom us all," the priest said coldly. "Mark my words, Lord Gerin." He wheeled about and left the room. Gerin closed and locked the door.

"I don't know what to think," he said. "Is it possible to use magic to enter the dreams of others? You read more of Hollin's books than I do."

"I don't know. There are spells for affecting the dreams of others, but they're difficult and require the use of magical devices. Are you suggesting a wizard is behind this?"

"What about the name "Asankaru"? Does that mean anything? The name of some wizard expelled from Hethnost, maybe?"

She scowled. "No, I don't recognize the name. But as soon as Hollin's back, we'll ask him."

"Check the books in the workroom to see if you can find anything about Asankaru or the Storm King." He paused, then sneezed. "Telros preserve me," he muttered as he wiped his nose. "If different people are having the same dream—a dream that's making some of them kill—then magic of some kind must be the cause of it."

"I'll go right away. I almost hope it *is* a wizard."

"Why do you say that?"

"Because the alternative is that Petring might actually be right."

Gerin was in his study the following morning when Master Aslon appeared. "A message from your brother, my lord," he said with a bow of his head. He handed Gerin the small roll of parchment. "I'll leave you to your reading."

"Where can I find you, Master Aslon, if I need to send a reply?"

"In my work chamber, my lord."

When the old man was gone, Gerin broke the seal and began to read.

He could scarcely believe the message. He read it twice, certain that he must have misunderstood it despite Therain's clear, direct statements.

A Neddari army was forming on their border. Therain had written: *If they march upon Agdenor, the castle will eventually fall without your help. I am sending more men to watch them, but I can see no other reason for a force of this size to be mustered except to invade Khedesh.* He went on to describe the capture of the Neddari archer and his words concerning "unbelievers" as further validation that Khedesh was in imminent danger of invasion.

The first part of the message was shocking enough, but the second part took Gerin's breath away. He read how Castle Agdenor was being plagued by a murderous group called the Heralds of Truth. They followed a mysterious being called the Storm King who seemed to have the ability to appear in the dreams of others.

> *I have dreamed of him myself, as have my castellan and Master. Our dreams are the same: a crowned figure of terror concealed by mist who commands us to kill. There have been unexplained deaths in addition to the murders committed by the Heralds. People dying for no reason that my Master can find. Is this magic of some sort? Is a wizard behind these dreams and deaths? I don't know what to do other than ask for your help. How can I defend myself against magic?*

Gerin summoned Reshel, Balandrick, Matren, and Master Aslon to his study, where he read them Therain's message.

"It seems we have three problems to contend with, which might all be related," he said when he was through.

He raised his index finger. "There is the problem of the random murders, which seem to be similar to the Heralds of Truth at Agdenor. They may also be elsewhere in the realm, which we shall have to find out."

He raised another finger. "There is the problem of the Neddari army gathering on our border."

He held up a third finger. "Then there is the problem of these unexplained deaths, which may or may not be related to anything else going on. Are we in agreement that these are the main problems we face?"

"Yes, but you forgot about the Storm King," said Balandrick, who was sitting so close to Reshel that their shoulders almost touched.

"No, I didn't forget," Gerin said. "The Storm King may be the connecting thread between these problems." He paused to collect his thoughts. There were a number of ideas swirling through his mind and he wanted to make sure he stated them clearly. "It seems that the Storm King can enter the dreams of others. The Heralds—I'll use that term to apply to both the murderers at Agdenor and here—follow him and kill at his command. It may also be that the unexplained deaths like Nandis's are somehow related to this. If the Storm King *can* enter dreams, then maybe there's a way he can use those same powers to kill."

"But Nandis wasn't asleep," said Reshel. "She certainly wasn't dreaming when she died."

"I know. I can't explain it. Maybe there is no connection. But it seems far too coincidental that all of this is happening at the same time."

"It's almost too frightening to contemplate," said Master Aslon. "A being that can strike someone down without ever being seen."

"I hope I'm wrong, and I admit I have no evidence, but it's something we have to consider until we know for certain what *did* kill Nandis and the others. My brother thinks the Storm King may be the leader of the Neddari army, the one who has managed to unite their clans. If that's the case, then this being—whoever or whatever he is—is attacking Khedesh on two and possibly three fronts. Through the Heralds of Truth, with the Neddari army, and the unexplained deaths."

"We have a very dangerous enemy," said Balandrick.

"We need to find out who the Storm King is," said Reshel, "and how he's entering the dreams of others."

"My lord, we have no idea *where* he is," said Master Aslon. "He could be in this very castle, or in Padesh, or in a cave in the hills somewhere between here and Agdenor. And if the Storm King and the Neddari warlord are one and the same, then he is in Neddar surrounded by tens of thousands of men far from our reach."

"What shall my reply be?" Gerin said. "Therain's asked for our advice, and I don't want to delay my message. But what are we to tell him?"

"I think he should move with all haste to learn who commands the Neddari army, my lord," said Matren. "If he can learn that, it will answer many of our questions."

"I agree," said Balandrick. "That should be his priority."

"In the meantime," said Aslon, "we should do whatever we can to root out the Storm King's followers to see if we can learn of his whereabouts. My lord, my lady, is there any way your powers can assist us?"

"There's nothing I know of that could locate such a creature," Gerin replied.

"I'll have to consider it some more," said Reshel. "I'll see if I can find anything in our workroom that might help."

"Balandrick, I want you and your men to do everything in your power to capture one of these killers alive. If Therain can do it, then by the gods so can we." Gerin looked at each of them. "If there's nothing else, you may go. I need to draft my response to my brother." *And hope that he's wrong. Otherwise we'll soon be at war.*

Abran was walking quickly through a colonnade in the Tirthaig, his cloak pulled tight around his neck to keep away the cold bite of the winter wind blowing from the sea, when a messenger hurried to him. He was a young man with a scraggly fringe of dark beard upon his otherwise boyish face, his breath puffing from his mouth in small white clouds that vanished almost as quickly as they appeared.

"Your Majesty, a message has just arrived from your son the Duke of Agdenor," the young man said. Beneath his hood, his cheeks and nose were ruddy from the cold. He handed Abran a sealed cylinder, then backed away with a bow. "The Master of Birds felt you should have this immediately."

Abran nodded and dismissed him with a wave of his hand. He pulled off his gloves and rubbed his hands together vigorously as he climbed a long, twisting flight of stairs that led to his study, which he maintained in one of the garrets of the palace, near his sleeping quarters. The room was long, with a slanting outer wall, facing north, into which four dormered windows had been set. The marble floor was covered with richly colored rugs of the finest Neldemarien wool. There was an enormous hearth in the long wall opposite the windows, with a mahogany mantel so huge it seemed to Abran that an entire tree trunk had simply been squared off before being sunken into the stone. Very old and intricate tapestries hung between the windows, showing the coming of Khedesh to these lands, the conquering of the Pashti, the construction of Almaris, and a grand vista of the Tirthaig itself.

A servant was in the room tending to the fire, prodding the burning logs in an attempt to coax the greatest amount of flame and heat from them.

Abran removed his cloak and threw it on a chair. The servant rose from the hearth, gathered up the cloak, and hung it near the fire. "Is there anything I can get you, Your Majesty?"

Abran sat at his desk and broke the seal on the cylinder. "Some spiced wine, Yurente. And some bread."

Yurente Praithas bowed his head to the king. "Of course, Your Majesty. At once." He turned sharply on his heels and left through a servant's door at the far end of the room.

The frown on Abran's face deepened as he read the letter from his son. "Gods preserve me from the madness of foreigners," he muttered to himself.

Yurente returned with a platter of bread and a large goblet of spiced wine, which he set down on the corner of the king's writing desk.

"Send for Minister Waklan, Yurente," Abran said. "Impress on him the need for haste."

"Yes, Your Majesty. I'll see that he comes at once."

Jaros Waklan was the Minister of the Realm and senior member of the King's Council. He had served King Bessel loyally for more than thirty years, ever since he negotiated a peace between two noble houses, the Aumelars and Thoreks, who'd threatened open warfare against one another over the suspicious death of Baron Aumelar's oldest son.

Waklan's bald head was fringed with short white hair, and a trim beard covered his pointed chin like a patch of downy fur. His surcoat bore the emblem of his office, an eight-rayed star above a solitary mountain.

He looked aghast as Abran read the contents of Therain's letter to him. When he finished, Abran handed the Minister the paper so he could read it for himself.

"Quite a dilemma," said Waklan as he looked over the tightly written script. "I don't know your son, Your Majesty, so forgive my bluntness, but is this credible? He is very young. Could this be a Neddari celebration of some kind that is being misinterpreted?"

"I understand your feelings, but the Neddari warrior's words about a war against the unbelievers seems to remove all doubt about their intentions. And though my son is young and inexperienced, the men who provided him with this information are not. They are seasoned soldiers whose sworn duty is to watch the border with Neddar for precisely this kind of activity."

"Yes, Your Majesty, I meant no offense against your son. But this is as yet a *gathering* of Neddari. An army it may be, and it *may* be their intent to use it against us. Yet there's been no dispute with their leaders, no indication of any kind that they mean to go to war with us. No threats, no demands. They have harried some villages along our border recently, that is true, but those attacks have decreased of late. A nuisance to be sure, but our own captains reported that they believed the attacks were the work of a single clan, perhaps even of a smaller group within that clan. We have only the secondhand word of one Neddari soldier, who is now dead."

"What do you suggest? I need to reply to my son."

"We must surely tell your vassals that a large force of Neddari is gathering near our border and ask them to prepare to march should they cross into Khedesh. But what if nothing comes of it? We cannot march thousands of men hundreds of miles for no reason. The threat must be clear and undeniable. So far it is not. If we are told that the Neddari have entered our lands, then we march. But not until then. There are too many other problems that press us. The Threndish are harassing our settlements in Dorlinden, and just last week we received word that two merchant ships vanished on route to Brangáran, raising fear that pirates have returned to our shipping lanes. We have troubles enough. We must be cautious but prudent in how we deploy our forces."

Abran was quiet as he drummed his fingers on the desk and took a bite of bread. *The gods damn these practicalities of my office,* he thought. *This is my son. I need to do what's right by him.* But would mobilizing his vassals help Therain if the Neddari did not march against them? Both his own reputation and Therain's credibility would take a grievous blow.

"Summon my scribe," he said at last, hoping his decision was the right one for them both.

21

Five days had passed since Gerin had sent his messages, with no word yet from Therain. If no reply came soon, he would send a mounted messenger to Agdenor. He was growing increasingly anxious about the situation with the Neddari. He told himself that an army that large could not take Agdenor by surprise—there was no need to worry that the castle was already under siege or had fallen. Therain certainly would have sent word if the army had begun to move. Still, without firm information about the situation, Gerin's imagination filled in the void, and at the moment his imagination was overly active and increasingly gloomy.

Two days later, on the fourth of January, the Heralds of Truth—as he now thought of them, though there was no evidence that the killers here used that name—murdered a serving girl in the castle. The castle guards cornered the killer in a fifth-floor hallway, but he hurled himself through an outside window before he could be taken.

"He was in this castle right under your noses and you let him kill himself!" fumed Gerin. Balandrick stood at rigid attention with his helm under his right arm. He stared straight ahead and did not look at the crown prince as Gerin stormed about the room. "I need one of these men alive, Balan! If we're going to find out anything about their leader, we need to question one of them, and we can't question them if they're *dead*. I don't care if one of your men has to hurl *himself* from a window, I want one of these murderers captured." He paused. Some of his anger left him, and he lowered his voice. "I know your men did what they could. But this is very, very important."

"I know, my lord. I understand the importance of the situation. We'll not fail you again."

"Who was he? The killer who threw himself out the window?"

"His name was Stanles Terring. One of the gardeners. Killed the girl with a pair of his shears. Cut her head clean off."

"A heavy man with just a fringe of gray hair?" asked Gerin, making a circle around his head.

Balandrick nodded.

"I remember him. He seemed like a kind old man. Hardly the sort to cut off a girl's head."

"He lived here all his life. I guess you can never truly know what secrets a man carries in his heart." Balandrick shook his head in disbelief. "Just before he jumped through the window he shouted that the Storm King would raise him up once more. What I saw splattered on the courtyard didn't look too likely to be rising anytime soon." For the first time he looked directly at Gerin. "What kind of dreams can drive a man to commit murder? For the grace of the gods, I can't imagine having a *dream* that would make me go out and kill."

"Neither can I, Balandrick. Which is why you have to capture one of these men alive. It may be the only way we'll ever find out."

A few days later Gerin himself dreamed of the Storm King. He sensed that there was something strange about this dream, something dark and perilous, the moment he slipped into it. There was a feeling of *truth* to it, as if it were as real as the castle in which he slept. This was no fantasy of his sleeping mind. And the peril he sensed was just as real. He was certain that his life was in danger while this dream continued, but he still could not wake himself.

A gray fog swirled around him. There was something familiar about this place, but he could not say what. A sense of power was all around him, like a scent in the air. It was not magic—at least not the magic of wizards—but power nonetheless, and the feeling of familiarity grew stronger as the mist closed in around him.

He did not have a body here, and there was no ground beneath him, only the fog, which glowed as if reflecting the embers of a dwindling fire.

He saw something in the distance. As it drew closer he could see that the shape was a monstrous figure. He wanted to flee but could not even look away as it approached.

It stopped at last, looming over him. There was a silver crown visible upon its head and a dark shadow fell across its face, though he could see two silver sparks where its eyes should have been.

The figure filled him with terrible dread. When its glowing eyes looked down upon him, he understood how someone would kill for this being, if only from fear alone. The hatred that he sensed in it was like an inferno—a hatred of all things so intense that Gerin would have done anything to make it stop, to turn the Storm King's attention toward someone else, *anything* else. It made him want to scream.

A voice boomed from the figure, deep and ominous and filled with the threat of violence. "I am Asankaru," it said. "You are the summoner. I have found you at last. You are the one who has called me from my troubled sleep, but I am not yet complete. You must finish what you have begun."

The Storm King vanished. The bloodred mist faded. All was black. The dream ended, and though Gerin thrashed about in his bed, he did not awaken until morning.

"So the Storm King called you a summoner," said Reshel at breakfast after Gerin had described his dream. "Don't you find it more than a little strange that a Neddari sorcerer called you a god-summoner when he saw you? And now we have this Asankaru naming you the 'summoner' at the same time the Neddari are massing on our border, supposedly at the behest of their Slain God. It certainly lends weight to your idea that their leader is also the Storm King."

"Magic has to be involved with this," he said. "My magic. But I can't think of anything I've begun that I haven't finished. I just don't see what it can be."

Reshel looked up at him, her eyes sparkling. "I can think of something, and now I know why the dream *I* had seemed so familiar to me." She folded her hands and took a moment to compose her thoughts. "Remember how I told you I thought the dream I had of the Storm King seemed familiar somehow? There was a . . . a *sensation* to the dream that I'd felt before, but I couldn't recall where I'd experienced it. Your comment about magic brought it all back to me. Gerin, it was your sounding of the Horn of Tireon. When you blew that horn, it woke every wizard in Hethnost. The feeling I had then is the same I felt in my dream."

"You're sure about this?"

"Yes. Completely. I can't believe I didn't see it before. I guess I just never thought to connect the two, but they're definitely the same. Something you did with the horn has caused this."

He tried to remember that night on Maratheon's Hill. Everything was clear until the end, just before he blacked out. But there was something . . . he could almost see it. He'd been lying on the ground in agony, his mind in two places at one time, when he looked up one last time before blacking out. There had been—

There had been a shape standing over him.

Startled, he described the shape to Reshel. "That must be it," she said. "The doorway you opened with the Horn of Tireon. Somehow the Storm King came through it from that other world. That's the figure you saw."

"I thought the Warden of Healing finished the spell to close the doorway, so why would this being say I had to finish what I'd begun?"

"The Warden said he *thought* he closed the doorway; he wasn't completely sure."

"Let's assume you're right, that the doorway I opened allowed this being to enter our world from some other place. A being we now know as the Storm King that the Neddari worship as a god. Whether it really is a god is something we have to find out. The *kamichi* saw this in a vision and came looking for me to make sure I fulfilled it. This being, once he's entered our world, then goes to the Neddari and unites their clans by claiming it is their lost god returned."

"Why do you doubt that this really *is* a god?" she asked. "It seems from what we're saying that it very well may be something divine."

"Because the doorway I opened was to the world of the dead. That's where Naragenth was; that was the purpose of the spell. That's enough to make me believe that whatever came through the doorway was not a god, since gods don't die and would not be in the world of the dead to begin with."

"So that leaves us with something that was dead that is now *posing* as a god of the Neddari. Something that has the power to enter a person's dreams and perhaps kill at a distance and leave no discernable cause."

"There's still the question of what I'm supposed to finish. Even if the doorway isn't closed, how would it benefit the Storm King for me to finish the spell and close it all the way?"

"That's something else we can't answer."

"But maybe the Warden of Healing can. I want you to return to Hethnost to see if the wizards can help us unravel this mystery. Tell them what's been happening here. I can't leave Khedesh with a threat on our border. I won't command you to go. If you refuse, I'll send Balan or someone else I can trust. But I hope you'll do this. You're the one best suited to go to them for help."

"I'll go," she said without hesitation.

"You will have a large bodyguard of soldiers to go with you. I want no repeat of our little battle with bandits. Can you be ready to leave by tomorrow?"

"If the soldiers can be ready, so will I." She rose to leave, then paused. "Gerin, if you're right and the Storm King entered from the world of the dead, then what was he when he was alive that he can command such power? Who was Asankaru?"

"That's one of the things I'm hoping you can find out."

Shortly after midday, Gerin received word that Therain had arrived in the castle. He was shocked by the news. "He's waiting for you in the Sunlight Hall, my lord," said the servant. "He said he must see you at once."

"Summon the castellan, the captain of the guard, and my sister and have them meet me there," he said. *If Therain's come in person, the news can't be good,* he thought as he left his salon.

Therain was seated at the long table in the hall, devouring food as if he had not eaten in days. A plate of lamb slathered with gravy and a platter of bread, butter, cheese, and apple tarts were on the table in front of him. Therain glanced up at Gerin and then returned to his eating.

"Hello, Gerin," he said with a mouthful of bread. "I had your servants bring me some food and told them to fetch some for my men. We've had a hard ride and not much time to eat."

Gerin eyed his brother closely. He was dirty, his clothes worn and weather-stained, and he looked as if he'd lost at least ten pounds. His cheeks were gaunt and stubbled with a week's worth of whiskers. The rings of flesh beneath his eyes were dark and swollen, but his eyes themselves were bright and animated—almost too animated, Gerin thought, as if he had seen things that he would rather have left unglimpsed. His pupils darted about the room as though he feared something would jump from the shadows at any moment.

"Did you get my message?" Gerin asked as he sat down. "Are you all right?"

Therain barked a laugh. "Yes, I got it. It came the day I left to go see the Neddari army for myself. As for being all right?

Well, I am now, but it remains to be seen how long that will last. I'm afraid I have a lot to tell you, and none of it's good."

"What I have to tell you won't be much better."

Reshel and Balandrick entered together. Reshel gave her brother a kiss on the cheek and patted his arm. "It's good to see you, Therain."

"You may not think so after you hear what I have to say."

Matren entered and sat down, his face pinched with concern.

Therain finished chewing a piece of cheese. "I hardly know where to begin. Every day on the road I thought about what I would tell you and how I would say it, but there's so much, I can't seem to wrap my mind around it." He craned his neck back and stared at the lofty ceiling. After a long moment he lowered his head and folded his hands on the table. "You got my message, so you know what was going on in Agdenor. The Heralds and the dreams of the Storm King, then word of the Neddari army. After I'd sent my messages to you I decided to see the Neddari army myself. My counselors and I had concluded that only a strong leader could keep the Neddari clans together, so our best hope was to strike first and kill the leader if we could. If their leader was dead, the army would fall apart before it ever marched, or so we hoped. But since assassinating a Neddari warlord on Neddari lands would be an act of war on the part of Khedesh, I felt I had to go in person. I had to be the one to make the decision on the field.

"I waited a few days after I sent the messages to see if you would reply. Your message arrived on the day I had determined to set out, but it didn't help me decide anything. I was shocked to learn that the Heralds were here and that you were having the dreams too, but knowing about it couldn't help me with the problems I had at hand. So I continued with my plan.

"I left with a hundred soldiers that afternoon. We received a nasty shock when we reached the hideouts in the hills above Neddar where our scouts were to have been. They were there all right, but they'd been hanged from trees and burned.

"The bodies were in a sheltered hollow just east of where

the hills drop toward Neddar in long wooded slopes. It was drawing toward evening when we finally reached the edge of the hills. I could see the fires of the army below us. The encampment was huge. My men estimated that the army had grown to about thirty thousand. We could see how it was broken into smaller units, which Captain Melfistan said represented each of the different clans."

"Captain Melfistan?" Gerin said. "The same captain who chased the Neddari here?"

"Yes. A good man. He thought that the signs of the clans keeping to one another was a good thing. He said the Neddari had no experience managing an army of that size. Without good field commanders who knew how to work together and a solid chain of command—which he said the Neddari clans don't have, they're more like large extended families—it wasn't going to be easy for them to keep it together. Just keeping it fed was going to be trouble for them. But he also thought that meant they would have to move soon. He did not believe they would wait for spring.

"We set a watch and made a camp in the hollow, but lit no fires ourselves. I had just sent some men to see if they could find where the Neddari leader was when we saw a group of Neddari approaching us up the slope.

"They were already pretty close to us when we saw them. I cursed up a storm and then ordered a retreat. I didn't see the use in getting into a fight for no reason. We'd have had to fall back anyway. Even if we wiped out this first group, they'd just send more against us now that they knew we were there. But I can tell you I was furious that our trip had been wasted. There was no chance of us getting closer.

"We were pulling back when our lookouts rode into camp and said mounted Neddari were coming fast from the north and were going to be on us in minutes. Just then the Neddari below us decided to forgo stealth and ran toward us in the open. Their archers began firing blindly at us, sending their arrows in a high arc over the top of the hill. One struck a tree not a yard from my head.

"My men were starting to gallop up out of the hollow when three men in red robes appeared ahead of us on the hollow's rim." Therain rubbed his hands together. "And by 'appeared,' I mean they just . . . formed out of thin air. They were just suddenly *there*. I have no idea what they were. Sorcerers or ghosts. They were tall and very thin, with eyes that looked almost too large for their faces, and blue caps that fit tightly to their heads. Each of them carried a tall staff made of some kind of dark wood. I was close to the rim and saw them quite clearly even in the failing light. They did not actually *glow*—at least not from within, like a candle or lamp, where the light shines from the inside out—but they were brighter than they should have been. There were other things about them that looked . . . not quite right. Their proportions seemed somehow wrong. Fingers and necks that seemed oddly long, and their heads looked taller than they should have. They did not really look like men.

"Keep in mind this all flashed through my mind in a moment or two. They scared me half to death, but we didn't stop our charge up the side of the hollow. They weren't mounted, and if they wanted to get trampled by our horses, that was all right with me, as long as we got out of there.

"The first of my men reached one of the Red Robes and tried to cut him down where he stood. His sword passed right through the man with no more effect than if he'd chopped through smoke. I swear I would not have believed it if I hadn't seen it for myself. His blade hit him squarely on the shoulder and just passed through. Brill was so startled he nearly unhorsed himself."

"There are illusions that wizards can create that could fool you in this way," said Reshel. "Did your man Brill notice any disturbances in the robed figure when his sword passed through it? A violent intersection with a physical object can momentarily disrupt an illusion." She spoke calmly, and Gerin suspected she had slipped into a semitrance state in order to better concentrate on Therain's story.

"I have no idea what he noticed. The Red Robe's staff

exploded with blue fire. He pointed the staff at Brill as he rode past, and the same blue lightning erupted from Brill's eyes and mouth. Can one of your illusions do that? I'm telling you this was a ghost or spirit. Brill was dead before he tumbled from his horse, with greasy smoke pouring from his head. My own horse reared and almost threw me back into the hollow, but I managed to hold on.

"More of my men tried attacking the Red Robes. Four of them ended up dead for their effort, all killed with that blue fire. Thank the gods it seemed to take something out of them to use it or we'd all be dead. It looked like they had to pause to recover for a little while after each kill, which allowed the rest of us to scramble out of the hollow. By that time we did everything we could to stay as far away from them as possible. I shouted an order for my men to head east and regroup at Neythin's Hold, then galloped like Shayphim's Hounds were biting at my heels. The Red Robes did not follow us.

"The Neddari coming from the north made the mistake of riding down the western side of a dense wood that ran almost to the lip of the hollow. Maybe the terrain to the north forced them to take that route, I can't say for sure, but whatever the reason, it saved our lives. I suppose they thought they would surprise us while we were still down in the hollow, but we were out and a mile or more away when they reached it. They tried to pursue us, but we had too much of a head start. We rode all bloody night. Killed three horses when they tripped in the dark, and we had to double up the riders. I left most of the company in Calad-Ethil and continued on toward Agdenor with the rest. I stopped there for only a few hours to get fresh horses and some provisions before riding here."

He looked hard at his brother, then swiveled toward Reshel. "What in the name of the gods *are* these Red Robes? They have magic of some kind, that's for certain. I'm sure they're connected to these dreams and deaths we've been having. I'm desperately in need of advice—how can I defend myself from these things if they march on Agdenor?"

"I can't tell you what the Red Robes are, Therain, because I don't know. Not yet."

"Can you tell me anything?"

Gerin described his own dream of the Storm King and how he and Reshel had come to believe that he had released it during his attempt to summon Naragenth from the grave.

"That means it's all part of that *kamichi*'s spell, doesn't it?" said Therain. "He *wanted* you to release this thing, this Slain God or Storm King or whatever it is."

"Yes, I think so."

"But to what end? So it would unite the Neddari and lead them to war?"

"We don't know. I've asked Reshel to go to Hethnost to see if the wizards can tell us anything. It seems to me if anyone can put the pieces of this puzzle together, they can."

"And if they can't?" Therain asked. "What then? What do we do about that army?"

"If it marches into Khedesh, we'll do what we'd do to any invader. We'll gather our strength and destroy it. I will not suffer our kingdom to be invaded. I've already sent messages to my vassals commanding them to prepare their forces. They'll come to Ailethon should the Neddari cross our border."

"Mine are already gathering."

"I want you to return to Agdenor tomorrow. You and your men rest tonight, but ride home as fast as you can. Reshel, I still want you to leave for Hethnost in the morning."

"I'll be ready. Don't worry about that."

It was very late that night before Gerin went to bed. His head was swimming with thoughts and he needed rest to clear his mind. *I hope I don't dream about this,* he thought as he pulled on a nightshirt. He also fervently hoped that he did not dream of the Storm King again.

He was sitting on the edge of his bed when the world around him changed. His vision dimmed as if he had closed his eyes, though he had not, or the light in the room had gone out. His body seemed to vanish; he could no longer feel the bed beneath him. He tried to reach out with his hands—hands he could no longer see—but touched nothing. *Have I fallen asleep?* he wondered. *Am I already dreaming?*

The darkness around him became gray and indistinct, as if hazy morning light were trying to shine through a thick bank of fog. He turned to look around. Or he thought he did, but without his body as a reference and no variation at all in the gray featureless haze, it was impossible to tell if he'd moved.

He heard sounds in the distance, faint and vague but growing closer. He soon recognized the sound of battle: the sharp ringing of steel against steel, the thrumming of bowstrings, the sounds of men shouting orders, speaking in a strange tongue he could not understand. Other men screamed or groaned in agony. As the sounds drew closer, more and more layers appeared: women weeping and shrieking in horror, children crying, swords crashing together, heavy armor clanking, booted feet rushing forward like a wave—

Then it was gone, as suddenly as it had come. He was still seated on his bed. His eyes were still open. He did not think they had ever closed.

What in the name of the gods just happened to me? he wondered. The calmness that had filled him during the . . . vision? waking dream? He had no idea what to call it. It had vanished, leaving a cold pit of fear and worry in its place.

There was something else that lingered, he realized. A faint sensation of being *pulled,* a compelling summons to come westward . . .

It was far too late to wake Reshel to ask her what she thought. She would be rising early to leave for Hethnost. Let her sleep. He would talk to her in the morning. He lay down and stared up at the dark ceiling. He could still hear the shouts and screams and the clash of steel echoing through his thoughts when he finally fell asleep.

* * *

The sun had not yet risen above the castle walls when he described his experience to Reshel. A cold wind swept down from the north and rattled the panes when it gusted against the keep.

She performed a spell to see if magic had been used on him. He could feel the spell moving across him as she spoke, a faint warmth that caressed his skin and penetrated to his bones. It would have been enjoyable if he'd not been so concerned. He realized he should have done this himself right after the vision ended, but he'd been so weary that it had not occurred to him. *I can't be so careless,* he thought, *or everything could be ruined. I have to be clear; I have to think.*

"There's *something* here," she said at last, letting her hand fall to her lap as she ended the spell. "But I'm not sure what. It's not the magic of a wizard. It may not be magic at all."

"I don't understand."

"It's like when the Warden of Healing blew the Horn of Tireon to save your life. There was a wind that blew through the room, though it wasn't really wind at all. It was power of some kind, something that linked the horn to the other world you had crossed into." She slapped her hands on her thighs. "That's it! It must be! The vision you had last night must have been caused by your crossing back into that other world."

"How could I have crossed over? The Warden of Healing severed the link that connected me to the world of the dead."

"He severed the link, but he wasn't sure if the doorway you'd opened had been completely closed. If it was left open, maybe it's somehow found you and regained its connection. Maybe the Storm King was brought here with the power of the horn, and his touching you in a dream brought the doorway to you."

Gerin considered what she'd said. The thought that all of this could be happening because of *him* was like a crushing weight upon his shoulders. He saw Nandis's dead face, imagined what she would say to him from beyond the grave if he called her as he had called Naragenth: *I'm dead because of you. It is your fault.* He thought of all the others who had died, and those who *would* die at the hands of the Heralds or the Neddari. How many would it be in the end? How much blood would be on his hands?

But it's not my fault, he told himself. *I didn't mean for any of this to happen. I never intended for anyone to die. I just wanted to find Naragenth's library. The* kamichi *is the one who's responsible. His spell is what forced me to do what I did.*

No matter what anyone told him, no matter what he told himself, he could not eradicate the sense that he had failed. That there was a flaw in him that had been exposed for everyone to see, a flaw that could never be fixed, never be forgotten.

"I hope the wizards can tell us something for certain," he said, hoping his words would help him rise above the bleakness and despair he felt himself sinking into, like some animal trapped in the sucking muck of a swamp. *How will I ever set things right?* he wondered. "I'm tired of playing guessing games."

"I wrote down a lot of what we've talked about so I won't forget anything," Reshel said. "I'll add this to the list while I'm on the road."

They gathered near the practice yard in the outer bailey. Heavier clouds had rolled in from the north, and the light in the bailey seemed dim and somehow sad to Gerin, as if mourning the departure of his brother and sister. He stood with a black wool cloak lined with fox fur pulled tight around his neck. Nearby, Therain spoke softly with his men; there was a gentle but steady wind blowing through the bailey that prevented Gerin from hearing what he was saying.

Reshel waited with her escort—a small, slender young woman in layers of white and blue surrounded by hulking soldiers who were well-armed and protected by plate and mail and steel helms.

"You're traveling light," he said to her, eyeing the packhorses standing by the soldiers.

"You've impressed upon me the need for haste. I packed for speed, not comfort."

He hugged her. "Fare well, and be safe. May Telros watch over you and protect you."

"And you," she said as she pulled away. Therain came over and also wished her a safe journey. "Send word as soon as you're able," he said.

A servant from the stables helped her mount Dari, then handed her the gray mare's reins. Her soldiers swung up onto their horses and waited for her command. She smiled at her brothers once more, then pulled Dari about and trotted toward the gates, followed by the guards.

"Time to get going," said Gerin to his brother. "Your castle and your men need you."

Gerin stood there for a long time after they had disappeared, already anxious for Reshel's return and news from the wizards.

22

Riding hard, Therain and his men reached Agdenor at mid-morning two days after leaving Ailethon. The Heralds of Truth had struck again, setting a fire in Rengel that killed seven people. The smoke was still drifting across the river when they emerged from a steep-sided cut in a hillside. At first Therain thought the smoke was coming from the castle and his heart froze. It was not until they drew closer that they realized the smoke was coming from the nearby town.

One of the Heralds had died in the fire, and another had fallen on his knife rather than be captured by the townsmen who had cornered him. His body had been beaten beyond recognition, then hanged from a gibbet at the entrance to the town and burned; after the flames went out, they hung a sign on him that read, DEATH TO THE HERALDS!

There had also been another unexplained death in the castle, and fears of plague were becoming more widespread. Therain could do little to combat it since he could not say it was *not* a plague—and Gerin and Reshel's conjectures made it seem almost a plague bred from magic rather than disease. Master Evernyes had learned nothing else in Therain's absence either of the plague's source or how to combat it.

"What other news do you have?" Therain asked his castellan after hearing of the latest death. "Is there anything I'm going to want to hear?"

Velarien cleared his throat. "My lord, we've received messages from several of your vassals. Three lords said they feel that a gathering of Neddari on Neddari soil is not threat enough for them to call their men-at-arms and march to Agdenor. They feel that until the Neddari set foot in Khedesh itself or demonstrate a clear and hostile intent to us, the terms of their fealty agreements with you have not been met."

Therain wanted to pound his fist into the wall. "At least some have obeyed me."

"Five so far, my lord."

"They play games," said Wilfros. "They feel there's no point in marching here only to camp in the cold, waiting to see what the Neddari will do."

"Technically they're correct," said Therain. He guessed correctly that the written messages to him contained more of the same: *The threat is not enough for us to empty our castles and towns.* His vassals were probably scoffing at him in private, calling him "the lord whelp" and saying he knew nothing of the Neddari and was panicking at his first sight of them. *I hope they're right,* he thought. *I hope this all comes to nothing. Let them laugh at me if it means no war. Let them laugh all they want.* But they had not seen the Neddari. He had, as had men who knew and understood them and could say unequivocally that this gathering was unprecedented. "Their oaths to me do not require them to obey my summons just yet, so we must make certain we're vigilant in watching the Neddari. As soon as it's clear that they're marching toward Khedesh, I'll issue my summons again. If my lords again disobey me, I'll take one of them and hang him from the castle walls as a traitor and oathbreaker. They can test me, but if they endanger Khedesh through their stubbornness and arrogance, I'll see the lot of them executed."

Therain retired to his rooms to rest. He'd been asleep for only a few minutes when there was a knock at the door. He awoke groggily and tried to ignore it, but the knocking persisted. With a groan, he rose from his bed.

Master Evernyes stood in the hall with a small leather pouch. "My lord, I'm terribly sorry to disturb you, but I thought you would want this right away. It is a message from your father the king. The bird arrived only a little while ago. I came as soon as I realized what it was." He handed the pouch to Therain.

"Thank you, Master," he said. "You were right to come at once."

Therain went to his desk and rubbed his face to try to wake himself up; he felt as if his head had been packed with straw. His father's stag-head sigil had been pressed into gold wax sealing the paper.

Therain, I hope this message finds you well. While I am alarmed at the gathering of such a large number of Neddari so near to our borders, until they make some decisive move against us, I have no justification for calling my vassal lords. I hope you understand the situation. Their oaths to me do not require them to obey my summons unless the threat to the sovereignty of Khedesh is clear. While I could push my demand and force even the recalcitrant nobles to heed my call, if the Neddari then do not enter our lands, my power and credibility would be severely damaged—as would yours with your own vassals. In the Assembly of Lords there would more than likely be demands that I pay reparations to the houses. This is something I simply cannot afford. You will find yourself in the same situation with your own vassals, I am sure. I have sent messages to the lords closest to Almaris, telling them what you have told me and asking that they make preparations to march to your defense immediately should word come from you that the Neddari have invaded Khedesh. I expect that you will watch them closely and notify me at once if they move toward our border. I have ordered my own soldiers here in Almaris and the commanders of the Naege to prepare for a march. If

*they do indeed invade, I will come to your aid as swiftly
as I can. May the gods guide and protect you.*

　　　　　　　　　　　　　　　　　　　　Your Father

Therain leaned back in his chair and folded his arms, surprised at how hurt and disappointed he felt. He understood
his father's reasons perfectly, but it still felt as if his father
did not trust his judgment. He thought that if Gerin had sent
the same message, his father would have mustered half the
kingdom at once. He could imagine his father thinking, *It's
just Therain, I'm sure it's nothing to worry about.* He knew
that was not fair, and more than likely not even right; his
father would face the same problems from the houses no
matter who had warned him of the Neddari. But that did not
make his hurt lessen or go away. *At least some of my lords
trust me,* he thought. *At least some are heeding my call.* A
small consolation, but it was all he had.

Baron Jerrin Tovos of Harrendel was the first of Therain's
vassals to arrive, bringing four hundred foot soldiers and fifty
horse. Count Tomalos Imrelain of Molaeros marched across
the Holly Bridge with six hundred foot soldiers and eighty
horse, blowing his trumpets and waving his blue and red
fox-head banners as if he were a conquering hero returning
home after a lengthy campaign. Therain considered him an
insufferable braggart and bore, and his ready agreement had
come as something of a surprise. He had expected Imrelain
to be one of those lords who would stick to the letter of the
law and wait until the Neddari entered Khedesh before
marching. But he would gladly endure the man's ceaseless
boasting as payment for his support.

　Imrelain's men were still filing into the castle when the
count spied Therain in the courtyard and rode over to greet
him. The pleasantries had scarcely been dispensed with
when Imrelain asked that his taxes be cut in half for the next
year. "I've brought my men as you asked, my lord, though
my oath to you does not in fact require it." He stroked his

beard and regarded Therain with narrowed eyes down the length of his long, crooked nose.

"We can talk about remuneration later, Count," said Therain pleasantly. "At the moment we have a castle to fortify and defend."

"I have incurred great cost, my lord, to bring my soldiers here, who may in the end do nothing more than wait out the winter upon the hill and practice their swordsmanship if you are wrong."

"And where they'll be housed and fed at *my* expense. As I said, we can discuss this later. I think now you should see to your men."

Imrelain's mouth tightened. Therain did not flinch from his gaze, and made it plain from his expression that the conversation was over.

"Very well," said Imrelain, spurring his horse forward. "We'll talk about this matter some other time."

Therain ordered a dike to be dug along the southwestern shoulder of Henly's Hill and an earthen rampart set behind it. The dike stretched in a wide curve from the sheer side of the hill on the north to the equally sheer slope on the east. Teams were sent to the pinewoods and oak thickets in the uplands east of the Azren to fell trees and bring them back to the castle in wagons. Sharpened wooden stakes were hammered into the dike walls, and the rampart was reinforced with logs on its inner side. More stakes were placed along the top to form a palisade. A thirty-foot-wide opening was left in the center, which could be closed with a gate of rough-hewn timbers lashed together with stout rope.

Once two thousand soldiers had entered the castle, Therain ordered the remainder of the men to make camp on the far sides of the rivers. He divided what cavalry he had into thirds and sent two groups to each of the camps, keeping the last at Agdenor. He named Lords Urthailes and Stehlwen as commanders of the far camps, since their men comprised the bulk of those forces.

* * *

Therain was on the southern slope of Henly's Hill inspecting the dike and rampart when a messenger arrived from the border.

"My lord, the Neddari army has begun its march." He had removed his helm and held it loosely beneath one arm. The young man was breathing heavily, his cheeks flushed from the chill winter air.

"In which direction are they moving?"

"Toward us, my lord. We estimate more than forty thousand men, plus servants."

Therain dismissed the messenger and started up the slope toward the castle. It was time to call the rest of his vassals and send messages to his father and brother.

He gathered his scribes and sent his messages, then paced the walls of Agdenor, staring down at the dike and the townlands to the west. The dike seemed a woefully inadequate defense against an army so large, but there was little else to be done. He'd commanded the soldiers camped beyond the rivers to build trebuchets. The Neddari would be facing an enemy force on three fortified fronts; they would suffer greatly no matter their size. If they camped around the hill, they would be pounded with missiles from the far banks of both rivers, with no easy way for them to cross. When Gerin arrived with his own vassals, the situation for the Neddari would get worse. If they were planning on moving into the heartlands of Khedesh, they would find that reaching their goal would be far more difficult than they imagined.

But was that their plan? For the first time he wondered about their goal. The Neddari had no need for land; they already had plenty of their own. As far as he knew, they did not lack for livestock or farmlands or mineral-rich hills to mine for the making of their tools and weapons. So why attack Khedesh? The two nations were not friendly and sometimes skirmished along the border, especially when the Neddari came hunting for slaves, but they had no reason or cause to make unprovoked war against the Khedeshians.

Is this a holy war? he thought, remembering the words of the captured Neddari warrior. *Do they intend to convert us to their beliefs or eradicate us as infidels?* He wondered if the fervor of a religious war would make the Neddari even more formidable as foes, especially if they believed one of their gods walked among them. How would *he* fight if he believed—truly and deeply believed—that Telros himself were riding with him into battle?

23

"I don't know how she died," said the Warden of Healing, staring down at the body of Viramele Dreithes. She lay where she was found, crumpled in the doorway to her apartments, her arms flung out over her head as if she'd died grasping for something just beyond her reach. "She was not murdered. There is no wound or trace of poison that I can find. She shows no signs of the sudden aging that befall us before our lives end. There is no damage to her heart or brain."

"Then why is she dead, Kirin?" demanded the Archmage.

"I cannot say."

"How can that be?" The First Siege glowered down at the body as if it were a personal affront. "Are you certain magic was not used against her?"

"I'm certain no *wizard's* magic was used against her. That, I would have found. And I know of no other power that could kill a wizard like this."

"I've heard that two people from the townlands have died mysteriously over the past few days," said Marandra. "Is this the same thing? Do we have a plague on our hands?"

"I've heard about those deaths as well, Archmage. If this is a plague, I've not seen or heard the likes of it before. There are no symptoms, no signs of sickness."

"That is an unacceptable answer," said the First Siege.

"Our sister is dead. We need to know why. If she died naturally, we'll give her to the fire and pray for her Released spirit. But what if she *was* killed, or died of some sickness you have never before seen? That, too, must be known so we can protect ourselves."

"I'll do what I can, First Siege."

"Perhaps you should visit the towns where the others died," suggested Marandra. "There may be something there you can learn."

"What of Viramele, Archmage?" asked Kirin. "When will we Release her?"

"Tomorrow night," she said. "You have until tomorrow at sundown to study her to see if there is anything else to be found." She put her hand on his shoulder. "I have confidence in you, Kirin. If there's something to find, you'll find it."

"I do not share your confidence, Archmage. But I'll do my best. She and I were close friends."

Marandra returned to her manor house and sat in silence. She hated death, especially the death of a wizard. *There are so few of us left. Each one lost brings us a little closer to that final end.* But to have a death that could not be explained, a death that might even be murder . . .

She went to her balcony and looked across Hethnost. What would become of this place when at last the final wizard died? Would anyone live here, or would it become a place to be feared and avoided, haunted by the ghosts and memories of those who had forged their lives within these walls? *Do not go there,* she imagined some wayward traveler saying to another. *It is a place of silence and dread. Beings of great power and majesty once lived there, but they are gone, gone and forgotten; nothing remains but their bitter memories cursing their fate. If you walk there you will arouse their angry spirits. It is best left alone.* She thought of Hethnost falling into ruin, its towers toppling, the roofs of the buildings collapsing, its foundations weakening and finally giving way, the volumes of the Varsae Sandrova dissolving to dust. The death of Hethnost. In a way, that death would be the worst of

all, the most painful and final. She was glad she would not
be present to see it.

Kirin's examination of Viramele's corpse yielded nothing.
He visited the towns where the others had died, only to find
that the dead had already been buried. The Warden spoke
to those who discovered the bodies but learned nothing
more. They asked him if a plague had come among them
and if the wizards could protect them. "I do not think it is a
plague," he told them. "But other than that, I'm certain of
nothing, and there is no protection I can grant for something
I do not yet understand. I'm sorry."

Viramele was given to the Releasing Fire at midnight two
days after her death. Her body was placed on a bier in the
Circle of Awakening, her end as a wizard occurring where it
had begun. The mood of the gathered wizards was grim and
uneasy. They all spoke the words of the spell and directed
the fire into her body, around which they'd created a Warding to contain the fire and increase its potency. The Warding
filled with white-hot flame that consumed everything within
it. When the spell ended, nothing remained of Viramele or
the bier except waves of heat that quickly dissipated in the
cold night air. She was gone, her spirit Released from its
prison of flesh. Afterward they gathered in somber groups to
speak about her life and whisper about what might have
killed her.

Hollin returned with the Archmage to her chambers after
the ceremony. "There is something sinister about her death.
I feel it in my bones. There was nothing wrong with Viramele, no reason for her to just die in her doorway."

Marandra had removed the Ammon Ekril and was sitting
before a mirror brushing out her hair. Hollin put his hands on
her shoulders and gently rubbed her neck. She found his
presence comforting, a steady reassurance that things would
always be right. *But things are not right,* she thought. Something had soured in the world. And Hollin would return soon
to Ailethon. Their relationship had been cooling these past

few years, but his absence had affected her more deeply than she would have thought possible. She had missed him, as surprising as that was. Not at first—her sense of relief at his departure had filled her with guilt—but as the weeks grew into months, she felt a hole appear in her life, a presence in her heart he had once filled.

Now he was back, if only for a short time. There was something subtly different about him, too; though he said all the right things, looked at her as he always did—with a devotion that confounded her because she felt she did not deserve it—something felt false to her, as if he were acting for her benefit.

As if his heart were elsewhere. That he had moved on from her but could not yet bring himself to tell her.

I've been growing tired of him, but now that he seems prepared to end it, I don't want to lose him. How incredibly selfish of me. And foolish.

"I fear you're right," she said. "I wish Kirin had learned something in the towns." She leaned her head back against him and sighed.

"Do you think this has anything to do with what we learned from the sheffain? Could this be a result of the two worlds growing closer?"

"I asked Rahmdil to explore that very question. He was unable to say with certainty one way or the other, though he is continuing to study the matter."

"I'm surprised he told you that much if he wasn't certain. That man can be more cryptic than the Oracle of the Midkaril Rock," said Hollin.

"I'm filled with a terrible dread I can't explain. As we spoke the words tonight to Release her, I had a premonition that she was only the first."

"I hope you're wrong about that."

"So do I."

A serving girl in the kitchens died, and a two-hundred-year-old oak tree suddenly withered and died, its leaves clustered on the ground beneath its dry and brittle branches like pieces of ancient parchment. The inhabitants of Hethnost began to keep to themselves, staying away from public places for fear of a plague, though no one yet spoke such things aloud.

The serving girl, Lannah Gell, had died while speaking to her father, Urley, one of the kitchen cooks. He was inconsolable with grief over her death. His wife had died in childbirth, and he had devoted his life to raising Lannah. "My baby girl, my baby girl!" he wailed as he cradled her body. After she was buried, Urley sat down beneath a great willow tree and slit his wrists, letting his blood flow out onto the hard cold earth. A wizard passing by the next morning saw him propped against the trunk, his chin resting upon his chest. She thought he was sleeping until she saw the blood on the ground and the tears frozen on his face.

When Reshel arrived at Hethnost, she asked to be taken to see the Archmage right away. "My news is urgent and will not wait," she told the guards at the gate.

Hollin spied her upon one of the paths. "Reshel! It's good to see you, but why are you here?" He gave her a quick embrace. "This is not the best of times to be returning, I'm sad to say. There have been some unexplained deaths—"

"I know. That's why I've come."

"You know something about this?"

"I think I do. But there may be more that I can find out here." She squeezed his arm. "I don't mean to be brusque, but I need to speak to the Archmage. She should be the first to hear what I have to say."

"I'll come with you."

The Archmage summoned her other advisors before allowing Reshel to speak. They were seated in a council chamber in the Archmage's manor house; most of the space was occupied by a large round table of dark wood with a patterned gold inlay around the rim. *A place where equals meet,* Reshel thought. Unlike the chamber where Gerin had faced them after the blowing of the horn.

"How have you been, Reshel? Hollin tells me your training is going well. What of your life as a princess?"

"It's been fine, Archmage. Hollin's a good teacher."

A few minutes later the First Siege, High Ministers, and remaining Wardens arrived.

"Reshel claims to have news of the deaths that have troubled us," announced the Archmage. "She's come to tell us what she knows and ask our guidance and help in return. You may speak now."

Looking at all the stern faces staring at her, Reshel felt naked and small. She cleared her throat and told her tale.

She did not look at her notes once. She told them what had happened in Agdenor and Ailethon and why they believed this was somehow related to the Horn of Tireon. She described the dreams of the Storm King and Gerin's strange vision in which he heard the sounds of a nearing battle, as well as Therain's encounter with the mysterious and deadly Red Robes.

"We have had no dreams here," said Kirin when she was finished. "At least I have not heard of anyone having dreams such as you described."

"There are many protections around this castle and its lands," said Hollin. "Many were set in place when Hethnost was first built, and many more were added over the centuries. It may be that this intricate and powerful web of spells is what has prevented the dreams of the Storm King from reaching us."

"I'm surprised none of the townspeople or villagers have come to us about these dreams," said Kirin. "I was just among them. It seems they would have said something to me."

"They may not have discovered that more than one of them is having the same dream," said Sevaisan. "They may think them simple nightmares."

"We should make inquiries to see if this dream has reached these lands," said Hollin. "If it has, then the power behind it has a long arm indeed."

"Who is Asankaru?" Reshel asked. "Is he truly a spirit

that has come through the door Gerin opened with the horn?
It seems that *he* is the reason for the compulsion placed in
my brother, but we do not know why Asankaru would tell
Gerin he needed to complete what he had begun. We have
many pieces of this puzzle, but are missing the means to put
it all together. Is there anything you can tell me?"

"Not yet," said the First Siege. "But what you have told us
explains much. We'll examine the Horn of Tireon again to
see if it will yield its secrets. And we'll search for the identity of Asankaru."

An idea occurred to Reshel. "Could Asankaru be a wizard
of the Baryashin Order? Could their black magic have somehow allowed him to return to this world through the door
Gerin opened?"

"An interesting thought," said the Archmage. "We will
pursue it. You will assist us in our search. I suggest you eat
and get some rest, then join Hollin in the Varsae Sandrova so
he can assign you a task."

She bowed her head. *They've accepted what I said,* she
thought. They didn't think her ideas were ridiculous or foolish, which she had secretly feared. "Yes, Archmage. I'll do
as you say."

Reshel found Hollin in a third-floor antechamber in the Varsae
Sandrova. He commanded her to help the archivists search
through the records of wizards from the era of the Baryashins
to see if the name Asankaru was among them. Some of the
Wardens and archivists studied everything they could find on
the order, including the book of spells linked to the Horn of
Tireon. Reshel spent long hours in the library reading through
books and sheaves of loose paper, some of her research overlapping what other wizards were studying. She found herself
asking questions about what they had learned, and being
asked questions in turn. Marandra received daily reports on
the progress of each group, but for all their efforts, the name
"Asankaru" was as yet nowhere to be found.

She heard whispers that the wizards studying the

Baryashins had made some disturbing discoveries, but no one would tell her what they were. Even Hollin said only: "There are things the Archmage will reveal when she is ready, and not before."

She did not have to wait long to find out what it was. As the mid-morning bells sounded on the fifth day since her arrival, Hollin appeared at her small reading room and said, "We've been summoned by the Archmage."

A group of wizards were standing on the floor of the atrium beneath the library's dome, talking in hushed tones. The tables and chairs had been rearranged to form rows facing one side of the large circular room. A few other wizards entered after Reshel, and then all the doors were shut.

The Archmage and First Siege appeared from a closed room. "Please, sit," the Archmage announced. She stood between two of the fluted columns supporting the upper levels of the room. "There's much to discuss." She waited while the wizards seated themselves at the tables.

"I wish to thank all of your for your work. Since Reshel Atreyano's arrival, you have all striven to find answers to the questions she and others have raised. What is responsible for these mysterious deaths? And who is Asankaru, the Storm King who has the power to appear in dreams? We believe we have answers to those questions. Hollin will speak first."

Hollin stood and moved to the front of the room. "We have uncovered the identity of Asankaru. At least we believe so. The records are very old—all of them predate the founding of Hethnost by centuries. They were fragile, and the Osirin archaic and hard to decipher in places, even for the Archivists, but despite those obstacles we feel we've learned a great deal.

"The name 'Asankaru' belonged to the last king of a race who named themselves the Eletheros. The Atalari called them the 'Aneldromari,' and feared them as creatures of darkness and evil."

Reshel frowned. The name Aneldromari meant, roughly, "shadow-earth-people." *What a terrible race they must have been to earn such a name,* she thought. *No wonder they were feared.*

"A dark name for a dark people," said Hollin. "The records are sketchy, but from what was written, the Eletheros lived in dwellings beneath the earth and had mysterious powers that they used for evil purposes. Apparently, some among the Atalari believed they were a race of demons or demon-spawn who sacrificed their enemies upon altars to the dark gods they worshipped. Their spirits, upon death, were believed to have tarried in this world to torment the living rather than departing this world for the afterlife. They warred often with the Atalari until our ancestors succeeded in driving them from the north-lands. The uprooted Eletheros settled somewhere in the South. It is not known for certain where they made their new home, but it may have been in the lands where the Neddari now live.

"Asankaru was the king and warlord who commanded an Eletheros army in a war against our ancestors that occurred at least six thousand years ago. The oldest accounts we found speak of his power to bend the weather to his will and shape it as a weapon. In the final battle between the Atalari and Eletheros, Asankaru is said to have summoned severe storms with twisters, lightning, and hail. We read a copy of an account that had been written by an Atalarin soldier who said the Eletheros might have won the day if the Storm King could have continued his attack. Apparently he spent his powers quickly and could not recover them before the Atalari killed him and destroyed his army. We surmise that somehow the spirit of Asankaru has passed through the doorway Gerin Atreyano opened."

"What about the Red Robes my brother Therain saw?" asked Reshel.

"Asankaru is said to have had warrior magicians who were his most trusted servants. It may be that he was able to summon them through the doorway with his own powers, or they may have passed through of their own volition. There's no way to know, but I think it likely that the Red Robes are indeed Eletheros as well."

"What of the Storm King's words to Gerin in his dream?" asked the First Siege. "Reshel told us that Asankaru called him the 'summoner' and that he had 'to finish what he had begun.'"

"Yes," said Reshel. "He was the only one who heard those words. I myself dreamed of the Storm King, and that is not what he said to me."

"That delves into the matter of the Baryashin Order, which was studied by others. But we feel that Asankaru and his followers have only partially reentered the world of the living. They can assume a shape but do not have a true body. They are indeed phantoms or ghosts. They may have some material presence to interact with this world in limited ways; for instance, to walk upon the earth or perhaps pick up small objects. That is most likely why weapons pass through them harmlessly. Their physical presence is not strong enough to allow swords or knives to hurt their ethereal forms.

"And they have retained their powers, as your brother witnessed, but perhaps not to the same degree as when they were alive." Hollin drew a breath and his own expression darkened. "It may be that Asankaru is trying to live again. Live as flesh and blood, alive as we are alive."

Someone muttered, "Impossible!" Others called out questions to him, while a few turned to speak to their companions.

"Silence!" shouted the Archmage. At once the room was quiet. "We will have order here, not chaos. Kirin, please join us and tell us what you've discovered."

The Warden of Healing joined Hollin at the head of the table. "We were commanded by the Archmage to study the Baryashin Order and the Horn of Tireon. We've learned much that might answer your questions.

"As some of you know but others may not, the members of the Baryashin Order were dedicated to finding a means to eternal life. They discovered that they could not keep their bodies alive forever—the flesh must one day perish. Its life can be greatly prolonged, but not to the degree the Baryashins sought. It is an immutable law. Tireon al-Vashkiril created the horn as a means of transferring their spirits into other living bodies, preferably children's, whose personalities could be more easily destroyed by the invading spirit. Children also have much longer lives ahead of them.

"It may be that Asankaru is looking for a body to house his spirit, a vessel in which to transfer his essence. We think that is the meaning of his words to Gerin. He must complete the process of the horn and provide Asankaru with a living body. Only Gerin can do this. He is the summoner. He is inextricably linked to Asankaru because of his sounding of the horn, linked in ways we don't fully understand. Unless he were to die, Prince Gerin is the only one who can complete the ritual of the Baryashins."

"Then that part is simple," said a wizard named Terya Uldamaris. "Gerin does not and will not have the horn. Asankaru has no hope of regaining a physical body."

"Is there a way to expel Asankaru from the world of the living?" asked Hollin. "Can he be forced back through the door that Gerin opened?"

Kirin's expression darkened. "What both Terya and Hollin have said lies at the heart of our dilemma. In our probing of the horn we made another dreadful discovery. The horn's power is still active, holding open the doorway between the worlds of the living and the dead. I thought I had closed it when I revived Gerin, but that is not the case. Gerin was brought back to this world from the other, which allowed the door to close, but not quite all the way. Asankaru's very presence keeps it from being completely sealed."

"Then he must be forced through it," said Hollin. "Is there a way to close the door even while he's here in our world? Would that very act return him to the world of the dead?"

"I'll answer your question, Hollin, but there's another matter I want to explain first. We believe that this open doorway between worlds is the reason for the unexplained deaths—it throws the worlds out of balance. The realm of the dead is coming into contact with our world, and where that happens, death occurs instantly, like a black wind blowing through Osseria. The very nature of this power is anathema to life itself. So far as we can determine, it strikes randomly, with no way to know where it will next touch our world. But it will only grow worse over time, as the doorway slowly widens because of Asankaru's presence here. After Gerin's healing, the doorway was nearly shut, its power so slender it could not be found. But the longer Asankaru remains in this world, the larger and more dangerous the doorway will become."

"What if he somehow succeeds in regaining a physical body?" asked Reshel.

"Then it may be impossible to ever seal the connection between the worlds, and all life in Osseria could be destroyed."

Another murmur ran through the wizards, but this time the Archmage did not silence them. Reshel watched Marandra's expression closely. She seemed both horrified and enraged by what she had just heard.

"This is intolerable," said the Archmage. The Ammon Ekril glittered and flashed upon her brow as if somehow infused with her anger. She turned to Kirin. "Can we destroy the horn to undo its power and close the door?"

"I would advise against such action, Archmage. We thought of that ourselves, but we have no idea what the horn's destruction will do. Its magic would be released in a sudden, uncontrollable torrent, and there is no way to know the outcome. It could result in the very thing we are trying to avoid."

Fury gathered around the Archmage with such intensity that Reshel sank back into her chair. "Then what course of action do you recommend? We cannot simply do nothing."

"We realize that, Archmage." Marandra's anger seemed to actually calm Kirin. "There is a spell that will close the door. It's a spell of Compulsion that will force Asankaru back into the realm of the dead, which will seal the worlds off from one another. The Baryashins created the spell to force their own spirits into the bodies they had prepared. They were concerned that a recently disembodied spirit would become disoriented and forget its goal. Instead of possessing the waiting body, they worried it would journey at once to the world of the dead as in the natural course of death. The spell of Compulsion was to be used by the living Baryashins performing the ritual to force the spirit to remain in this world."

"Then we should perform this spell at once," said the First Siege. "There is no time to waste. Even as we speak, others could be struck down by the touch of the world of the dead."

"It is not that simple, First Siege," said Kirin. "We cannot perform it. As I said before, Asankaru's presence is bound to Gerin, who blew the horn that summoned him. Inadvertently, yes, but still, only Prince Gerin can perform the spell of Compulsion."

"Then we must take the horn to him," said the First Siege. "We'll take the horn and the Baryashin spellbook and whatever else is necessary for him to compel Asankaru's spirit. Kirin, you will have to guide him—"

"A moment, First Siege," interrupted Kirin, raising his hand. He looked as if he had swallowed something foul and rancid. "The Baryashins' power was built upon murder and death. The spell of Compulsion requires great power. A very *specific* kind of power. In order to complete the spell, one who is innocent and pure of blood—a child or virgin—must be sacrificed."

The wizards once more voiced their dismay. A jumble of voices enveloped Reshel until the Archmage silenced them with a gesture.

"That, too, is intolerable," she said. Her low voice sounded even more dangerous to Reshel. "We cannot kill an innocent *child* to complete this spell."

The Warden of Healing looked down. "I don't know what else to tell you, Archmage. We've studied this very matter. The spell will not work without the sacrifice. It's the primal catalyst of the Compulsion."

"Then create another spell," she said through clenched teeth. "One that does the same thing without the need for spilling innocent blood. I will not commit murder or condone murder to be committed. *I will not.* Find another way."

Kirin nodded but did not look hopeful. *He doesn't think it can be done,* thought Reshel. *He knows that what she's asked of him is impossible.* A coldness filled her as she watched the Archmage wheel about and storm from the atrium. Kirin remain where he was, his eyes locked on the floor.

24

Reshel sought out Kırın and found him in one of the study rooms. He had several leather-bound volumes open on the table before him and several unrolled scrolls, a few of which were so old and brittle they seemed ready to crumble to dust at the merest touch. He was taking notes in a slender book, writing very fast, reading and then scribbling something down, only to cross it out moments later. The magefire lamp suspended above his head cast a cone of warm yellow light upon the table. Gloom settled heavily in the corners of the room, as if his mood had seeped out of him and into the very air of the chamber.

"Hello, Warden," she said quietly.

Startled, Kirin looked up at her. "Oh, hello, Reshel. What can I do for you?"

"I want to help," she said, taking a step into the room. "I know I'm not finished with my training—in fact, I've scarcely begun—but that doesn't mean I have nothing to contribute. I can't see why it would hurt to have another set of eyes looking over other spells to see what might be made to work, or thinking about ways to solve this problem."

He smiled. It was a tired smile, but she was glad nonetheless to see it. "I know, Reshel. I'm sorry. You shouldn't have been kept out. We aren't used to having you here, and when we assigned tasks, you were overlooked." He put his pen in its well and wiped his hands. "If you're going to help us search for alternatives, you first have to understand the spell of Compulsion. It is horrifying magic, and under other circumstances I would not let you come near the Baryashin spellbook. But if we're to use you, it's something you'll have to read."

He led her to a nearby room that was sealed with both physical locks and magic. He produced an amulet to first undo the spells, removed a key from one of his pockets and unlocked the door. "Wait here," he said, then stepped inside and closed the door. In a moment he reappeared with a thin book bound in black leather.

They returned to the room where she had found him. He slid a second chair close to the table and gestured for her to sit.

"This is the spellbook of the Baryashins, which your brother used to call Naragenth. The spell of Compulsion is here." He opened the book toward the back and flipped through several pages before stopping. The runes of death and spirit had been written at the top of the yellowed page, intertwined by a strange symbol she did not recognize, like two loops twisted back upon themselves.

"That is the symbol of the Baryashin Order," he said, pointing to the twisting loops. "They saw themselves as an eternal power that would allow the spirit to elude death. But in the end all they did was create death. A terrible waste, and a blight upon us and upon Hethnost."

He returned to his seat and took up his pen. "You need to understand that spell. Learn it well. If you are to help us find a way to create the same power without the use of a sacrifice, you will have to know it completely. I won't say do not fear it, because it is something to be feared. When you've shown me you have sufficient understanding, I'll bring other books of dark magic for you to read, to see if they contain any spells that might be of use to us. You may not take them from the Varsae Sandrova, and you may not have them outside of my presence. Do you understand?"

"Yes, Warden. But I won't attempt something foolish on

my own. I know the rules and obey them." She tried not to
sound slighted, but it was hard.

"You need not take affront at this. You've not been singled out. Only the Wardens, archivists, and the Archmage
herself may have these books alone. Even the High Ministers would not be allowed to take them. These precautions
are for everyone's safety. Some of these spells are so dangerous that simply the act of reading them can trigger unknown and potentially deadly consequences."

That surprised her. "Thank you, Warden. I understand."
She folded her hands, looked down and began to read.

It did not take her long to learn the spell. It was surprisingly simple compared to the one she heard that Gerin had
used to summon Naragenth. Apparently opening the doorway and calling a spirit was harder in some respects than
compelling and controlling a spirit, though the latter required a specific kind of power—namely, a blood sacrifice—to work.

The idea of committing murder to acquire the necessary
energies to compel a spirit was dreadful enough, but the eager, almost excited tone in which the spell had been written
made the horrific and unspeakable acts described seem even
more obscene. She read it several times over the course of
an hour, then asked the Warden if she could be excused for a
few minutes to take a walk.

"Of course," he said. "I know how disturbing this is. Take
all the time you need. And if you think—"

"No, Warden. Please. I'm fine," she said, trying to sound
more sure than she felt. "I just feel . . . *unclean*. Tainted by
the very act of reading it."

"Knowledge can be a very dangerous thing, Reshel," he
said. "We are changed by what we learn, whether good or
bad. For good people, learning the dark things that others
are capable of can change us the most. Knowledge can never
be unlearned, which is why dangerous knowledge—like that
created by the Baryashin Order—was kept safely locked
away. Such knowledge always comes with a price."

* * *

While Reshel was wandering through the upper floors of the Varsae Sandrova to clear her thoughts, Hollin and Marandra were approaching a room on the ground level many floors below her. Located off a narrow corridor near the offices of the Archivists, the room was locked with a special key amulet in the sole possession of the Archmage. It appeared on no map or diagram of the Varsae Sandrova, and was not mentioned in any of the histories of the library. Anyone passing through that corridor would see only stone walls unbroken by a door or window. But there was a door, hidden halfway along its length, and it could be opened if one held the proper key. The spells that guarded it were created so a wizard could not detect them even if he searched for them directly; seeking spells would pass over the spells as if they did not exist.

The Archmage and Hollin were careful not to be seen, passing quickly and silently through the hallway until they reached its center. The Archmage pulled out a small silver chain that hung around her neck. Attached to the chain was a sapphire held in a delicate filigree of silver, fashioned in the shape of a leaf. The *lhasa* rune, the rune of dreaming, had been worked into the surface of the leaf in an intricate braid of wire.

She drew magic into herself and spoke several words in Osirin. A blue light flashed deep in the heart of the sapphire, then a faint blue outline appeared on the wall in the shape of a door. She pushed, and it swung inward in complete silence. She and Hollin stepped through and closed the door behind them. The blue outline vanished, leaving no trace of where the door had been.

As soon as she entered the room, Marandra's key amulet caused a small magefire lamp held in a wall sconce to brighten. They found themselves in a small square space with nothing in it but the lamp and a second door, set opposite the one they had just passed through. This one, fashioned of old, heavy wood, was visible, and they wasted no time opening it. On the other side was a narrow twisting stairway made of stone. They began to descend, Marandra leading the way.

She'd gone ten steps when her key amulet lit another magefire lamp. The lamps were set at regular intervals along the winding stairway and would remain burning until the key amulet passed them again. The stairs continued down deep beneath the Varsae Sandrova but did not intersect its many layers of subterranean corridors and vaults. There was but one way in or out of the stairs, and that was through the door they had passed.

They continued on the stair for a long while, descending in silence. Marandra did not like being on the stair. She did not like venturing into any of the subterranean passages beneath the Varsae Sandrova, though she had never shared this secret with anyone, not even Hollin. It embarrassed her to feel frightened of a place simply because it was below the ground. The thought of so much weight above her was terrifying, threatening to close in and trap her far from the light of day. She knew she was being foolish, but no matter what she told herself, her fright remained. She was not afraid when in buildings with many stories above her, so why should she fear being underground? She could not answer that question, which vexed her even more. Over the years, she had managed to control her fear to the point where it was now little more than a lingering discomfort, though occasionally and unexpectedly a sudden overwhelming dread would rise up and clutch her heart like a cold hand, taking her breath away and forcing her to pause to recover. So far on this descent that had not happened, though she walked with deliberate care in case her legs went suddenly weak.

The stairway ended at an arched opening, carved ages ago through the limestone wall. Beyond the opening was an impenetrable darkness.

As soon as Marandra passed through the archway, a dozen lamps seated upon twin rows of pedestals flared to life. They found themselves in an immense cavern, its distant ceiling beyond the reach of the lamps, which were hooded to cast their illumination downward. The far side of the cavern was more than one hundred feet distant, and more than three times that in length. Rough columns of stone rose around them like the trunks of strange trees, their surfaces slick and glistening with moisture. Directly in front of them the columns of stone had been cleared in a straight line to form a path. The lamps stood six to a side along the path's edge, and at the end there was a lake.

It filled the cavern from the end of the path to the far side, where there was no ledge or shore, just a sheer wall of stone. Only in this spot was there a dry shore, where the rock of the cavern rose up out of the water in a ragged semicircular bank. The surface of the lake was utterly still, with no waves or swells to disturb the dark waters. It looked to Marandra like a great sheet of black glass.

She had never before used the power of the Tivar Lhasaril, the Lake of Dreaming. It shared its name with the lake that lay at the entrance to the Valley of Wizards, where it was said that Venegreh, while sleeping near its shore, had his vision of the building of Hethnost. The lake in the valley was believed to be enchanted with the power to grant visions or portents of the future. Over the centuries many wizards had slept there, and a handful had indeed experienced dreams that later proved to be true.

But that lake had no powers of its own. The true Lake of Dreaming was here, buried deep beneath the earth. Venegreh had not known of it. It was not discovered until long after he was dead. Once it had been found and its properties discovered, the Archmage at the time, Sardovus Erleng, had decided its powers would be held by the rulers of Hethnost alone. He feared that wizards would paralyze themselves with indecision when faced with difficult choices, that they would try to use the lake to show them what they should do rather than decide for themselves. *To know the future is perilous,* Erleng had written in his private diary. *The power of the lake is very great, but what it reveals does not always come to pass. I believe it shows what is likely or probable rather than what will or must be. It should be used only in the most dire of circumstances, and only then with great caution and care.* Marandra had reread his words just hours ago, before deciding to summon Hollin and come here to see what the lake could tell them.

My need is great, she thought as she walked down the path to the lake's edge. At the end of the path, on the very edge of the lake, a stone slab was set upon two thick legs of rock. Marandra placed herself upon the slab and folded her hands upon her stomach. "Watch over me, Hollin."

"I will." He placed his hand over hers and smiled down at her. "May Venegreh guide you and keep you safe."

She returned his smile, then closed her eyes. She quickly fell into a trance, and within a few minutes was asleep.

She came awake with a start, her body shuddering as if cold water had been poured on her face. She felt disoriented, and her vision seemed clouded. "Hollin?" she called out. She heard the fear in her voice. "Are you there?"

A hand squeezed hers. "I'm here." Her vision cleared and she saw him leaning over her. A wave of nausea swept through her.

"Are you all right?" he asked.

She swallowed. Her throat felt very dry. "I'm fine. A little weak. Just let me lie here a while." The nausea passed. "Did you bring any water?"

"No. I didn't think to. But the lake is right here—"

"No. It's forbidden to drink from it. I'll be fine." Fragments of her vision flashed through her thoughts. *Is there no other way?* she wondered. She opened her eyes once more. "How long was I asleep?"

"I would guess between one and two hours."

She sat up slowly, holding his hand for support. He put his other arm around her shoulders, and she let herself lean against him.

"Can you make it back up the stairs?"

The thought of the long climb back up filled her with dread. "I'll be fine. Just give me a few minutes to regain my strength." Her throat felt like she had swallowed dust and ashes, but there was nothing to be done until they were back in the Varsae Sandrova. She would not drink from this lake if she were dying of thirst.

"You had a vision, didn't you?" he asked after a while. "What did you see?"

"Yes. It was very powerful, and terrifying. I'm not ready to speak of it. Come, let's go."

"You want us to leave in the morning?" asked Kirin, staring at the Archmage in disbelief.

Reshel was also surprised. She had been poring over a book of black magic more than a thousand years old, written by wizards who had served the pirates of Lingul. She looked from Kirin to the Archmage and then to Hollin, who stood beside her in the doorway. Something had happened, she realized, but she was certain Marandra and Hollin were not going to tell them what it was.

"Yes," said the Archmage. She looked weary to Reshel, as if she had not slept in days. She spoke to Kirin, but glanced toward Reshel from the corners of her eyes, which unnerved Reshel. "You, Reshel, Hollin, and an escort of the Sunrise Guard will take the horn to Prince Gerin at Ailethon."

"But Archmage, we've only just begun to search for another spell to Compel Asankaru," protested Kirin. "What purpose is served by going to Prince Gerin if we have nothing to offer him?"

"You may take whatever resources you need and study them on the road. Time is of the essence. You are to get the devices of the Baryashin Order to Ailethon as soon as possible."

"What have you learned?" he asked.

"I've learned nothing," she said sternly. But her eyes flickered toward Reshel. "But I've guessed many things that I cannot share with you." Her expression softened and she stepped forward and placed her hand on the Warden's shoulder.

"Kirin, you must trust me in this. To tell you what I suspect may undo the very thing we're trying to achieve. I dislike speaking in riddles, but that is the best I can do." She looked at Reshel directly for the first time, smiling at her maternally. The warmth of that look startled Reshel so much that she lowered her eyes to the table. The Archmage placed a finger beneath her chin and gently raised her head. "And you, young wizard," she said softly, with a gentleness that was unlike her, "are stronger than you know. Remember that when this struggle seems darkest."

"Archmage? I don't understand."

Marandra did not answer. Instead she said, "Tell your brother to do what must be done to rid the world of Asankaru. He, too, must be strong when the time comes." She tucked a loose strand of Reshel's hair behind her ear, then left the room. Hollin vanished with her.

"What was that all about?" Reshel asked Kirin.

"I have no idea. The Archmage has always been a very direct woman. I've never seen her so cryptic. She has learned or guessed something, and it would be best for us to obey her."

25

A cold rain fell the night before the Neddarı
army arrived at Agdenor, a sad silver curtain that damp-
ened the already dark moods of the Khedeshians. The rain
turned to a drizzle, then a faint mist, then ceased altogether
an hour before dawn, when a thick fog rose from the rivers
and drifted across the land.

In full armor, Therain walked the battlements near the gate
towers, with Captain Hiremar and his personal guards close to
him. Therain's stomach was in knots as he waited for news.
His outriders had been shadowing the vanguard of the enemy
for days as it crossed Calad-Ethil. Villagers and townfolk had
fled before the enemy, taking with them what they could and
burning any food they had to leave behind. Many had come to
Agdenor seeking refuge, but the castle's population had already swollen with the arrival of the vassals and their soldiers,
and he was forced to turn nearly all of them away, sending
them across the rivers into the holds and keeps of the very
lords now camped at Agdenor.

Nothing was visible more than thirty or forty feet out
through the fog. The men moving through the courtyard
were little more than murky, ghostly shapes. It made him increasingly nervous, knowing there was an enemy out there
that he could not see.

"They're coming!" someone cried. In the fog, he could

not tell where the voice was located. It seemed the speaker was everywhere and nowhere at once; he knew, though, that this particular voice had to be coming from the direction of the approaching army. "They're coming!" the same voice shouted again. "Prepare the defenses!"

The knot in Therain's stomach tightened. The fog had thinned somewhat since the early morning, and he prayed it would burn off quickly. He did not want attacks made against his defenses by enemies he could not see, and the fog would make it difficult for the troops beyond the rivers to harry the Neddari. As he stared into the gray haze, it occurred to him that the fog would hamper the Neddari as well. But he still did not like it. He said a prayer of thanks to Telros when a steady wind began to blow from the west.

"Elmen," said Therain in a low voice, "why didn't you send Vaiseth and Lorel to Ailethon? It's certainly a privilege of your station to send your family to safety."

Elmen paused before answering. "My lord, my wife and daughter are everything to me. I could not bear to be apart from them for as long as a siege might endure, and they will not be parted from me. I'm certain we'll prevail, and I saw no need to be separated from them."

The wind picked up even more; the fog at last began to clear. The Neddari army was less than two miles from the foot of Henly's Hill, darkening the brown grassy plain like an oncoming flood. Therain's blood ran cold when he saw its size. Several thousand horsemen formed the vanguard, carrying banners and spears and wearing mostly chain mail over leather jerkins, though some, perhaps the captains, wore plate armor and crested helms; behind them came foot soldiers armed with swords and spears, forming a wide line like a river that vanished into the hazy distance. There were perhaps a thousand drogasaars with them as well, their upswept, batlike ears looking like horns rising from their dark-skinned heads. Scimitars were slung across their backs, hilts up, two for each of the creatures. Therain heard a murmur run through his men as they first caught sight of their enemy.

There was nothing to do but watch while the Neddari army neared the hill and began to spread out around it, beyond the range of Khedeshian longbows. Therain's forces and their trebuchets on the far sides of the rivers were clearly visible now, and the Neddari kept the flanks of their army well away from the rivers, which was exactly what Therain wanted. *They may have greater numbers, but if we can keep them bottled up tight, they can only come at us from one fairly narrow corridor. Their numbers won't do them much good.* His forces across the rivers could make sorties against the flanks of the Neddari if they tried a head-on assault of the castle.

"They're deploying exactly as we hoped," said Captain Hiremar. "Hemming themselves in so that when they stick out their neck we can chop it off."

"Let's hope the Neddari are cooperative when the time comes. But I don't like having to depend on an enemy doing the obvious. They have to know the difficulties and dangers of a siege from their position. I'm sure their captains are devising strategies of their own to thwart us."

"Perhaps, perhaps not. They have no siege engines, so they'll have to build them, which will take time. Their men seem well-provisioned and there's a sizable train behind the main host, but it will still take much to feed this many men, and their supply lines do not run all the way back to Neddar. There's little forage left here. Your brother will be coming with reinforcements, and your father after that. All we need do is hold out until then and we will rout them before us."

"I hope you're right. What you say is perfectly reasonable. It seems almost inevitable. But I doubt the Neddari have come here without plans of their own. I'm telling you, Elmen, they have a plan to defeat us that seems as inevitable to them as yours seems to us, and we can't forget that. To think any other way will get us killed."

"Yes, my lord."

"We can't forget the Storm King, if he's truly the one who leads this army. He's a sorcerer, and I doubt we've seen the full extent of his powers. And there will be the Red Robes to contend with."

Servants began to erect tents well behind the vanguard of the army. Night was coming, and servants moved about the camp building fires and hanging cookpots. Therain looked for the Red Robes. He did not see them, but he knew they were there. He feared them and their powers. How could he defend against ghosts who could kill with magic? For all he knew, they could tear the castle down around his ears without a Neddari soldier ever getting any closer.

"I'm going down to the rampart. If they send an embassy, I must be there to answer."

His men cheered him as he descended one of the stairways from the wall with his guard behind him. He smiled despite the grimness of the day. "Send the bloody Neddari to Shayphim, my lord!" called out one soldier. Other men shouted their approval and raised their swords and shields. *I can't let them down,* he thought as he passed through a postern door near the gates. He was no longer the lord whelp to them—he was their commander, their duke, the one who would bring them victory. *I have to figure out how to win.*

As he walked down the hill, surrounded by his guards with their shields held high, the soldiers on the rampart turned and cheered. He recognized Davin Simmolo, the soldier who had first brought them word of the gathering Neddari army, conferring with another man whose long graying braid identified him as Captain Melfistan.

The captain in charge of the soldiers on the rampart, Bael Arvandi, had been conferring with several of his lieutenants in a tent near the gate. He emerged at once upon hearing that his lord was nearing. When he saw Therain, he bowed his head and saluted.

"My lord, I welcome you. Would you care for some mulled wine? There is some in my tent."

Therain shook his head. "No, Captain, but thank you for your offer."

"Of course, my lord. They've done little so far but make

their camp ready. They're beyond the range of our bows, I fear, though our trebuchets might be able to reach the forward edge of their van."

"We'll wait to attack," said Therain. "But make certain your men are ready. When the Neddari move, I want them to have to charge through a hail of missiles to reach us. Keep the range of the trebuchets short. I'd rather use them to hinder an attack than force them to move their camp back a little."

"As you command, my lord."

Therain climbed the roughly squared logs to the top of the rampart. He looked out from between angled stakes pounded into the earth and sharpened to a deadly point. The size of the army arrayed against him again filled him with dismay. A servant brought him heated spiced wine at the command of Captain Arvandi. Therain sighed and accepted the cup. He drank it while the Neddari continued to prepare their camp. There was still no sign of the Red Robes.

"We will prevail, my lord," said Elmen beside him. "Agdenor is strong, and its defenders are stronger. And we have you to lead us."

The lord whelp, indeed. They look to me now to calm their fears, but what will they say if I fail them?

A short while later there was movement along the forward lines of the Neddari camp—several men emerging from one of the larger tents, and soldiers lining up in formation near them. Horses were brought, and three men mounted. Others then mounted, and even at this distance Therain could see that some of the men in the latter group were very different from the rest. A dozen seemed regular soldiers, three carrying standards whose markings Therain could not make out. But the other men carried staffs and wore no armor that Therain could see, though it had grown too dark to be sure.

A path opened before them and vanished in their wake as soldiers and servants moved aside to let them pass. They soon passed beyond the forward line of the army and increased their pace as they crossed the long stretch of open land that ran to the foot of Henly's Hill.

He could now see that three of the men wore full armor of strange design, and elaborate helms painted white and red, with tall plumes rising from the crests. *Those will be the captains,* Therain thought as he watched them near the hill. The strange men with no armor, he saw, wore dark clothing and heavy cloaks with hoods they had thrown back to reveal long hair bound into many braids.

"Captain Arvandi, who are those dark men with the staffs? Are they the *kamichi*?"

"Aye, my lord. Foul magicians who call unclean spirits to kill for them. They can't send their elementals far or hold them long in this world, but they're still very dangerous." The captain told one of his men to have their archers ready themselves. "If those *kamichi* start to call their elementals, they're to be killed at once. Don't wait for me to give the order. Tell the men to use their judgment in this." The soldier hurried off down the line of the rampart.

The Neddari reached the foot of the hill and began to climb the wide road that led toward the closed gate in the rampart. They stopped fifty feet from the defenses.

"Who among you is the leader of this place?" shouted one of the men with plumed helms. He had a sword strapped to his side. "I am Delgo Nerat Igrulun, chieftain of Clan Térutheg, Overchieftain and Warlord of the army of the God Who Has Returned." His accent was so strange and thick that it took Therain a moment to understand what he'd said. "I would speak with your high captain, or whoever commands this fortress of rock."

Therain straightened and moved to a part of the rampart where he could better see and be seen. "I am Therain Atreyano, Prince of Khedesh, Duke of Agdenor, Warden and Protector of this castle and all its lands in the name of my father the king," he called out. "You have violated the sovereign nation of Khedesh with your unlawful and unprovoked invasion. Even now the king and our eastern lords are mustering a mighty host to destroy you. If you depart now you will be allowed to return to your own lands unmolested and we will neither follow you nor attempt to exact retribution for your actions. But if you remain, you will be shown no mercy."

"Brave words for a man whose house of stone has just become a cage," said Igrulun. "The God Who Has Returned cares nothing for your country or king. All people will bow to His will and worship Him in the end. Any who do not will perish on our swords. Their spirits will be sent wailing into the Sea of Lamentation in the depths of the earth." He thrust his fist above his head. "Hear me, Therain Atreyano and people of Khedesh! You cannot hope to stand against our might. The God Who Has Returned is among us, and His power will cast you down if you do not submit to Him. These are the terms for your surrender:

"First, that the god-summoner will be brought to this place along with the Horn of Calling, so that the God Who Has Returned can become fully manifest in the world.

"Second, that you and all your people, and all the people of this kingdom, and all your children and their children, will lay down your weapons and swear never to take up arms against us again.

"Third, that you and all your people, and all the people of this kingdom, will proclaim and acknowledge the overlordship of the God Who Has Returned, and swear—"

"I have heard enough, Igrulun," said Therain. "Your terms are rejected utterly. We are not a craven people who will bow our necks to invaders at the first show of arms. Caged I may be, but this cage is strong, and you may find that you will batter yourself to your death trying to enter it. You have heard my terms: leave now and you will live, remain and continue this folly, and you and your men will never see the lands of your fathers again." He turned away from the rampart and stepped out of sight.

"You have doomed yourself and your people, Therain Atreyano," called out Igrulun. "Remember your choice when you feel the bite of our swords!"

"Well done, my lord," said Elmen. "Well done."

"Make certain the men are prepared. It will not be long now before they attack."

"Those were good words you spoke, my lord," said Captain Arvandi. He sounded surprised. Therain had heard from Elmen that Arvandi was one of the men who had called him "the lord whelp" and spoken disparagingly of his inexperience. "Brave and defiant and merciful all at once. You have a gift of speech."

Not long after Igrulun and his company returned to the camp, several shapes emerged from the largest tent. The Neddari nearby stepped away as if they feared to approach them. *The God Who Has Returned, indeed,* thought Therain. The spirit Gerin had unleashed had apparently managed to convince the entire Neddari people that it was an ancient god of theirs that had returned from . . . where? Why would a god disappear? Where would it go? And, most importantly, what could kill a god?

The flesh of his arms and scalp crawled when he beheld the Red Robes striding forth, their staffs held in the crooks of their arms. The eerie brightness about them was still present. There were seven in all, their blue skullcaps visible with their hoods thrown back. They moved with long but easy strides, filled with a confidence, an arrogance, that Therain could sense even from a distance. *What are they?* he wondered. He'd never heard of such beings, even in stories. Where in the name of Telros had they come from?

Then he saw another figure following them, shining like the Red Robes. He wore white armor with markings of gold upon the breastplate; his long black hair was tied into many braids, and sparks of light shone in his eyes like points of liquid silver. He carried no staff or weapon that Therain could see.

"Captain Arvandi, as soon as they are in range . . ."

"Yes, my lord," said the captain, turning away from one of his lieutenants. "I've already given the order to the archers."

He stepped next to Therain. "What are they, my lord? Are these the ghost creatures that you met?"

"Yes. And I think the figure in white armor is the Storm King himself."

The Red Robes reached the base of the hill and began to climb the road. Therain heard a soldier bark a command; a second later a score of archers unleashed their arrows. The missiles whistled through the air in a high arc.

But as Therain had expected, the arrows passed through the bodies of the Red Robes and Storm King as if they did not exist. They landed in a tight cluster on the road, where most of the shafts shattered upon the stone.

"The gods preserve us and protect us," muttered Captain Arvandi. "They truly are ghosts."

Therain heard a shout of, "Again!" He heard the thrum of the bowstrings and the whistling of the arrows; but again they hit their marks without causing harm.

"Captain, have your men save their arrows," said Therain.

Arvandi seemed shaken by what he had seen. "As you command, my lord." He spoke to another of his lieutenants, who hurried off to relay his order. "If we can't use our weapons against them, how can we defeat them?"

I have no idea, thought Therain. He needed Gerin or Reshel or Hollin, and had none of them. "Let's see what they intend to do, Captain," he said. "If we can't harm them, maybe we can at least thwart their purpose."

The Red Robes stopped about a hundred yards from the timber gate in the rampart. They formed a circle around the Storm King, then placed the ferrules of their staffs on the ground and angled them in toward their master. The figure in white armor stood with his fists clenched at his sides. The silvery points of light in his eyes shone bright in the dark hollows of his sockets, as if some secret fire were burning deep within him.

"I am Asankaru!" shouted the figure. Therain heard his voice as clearly as if the Storm King were standing but a few feet away. "We have not forgotten your crimes! The time has come for justice!"

He raised his arms and shouted words that Therain could not understand. Sparks of light appeared around Asankaru's head like a swarm of fireflies. Wind suddenly howled up the hill toward them, strong gusts that forced Therain to squint and peer through his fingers to see anything at all. Asankaru had thrown his head back and stared up at the dark sky overhead. The staffs of the Red Robes began to glow with a blue light that rippled up and down their length.

Therain looked up and saw black clouds forming with incredible speed against the night sky. Hanging low overhead, the clouds spun with a mad energy, churning like the surface of a storm-swept sea, if the sea were turned upside down and hung above them. Lightning flashed, followed immediately by deafening cracks of thunder that rattled his bones. *Miendrel is laughing,* he thought. *The god of war has ever loved the clash of battle.*

"My lord, back to the castle *now*!" shouted Elmen. He grabbed Therain by his upper arm and tugged him away from the front of the rampart.

Therain nodded and took several steps back, though he kept his eyes fixed on Asankaru, awed by what he was seeing. The display of magic was far beyond anything he could have imagined. *So this is why he is named the Storm King.* Finally he pulled his gaze away and followed Elmen off the rampart, flanked by four others of his personal guard. He could see soldiers rushing about securing tent pegs and tying flaps closed while the campfires whipped about madly in the wind.

He glanced upward again as they ran up the hill. The sky looked as if it were boiling, a vast swirling maelstrom that spun faster and faster as he watched. Lightning flashed out of the whirlpool of clouds and struck a section of the rampart to the north. Men were blown off the ground and fell with their armor seared into their flesh. The sharpened stakes closest to the point of impact exploded into hundreds of flaming splinters that sliced men to bloody ribbons.

Therain clenched his teeth. The first of his men had fallen, but they would be far from the last.

Then came a thunderclap so powerful the very earth shook, heaving beneath him so violently that he stumbled and fell to his knees. He heard men shouting and screaming behind him and turned to look.

He was high enough up the hill to be able to see Asankaru and his Red Robes over the top of the rampart. The Storm King's body was engulfed in a shimmering column of translucent energy that flowed from the earth beneath his feet into the black churning clouds.

We're all going to die, thought Therain, frozen by the sight. *His power is going to kill us all.* A dark despair washed over him, a terrible regret that he would not see his father or brother or sisters ever again in this life.

Hands pulled him to his feet. "My lord, we must get to the castle!" shouted Elmen. Therain followed, though there was no hope left in his heart. What good were swords, spears, and arrows—what good were the strong walls of Agdenor itself?—against an enemy who could command such power?

The wind shrieked around them. They'd gone no more than a dozen steps farther when a driving rain began to fall. The freezing drops pelted them with stinging force where they struck exposed flesh. Therain was all but blinded. He could see perhaps twenty feet in front of him before all was lost in a blur of wind and rain.

He followed two of his guards, his gaze fixed on the backs of the men. He knew that two more were beside him and that Elmen was behind; other than that there was little he could discern.

The men in front of him halted, and Therain realized they had reached the castle. The men pounded on the postern door, which open to release a sliver of yellow lantern-light through the crack. "The lord of the castle has returned!" shouted one of the guards. "Open the door!"

The rain faltered, disappearing as quickly as it had begun. Therain felt as if he had just crawled from a river. He turned to see what was happening behind him. Asankaru was still engulfed in his shimmering pillar of magic, a watery column of light and power, surrounded by the Red Robes.

There was another grumble from the sky, as if some gigantic beast had growled in hatred and anger. Therain looked up once more and saw the black whirlpool of clouds form a funnel that began to descend like a finger of doom toward the earth.

26

Balandrick was on his way to his rooms from a meeting with Gerin and several company commanders when he nearly crashed into Claressa. She jumped back, startled, her eyes wide, her hands pressed against her chest.

"Forgive me, my lady," he said. "I did not see you. I'm surprised you're not carrying a lamp. I'd have seen you otherwise."

"This is my home, Balandrick, and it's not yet dark in here. It's nice to know I'm not invisible, though. There's so much going on in the castle, and I've been so thoroughly ignored for the past few days that I feared I'd become a ghost."

It's hard to imagine anyone ignoring you, Claressa, he thought. What he said was, "Not at all. There's just a lot for us to do that demands our attention."

"By *us* and *our* you obviously mean *men,* since what demands your attention is your preparation for war, which is a thing for men, and men alone. The fighting part, at least. The killing and the dying. The women are left behind, mothers and daughters and wives, to keep the hearths warm and wait to see whether their men return to them alive and whole."

He could not tell if she were speaking in a simple, matter-of-fact manner or with a more cynical, sarcastic intent. "Yes, my lady. That is indeed the way of war. Would you have it otherwise? Would you send women into battle with sword and spear and shield, to die with their guts strewn across the ground or their limbs hacked off?"

"No. I would that there was no war at all," she said sincerely, staring him straight in the eyes.

"You and I agree in that, but it seems the world does not share that view, and unfortunately when war is thrust upon us we must respond in kind or be swept away."

"Which way are you going, Balandrick?"

He gestured down a branching hallway with a staircase at its end. "To my rooms to catch a bit of sleep, my lady."

"Then our paths take us in the same direction. I'll walk with you." She threaded her arm through his—a gesture that surprised and startled him—then fell in beside him.

"From my window I can see the northern roads," said Claressa as they walked. "There were more soldiers marching toward the castle this morning. I don't know how many there were; I have no faculty for guessing such things. I don't understand how others can look at so many men and know their number. But even I can tell that Gerin's army is growing large."

"That it is, my lady."

At the top of the stairs, Claressa spoke abruptly. "It's plain to anyone who has eyes that you have feelings for my sister, Balandrick. And that she has them for you."

He felt a sudden clenching of his lungs and heart, but tried to make no outward sign that her words disturbed him. He and Reshel had decided before they reached Ailethon that they would not try to keep their relationship secret, though neither would they flaunt it. They'd had precious little time together before her departure for Hethnost. He was surprised Claressa had noticed anything at all, considering how little attention she paid to her sister. Then he remembered this was Claressa.

Still, it bothered him to have her aware of his feelings and speaking to him about it. "If it is so obvious, my lady, what is your point in commenting?"

"No point other than to get you to acknowledge it, which

by not denying it outright I suppose you have." She stopped
and turned to face him. In the lamp light, Claressa's features
possessed an ethereal beauty that literally made him catch
his breath. Yet it was also a cold, perilous beauty; she was a
Snow Princess, and were she ever to sit upon a throne, he
imagined she would be called—by subjects who both loved
and feared her in equal measure—a Winter Queen.

He much preferred Reshel's simpler beauty, the fragility
of her features that belied the iron-hard strength beneath.
And not just because of her wizardry, though that discovery
had allowed her to flourish in new and unexpected ways. She
and Claressa were both strong-willed and determined, he
realized; yet Reshel used her abilities to help those she loved
and admired, where Claressa was interested only in herself.

"I do care for her," he said, drawing himself up a little
straighter. "What of it, my lady? Forgive me for being blunt,
but what concern is it of yours?"

She tilted her head and a thin smile touched her lips; then
she turned and continued to walk. "It is no concern of mine,
Balandrick. But it may be a concern of my father's."

"Then that is between me and your father. Or Reshel and
your father."

"Does her wizardry not bother you in the least?" From the
tone of her voice, he knew they had at last come to the reason
she was talking to him in the first place. "That if you two were
to be wed, she would outlive you by hundreds of years?"

"It does not bother me at all. Either a husband or wife
must outlive the other. You may outlive the man you wed, or he
may outlive you. What if you die in childbirth, my lady?
He would outlive you by decades, and perhaps take another
wife. You will be dead, so what will it matter to you? If you outlive him, what will *he* care? Reshel will outlive both of us because of her wizardry. What does it matter to me, or to you?"

He felt her tense and knew he had angered her. "Of *course*
it matters."

"Then you must explain to me why, because it does not
matter to me. It seems to me that the only way in which it

could matter is because one is jealous of her magic and long life." Reshel had told him of Claressa's confession about her jealousy of Gerin when she learned he could become a wizard. She also told him that later, after speaking with Hollin and learning she could not become a wizard herself, Claressa had told him that she was no longer envious of her brother, having decided that the inability to share her life with others would in the end simply be too hard. Hollin had not believed a word of what she said.

Even if it was true then, it does not seem to be now, Balandrick thought. *And what will happen in years hence, when her beauty withers and fades while Reshel remains as she is now, frozen in time in the fullness of her youth? What will Claressa feel then? Will she go to her grave filled with bitterness and spite over what she can never have?*

She wheeled on him, yanking her arm from his. Her face was red with anger, her eyes glaring, her mouth drawn into a tight sneer. "You're all fools."

It appears my question has been answered, he thought.

She turned about and stalked down the corridor, vanishing into the gloom as if swallowed by a dark, stony throat.

Gerin left the meeting with his vassals and headed for his rooms. He'd received a message from his father earlier that day telling him that he'd received word from Therain about the movement of the Neddari and that he expected to field an army of twenty thousand men but could not begin his march westward for at least another five or six days. There were seven thousand men camped in and around Ailethon, and he expected two thousand more to arrive soon. His captains were ready to act, but first he needed to know what the Neddari were doing and how well Therain was weathering the siege. If it had not begun yet, it surely would soon.

Gerin was climbing a staircase toward his rooms when he heard someone charge up the steps behind him. He spun about, the long dagger he always carried with him already in his hand.

A man with a look of crazed rage on his face was only a few steps away from him, snarling as he thrust a long knife at Gerin's throat.

Gerin deflected the blade with his own and kicked out toward the man's chest. His attacker jumped back from the kick but overbalanced himself on the stairs, his arms shooting out as he tried to steady himself. Gerin stepped toward him and slammed the heel of his right hand into his chest. He heard ribs crack beneath his palm. The force of the impact lifted the attacker off his feet and sent him flying backward down the stairs, where he landed squarely on his back. His arms fell limply at his sides; after that he did not move.

"Guards!" shouted Gerin. "Guards! Come quickly!"

He retrieved the man's knife, which he'd dropped when he was hit, and descended the stairs. The attacker was unconscious. His breathing came in labored gasps. *He won't have to worry about breathing much longer,* Gerin thought as he stared down at the man. He was barefoot, to better conceal his movement along the floor. He must have snuck up as close as he thought he could get before rushing to attack.

It was very dark in the corridor, but still he thought he recognized the man. One of the castle servants, whose name escaped him.

A guard ran down the stairs, his weapon drawn, a lamp in the other hand. "My lord, what's happened? Are you all right?"

"This man tried to kill me, but I'm fine. More than likely another follower of the Storm King. See that he's taken to the dungeons and thoroughly questioned."

The man bowed as other soldiers rushed down the corridor. "At once, my lord."

Gerin sent guards to wake Balandrick with orders to meet him in the Sunlight Hall. He commanded soldiers to check on all the heads of noble houses who were staying in the keep in case this was part of a coordinated attack against the leaders of their forces. The last thing he needed was to find that some of his vassals had been murdered under his own roof. This felt eerily like the night when Stefon Malarik had attacked him, when his vassals had been here to reaffirm their oaths.

I've been a fool, he thought as he marched through the darkened halls of the keep. There were four guards with him now, two in front and two behind. He'd felt safe in the castle despite the murders that had occurred. Once they'd surmised that Gerin was personally needed by the Storm King to finish the summoning—whatever that meant—he'd felt immune to any attacks. They would not kill the object of their master's desire. Gerin was needed by the enemy, therefore he was safe from the enemy's killers. At least that's how he'd thought of it, and so he had taken no extra personal precautions.

When Balandrick arrived, Gerin gave a brief account of the attack. "I have a problem, Balan. The dream I had of the Storm King led us to believe that I was needed by him. But if that's the case, then why did one of his followers try to kill me? Is there something we missed?"

Balandrick pondered the question for a few moments. "Your attacker may have the answer to that question, my lord, but I think the answer is quite simple." He yawned hugely and covered his mouth with his hand. "My apologies. As I was saying, it may be that these killers don't know that their master needs you for some dark purpose. In the descriptions we've had from those who've experienced the dream, the summoning is never mentioned; you were the only one who heard that phrase. Those who fall under the influence of the Storm King are commanded to kill with the promised reward of resurrection after death. They're not asked to discriminate in who they kill."

"So you're saying this was a mistake? That I was attacked because the Storm King forgot to tell his followers to leave me alone?"

Balandrick shrugged. "Essentially, yes."

Maybe he doesn't know who I am, he thought as he returned to his rooms for the second time that night. *He sensed my identity somehow in my dream, but that doesn't mean he would know my name. He may have recognized me through the power of the horn or the doorway I opened, or the fact that I was lost for a time in the other realm. Even if he wanted to issue a command to his followers to leave me unharmed, maybe he can't.*

The corridor outside his apartments was guarded at both ends, and there were other guards stationed at the door. The stairways were watched now, as were the hallways below and above.

He was lying in bed, trying to fall asleep, when the world vanished around him again and he found himself in a formless gray haze. He heard shouting in the strange language he could not understand or recognize, the sounds of battle, the wailing of women and children, all growing closer, ready to swallow him in its horrid violence—

Then his vision returned. He had been holding his breath, and released it now in a long exhalation. The westward pull was very strong. He did not truly understand what he was feeling; he did not hear a voiceless command saying, *Come to the West,* nor did he sense any kind of physical tug or pull in that direction. But somehow he knew with certainty that he was to go west, that something would be there waiting for him.

The visions had been occurring more often, and growing stronger each time. If he were indeed being pulled into the realm of the dead during them, as Reshel had theorized, then something was increasing the frequency with which they happened.

He had told no one else about this. There was nothing anyone here could do about it, and he did not want to undermine their confidence in his ability to lead. Reshel knew, but she was not here for him to speak to. He wondered how she was faring with the wizards. Was she on her way back by now? He hoped so, and he fervently hoped she had learned something useful.

Gerin slept a little before dawn finally came. He was

roused by Balandrick, who'd gone to the dungeons after leaving him. Balan told him that his attacker, Iamel Kandraivis, had broken and talked, that he'd acted alone and that no attacks against other nobles were planned. "The same ranting and raving about the Storm King as the others," said Balan with evident disgust. "He picked you as his target because he thought it would curry favor with his master. He wasn't commanded to assassinate you in a dream or any such nonsense like that."

"Very good. Do you think he's told us everything he can?"

"Yes, my lord."

"Then he can join his companions and await his master."

Kandraivis was executed within the hour and his head impaled upon a spike with the others on the wall, with a curse for Shayphim to take his soul nailed beneath it. His mother stared at her son's head from a window in the keep, weeping silently, afraid to be seen for fear of being thought a sympathizer to the cult of murderers. After a while she turned away, sick and heartbroken. She remembered the happy boy he had been, a little slow perhaps, but kind and goodhearted. A boy who had loved her and cared for her when her husband died, a boy who had fed the cats in the kitchens with sweet, gentle tenderness. Something had happened to him; some evil had entered him and turned him against the prince, and for that he'd died. She did not understand it. She sobbed and wiped the tears from her eyes. Now he was gone and she was alone and afraid in the world, wondering how the gods could be so cruel.

27

Therain stood transfixed by the sight of the twister descending from the maelstrom of clouds. The sound of it was deafening, a roar that seemed to drive the air from his lungs, and the wind was unbelievably strong.

There was a pull at his arm. "My lord, we must hurry!" shouted Elmen. Therain could barely hear him, though the captain's mouth was almost pressed against his helm. "We have to get into the castle!"

Therain allowed himself to be led through the postern door. He did not take his eyes from the descending whirl-wind or the incredible sight of Asankaru feeding the storm with his powers.

The door shut and the wind ceased with a suddenness that Therain found almost startling, though he could hear the roar of it beyond the door, like a wild animal stalking them, rabid and deadly, trying to find a way to reach its prey.

"The gods preserve and protect us," said Elmen, panting heavily. "My lord, what are we to do?"

Therain did not answer. Instead he pushed past the captain and ran to the nearest gate tower. He dashed up the steps un-til he reached the battlements. He had to lean against the door with his shoulder to open it against the wind, stepped out onto the rain-slick stones and pressed ahead until he reached the crenellated wall. Pieces of the tower's slate roof

had been torn away by the wind, exposing the underlayers of
wood like bones visible through open wounds.

Elmen, who had followed him, shouted once more into his
ear, trying to be heard over the roar of the wind. "My lord,
you can't remain here! You have to go to the Thorn!"

I'm a fool, he thought. They had no hope of standing
against such might. How could they even begin to fight it?
They were doomed, all of them, at least until Reshel and
Hollin came to counter the Storm King's powers. But by
then it would be far too late for anyone here at Agdenor.

"My lord, please! We must go!"

Therain did not move. He watched as the whirlwind
slammed into the ground between Asankaru and the earthen
rampart. Clumps of dirt and rock spiraled up into the air,
driven outward by the hammer-force of the twister. It thickened and darkened as it drew dirt upward into its funnel.
Therain could feel the very stones of the castle trembling.

Asankaru thrust his arms forward, and the twister began
to move.

As the whirlwind churned its way up the long slope of
Henly's Hill, it dug a wide scar in the earth. Therain could
hear a terrible grinding noise as the rocks and paving stones
of the road were torn up and flung about by the power of the
twister. Asankaru and his Red Robes did not seem affected,
and Therain wondered if that was because of their insubstantial state in this world or because their magic somehow
protected them.

The men in the path of the whirlwind scattered frantically
as it neared. Soldiers scrambled down from the rampart and
dashed in all directions. Horses tore up their pickets and ran
off into the darkness. Some of the tents had been blown into
the fires and were still burning despite the sudden torrent of
rain that had fallen, the flames rekindled from sheltered areas of the smoldering wreckage. Some of the soldiers and
servants had become entangled in the fallen tents and were
now burning beneath the debris, while others were trapped
in the path of the twister bearing down upon them. Therain

knew they must be screaming but he could hear nothing over the sound of the wind.

"My lord, *please*!" shouted Elmen, dragging at his arm. Therain shrugged him off without ever taking his eyes from the twister.

The churning funnel cloud, which had moved up the hill in a lazy zigzag pattern, crossing back and forth across the road like a drunkard attempting to walk home, struck the timber gate nearly dead center. The gate exploded in a shower of deadly debris. Men fifty and sixty feet away were killed by yard-long splinters of wood that drilled through their armor with the force of a crossbow bolt. A long section of the earthen wall collapsed into the ditch, shaking loose the timbers that had braced it.

The twister chewed through the encampment on the hill. A cloud of debris hung suspended in the air around the funnel— shrubs, bits of holly, wooden stakes, strips of tent fabric, cookware, knives, clumps of dirt, and other things Therain could not recognize, orbited the storm in a motion he found almost hypnotically dreamlike.

Most of the soldiers and servants upon the hill had been able to get out of its path. Some had run back to the castle and were flooding in through the postern doors—by Therain's own order, the gates were not to be opened under any circumstance, though he had not foreseen anything like this when he'd issued it—while others scattered along the line of the rampart, heading for the rivers. He wondered what his commanders on the far banks were thinking as they watched the whirlwind bear down upon Agdenor.

"My lord, we leave *now*!" shouted Elmen, pulling Therain away from the battlements. This time Therain allowed himself to be led away, though he continued to look back over his shoulder at the approaching funnel.

He pulled free of Elmen and ran to the captain of the watch, Teren Patserik, a hale man in his fifties with a graying beard. "Evacuate the gate towers!" he shouted at the captain. He could feel his voice giving out with the effort of trying to be heard above the wind. "Clear everyone out!"

"My lord, we can't leave the towers undefended!" protested Patserik. "We can't desert our posts!"

"How are you going to defend against *that*?" he shouted, pointing to the black mass of the twister. "I'm ordering you to evacuate the towers!"

Patserik looked pained but nodded. "Yes, my lord!" He turned away to convey Therain's orders.

They ran down the stairs as the order to abandon the tower was relayed through its rooms. Armored soldiers joined them on the steps in a hurried descent and then ran out into the courtyard. Therain saw men running out of the other tower and was thankful his order had reached them. The men on the curtain wall moved well away from the gate towers as the whirlwind neared.

He could see the top of the funnel above the wall where it merged with the clouds. It was very close now. Elmen and the guards ushered him away from the gates and onto the path that led to the Thorn. The keep's bulk loomed ahead of them. Therain slipped on the wet stones of the path and would have fallen had not one of the guards steadied him with a hand on his shoulder.

When they reached the bottom of the Thorn's main steps, Therain turned to see what was happening. He drew a sharp breath, and it seemed that his heart stopped beating in his chest.

The whirlwind slammed into the gate tower he had just vacated, striking it on the inner corner where the gate itself was hinged. The funnel cloud bent forward over the wall as its lower portion was impeded by the stone. But the gate and tower were no match for Asankaru's strength. The funnel surged forward as the outer section of the tower suddenly collapsed. It sounded like a mountain falling. Blocks of stone flew threw the air and thudded into the wet ground, or crushed those unfortunate enough to lie beneath the arc of their trajectories. The whirlwind sheared off the roof of the tower, which disintegrated into a flying mass of wood and tiles. The gate and lowered portcullis behind it were ripped from their mountings and hurled into the courtyard, where they crashed together in a twisted pile of wreckage. The stone arch above the gates fell down in a shower of rubble; dust billowed out from the debris and was scattered upon the roaring wind. Therain saw the guard to his left, a young man named Tevin Heshlir, mouthing prayers to the gods.

The inner side of the tower tumbled down, exposing the stairway and several guard rooms. Therain saw a long-bladed knife fly upon the wind and sink six inches into the stone wall of a nearby barracks.

"My lord, go inside!" shouted Elmen.

Therain turned, stared hard at the captain and wondered what kind of expression was upon his face to elicit such a re-action. The captain looked shocked and startled. *Perhaps I look like a man about to die. A man resigned to his fate.* And why not? That was exactly what he was.

He thought about his mother. Her face appeared in his mind. It seemed so long since she had died. He prayed for her often in the tabernacle in the Thorn, prayed that she had found peace after her long and dreadful illness. *I've missed you sorely, Mother. But I'll see you soon.*

The rest of the tower collapsed, the floors crashing down upon one another as walls and other supports gave way. Much of it slid into the gate tunnel or inward toward the now-deserted courtyard. A choking dust from the mortar and crumbled stone filled the air.

"Elmen, go to Vaiseth and Lorel!" he shouted. "There's no hope here! Go to them and be with them! Escape if you can, but be with them when the end comes if you cannot!"

"My lord, I won't leave you!" Elmen said, his voice hoarse from the dust. "It's my duty to protect you!"

"I release you from your duty! There's nothing you can do to protect me from this enemy! Go to your family! As my last order to you, I command it!" To the other guards, he said, "I release you as well from my service! Go to whatever family or loved ones you have here!"

"Please, my lord, I won't . . ." Elmen trailed off, staring at something over Therain's shoulder.

Therain turned back toward the wall and saw the funnel cloud grind its way through the corpse of the tower. A short segment of the curtain wall fell when the section of the tower it was attached to collapsed inward, dragging part of the wall with it. It was difficult to comprehend that so much destruction had occurred in a few brief minutes.

The twister churned into the courtyard, flinging up the debris from the fallen gates and tower. But then it stopped and thinned. The funnel began to dissipate, as if the energy that powered it had vanished. The cloud of debris spinning around the twister fell away toward the earth as the churning winds slowed, creating a ring of wreckage centered on the courtyard. The funnel grew less distinct, and then its base receded suddenly from the ground. After that it vanished quickly, seeming to evaporate into the air about it. The wind died almost completely. The silence in the twister's aftermath seemed preternatural, completely at odds with the scene of devastation before them.

"My lord, we've been delivered," said Elmen, his voice a hoarse whisper.

"The gods have answered our prayers," muttered Tevin Heshlir, his eyes closed in thanks.

"Perhaps," said Therain, "but there are other explanations than the gods. I rescind my releasing of your service! Perhaps we are not to die this night. Follow me!"

He ran toward the closest section of the curtain wall and scaled the narrow stairs. He needed to know what was going on outside. Given enough time, the twister could have leveled the entire castle. There would have been no need for a single Neddari warrior to do so much as fire an arrow until Agdenor had been reduced to ruins. Survivors within the castle would have been quickly overrun. So why had Asankaru stopped?

Therain leaned through a crenellation and looked down the slope of Henly's Hill. He could see fires burning out of control throughout the Khedeshian encampment. Men were moving to fight or contain some of them, but other fires burned with no one near. He could see bodies upon the ground and the wide dark scar that marked the track of the twister. He thought he could see the Storm King and Red Robes returning to the front lines of the Neddari army. What had happened? Had they seen the limit of Asankaru's power? Had he simply run out of strength? If that were the case, how much time did they have before he could send another twister at them?

In the courtyard, men were moving in to assess the damage. "We cannot repair the gates right now, my lord," said Elmen, "but we should work to erect some kind of temporary barrier."

"I agree. Summon Teiyeron at once," he said. There would be much work for the chief stonemason of the castle this night. "See that he's given everything he needs."

Cries arose from the hill; war cries and the answering shouts of Khedeshians. Therain and his guards looked down toward the rampart. "Blood and *bloody* ashes," muttered Elmen.

The Neddari, weapons drawn and shouting their battle cries, were charging up the hill.

28

Abran was standing at the window of his study, staring out across the northern expanse of the city. Its towers caught the fading golden rays of the setting sun, while the streets below filled with deepening pools of gloomy darkness. At a crisp knock on his door, he called out, "Enter!" then turned away from the frosty glass.

Yurente Praithas opened the door and stepped aside to admit Arilek Levkorail, the Lord Commander and Governor General of the Taeratens of the Naege, the immense, double-ringed fortress where the supreme warriors of Khedesh were forged. Arilek was in his fifties but muscled like a man twenty years younger, a soldier who strove to keep his body as lean and hard as the armor he wore to protect it. His head, like all Taeratens, was shaved, though his mouth was rimmed with a trim beard like a ring of reddish fire flecked with strands of gray. He wore black trousers tucked into tall boots, a black tunic trimmed with gold beneath a wool jacket with gold buttons, and black gloves. With a single deft motion he removed his hooded, fur-lined cloak and handed it to Yurente, who folded it over his arm with an equally dexterous movement. Though Abran could not see them, he knew that the sleeves of Arilek's jacket covered tattoos of twin concentric circles given to every man who completed his two years of initial training before being admitted to the exalted and elite ranks of the Inner Ring of the Naege, where he would continue to train—and teach others in turn—for the rest of his life. Some, like Odnir Helgrim, were sent to various powerful noble houses to teach the sons of lords the art of combat. The rest remained within the high walls of that secretive fortress, emerging only when needed by their king to fight the enemies of Khedesh.

"Greetings, Your Majesty," said Arilek with a bow of his head. His voice was deep and rough, as if the inner workings of his throat had grown worn and threadbare. But Abran was aware from firsthand experience—a visit to the Naege a few weeks after his coronation—that he could bellow commands with volume and authority, and would not have been surprised if the master of the Naege could cause a stone wall to crumble simply with the force of his shout.

"Hello, Lord Commander." Abran gestured toward two high-backed, cushioned chairs placed near the fire blazing in the room's hearth. "Please, sit."

"Is there anything you require, Your Majesty?" asked Yurente, still standing in the doorway.

There was already a flagon of mulled wine and two glasses set on a table between the chairs; Yurente had brought the flagon a short time ago, at Abran's request. "Pour us some wine, Yurente, and then you may go."

"Of course, Your Majesty." He shuffled across the room and filled both glasses as the two men sat down.

Abran rolled the glass between his palms several times before drinking. He held the wine in his mouth for a moment or two, allowing the heat to saturate his mouth and tongue, then finally swallowed.

Arilek finished half his wine with two quick gulps, then placed the glass on the table and regarded Abran evenly. "I'm not often summoned to the king's presence," he said, leaving unstated his real question: *Why am I here?*

Abran again rolled his glass between his hands, staring into the depths of the fire in thoughtful silence. "How go the preparations for our march to the west?"

"They are fine, Your Majesty." His eyebrows furrowed, puzzled. "If that is all you wanted to know, I'll send an adjutant to give you progress reports—"

Abran shook his head. "No, that is not all, and that is not why I summoned you. I would not waste your time so frivolously. You are here because I want to know how many men you are sending. There seems to be a discrepancy between my order and the number I received from you. I want to know why."

A look of annoyance flashed across Arilek's face. "You asked that we virtually empty the Naege, Your Majesty. Ten thousand Taeratens have not been called to battle in more than thirty years. I think it would be wiser if we sent half that number on this campaign and kept the rest in reserve."

Abran set his own glass down and stared hard at Arilek. To his credit, the Lord Commander did not flinch or look away; he did not even blink. *Then again,* thought Abran, *he would never have become Lord Commander if anyone—even a king—could so easily intimidate him.*

Which brought him to the crux of the problem. Not only was Arilek not intimidated by him, he was also not obeying him.

"Lord Commander, it does not matter how long it has been since such a number was fielded. All that matters is I commanded you to prepare ten thousand for a march to Agdenor to repel a Neddari invasion."

Arilek looked startled by the king's words and the force with which he spoke them. "Your Majesty, if I may—"

"You may *not*. I am not finished. You have been an able Lord Commander for seventeen years, that is not in question, but I think you have forgotten a crucial fact: the Taeratens exist for one purpose, and that is to defend the sovereignty of Khedesh *at the will of the king*. Nothing else. I asked for ten thousand Taeratens, you told me you would send five. Notwithstanding the fact that you disobeyed a command from your king, by whose authority you maintain your post, why is it that you sent only half the number I

.called for?" He sank back into his chair. "You may speak."

Arilek cleared his throat and shifted uncomfortably in his seat. *He's not used to being talked to this way,* thought Abran. *And that's the problem. He's been master of the Naege for so long that he's forgotten he rules there by my leave. My father had done little with the Taeratens for too long a time. Arilek's had free reign there for at least a decade, perhaps longer. It's understandable that he would chafe at finding a leash around his neck once more.* He folded his hands and waited for Arilek to speak. *Understandable or not, it's time he was reminded who is in charge here. His neck will be leashed, or it will be severed.*

"Your Majesty, I must first say that I did not disobey you, I merely suggested what I felt was a more prudent—"

"I asked for ten thousand, you told me you would provide half that number. I have your message on my desk. There was no hint of *suggestion* in it, Lord Commander. Your words were clear and succinct. 'The Naege will have five thousand Taeratens ready to march at your command.' There was no explanation of *why* you made this change, which is why you are now here." He gestured toward his desk. "Did you forget what you wrote? Shall I get it for you?"

Arilek shook his head once. A few beads of sweat had appeared on his brow. Abran could almost hear the other man's thoughts as he realized just how grave his peril was. If he did not please his king, if he did not do everything in his power to correct the error he'd made and prove his loyalty to the throne, he would quickly become acquainted with the dungeons of the Tirthaig and perhaps even the executioner's axe. He could easily be charged with treason for his disobedience. If he did not say all of the right things, he would most likely never leave the palace. Certainly he would never set foot within the Naege again. A king could not afford to have the general of the most powerful army in the kingdom tempted to lead his men in a revolt to maintain his position. Abran would appoint another Lord Commander, one whose loyalty and devotion was above reproach.

"Your Majesty, I apologize for my prior message," he said slowly, watching Abran closely for any reaction to his words.

Abran kept his expression blank, hoping to give nothing of his intentions away. *Especially since I will not know my intentions until he has had his say,* he thought. He did not dislike Arilek; indeed, he had a great deal of respect and admiration for the man and his accomplishments. But that made no difference. This was about the authority of the king, which Arilek had dared to question in a time of crisis. Abran could not permit that to go unchallenged.

"It was ill-worded and did not convey my desire to advise you of alternatives. In hindsight, that was wrong of me. I should not have questioned your command. You are right—it is the purpose of the Taeratens to serve the king, by whose authority we were created. We exist to serve, and to fight, and to die for Khedesh." He rose from his chair, put his right fist across his heart, then dropped to one knee and lowered his head. "I beg your forgiveness, Your Majesty. You will have your ten thousand men. And if you feel I have failed you beyond my ability to repair, I will step aside as Lord Commander."

Abran stood, pleased. "That will not be necessary. Rise, Lord Commander." Arilek straightened. Abran handed him his glass of wine, then picked up his own. He believed Arilek's sincerity. The Lord Commander had needed a reminder of the king's authority, nothing more. He was not a traitor or potential usurper, as Abran had quietly feared when he'd summoned him. He was relieved that he would not have to appoint a new Lord Commander on the eve of a campaign. "To our victory over the Neddari. May we send them to Shayphim for daring to invade our fair lands."

Arilek raised his glass. "To victory."

29

The Neddari sent their heavy cavalry first. The horsemen charged in close ranks, with foot soldiers behind them. The cavalry shifted into a wedge-shaped formation as they neared the rampart. The stake-filled ditch and earthen wall still held across most of the hill, leaving only the relatively narrow opening where the timber gate had stood as their means of reaching the castle.

Therain's men prepared their defenses. They loaded trebuchets with buckets and pots soaked in a resinous compound called Fierel's Fire, which would burn anything it touched. Even the surface of a river could be set aflame, and would burn until the compound had consumed itself. Men who were struck with it would perish, and any matériel hit would be destroyed. Soldiers with torches stood near the trebuchets, waiting to ignite the missiles moments before they were hurled upon the Neddari. Archers stood with bows in hand, clothyard arrows nocked, with full quivers upon their backs.

Therain looked to the north and could faintly see the slender gray line of the Samaro River. He could just make out the campfires of the army there, small flickering sparks in the darkness. He prayed that Lord Urthailes was prepared with his own trebuchets and archers to hammer the northern flank of the Neddari, who were keeping more to the north

and were out of the range of Lord Stehlwen's forces across
the Azren. His prayer was answered a moment later when he
saw the first flaming buckets streak through the air from the
far side of the river with bright tails behind them, like giant
shooting stars. The first missiles landed fifty yards into the
charging Neddari, sending a burning rain of death upon
them. Soldiers ignited like oil-soaked torches and ran madly
until they fell. More Neddari fell seconds later, pierced with
arrows that Therain could not see because of the distance. A
second volley of burning missiles was launched as soon as
the trebuchets could be reloaded, and again landed with
deadly effect.

But though Urthailes and his men inflicted damage to
the northern flank of the army, the rest of the Neddari
charged mostly unhindered. Therain could only watch as the
Khedeshian soldiers at the ramparts frantically closed ranks
where the timber gate had been. Archers and crossbowmen
began to fire their arrows and bolts at the nearest horsemen.
The sound of the cavalry's approach was a deep rumble that
Therain could clearly hear upon the curtain wall.

As the enemy drew closer to the opening in the rampart,
the Khedeshian archers fired from close range, taking a
heavy toll on the enemy. The formation began to fall apart.

But though the Neddari faltered, they continued their
charge. Captain Arvandi ordered the soldiers holding the
breach to close ranks and overlap their shields. The pikemen
raised their weapons, bracing the ferrules in the ground, just
before the Neddari reached them.

By then it was too late for the horsemen to stop, and their
horses slammed into the pikes with ferocious force; Therain
could hear the animals scream as the steel points drove into
them, piercing muscles and organs and snapping bones. The
Khedeshians rushed forward, swords drawn, and began to
hack away at the fallen riders. Archers continued to fire at
the rearguard of the horsemen who were trying to maneuver
their steeds around their fallen countrymen. Khedeshian foot
soldiers attacked the mounted Neddari where they could

reach them, chopping at the legs of the horses to dismount the riders and choke the breach in the rampart with the bodies of men and animals.

To a large part they succeeded. The Neddari cavalry was mostly annihilated; only a few riders managed to break through into the ruins of the Khedeshian camp, and though they did succeed in killing some soldiers, they were quickly brought down.

But the Neddari infantry—including several hundred drogasaars—was not far behind. Rows of men and beast were nearly to the scene, and the Khedeshian archers turned their sights to this new threat. They cut down many in the forward line, but those behind them raised their shields to ward off the rain of arrows. More Khedeshians tried to block the breach where the gate had been, scrambling over dead and dying men and horses. They knelt and formed a shield-wall, then waited for the Neddari to batter themselves against it, hoping the earthen dike would keep their enemy from spilling out around them.

The Neddari hurled themselves on their enemy, their war cries ringing in the night. Drogasaars leapt high into the air, their scimitars flashing, their roars carrying even over the sounds of the pitched battle. Many were shot through with arrows in mid-leap and tumbled dead to the ground. Those that managed to land behind the dike wall unharmed began to furiously cut down the nearest Khedeshian soldiers, their scimitars whirling and slicing with deadly precision. Some continued their incredible leaps up the hill toward the castle, blades hacking through anyone who attempted to stop them.

But they were quickly overcome by sheer numbers. Therain saw one Khedeshian—he could not be certain, but thought it was Captain Melfistan—hurl a knife into the eye of one of the drogasaars, felling it instantly. Another soldier hacked through a drogasaar's forearm. It wheeled around, shrieking in pain, dark blood pumping from the stump of its arm; but before it could bring its other scimitar to bear, the soldier drove the point of his weapon into the creature's face. Other men converged on the remaining drogasaars near the earthen rampart; despite their skill with their scimitars, the drogasaars could not keep so many soldiers at bay and were soon hacked to pieces. The creatures leaping up the hill never reached the castle. Archers upon the walls picked them out of the air before they could get within two hundred feet.

At the ruined gate in the rampart, the Khedeshian archers devastated the flanks of the Neddari infantry—the leading enemy soldiers could not force their way past the overlapping shields blocking their way. When the Neddari tried to reach over the shields, Khedeshians waiting behind the kneeling men cut them to bits. Soon there was a heap of dead and dying men upon the ground, groaning and screaming in agony.

But there were simply too many Neddari. Despite their terrible losses, they did not retreat. They surged forward and pressed once more against the shield-wall, and this time they forced their way through. They formed their own wedge of soldiers behind shields and overran the Khedeshians with sheer numbers. The Khedeshians at the center of the shield-wall were driven backward and trampled. They had no chance of rising once they fell; the surge of Neddari could not be stopped. The Khedeshians were forced to fall back—Therain could see Captain Melfistan screaming orders and gesturing for his men to race up the hill—after failing to stem the flood of enemies that now came pouring through the breach.

Some men foolishly remained behind, hoping to retake what was now irrevocably lost. Therain watched helplessly as a Neddari ran his sword up into Captain Arvandi's throat. The captain's body disappeared a second later beneath the swarming mass of Neddari.

"My lord, shall I send men down to help them?" asked another of the commanders upon the wall.

Therain shook his head. "No. With the gates thrown down, I need every last man here for the defense of the castle.

There's no point sending your men to be slaughtered. I hope the men down there have enough sense to retreat to the castle before they're all killed."

"But my lord, that means we'll yield the upper hill to them!" said the lieutenant. "They'll be beneath these very walls!"

"Lieutenant, the hill is already theirs. There's no hope of stemming the tide at the breach. If our men continue to fight, most of them will die. I would rather have them here and alive than dead on the field. In either case, the Neddari will soon be beneath these walls."

"Yes, my lord."

"Make certain the other commanders are ready. And see that Captain Vailes and his cavalry are ready to move at my word."

"I'll see to it personally, my lord."

The battle on the hill was moving inexorably toward the castle. The Khedeshians had abandoned the rampart and were attacking the wedge of Neddari, who were coming through the breach like a giant arrowhead aimed directly at the ruined gates of Agdenor. There was a break in the clouds—Therain was hopeful when he saw this, considering it a sign that the Storm King's power would not quickly return—and the light of a yellowed moon shone down on the hill, pale and sickly, as if the glow were filtered through a layer of malice and disease. The trebuchets upon the castle walls were finally used when the retreating Khedeshians passed within the minimum throw distance of the weapons. Look-outs on the wall shouted that all was now clear; others relayed that information to the men in charge of the weapons, who lit the buckets of Fierel's Fire within the throwing sling before releasing the counterweight.

As the battle neared the castle, Therain saw the soldiers upon the walls rushing about in final preparations of their defenses. Some stoked fires beneath buckets of sand brought from the shallows of the river, while others prepared huge

cauldrons of oil braced with pulleys and fulcrums designed
so their great weight could easily be raised above the wall
and tipped forward. Archers stood at the crenellations with
pitch-tipped arrows nocked lightly in their bows; they would
be set afire and used to ignite the oil once it had been poured.
Smaller cauldrons filled with Fierel's Fire were also moved
into place, but most of that precious substance had been
handed over to the captains of the trebuchets. Some of the
cauldrons and buckets of sand were moved to the shattered
ends of the wallwalk where the gates had been. Archers and
crossbowmen took up position in the rubble of the gate towers, hiding as best as they could amid the crumbling and
shifting debris.

Some of the Neddari carried scaling ladders. They had no
siege towers, but the gaping hole in the thick curtain wall
where the gates had once been made their lack less critical.
Huge blocks of stone and smaller rubble and debris had
been strewn in the remains of the gate tunnel, but provided
no serious barrier to entering the castle. There had been no
time for the stonemasons to work on even a temporary solution to the ruined gates. Instead, the soldiers who had abandoned the towers before their destruction formed another
shield-wall like the one their countrymen had made at the
breached rampart; there was little else they could do.

"My lord," said Elmen. "It's too dangerous for you to be
upon the wall."

They withdrew to the courtyard. Therain could see his retreating soldiers finally reach the castle, where they turned
and used the last of their strength to run into the gate tunnel
while the archers and crossbowmen tried to hold back the
enemy. An opening appeared in the shield-wall so the men
could dash past into the courtyard. They were tired and
bloody, but at least some had survived the onslaught at the
rampart.

The Neddari were not far behind, however. The greater
part of the attacking host rushed at the ruins of the gates,
while smaller parties with the scaling ladders spread out to

either side along the base of the wall. As they drew closer to the castle, they braced the feet of the ladders in the soil and then swung them up against the battlements.

When the topmost Neddari had climbed about three-quarters of the distance to the top, the Khedeshians sprang into action. Using heavy cloth to further insulate their gloved hands, they dumped buckets of heated sand upon the attackers. The scalding particles blinded some of the Neddari, who looked up at the moment the sand was dropped. The sand slipped beneath the mail and jerkins of everyone it landed upon and burned into their flesh. Neddari on the scaling ladders screamed and flailed before losing their balance and crushing soldiers on the ground.

The Khedeshians continued to dump sand over the walls until they ran out. Then they poured oil on the ladders, set them on fire, and pushed them away from the battlements. Those Neddari who had not been scalded or shot with arrows retreated from the wall, leaving the burning wreckage of the scaling ladders behind.

The Neddari attacking the gates suffered terrible losses as they fought their way toward the shield-wall. Arrow-riddled bodies littered the road. When they were a dozen yards from the walls, the defenders poured out their cauldrons of oil, which flowed down the road to form slicks on the uneven stone surface and pool against the bodies of the fallen. Nevertheless, the Neddari did not slow their charge. Arrows and bolts found their way between shields to thud into the unprotected flesh of faces and throats.

Therain turned to Elmen and issued a command, which in turn was relayed to two waiting messengers who dashed off in the darkness. *We can't hold anything back,* thought Therain. *We must use all our weapons now, or we will fall.*

When the Neddari were nearly to the wall, Khedeshians in the ruins of the gate towers hurled torches onto the oil slick. A sheet of orange flame shot upward and rushed to engulf the front lines of the enemy. Men screamed and tried to turn back from the fire, but the press of soldiers behind them would not allow it. Some slipped on the road surface and fell, to be trampled and burned. Others dashed off the road with parts of their clothing or hair on fire, and rolled frantically in the withered grass, only to be shot through by the archers on the wall.

The Neddari behind the forward lines skirted around the edges of the burning oil and rushed toward the gaping rent in the wall. Archers and crossbowmen continued to fire, but there were so many Neddari it seemed that three sprang forward for each one that fell. The defenders poured more oil and set it ablaze, creating a conflagration where the gate of Agdenor had once stood.

It was not enough. The Neddari charged past their dead and dying countrymen and entered the ruins of the gate tunnel. Some leaped onto the crumbling wreckage of the towers and hacked at the archers who had inflicted so much harm on them. The rest rushed forward and slammed into the shield-wall, trying to break through it so they could enter the castle proper.

The shield-wall held, but not without effort or loss. Long swords chopped through helms and hacked off limbs. Men screamed and bled and died. There were so many men fighting at close quarters that Therain could scarcely make out what was happening. The Khedeshians surged forward, trying to force the Neddari out of the castle and back onto the hill. The Neddari within the castle were quickly slaughtered by the Khedeshians attacking on three sides, and the surviving Neddari fell back to the road.

Then Therain heard the horns of Captain Vailes and his cavalry.

Thank the gods! It seemed to him that he'd issued his order for the captain to attack the Neddari ages ago. He wanted to rush forward and climb the walls for a better view of the battle, but thought Captain Hiremar might actually knock him senseless if he tried such a thing. He knew he had to remain where he was. If this failed and the Neddari were able to force their way back into the castle . . .

The cavalry horns sounded again, and the men upon the walls let out a great cheer as they watched more than two hundred horsemen converge on the Neddari from the north and south. They charged with lances lowered and banners waving.

The Neddari saw what was coming, but by then it was too late. The few who remained within the gate tunnel retreated or were cut down. The Khedeshian heavy horse thundered into them and cut the force in two. The Neddari caught between the cavalry and the castle, standing on ground still burning in many places from the oil and Fierel's Fire, were crushed between the horsemen and the foot soldiers who now surged out of the castle, led by Captain Melfistan and what remained of his company. Wounded, confused, and now hemmed in, the Neddari were soon dead to a man.

The Neddari on the downslope side of the cavalry fought for a brief while before deciding there was no hope in the attack. The surviving captains sounded their retreat. They turned and fled down the road toward the shattered rampart. Captain Vailes and his men pursued them part of the distance, cutting down the stragglers from behind. The horsemen turned back before they reached the rampart, where a fresh force of Neddari now waited on its lower, western side. They rode back to the castle, cheering and waving their swords. The first battle had ended, and the victory was theirs.

30

Therain listened to his men cheer and felt himself grinning despite the horrors of the night. By the gods, they had held. Even after the madness of Asankaru's whirlwind and the damage it had caused, his men had kept the invaders at bay.

But his relief was tempered by the knowledge that this was just the beginning of what they would face. The gates were smashed to rubble. Fires burned beyond the wall and in the courtyard, and the stench of blood and burned flesh filled the air. Severed limbs were strewn across the bloody earth like discarded refuse; dying and wounded men screamed in agony and cried out for the gods and their mothers to help them. Horses with broken backs or hacked-off legs writhed in torment on the ground, their own cries in some ways more piteous because they did not know the reason for their suffering. *And this is just the first night of the siege,* he thought as he stared at the wreckage around him. Before tonight he'd believed they could have held out for months if necessary. Now he prayed they could last a week.

He walked into the courtyard, shouting commands in his hoarse voice. He ordered the stonemasons to construct whatever kind of temporary curtain they could to seal the breach where the gates had been. He shouted for Master Evernyes and his healers to tend to the wounded, and commanded one company of relatively unharmed soldiers to put down the wounded animals and locate any survivors among the Neddari. The Neddari dead were to be placed in a great pile a short distance down the hill and burned. The Khedeshians who had fallen, he ordered to be buried in a mound outside the castle wall. Torel Vailes returned with a report of their pursuit of the Neddari back to the rampart, but he tempered his comments with the observation that the enemy had moved a considerable number of men up Henly's Hill and now controlled all the lands beyond the dike. "My lord, I'm not certain, but it appeared the enemy had shifted its northern flank so as to be out of the range of Lord Urthailes and his trebuchets, whose range they apparently underestimated," said Vailes, his narrow face lost in the shadows beneath his helm. "Some of my outriders spied groups of archers moving back toward the river, probably in anticipation of a crossing by our men."

Therain listened carefully. Urthailes and Stehlwen had both been preparing boats and barges to carry large numbers of soldiers across the rivers swiftly should the need arise. But the Neddari had anticipated that and were moving troops of their own to counter it.

He was quiet while he considered his options. "Captain, send messengers to tell Lords Urthailes and Stehlwen that when there is another frontal assault on the castle they are to send troops across the rivers as quickly as possible to attack the enemy's flanks. They should be prepared to face heavy fire from Neddari bowmen if they cross. I also want your cavalry to charge the Neddari archers when they attack the crossing. I don't want the assault on our men to go unanswered. We'll do what we did earlier—hammer them on three sides and either destroy them or force them back."

"Yes, my lord. I'll see to it at once."

"Captain, you did well out there. Everyone in this castle owes you their lives. Thank you. I won't forget it."

Vailes brightened. "Thank you, my lord."

"I heard your son was wounded in the attack. Mykel, is that his name?"

"He took an arrow in the leg. The wound is not serious. The shaft glanced off his armor and struck at a shallow angle in his thigh."

"I'm glad he's well. See that you both remain that way."

"Thank you, my lord."

The night passed quickly. Therain continued to issue commands and receive reports. He did manage to sleep for about two hours, only to be awakened by Elmen with word that a group of the Heralds of Truth had been caught trying to poison one of the castle's cisterns. He ordered them bound and thrown living onto the pile where the dead Neddari were being burned.

He climbed to the top of the wall to survey his enemy. The hill on the far side of the rampart was swarming with Neddari. Therain watched them and considered his strategy once more. Should he allow the next charge by the Neddari to reach the castle, or should he send his forces out to meet them on the hill? After pondering for a while, he decided he would make his stand at the castle. Teiyeron and his masons had worked feverishly to construct a chest-high wall across the broken section of the castle. Therain did not trust it to withstand a major assault, but if they faced no more storms, their other defenses should keep the Neddari at bay. *Let them break themselves against us. Let them learn the strength of our walls and feel the bite of our arrows and burn in our fires. They'll pay dearly if they attack again.*

As he thought about the first attack, he wondered why they had not sent any *kamichi* and their elementals at them. He'd been told that the elementals could not be sent far or remain long in this world, but he'd expected them to be part of the initial assault. Was there some reason they were held back? He still did not know what they would do if the Storm King sent another whirlwind at them. He needed magic to defend against magic, and that was the one thing he did not have.

The sky grew ashen in the east. The sun would soon rise. And with it, he knew, would come a second attack.

* * *

As the night waned, Delgo Nerat Igrulun pondered what course of action he should take. Braziers burned in the corners of the tent and there was a flickering oil lamp on the table. He took a bite of roasted beef and followed it with a long drink of wine. After their humiliating defeat at the castle, he'd spoken to his field captains and ordered them to prepare their men for another attack in the morning.

His thoughts turned to the disciples of the God, the Seven who had returned with Him from the Unnamed Lands. The truth be told, in his heart of hearts he disliked the God's disciples. No, he hated and feared them. He would not lie to himself, now that he knew they could not read his thoughts without touching him with their staffs and incanting their magic, their Communing, as they had when they first appeared to Clan Térutheg. It was how they had learned their speech, which the foreign conqueror Helca had forced the mighty Neddari people to speak after he had smashed the clan warriors and demanded that they pay tribute to his distant throne. A speech they still used despite the fall of the conqueror's empire many ages ago. Though their *kamichi* spoke Hakán in their secret ceremonies, it had long ago fallen out of daily use.

Proud and arrogant, disdainful of him and his station, the disciples of the God Who Has Returned treated him as if he were little more than a clan-slave. He understood that the God Who Has Returned needed his disciples—whom he named war priests in a usage that Igrulun did not fully understand—as he needed the *kamichi* of his clan, willful though they also were—especially their chief, Pendrel Yevan Hirgrolei—and he was mindful of their powers. But he disliked the war priests and was jealous of their status and privileges with the God, just as he was jealous of the *kamichi*, whose powers were not his to control.

Just before the God Who Has Returned had sent his whirlwind into the castle of the unbelievers, Igrulun had forbidden the *kamichi* to take part in the assault. "The strength of our warriors is enough to win the day," he'd told Hirgrolei. "We have no need of you and your fickle spirits."

The *kamichi* clenched his staff and glared naked hatred at him. "It is my right to take part, Igrulun. It was *I* whose vision saw the return of the Slain God. It was *I* who found the god-summoner and placed a *tendrun'avi* upon him to ensure the vision was fulfilled. You scoffed when I told you the purpose of my quest, but now you see its truth! You cannot refuse me or my brothers. Without our powers to assist you—"

"Without you on the field of battle, our warriors will be able to kill our enemies instead of protecting you, since you disdain the accoutrements of war. Because you will not carry so much as a shield, it is up to the warriors to save you from the spears and arrows of the Khedeshians. The God will break their walls and smash their towers. There is no need of you or your spirits. It is the time of the warrior now."

"You cannot refuse me the right to attack the unbelievers, Igrulun! We, too, serve the God Who Has Returned!"

"You will address me as Tevi Igrulun and show me the proper respect. This is not a dream-quest or crusade of vengeance, Hirgrolei. The *kamichi* have no say here. I am the Overchieftain and Warlord, and in matters of battle my will is paramount. The old ways are changing. I will say who goes to battle and who stays." A thought came to him. "If you are so willing to fight the unbelievers, I will not forbid it, Hirgrolei, but neither will I give you any of my warriors to protect you. Carry your own swords and shields or use your spirits to defend yourselves."

"You defy the traditions of our people, Tevi Igrulun. You refuse what has been the right of the *kamichi* since Urgden Zeya Maldrúlu first discovered the World That Is Above. We are both healers and slayers for the clans, but it is not our way to bear sword or shield or mail. That is for the warrior, and it is for the warrior to shield us in battle. That is the way of our people. Ours is a different path, and you risk everything to defy it."

"The God Who Has Returned changes everything, Hirgrolei. The old ways have been swept away. You yourself have said it. Nothing will ever be the same. You may join the battle if you wish, but without the protection of my warriors. The choice is yours."

And stubborn man that he was, a man too rooted in tradition for his own good, Hirgrolei and his *kamichi* had remained in the camp. The *kamichi* of the other clans and their Chieftains had also protested, but as Overchieftain and Warlord, Irgulun ruled all the clans in the matter of this war, chosen by right of combat when the clans gathered at Ziren-Bellek by the command of the God Who Has Returned. And so they had assaulted the broken castle without *kamichi* or elemental to aid them.

But the first attack, against all reason, had been repulsed. When the God's whirlwind faltered, Irgulun had felt an icy chill around his heart. The pillar of light that the God had called forth from the earth and sent into the heavens to create his storm of wrath had faded and vanished upon the breath of the air. He watched as the God, his face a mask of fury, turned and left the circle formed by his war priests. The men parted before Him, wordlessly, as He went to His tent, where He had remained ever since. Irgulun had stopped one of the war priests, Tageluron, and asked, "Why has the God halted His storm before our enemy is vanquished?"

He thought that the war priest would strike him dead. His strange face had filled with rage. "It is not for you to question our Lord Asankaru. He has done all He will. It is for you now to show your loyalty by taking the fortress of the unbelievers and delivering the summoner and the Horn of Calling into His hands."

He realized something about the God Who Has Returned that he dared not speak aloud. *The God's whirlwind had faltered because His strength failed Him.* It was not because He had decided to test the loyalty of His followers, as His war priests suggested. The God had reached the limits of His power.

It may be that the God's strength will not be complete until He has fully Returned to this world. The God had made it clear that His Return was not yet finished. His spirit was in this world, but only a glimmer of His physical form.

Irgulun stared at the flickering lamp, but what he saw in his mind was his first meeting with the Returned God many months ago. He had been hunting in the Kalóros, following an old trail that led northward through the tall pines of the wood. The light was dark and murky when it finally reached him on the needle-strewn path, the way sunlight looked when he swam deep in the lake at Olgren-na-Pugúlo in the shadow of the Gray Wall. Night was approaching, but the hunt-lust was upon him. There was a great black bear in the rocky hills rising ahead of him, the slate-gray slopes dotted with clumps of pine and oak. He'd struck out alone after finding the remains of a deer freshly killed by the bear and deep claw marks upon several of the trees. The bear had claimed these lands as his own, but he would take his knives and wrestle with the bear and cut out his heart and eat it. He was the master of these woods and hills, and no one, neither man nor beast, could claim otherwise.

It was while riding on this trail that Irgulun first met the God Who Has Returned. He was nearing the crest of a high steep ridge when he saw a figure appear ahead of him. Rage had filled him at the sight of an interloper in his woods, and his only thought was to kill him. He drew one of his knives and in a single motion hacked through the neck of the tall man as he rode past him. His weapon passed through the man's neck with such ease that he had to jerk his arm to a halt to prevent the powerful swing from striking his horse's neck. He wheeled Arilosi about, fully expecting to see a body lying on the rocky path without its head. Instead he saw the man staring at him with eyes that held so much power that he could not move. For the first time in many years, he felt afraid. What was this being who could defy death? Irgulun knew his aim had been true and that his blade had struck where he had willed it. Why was the creature not dead? *Is this some spirit come to haunt me, the shade of some enemy I have killed?*

But the being before him did not look like a man. He was tall and thin, with overly large eyes that glinted with silvery light, and strange proportions to his face and limbs. He wore white armor with markings upon it the likes of which Irgulun had never before seen. His black hair fell in long braids past his shoulders, tied with many strips of colored cloth. And his entire form glowed with a pale light of its own, as if the light of the moon had been narrowed to a single beam that fell only upon this creature.

"Who are you?" Irgulun had asked. His fear had faded a little, replaced with a strange curiosity. Strange, because Delgo Nerat Igrulun was not usually a curious man. "What are you doing in my woods? I could have you killed for being here without my leave." He did not bother to add that he had already tried to kill him and failed.

In reply the being frowned at his words. *"Arq'il lazk peza torqud Eletheros?"* His voice sounded peculiar, as if Irgulun were hearing it within his mind as well as with his ears.

"I do not understand your tongue," he said, shaking his head. "Are you a spirit of the wood, some dead man slain here long ago?"

The being's frown deepened. "You speak the summoner's vile language." He strode forward; Arilosi reared so suddenly and unexpectedly that Irgulun was thrown from his saddle. He sprang to his feet and drew his other knife, but before he could lunge at the stranger his body froze. His fear returned. *He could take my knives and slit my throat, and there is nothing I could do to stop it!* he realized as he fought against the paralysis. But his struggles were useless. The power that held him was as unbreakable as iron.

The being touched Irgulun's temples. He felt only the lightest pressure from the long fingers, as if they were made of currents of cold air. Irgulun's straining body went even more rigid when he felt a coolness enter his mind, as if the fingers had somehow slipped into his skull. He stared defiantly into the creature's enormous eyes. *If this is to be my death, I will*

*not look away from my slayer. I will curse him and drag his
spirit screaming with me to Nurvos when I die.*

The coolness in his mind began to shift and probe. Old
memories sprang involuntarily to the surface of his thoughts,
then were suddenly drawn away; he could almost feel them
sliding into the being who held him in its accursed power. *He
is stealing my memories!* Even the strongest of the *kamichi*
had no powers to match this.

It took him a moment to realize that his thoughts were not
being stolen. The memories that came to his mind remained
with him even after they were drawn away, as if copies had
been made that the being then consumed. *Consumed.* That
was the right word, he realized. His memories, or their
copies, were being devoured by this being, absorbed into his
own mind so that his thoughts would now belong to it.

The thoughts that were drawn from him began to center
around the history of his people. Legends and stories he had
been told as a child flashed through his mind. Was this a
god? Had one of the divine come down to his woods to demand something of him, or punish him for some crime or
offense?

Then he lost himself completely. Memories appeared faster
and faster until he could only wait, utterly overwhelmed,
while they were rooted through and drawn out of him.

Then it was done. He jerked suddenly as the being withdrew his hands and stepped back. The power that bound him
also vanished, and he dropped his knives and sagged to his
knees. Sweat ran down his face and dripped off the end of
his nose. His head ached horribly, but at least the power was
gone and he could form his own thoughts again.

He picked up his knives with shaking hands and stood
slowly. "Who are you?" he croaked in a hoarse whisper. It
was all he could manage. "What have you done to me?"

The being continued to stare at him with its strange eyes. "I
am Asankaru," he said in that odd voice that sounded in both
ear and mind. "I Communed with you to learn what manner
of creature you are. You look similar to Eletheros, but you are

not Eletheros. Nor are you a hated Atalari. You are a small creature, short-lived and without power." He turned about to survey the dark pines of the Kalóros. Irgulun considered driving his knives into the stranger's back when it turned away from him, but decided such a brash action would be unwise despite the insult. *I must learn more before I can decide what to do next.* Again, this was strange for him. He usually acted without thinking, allowing his body to decide for him. But this was most certainly not a usual situation.

Asankaru looked at his hands. "I have been gone for many ages, Delgo Nerat Igrulun. Ages beyond reckoning. But I have not forgotten what was done to me."

"How do you know my name?"

The being who named himself Asankaru laughed. "I have Communed with you, Delgo Nerat Igrulun. All that you are is part of me now." He looked at his hands again. His whole form glowed with its strange radiance in the deepening gloom of the woods. "But I am not yet whole. I do not fully understand what has happened to me." He seemed to be speaking more to himself than to Irgulun.

"I know not of what this phantasm body is made," said Asankaru, staring down at his armored form. "It has substance but no true flesh. I can will it to become unseen and move about with great speed." He disappeared abruptly, as if his body had been made of nothing more than motes of dust. A second later he reappeared a few feet away from where he had been. "It is how I came to be here after my passage through the Door of Night. I was drawn here, to the lands where I dwelled long ago." Irgulun, stunned by what he had just witnessed, could not read the expression on Asankaru's alien face but thought it might be amusement. Once more he wondered if this were a god before him.

"My return is not yet completed. I do not understand all that occurred, but there was a summoner that opened the doorway through which I passed. I must find him so I can be made whole once more."

"You said you went away long ago," Irgulun said in a

hushed tone. *And that these lands were once his home.* He had no idea what to make of that. "Ages beyond reckoning. Where did you go?"

Asankaru laughed once more. "I was dead, Delgo Nerat Igrulun. Slain in a war against the bitterest of enemies."

It is true. The God Who Was Lost has returned to us. He dropped his knives and fell to his knees. "You have come back to us as was prophesied long ago. I beg Your forgiveness, Lord Asankaru. I scoffed at the *kamichi*'s tales of the Warrior God of our people who fell long ago in a battle against the Dark Ones. The *kamichi* teach that the Slain God would one day return from the grave to lead us, but I did not believe, even when one of the *kamichi* had a vision of Your Return and went to seek the one who would guide You. Forgive me, please, Great One. I was wrong. I have seen Your power and heard Your words. You live again. Command me and it shall be done." He bowed his head.

"Rise, Delgo Nerat Igrulun," said the Slain God Asankaru, the God Who Had Returned. "Serve me well, and you shall have a great reward."

The Slain God's war priests had appeared soon after, mysterious and contemptuous, creatures that filled Igrulun with a deep and nameless dread. They too had Communed with others of the clan to learn their speech and their ways. Word spread of the God's Return like a fire through the grasslands at high summer. Irgulun called for a gathering of clan Chieftains and the high *kamichi* at Ziren-Bellek, the enormous wooden hall that belonged to no single clan but rather to all Neddari, perched atop Parglati Qesh in the shadow of the Gray Wall. There the clan Chieftains swore their oaths to the God and put aside all their quarrels and blood-feuds. By the God's command they were to create an army that would go forth into the land of the unbelievers and slay all who would not acknowledge Him. The Chieftains had returned to their clans to gather their warriors and prepare for war. They would first conquer the lands of the Khedeshians, where the

God believed the mysterious summoner lived. "I can feel his presence," He had said. "It is faint, little more than a scent upon the wind. But I know he is out there, somewhere." He had gestured to the northeast.

The warriors slowly amassed their army—an undertaking the likes of which had never been attempted in the history of the Neddari, not even in the days of Helca the Conqueror, when the clans had fallen to him one by one. The God sent His powers forth into the dreams of the unbelievers to recruit them to His cause and find the summoner if He could. How the God would know the summoner through a dream was something Irgulun did not comprehend, but he did not doubt the God's words or His powers.

Then the strange deaths had come. Hale warriors and strong women died for no reason the *kamichi* could discover. Three *kamichi* themselves had died. Elgari Orlet Veicomar, the old seer of his clan, toppled over dead while instructing an apprentice. Irgulun had asked the God about these deaths and if He could protect His people from it or tell them its cause.

"I have dwelt long ages in the realm of the dead," the God had said. "All things perish, Delgo Nerat Igrulun, even as I once did. It is the way of things, and not even a God may compel death to stay its hand."

"I understand Your wisdom, Great One, but these deaths are strange and unnatural according to our healers."

"Perhaps your enemies send dark powers against you," said the God. "The summoner I seek has powers of his own. His people are your enemies, are they not? It may be that when we find him we will find the answer to your deaths."

And that is all the God had said. The deaths had not stopped. Twice or thrice a month someone perished in a manner the *kamichi* could not explain. One of Irgulun's own clan-slaves had fallen dead at his feet in his bedchamber.

Irgulun's eyes snapped back to the present and he straightened in his chair. *Dare I ask the God for another of His whirlwinds?* He feared to ask for something the God would not freely give. Would the God think him weak for beseech-ing Him?

He did not ponder the question long. *I will not ask.* The God had done what He would, either by choice or necessity. *It is my part to finish the unbelievers, or I am not worthy to be Overchieftain and Warlord.*

A clan-slave drew back the tent flap so one of the seven dis-ciples could enter. The divine light that shone upon the disci-ples and the God, the Light from Beyond, as Irgulun thought of it, was still visible, though less obvious in the interior of the tent. It was brighter when they stood alone in the night, a sil-very sheen that looked as if they had somehow wrapped them-selves in cloaks of starlight.

"Our Lord Asankaru commands your presence," said the war priest. His wide eyes stared at Irgulun coldly. *They never call me by name or title.* He despised the manner in which they showed their contempt, but there was nothing he could do but hold his tongue. He served the God Who Has Returned, not them, and if they stood higher than he did in the eyes of the God, still he owed them nothing. He did not disparage them openly, but neither did he show them honor or respect.

He followed the war priest to the tent of the God. The Lord Asankaru was seated on a high-backed chair with the other war priests around him. They all watched Irgulun with their cool stares as he approached and knelt. "Command me, my Lord Asankaru."

"Rise, Delgo Nerat Igrulun," said the God. Irgulun did as he was bidden, pleased that the God had used his name. *It matters not what the war priests think, only the God,* he re-minded himself. "You have witnessed my power firsthand. You have seen me break the walls of the unbelievers with the storms that are mine to command. But I am not yet whole, and my strength wanes before it should. I am telling you this because you are my sword and spear, and must finish this siege without further aid from me. Were my body complete I would not have stopped until their fortress was thrown down utterly and scattered to the winds, but that cannot be until the summoner and his horn are brought to me. *I must be made whole*. When that is done, we will sweep across the lands with sword and storm and no one will stand against us. The puny kings of this era will swear to me or perish."

I was right, thought Irgulun, surprised by the frankness of the God's words. *The whirlwind ended because His strength failed*. He felt honored that the God had admitted such a thing to him.

"My Lord, I have already commanded the warriors to prepare to attack when day arrives," he said. "The fortress will fall to us soon. The Khedeshians will not be able to long withstand our might."

"Yet you were at their walls and they drove you back," said one of the war priests. His tone was like ice. "Who is to say they will not do so again?"

"*I* am to say," said Irgulun, unable to keep the defiance from his voice. "Sieges are not won in a day. That is why they are sieges. If need be, we will build engines to further break their walls. Their fortress has already been grievously wounded."

"And while you sat in your tent they have set about repairing that wound," said the war priest.

"Then we will smash it again."

The God held up His hand. "Delgo Nerat Igrulun, I grow impatient. I hunger for flesh and the return of my strength. Prepare your warriors, but my war priests will go first. Their powers have not been so expended as mine, and though their strength is not as great, there is still much they can do to help you win the day."

Irgulun bowed his head once more. "As you command, my Lord." He looked up and stared hard at each of the war priests, undaunted by their barely concealed hostility. "I will await your signal, and then the castle will fall."

31

Therain was back upon the wall well before dawn. The night had grown bitterly cold. A freezing rain had fallen toward morning, and a thick mist rose from the rivers and drifted across the hill. *We won't be able to see them until they're upon us.* He ordered men with horns to stand watch down the road and signal at the first sign of a Neddari attack. *At least the fog will help Urthailes and Stehlwen cross the rivers unseen.*

A thick column of black greasy smoke still rose from the mound of dead Neddari and swirled amid the gray mist. Therain thanked the gods for the faint east wind that carried most of the smoke and stench down the hill rather than into the castle.

"My lord, here is some mulled wine," said Elmen, appearing out of the fog. "It will help warm you."

Therain took the cup in his gloved hands and took a long swallow of the hot liquid. "Thank you, Captain."

As Therain pondered the heavy fog, an idea came to him. "Summon Vailes and his horsemen and the field captains. We need to send messages to Urthailes and Stehlwen at once. I want them ready to move within the hour. Less if possible."

"You mean to attack, my lord?"

"Yes."

"A risk, my lord. Why stick our necks out toward the swords of a larger foe? Would it not be better to remain here behind the protection of our walls?"

"Of course it is a risk. But I want to hurt them, Elmen. And do something unexpected. I realize we'll do little more than bloody their nose, but if they're caught unawares, we may cast doubt upon them. We beat them back once when they did not expect to lose. They may already be somewhat off balance. I would prefer to keep them that way."

"I understand, my lord. A bold plan."

"Once this fog lifts our chance will be gone. Have the men assemble in the courtyard."

"Yes, my lord. At once."

Messages were dispatched to Lords Urthailes and Stehlwen. Therain prayed they were prepared and would move quickly; his attack would be much more effective if it fell upon three fronts. If not, they would be compelled to withdraw quickly before the Neddari could maneuver their forces to surround them and cut off their retreat.

He commanded that his black destrier Urha be prepared for battle. Therain intended to lead his troops personally and would brook no argument when Elmen raised his inevitable concerns. He wanted to hurt the Neddari, to punish them for the Khedeshians they had killed and the harm they had brought to his home. It would not suffice to wait in Agdenor; they must feel the bite of *his* sword wielded by *his* hand, not just those of his soldiers. He wanted to kill the Storm King most of all, but knew that Asankaru was beyond his power to harm. *That must wait for Gerin's arrival,* he thought. He wondered if his brother and his vassals had yet begun their march.

Half an hour after he'd issued his command to prepare for an attack, two thousand foot soldiers and three hundred horse waited in the courtyard behind the ruined gates and their shattered towers. The wreckage of the gates and other rubble and debris had been used to make the small curtain wall across the mouth of the gate tunnel. Set into the low wall were two separate gates of steel-banded timbers that were now thrown open. The light in the courtyard was dim and diffuse; fog drifted through the castle, so it seemed to Therain that he faced an army of phantoms, grim and determined, their breastplates and helms dark and threatening, their banners hanging limply from their staffs in the still air.

His squire Hurother held Urha's reins while Therain mounted. Captain Vailes waited upon his horse Regga with his son at his side. Mykel, his leg bandaged beneath his armor, sat astride his gray charger and bowed his head to Therain. "M'lord, we await your command."

He looked across the courtyard. Men highborn and low waited on his word. *I wonder if any of them think of me as the lord whelp now?* Among the mounted soldiers, he saw Baron Darus Halfrey of Stocktill and his sons Daril, Raliene, and Domas; Raliene, the youngest, was not yet seventeen and had but a fringe of downy beard upon his cheeks, but he had fought bravely against the Neddari and killed three of them himself. Earl Eljon Sheridel of Durenhal waited atop his magnificent white destrier, with his son Elbran riding beside him and his nephew Collem Jorys as his standard-bearer. Old Lord Perren Dulgran of Enderholt, his rheumy eyes rimmed with red from weeping for his lost son and grandson, clutched his lance as if to keep himself from drowning in his grief. Dulgran had asked to be in the van of the attack, and Therain had not the heart to refuse him. He saw other lords and their men and his own soldiers of the castle. There were men from the outlying towns who wore bits of mismatched plate and mail scrounged from the castle armory or scavenged from the dead.

"Brave men of Khedesh!" he shouted. "Despite the unholy sorceries of the Storm King, we have held Agdenor against their attack! Now we take the attack to them! We will strike their lines swiftly and then return to the castle. Do not tarry! I do not want us surrounded upon the hill. Strike hard and fast, then return. Kill their commanders, burn their tents, set fire to their provisions, slay their steeds! Make them rue the day they set foot upon Khedeshian soil!"

"*Lord Therain! Lord Therain!*" shouted his men, thrusting their weapons into the air.

"To me, men of Khedesh!" He turned Urha about and rode through the gate, flanked by Elmen and his guards.

Delgo Nerat Igrulun had returned to his tent to don his armor and weapons when he heard distant shouts and the ringing of steel. He ran outside and looked up the hill. The fog had thinned a little, and through it he could dimly see a battle raging at the ditch.

Horns sounded—Khedeshian horns—and then a volley of burning pitch-tipped arrows fell around him. Three punctured his tent and set the rugs within aflame. Other tents were struck with the burning missiles; within moments the canvas erupted with gouts of fire. He saw with horror that the God's tent had begun to burn. Black smoke curled from three widening holes as the ropes and support poles within caught fire.

Ten feet away a warrior fell when an arrow pierced his skull. The burning tip broke through the back of his head and pinned it to the ground. "To me! To me!" he bellowed. "We are under attack!" He had carried his sword with him from his tent but had left his helm and breastplate behind.

The Khedeshians had annihilated the Neddari on the castle side of the rampart. *I should have torn it down,* Irgulun realized. By leaving the rampart in place he had succeeded only in hampering the advance of his own men against the castle. The Khedeshians had broken through the center with their horse, followed by their foot soldiers; now archers and crossbowmen took up positions along the rampart and killed the Neddari trying to close in on their flanks. *Without that ditch and wall we could surround them and crush them.* But he knew the Khedeshians would withdraw before he could mount an effective counterattack.

Still, he could not simply wait for the enemy to do their

damage and retreat. "To me, I say! We must drive them back!" Many of the horses—including his own—had torn up their pickets, terrified of the growing fires in the nearby tents. He saw the war priests and the God Who Has Returned walk calmly from their tent while the flames engulfed it. The priests looked at him with expressions of cold derision, and he knew they would not be helping him now. The God stood still as stone. Igrulun wondered if he should just fall on his sword and be done with it. Humiliation overwhelmed him. Bits of burning canvas fell through the air like black snow. One landed on his head and almost set his hair on fire before he smacked it out. An acrid stench blew through the camp.

But he did not fall on his sword. Not yet, at least. He would not abandon his men. If the God demanded his head as the penalty for his errors, then so be it, but first he would drive the Khedeshians back to their castle and make them regret their arrogance. He brandished his sword and ran toward the stony foot of the hill, shouting the war cry of his clan in the old Hakán speech, the only words of it he ever spoke, *"Elak merithki! Elak merithki!"*

His men saw their helmless Warlord racing toward their enemy and rallied to him. Suddenly a thousand men were running up the hill, shouting their war cries. Igrulun felt the warrior lust run hot in him. He needed to spill blood.

The Khedeshian horse had cut a line through the center of his men. They followed the course of the road in a close wedge while the foot soldiers spread out behind them, killing and burning. Fire and smoke sprang up all across the hill, but only on this side of the ditch and dirt-wall. *If the fires burn out of control, the ditch will protect their castle but not us.*

Then there was no more time for thought. He crashed headlong into a Khedeshian with a two-handed great sword who nearly took off his head with a single vicious swing of the blade. Irgulun ducked beneath the weapon and stabbed upward with his own, driving the point through the man's stomach and out his back. He wrenched his blade free and let the man topple.

Irgulun could not say how long he fought. Not long, surely, though it seemed hours passed as he and the cluster of Neddari around him hacked and stabbed at their enemies, killing and being killed. An arrow passed so close to his head the wind of it moved his hair. The man behind him was not so lucky; the shaft punctured the hollow at the base of his throat, driving a spray of blood from his mouth. Irgulun heard him grunt when he took the arrow, but that was the only sound he made before he died.

He spied the Khedeshian leader upon his horse, ringed by his guards, shouting orders with his sword drawn. There was blood upon the blade. Irgulun wondered if this were a field captain or the leader of the castle who'd exchanged words with him. He had never clearly seen the man who'd spoken to them from the dirt-wall. *No matter who he is, we will be better off when he is dead.* He turned and hacked off the arm of a man just below the elbow, then kicked him into one of the fires the Khedeshians had set. The man tumbled backward into the flames and rolled helplessly, screaming as he was roasted alive in his armor, his blood sizzling in the heat as it spurted from the stump of his arm.

His men followed as he made his way toward the Khedeshian leader. But they'd only moved perhaps ten yards closer when he heard the Khedeshian leader call for a retreat. "Fall back to the castle!" he shouted. His order was repeated by other field captains to their men.

The Khedeshians fought every step of the way back through the opening in the wall. Once they passed through it, they turned and ran full speed up the road.

"After them! After them! Do not let them get away!" Irgulun shouted. He would chase them all the way to their ruined gates and kill them to a man, and then pull the castle to the ground in retribution for his humiliation. He would flay the skin from their leader with his own hands and feed it to his dogs before he cut out his heart. The Khedeshian leader and his guardians tarried on the far side of the dirt-wall while his men retreated past him. Irgulun shouted his war cry once more, then pressed the attack.

He and his men passed through the earth-wall to the upper part of the hill, hacking at the Khedeshian stragglers. At least half of the Khedeshian horse remained behind to protect the foot soldiers running toward the gates. Irgulun did not care. He would kill them all. *I will not disappoint the God again.* His men were now pouring through the rampart behind him and spreading out as they charged up the hill. If the Khedeshian horse did not retreat to the castle soon, his soldiers would encircle them and smash them against the hard stone walls. *Let them stay. I will make them pay for what they've done to me.* Arrows began to fly from the battlements. His men were packed so tightly together that every arrow found a target.

He lunged at a retreating Khedeshian and drove the point of his sword into the back of the man's thigh below his hauberk. He'd no sooner hit the ground than Irgulun chopped through his neck, nearly severing it. Blood gushed onto the ground and the man went limp.

He looked up and saw that the Khedeshian cavalry had turned about and were now facing him. The walls of the castle loomed out of the fog, tall and dark, with dim shapes moving along its battlements. Were they going to attack him? He glanced over his shoulder—at least two thousand Neddari were behind him now, charging the castle. Were these riders madmen? Surprise had been their ally before, but now they faced overwhelming numbers. He did not understand what they planned to do.

Then he heard the horns and the thunder of horses. He stopped and turned. The horns sounded once more. Khedeshian horns, from behind him and to the sides. A cheer rose from the defenders on the castle walls. "Urthailes and Stehlwen have come!" he heard them shout. The foot soldiers he had pursued to the castle turned about and attacked while the cavalry charged. He and his men were beset on three sides.

A gray-fletched arrow pierced his upper arm. The force of it spun him around. He dropped his weapon and clutched at the shaft; its tip protruded from the back of his arm, dripping dark blood. He was bending down for his sword when the Khedeshian cavalry reached him. Just as the fingers of Irgulun's left hand grasped the hilt of his weapon, a horseman drove his lance into his back. The last thing Irgulun saw before his sight dimmed forever was a long point of gore-drenched steel protruding from his chest.

Therain was climbing the stairs to the battlements of the curtain wall when Lords Urthailes and Stehlwen sounded their horns and smashed the flanks of the Neddari. Therain's own cavalry and foot soldiers had turned and were driving back through the center of the Neddari who had pursued them. The enemy was now trapped between the castle and the earthen rampart, with an escape route too narrow to allow them to quickly flee the field. Some tried to clamber over the rampart and were shot by mounted archers or pierced with lances; others fell upon the stakes that remained at the bottom of the dike. A few escaped over, and more were routed back through the blasted gate opening in the earthen wall, but most of the Neddari who had come up the hill were killed.

"Well met, my lords," said Therain as Urthailes and Stehlwen joined him atop the battlements. Urthailes's face was streaked with blood from a glancing blow he'd taken from an axe. "Put a wicked dent in my helm," he said, holding it out for Therain to examine. The nose- and cheek-guards were covered with intricate scrollwork fashioned in the design of twining grape vines, the sigil of his house. There was a deep crease above the right temple.

"Do you need a physician?" asked Therain.

"I'll be fine, my lord. Just a shallow cut to my scalp. Let the healers work on those who are truly in need."

"My lord, do you wish us to retake the rampart?" asked Urthailes.

"I'd leave it be," said Stehlwen. "We've driven the Neddari

back from this side of it, but they moved some of their camp forward after they took it last night. Even with the hurt we've given their front lines, they're still too close. Our men could not make repairs without getting cut to pieces by their bowmen. It would be a waste of lives and gain us little."

"I agree," said Therain. "Pull back any men that are patrolling it. Where are your men now?"

"I sent anyone not wounded back across the rivers," said Urthailes. "I don't have enough men to hold the near bank. If the Neddari threw their might against us, we'd be crushed between them and the river."

"Good. That's where I want you. Send your men back to your camp if you have not done so already, Lord Stehlwen. Should the castle fall, at least you'll have clear means of escape."

"My lord, don't talk of such things," said Urthailes.

"I must. We're facing a foe with powers beyond our reckoning. Agdenor is strong, but against the Storm King's might I don't know how long we can stand."

Urthailes looked unhappy with talk of defeat and turned his gaze down the hill.

"We've dealt the Neddari a nasty blow," said Stehlwen.

"Yes, a good blow to be sure, but not fatal," said Therain. He looked down at the ruined gate tunnel. "As you can see, Agdenor has been grievously damaged. My gates seem to have gone missing. If the Storm King should send another twister at us . . ."

Lord Stehlwen's expression grew dark. "I've never seen the like of that, my lord. I'll tell you plainly, I was terrified of it, as were my men. I'd wager more than half of them fell to their knees and prayed to the gods with the fervor of a newly christened priest."

"Mine as well," said Urthailes. "A bit of dark and powerful sorcery that was."

"I know what it was. What I *don't* know is how to defend against it."

"I fear I cannot help you with that, my lord," said Urthailes.

"Perhaps if your brother or sister were here they could suggest a defense, but I can fight only men, not magic."

Yes, dear brother, where in the name of Shayphim's bloody Hounds are you? Are you waiting for Father to arrive before you march here? He dearly hoped not, but then realized that Gerin had no way of knowing about the Storm King's power and what had happened to Agdenor. He needed to send word to him. *I should have done that already,* he chided himself. *I need to know when he will come.* He took his leave of the lords and went off to find his scribes.

The Neddari camp was in chaos. Tevi Igrulun had been slain on the battlefield. His body had not been recovered, but many had seen him fall. The God and his war priests had watched the slaughter with hard, scowling faces. After they emerged from their burning tent, they had not moved for many hours. Glowing embers passed harmlessly through their ghostly bodies. Warriors and clan-slaves ran past the God and His servants to battle fires or join the fighting, but the God paid them no heed.

The Khedeshians had killed more than two thousand warriors and clan-slaves. The fog had cleared, but a pall of ashen death hung above the camp. Many warriors blamed Igrulun and said that if he had not died in battle they would have killed him for his failures. The *kamichi* spoke loudly of his refusal to allow them to join the first attack on the castle and said the God had allowed the attack to fail to punish Igrulun for his pride and arrogance.

Midday arrived and the last of the fires was finally extinguished. The wounded who would survive were taken to the *kamichi* and plant-healers to be treated for their injuries; those whose wounds were too grievous were quickly and cleanly killed to end their suffering. It was hard, grim work, but the men doing the killing told themselves that the God would raise the fallen once His stolen powers were returned to Him. That was why they were here in these strange lands fighting the Khedeshians in their castle—to find the summoner and his

horn so that the Slain God's Return could be completed and
His might and majesty restored. "And then He will reward us
for our faithful service," they said to themselves. Eternal life
would be theirs for the asking.

In early afternoon the clan Chieftains and *kamichi* leaders
gathered before the God. The war priests watched them with
cold hatred upon their strange faces. *This is Igrulun's doing,*
thought Pendrel Yevan Hirgrolei. *He was a fool who has
brought the Slain God's wrath down upon us all.*

"Great One, Tevi Igrulun has fallen," said Odan Iktoret
Perochan, Chieftain of Clan Evrosúlar. He was a tall man
with a thick neck and shoulders and a heavy slab of stomach.
A two-handed broadsword was slung across his back, the
hilt-guards rising above his head like a set of steel antlers.
"You must appoint a new Warlord and Overchieftain in his
stead. The war-host must have a lord to command it."

The Slain God turned his gaze toward Perochan, who paled
beneath the power of it. "Who are you to say what I must
do?"

Perochan bowed his head. "Forgive me, Great One. I mis-
spoke. Command me and it shall be done."

"Is the one here who foresaw my return?"

Hirgrolei stepped forward and bowed. "I am here, Great
One."

"It was you who set the summoner on the path that led to
his opening of the Door of Night, was it not?"

Hirgrolei did not yet raise his head. "That is so, Great One."

"Then you shall take command of this army." Hirgrolei
raised his head as a murmur of shock ran through the gathered Neddari. Never before had a *kamichi* been granted command of the clan warriors. *Indeed, the old ways have truly
been swept away,* he thought. He saw the looks of horror on
the faces of the clan Chieftains, but none of them had the
courage to voice an objection to the Slain God's command.

"Prepare another tent for me at once," said the God Who
Has Returned. "And see to the defense of the encampment.

You are the new Warlord. See that you do better than the last, or you will suffer his fate."

"Yes, Great One. I will see to your tent and plan another attack. We will not fail you again." He would have to choose one of the clan Chieftains to be his second-in-command. Hirgrolei was no warrior and did not know their ways; he would need the counsel of one skilled in the art of combat. He was not so prideful as to think he could carry out the Slain God's wishes without help. *That was Igrulun's undoing,* he thought. *I will not make the same mistake.* He glanced around the room. Perochan would be a good choice. A shrewd man who would understand the wisdom of assisting him. He would speak to him as soon as they were dismissed.

"You may plan all you will," said the God, "but do nothing until I command you. My war priests will prepare the way for you when the first stars rise and their power waxes full. See that you do nothing until then."

Hirgrolei bowed once more. He would not question the God. That, too, had been Igrulun's way. *A strong Chieftain, but a fool. He trusted himself more than the God.* Obedience was what the God required, not questions or demands for explanations. *We will not fail you again.* He would speak to Perochan about preparing the warriors, and await the God's command. He bowed his head once more. "Yes, Great One. Your will shall be done."

32

A bran made his way down the cobblestoned
surface of Nathrad Road upon his brown and black destrier Marhil, past Tanners Way and the Street of Kings, lined
with massive marble statues of the previous rulers of
Khedesh and the cleared spot waiting for his father's statue,
past stoop-shouldered men and shawled women standing beside barrows and carts filled with vegetables and fruits, past
guild houses and inns, blacksmiths' forges and cobblers'
shops, fish markets and merchants dealing in wool, silk,
leather, and linen, on his way to the Okoro Gate. He was surrounded by a phalanx of Kotireon Guards—charged with
protecting members of the royal household—who would escort him to the wall of the city, where he would meet the
Taeratens responsible for his safety outside of Almaris.

By law, the Kotireons had jurisdiction only in the capital
and its surrounding environs; this campaign would take the
king across the breadth of Khedesh, and so his safety would
be entrusted to Taeratens who had sworn special oaths to
protect Abran no matter the cost to themselves. They were
officially called the King's Guard, but they were also referred to as Red Helms because of the deep crimson color of
their helmets. There was a story that the helms had been colored red by the blood of the first Taeratens to swear the Oath
of the King's Guard two hundred years earlier. The tale said

that they had slit their palms and smeared their blood onto the helms while chanting the oath to King Toreyan Atreyano. The power of their oath was so great that it had stained the metal of the helms red forever after. It was said that if a King's Guard ever wavered in his duty while wearing his helm, the steel would turn black, and that if his thoughts were treasonous, he would die instantly.

These thoughts passed through Abran's mind as he rode beneath the Okoro Gate and toward the Field of Nenweil, where his commanders and marshals waited. His army was encamped around the city walls, tens of thousands of men about to march to war. It had been many long years since he'd led men in battle, and the thought was like a fire in his veins. He was troubled that his sons were embroiled in this war—especially Therain, as young and inexperienced as he was—but he had no doubt that they would comport themselves well. After all, they were his sons.

He reached the area of trampled earth where the leaders of the army awaited him. The tents had been folded and packed away onto wagons.

"Your Majesty," said Lord Commander Arilek Levkorail as Abran approached. Arilek held his right fist to his chest and bowed his head. "The army will be ready to march within the hour."

A servant rushed to steady Marhil as Abran dismounted. The golden stag's head gleamed upon Abran's breastplate as he shifted his cloak forward on his shoulders.

"Good. Has there been any further word from the west?"

"No, Your Majesty. We've heard nothing else since the last message from your son."

Abran nodded and sat down on a small folding chair. The King's Guard took up position behind him. "We have need of haste. This will be a hard march."

"The men are ready, Your Majesty."

He received updates on the total number of soldiers presently in the army—more would join them as they marched eastward from his vassals in those lands—a report on what rations the men would be allotted each day, and several other mostly meaningless bits of information that he listened to as attentively as he could. Arilek and others shouted commands to underlings, who rushed to carry them out. He tried to pay attention, but his mind was elsewhere. He was worried about Reshel. *By the gods, Gerin had best keep her safe and out of harm's way.* He feared that she might be called upon to use her magic in some way to counter the powers of the Neddari. *She'd better not go anywhere near the fighting,* he thought. *A battlefield is no place for a woman, wizard or not.* That Gerin's magic was somehow involved in starting this war galled him. He felt certain that more troubles would follow from his son being a wizard, but it was too late to change that now.

He gestured for one of Baron Sidden's lieutenants to come to him. "Yes, Your Majesty?" said the young man, bowing low. There was a nervous quaver in his voice that he tried unsuccessfully to hide.

"Bring me paper, pen and ink, and a writing table," he said. "I need to send a message to Prince Gerin. And make sure you can find the Master of Birds in all of this immensity. This must be sent right away."

"At once, Your Majesty," he said with another bow, then rushed off to fulfill the command.

He could not assume anything about Reshel anymore. Her magic changed everything. Not for the first time, he wondered if he had made a mistake in allowing her to train to become a wizard. What need did a princess have of such powers? He understood why she would find it so alluring, his daughter the scholar and historian, but that did not make his misgivings go away. He needed to quiet them as best he could, which meant writing to Gerin and making it very clear that Reshel was not to go anywhere near the battle front.

While he waited, he prayed to Telros to watch over his children and keep them safe. What else was a father to do?

33

After sending his message to Gerin, Therain returned to the battlements. He was pleased with the outcome of their attack, but his satisfaction was tempered by the knowledge that when Asankaru sent another storm at them, there was nothing he could do to stop it. He knew it was only a matter of time before they fell. Maybe hours or days, or weeks if they were very lucky, but at some point another twister would follow the first.

He knew that the Storm King was not a god; that was a deception that had allowed him to gather and control the Neddari army now camped on Therain's lands. Was there some way to turn that deception to his use? Some way to show the Neddari that their god was false? *Nothing is so hard as to show a man he has been played for a fool,* Master Aslon had told him once. *Many will deny they have been tricked no matter if the proof of the lie is waved before their noses. A man's pride can be a strangely delicate and stubborn thing when challenged. Some would rather die than admit their deepest beliefs are wrong.*

Therain could think of no way to prove the Storm King a false god except by defeating him, and if he could do that, he would have no more need to prove him false. But even if they did defeat Asankaru, he still was not sure the Neddari would believe they had been misled. *When the Storm King is*

*finally brought down, they will probably tell themselves our
gods were stronger, or that we used treachery or wizardry, or
that they themselves were not strong enough followers, that
their own faith had faltered. Anything that will allow them to
maintain their belief.*

The Neddari were still burying their dead. The fires were
all out, but smoke still hung low above the camp. More tents
had been erected to replace the ones that burned, only this
time they were placed farther back from the front line. He
saw men hardening sharpened stakes in fires and building a
crude palisade around the tents.

Teiyeron and his masons had returned to their work,
strengthening the wall they had erected in the ruins of the gate
tunnel. Men with barrows wheeled in blocks of stone and un-
loaded them in great piles, while other men used trowels to
slather mortar on the rock. The wall thickened and grew taller.
The rough wooden gates were reinforced with more bands of
hammered steel. Master Evernyes and his helpers brought
more buckets of Fierel's Fire to the soldiers on the wall; servants brought more oil and sand, as well as wood to stoke the
fires to heat them. Boys and girls from the kitchens ran about
with pails of water and ladles for drinking and chunks of
black bread, onions, and dried apples for the soldiers to eat.
Food was being carefully rationed in the event of a long siege.
Therain frowned at the thought and wondered if he shouldn't
just let his men eat their fill. It was doubtful this siege would
go long enough to deplete their stores. *Better to have them eat
it now than to leave it for the Neddari,* he thought. But he did
not change his order. To do so would be to signal that he
thought defeat was imminent, and he could not do that.

He was in the courtyard later that day when a messenger
appeared. "My lord, you must come at once. The Red Robes
are coming up the hill."

Soldiers had gathered along the battlements, many with
torches that flickered in the wind. Others had moved into the
ruined gate tunnel. Elmen shouted, "Make way for Duke
Therain!" as he and Therain and ran up the stairs.

The Red Robes had passed beyond the rampart and were on their way toward the castle. Their bodies cast the same silvery glow they had seen before. The Storm King was not with them. *Where is Asankaru?* He had feared their appearance marked the coming of the second twister, but why wasn't the Storm King with them? They couldn't create a whirlwind without Asankaru, could they? His jaw clenched and his teeth ground together. He hated not understanding what was happening. *They're marching right toward me, and I have no idea what they're going to do or what I can do to stop them.*

A young soldier stepped up to Therain and saluted. "My lord, should I command the archers to attack them?"

"Have them save their arrows. It will do no good."

One of the commanders farther down the wall saw fit to use a trebuchet to launch a boulder at the Red Robes. It slammed into the paving stones of the road with great force a dozen yards in front of them; the surface of the road cracked under the impact and threw up shards of rock. The boulder bounced into the air once, crashed down again and rolled right at the Red Robes. They did not break their stride. They did not so much as flinch when the boulder crashed into them . . . and passed right through them. Therain heard men curse and saw several make the sign against evil.

"What *are* these devils?" hissed Elmen. "I've never heard of their kind before. They're like spirits with the powers of sorcerers."

"I don't know," said Therain. "I wish I did. Maybe that would give us some idea of how to defeat them."

"What is their race? They are not men; that much is plain once you see them up close. And how are they related to the Storm King? Their powers do not seem to be the same as Asankaru's, yet it appeared they somehow helped him create the tornado he sent at us."

"Again, Elmen, I do not know. All good questions."

The captain paused, watching the Red Robes approach. "I

wonder if their power is bound up in the staffs they carry. If we could take one from them we might learn whether they can still command their magic without it."

"Since their staffs seem to be made of the same immaterial stuff as their bodies, I see no way to divest them of it. We cannot take what we cannot touch. But it would be interesting to know. The Storm King carries no staff, and did not need one to summon his twister."

As the Red Robes drew nearer to the castle, some of the men could not help themselves and loosed their arrows. None of their shafts had any effect, and they soon stopped trying.

The Red Robes walked with an odd fluidity, their steps so synchronized it almost looked as if seven images of one being were coming toward them. *It's like they're in a trance,* thought Therain as he watched them draw closer. He looked out into the Neddari camp, but the Storm King was nowhere to be seen. The Neddari, however, were massing on their side of the dike. He could see that in many places they'd knocked the rampart down and filled in the dike with earth after ripping up the stakes. *They won't be bottlenecked trying to attack us through the single gate we made. They'll come pouring through all those openings at once.*

Several lords begged their leave and scampered down the stairs to their men in the courtyard. Therain could see Kever Selystri shouting to the cavalry. Captain Vailes and his son had both been killed in the assault upon the Neddari camp, and command of the mounted soldiers had fallen to Selystri.

When Therain turned back, the Red Robes were almost upon them.

Despite the futility of the earlier attacks on the Red Robes, soldiers within the castle tried once more to stop their advance. Men hurled buckets of Fierel's Fire at them, which erupted at their feet and sprayed orange fire across the dried grass and stony road. But the fire did not cling to whatever insubstantial element composed their bodies, and they continued on.

Soldiers had dug a wide shallow trench where the gates had once stood and filled it with pitch. Just before the Red Robes reached the trench, a soldier threw a burning torch into it, sending up a sudden wall of roaring flame whose heat Therain could feel from the battlements. The Red Robes walked through the flames in their eerie synchronous march, their staffs held lightly in the crooks of their arms.

When they reached the chest-high wall that had been raised that day, they spread out until they were spaced equally along its length. A dozen soldiers rushed at them from behind and hacked at them with swords or tried to pierce them with spears. Therain watched, breathless, as the Red Robes wheeled about and touched the men with their staffs, which crackled with sudden blue fire. The men were hurled backward and fell to the earth with greasy smoke pouring from the seams of their armor.

As one, the Red Robes laid their staffs against the wall. Blue fire once more crackled up and down the black wood, then leaped to the stone and danced along its face.

The twisting blue fire washed across the stone until the entire wall was encased in a writhing sheath of living flame. The Red Robes then took a step back and slammed the ferrules of their staffs into the earth. Therain thought he heard them shout a word or phrase, but could not understand it.

The next moment, the wall exploded.

The sound was deafening—the force nearly lifted Therain off his feet. He would have fallen backward onto the wall-walk had Elmen and Randel Ergoen not been there to steady him. The wooden shutters in the embrasures were blown upward from the force of it; they all slammed down together with a loud *crack*. A few men fell from the wall-walk into the yard below.

There was only a smoking scar in the earth and some blackened bits of stone where the wall had once stood. Hundreds of men lay dead and dying in the courtyard, their bodies shredded by sharp fragments of rock. The cavalry had been obliterated: the horses that had not been killed in the explosion had thrown their riders and fled. Some of the animals were on their backs or sides, their legs shattered or severed, screaming in agony and terror.

The Red Robes were gone. He did not see their bodies lying anywhere in the courtyard. *How could there be bodies? They're dead already. They have no real substance.*

A hand gripped his shoulder and spun him around. Elmen was gray with dust; dark runnels of blood streamed down his face from cuts he'd received from flying bits of stone. *He's lucky he wasn't blinded,* Therain thought when he saw the two long gashes on his captain's face, both near his eyes. *I'm lucky I wasn't, either.* Another soldier lay nearby on the steps with a sliver of rock sticking out of his forehead.

Elmen pointed to the west. Therain felt his skin go cold.

Thousands of Neddari had charged through the openings in the earthen rampart and were racing up the hill at them. They would be there in moments.

"Bloody *bloody* hell!" he cursed. He cupped his hands around his mouth and shouted, "Anyone who can move, get into the courtyard to repel them!" *They're going to run right over us if we can't stop them here. Miendrel is laughing indeed.* His order was repeated by commanders within the bailey and deeper in the castle.

The Khedeshians who'd rushed to the gate tunnel crouched down and locked their shields, but they had no lances or spears, which had been destroyed when the Red Robes obliterated the wall. The Neddari horse reached the gate and rode right over them, crushing the soldiers beneath the hooves of their chargers. Some of their horsemen charged through the courtyard and into the bailey, hacking down anyone within their reach. Therain watched helplessly as an old serving woman trying to run away had the top of her head chopped off by a sword-wielding horseman. The bloody fragment of her skull skidded across the path like the lost lid to a jar. When her body hit the ground, her brains spilled out onto the grass.

As the rider turned, a Khedeshian archer put an arrow in

his throat. Other Khedeshian archers fired from tower windows and the wall-walk, killing more than a score of Neddari cavalry. There were so many bodies on the ground of the courtyard that the horses could not move without stepping on them.

He and his guards rushed along the battlements toward the north, crouching behind the inner parapet that edged the wall-walk. Therain paused once to look out through the battlements to see if Urthailes was coming across the Samaro. He thought he could see some movement near the bank of the river but it was too dark to be certain.

They descended a narrow stairway. When they reached the brown grass of the bailey, Elmen turned to him. "My lord, we should make our stand at the Thorn!"

"I should not leave the gates!" He drew his sword Baleringol and pointed to the smoking ruins, fifty yards away, where the Red Robes had worked their magic. The courtyard was filled with fighting men. Therain could see hundreds of Neddari pouring into the castle.

"The gates are lost, or soon will be! It's more important that you live!"

"I won't flee like a coward! I'll stay and fight!"

"We *will* fight, but not here!"

The few Khedeshians still in the courtyard were being slaughtered or driven off, and the fighting was spreading farther into the castle. The Neddari foot soldiers ran up the stairs to the battlements. Their archers took up positions within the castle and began shooting every Khedeshian upon the wall-walk. The men were almost completely defenseless; most did not even have shields. Some dropped behind the parapet to avoid the archers, but were then cut to pieces by the advancing Neddari swordsmen.

An arrow clanged into Donael Rundgar's steel shield, the shaft shattering on impact.

"My lord, we can't stay here!" said Elmen.

Therain cursed. "All right! To the Thorn!"

They ran down darkened pathways between the buildings

of the castle. While they were crossing an open greensward they saw a young serving boy impaled against a wall by a spear as he was trying to reach the door to one of the storage towers. Two fleeing washing women were run down by horsemen and trampled. A *kamichi* appeared at the other end of the sward, protected by a close guard of soldiers with tall rectangular shields. The *kamichi* whirled his staff and shouted a command, and a sparkling cloud of light appeared in the air above his head—a shimmering, swirling essence a yard or so across, filled with sparkling points of light like ethereal fireflies. *Elementals!* thought Therain, oddly fascinated by his first sight of the dangerous spirit creatures.

The *kamichi* gestured toward a Khedeshian soldier who was running at them with his sword lowered and shield raised. The elemental flew at the man and enveloped his upper body. The points of light within the elemental pulsed as the creature burned the life from the soldier, who had dropped his weapon and shield to claw futilely at his face. His body was a smoking ruin before the elemental drew away.

"Bugger that," muttered Therain. "Give me your bow," he said to one of his guards, a squint-eyed man named Estram Kint. They were well hidden in the shadows, and neither the *kamichi* nor his protectors had seen them. He pulled an arrow from Kint's quiver and nocked the bow. He drew back to his cheek, sighted, and released. The arrow passed between two soldiers and struck the *kamichi* in the side of the face, shattering his skull and knocking him from his horse. The elemental vanished at once. The *kamichi*'s guards shouted and looked around in confusion for the killer. Therain released two more arrows, both of which found their targets, before the Neddari sighted them and charged. A third arrow took the lead horse in the throat. The animal dropped like a stone, throwing its rider forward with such force that he broke his neck when he landed. The other riders had been following too closely and two more went down, tripping over the corpse of the first horse. Therain killed one more man with a well-placed shot through his eye. Only two riders remained seated. Both leaped over their fallen countrymen and charged at the Khedeshians. Therain fired one last arrow, wounding the horseman bearing down on him. The man dropped his weapon and slumped to his right. Therain dropped the bow and jumped as high as he could as the rider reached him, swinging Baleringol with all his might. The rider wore no gorget, and Therain's blade caught him squarely in the throat. The Neddari's head flew free and tumbled across the yard. His body remained in the saddle, headless and spurting blood, as his horse galloped off.

Elmen and Randel charged the last rider from both sides. The Neddari could not fight both and at once and veered suddenly toward the captain, who was the closer of the two. Randel dived forward, his arms completely outstretched, and severed the horse's foreleg just below the knee. The animal crashed down, screaming, and trapped its rider beneath its side. With both hands on the hilt, Elmen drove his sword straight down through the man's chest with such force that it pierced him completely and pinned him to the earth. The Neddari spasmed once as blood fountained from his mouth, then died.

Therain helped Randel to his feet. To Elmen, he said, "When we reach the Thorn, I command you to go at once to find your wife and daughter and get them out of the castle. You know the way."

"My lord, I can't—"

"You can and you will, or I will not only dismiss you from my service but see to it that you are banished from Agdenor forever." An empty threat, since it seemed apparent they would all soon be exiled, if they could remain alive through the night. "You have a duty to your family, and I will see you discharge it."

"I have a sworn duty to you, too, my lord."

"And you've done your utmost to fulfill those duties, but they are at an end. I know how much you love them, and I won't have them die alone and afraid while you are with me. Get them and flee. That is my command as your prince."

Elmen's face was hard and unreadable in the gloom. "Yes, my lord."

The screams of the dying echoed through the night. Therain set his jaw and hurried off into the darkness, wondering if he would live to see the dawn.

34

Late one night, restless and unable to sleep, Gerin left his rooms and made his way through the maze of corridors and stairways that riddled Blackstone Keep. Four guards fell in step with him when he left his chambers. He said nothing to them of his destination, and they did not ask him, though it was plain from his apparel—wool surcoat, hooded fur-lined cloak, and gloves—that they were going outside.

He descended to the main floor, his boots echoing loudly as he crossed the nearly deserted entrance hall to a side door where a single soldier stood at attention. "My lord," the man said with a bow of his head as Gerin approached. He unlocked the door and held it open as Gerin and his guards passed through.

On the other side of the door a narrow set of stairs descended steeply to a flagstone path about fifteen feet long that intersected a larger path running parallel to the wall of the keep. Gerin turned left on the larger path, making his way across the inner bailey toward a lone structure near the northeastern corner of the castle, nestled behind a stone wall pierced with a single gate of black iron. There were soldiers still awake in the bailey, standing around fires, warming their hands, speaking quietly to one another. They nodded or bowed to him as he passed, then returned to their conversations.

The soldiers carried torches from the keep that they lit in the fires of the makeshift camp of Gerin's growing army. They passed beyond the throng of men and made their way between several outbuildings that blocked the firelight from the camp. The darkness posed no problem to Gerin's sensitive eyes, but the men were another matter, and they raised their torches higher to push back the night.

Reaching the iron gate, Gerin withdrew a large key from his pocket and thrust it into the lock. He turned it once, feeling the lock resist for a moment before giving way and rotating. There was a loud click, and the gate swung aside on creaking hinges. He left it open and followed the path through a stand of pacca trees, planted in Khedesh as memorials to the dead, to the single door set in the mausoleum beneath the pediment. Gerin had always found the sight of pacca trees comforting; the way their oddly symmetrical branches thrust upward at sharp angles to the brownish-gold bark of the trunk, like a man forming a V with his raised arms, made him think that they were reaching toward the gods in eternal supplication, beseeching Bellon and Telros to watch over the recent dead.

The mausoleum was not large, twenty feet on each side, a square of white stone with a low-pitched roof and four marble pillars set along its face supporting the overhang of the pediment. Images of Bellon, Lord of the Dead and ruler of the shadowy realm of Velyol—where those who escaped the clutches of Shayphim went to dwell in gray silence—were carved along the front of the mausoleum on either side of the door. In the flickering light of the torches, Gerin saw Bellon's consort Sherenna guiding the dead through the gate of Velyol, small sad figures with bowed heads marching beneath his gargantuan and forbidding presence, while the Hounds of Shayphim howled in protest, kept at bay by Sherenna's outstretched hand.

"Wait here," Gerin said to the men.

"My lord, we should accompany you," said the lieutenant in charge. "Our orders are not to let you out of our sight once you leave your private chambers."

Gerin gestured to the black door of the mausoleum. "This is the only way in or out. If you stand guard here, you'll protect me just as well as if you came with me. I want to be alone."

"One of the killers could already be in the mausoleum, waiting to strike," protested the lieutenant.

Gerin closed his eyes and tried to keep his temper. *They're only doing their duty,* he told himself. He thought the likelihood that a Herald had managed to enter the locked mausoleum in anticipation that he would eventually happen by to be ridiculously small. He tugged on the door; it was still sealed, and the lock did not appear to have been tampered with. Still, he should not deliberately undermine the tasks assigned to his men.

"All right, Lieutenant. Send two of your men to make sure the crypts are empty. I'll wait here with you. When they report back, assuming everything is clear, I will then enter, *alone.*"

The lieutenant selected two of his men while Gerin unlocked the mausoleum door with a second key. Torches and swords in hand, they entered the small space, checked the interior, then made their way down the stairs to the crypts below.

It seemed an eternity passed before they returned. Gerin heard their footfalls in the underground passage long before the other men; the interior of the mausoleum suddenly brightened as the glowing torch-heads emerged from the stairs.

"The crypts are empty, my lord," said the taller of the guards as he came through the door.

"Good. Stand watch here." He turned away from them and entered the mausoleum.

Once inside, he spoke softly in Osirin. A tiny spark of magefire no larger than the tip of his little finger appeared above his head, bathing the cold stone in silvery light.

The interior of the mausoleum was a single open space, with four-foot-high marble pedestals set along the walls. Busts of the Atreyano dead were set atop the pedestals, their sculpted hair and blank white eyes covered with the dust of many long silent years. He turned around slowly, looking at each of them in turn, his long-dead ancestors, but did not linger. He walked to the long rectangular hole cut into the center of the floor, where a stone stair descended into the dark earth, and took the steps down, the spark of magefire following him like an obedient firefly.

The stairs were narrow and uneven, cut crudely from the bedrock of the hill. They delved down for nearly thirty feet, with rough stone walls on either side, before emerging in the long subterranean corridor of the Atreyano crypt. The corridor had an arched ceiling and many alcoves cut into the rock walls at this end, the oldest section of the passage dating back five or six centuries. In the alcoves lay the bones of his ancestors, covered with a thick accumulation of dust and cobwebs and bits of rotted burial cloth. Swords lay with many of the men, atop exposed breast bones, the blades rusted and dull, the hilts gripped loosely by brittle finger bones. The women had been buried with pieces of jewelry or other favorite ornaments; he saw bracelets encircling fragile wrists, rings adorning ghostly white fingers, and necklaces draped over exposed ribs. The names of the dead had been inscribed on thick metal plates bolted to the rock beneath the alcoves—in the glare of the magefire's light he silently read them as he made his way down the passage, which curved gently to the left.

The passage changed as he walked, becoming smoother, more polished, more refined; after fifty feet or so gray marble tiles had been inlaid into the stone of the floor and walls, and the ceiling was suddenly crisscrossed with ribs cut from the rock of the hill. The alcoves had been replaced by sealed crypts bearing bas relief likenesses of those contained within on the center of the crypt door, their names carved beneath the cold white faces.

He continued on, his heart growing heavier with each step. It had been a long time since he'd been here. Too long.

He reached the last crypt. The passage continued its gentle

curve through the bedrock of the hill for several hundred more feet, enough space to bury Atreyanos for generations to come before the tunnel would have to be extended or another one excavated. The light of his magefire was swallowed by the darkness ahead, so absolute he could see nothing in it, not even the suggestion of the walls or ceiling.

He moved a step closer to the final crypt. "Hello, Mother."

He looked at the face carved upon the long marble rectangle sealing the crypt. The relatively high angle of the magefire light cast deep pools of darkness across the eyes of the relief, so dark they looked like holes punched through the face. It did not look like his mother; he'd thought that from the moment he first saw it, standing here with his father and brother and sisters. His heart had thudded in his chest like the fluttering broken wing of a bird when the door of the crypt was set in place, closing with a loud echoing boom that signaled the end of his mother's life to him with more finality than anything else in the many months of her failing health. It seemed both a long time ago and very recent. VANYA ATREYANO, read the inscription below the face. No, it did not look like her at all. Oh, he could see the similarities— the prominent cheekbones, full lips, the shape of her nose, the flow of the stylized hair—but there was something missing, some vital essence his mother had possessed that this likeness lacked and could never gain. There was no magic, no spell, no secret word, that could instill this bit of marble with whatever it needed to truly represent his mother.

"I'm sorry I haven't been to see you in a while. So much has happened. So many changes in my life. Grandfather is dead and Father is king now. I'm the master of Ailethon and Therain is the duke of Agdenor. I know, that's hard to imagine, but it's true.

"But those aren't even the biggest changes. Both Reshel and I are wizards now. Can you believe it? A wizard wrote down a prophecy about me a long time ago, which is how they found me. There aren't many of them left anymore. They've been dying out for a long time, and it won't be too much longer before wizards have completely vanished from the world." He paused, a shiver running down his back that was not caused by the cold air in the crypt. "It's strange and unsettling, knowing that this woman saw my life, or parts of it, before I was even born. It bothers me when I think about it, which is why I try not to. I have enough to worry about without wondering if there's anything I can do to change any bad things that might happen.

"And it seems I'm not just any old wizard," he went on, "but a very powerful one. The *most* powerful, actually. How's that for an achievement? There has only been one other amber wizard since the Doomwar, and that was King Naragenth. The thought of having so much power, and living as long as I will, bothers me sometimes almost as much as the prophecy about me." He brushed his fingertips along the cool surface of the relief, down the side of the nose and beneath the right eye. "It's so . . . daunting.

"When Hollin told me I could become a wizard and how powerful I'd be, at first it seemed unreal, like it was happening to someone else. And I really didn't understand what it meant. When I visited Hethnost, the wizards there treated me like some kind of legend. At first they didn't even see *me,* they just saw this person who was going to turn their world upside down. It was intimidating. I know that's surprising. I've never been one to be intimidated by anything. But now I feel like I have to *become* a figure of legend, or I'll be a disappointment. I tried to find Naragenth's lost library precisely because I wanted to achieve a measure of greatness. Only I didn't find it, and I may have freed a creature from death who's now waging war with us."

He smiled and shook his head. "Gods above me, Mother, this is so complicated. I haven't even told you about the compulsion, or the fact that we've been invaded by the Neddari. I'm scared of what might happen and I'm worried for Therain, who's going to bear the brunt of their initial assault; and I'm sick with guilt because *I'm* the one who released Asankaru. I was under the influence of a compulsion when I did it, but that doesn't matter. A lot of people have died because of it, and a lot more are going to die before it's all over. It's hard for me to say, 'It's not my fault.' I didn't *know* I was under a compulsion—it felt like I was doing what I did because I wanted to. Even now, with the compulsion over, it still feels like it was my idea, so it's hard for me to blame someone else. I just hope that one day I can accept that it wasn't my fault, because I don't know how I'll live with the guilt if I can't.

"I have to go. I couldn't sleep and I felt this sudden desire to talk to you. Maybe you came to me and put that idea in my mind. I hope so. I wanted to come here and tell you everything I've been thinking. I miss you, Mother. If you were here, I'm sure you'd know the right things to say to make me feel better. But you're not here, so I'll just have to say those things for you and hope I get it right."

He turned and started walking back down the passage. After a few steps he paused, but did not look back. "I wonder if you could have been a wizard? If Hollin had arrived a few years earlier, could he have saved you?"

He was glad he would never know the answer. He was not sure how he would bear it if the answer to both questions was yes.

35

The castle was quickly falling to the invaders. Neddari soldiers shattered windows and then hurled oil-soaked torches into the buildings. Drogasaars loped through the shadows, their scimitars killing anyone they saw. Fires sprouted throughout the castle and black smoke billowed up into the sky. Men were fighting everywhere. The sounds of screaming and ringing steel and the roar of growing flames were all about them.

Therain and his men were attacked again on the steps of the Thorn, where Randel died with a spear in his belly. Estram Kint fell from the steps, screaming, after his arm had been hacked off at the shoulder by an enormous Neddari wielding a double-bladed axe. Donael slashed at the axe-wielder just behind the knee and sent him sprawling across the steps, then drove the point of his sword down through the back of his neck. Therain himself took a glancing blow on his thigh that his mail only partially deflected. The swordsman lunged at him again, but Therain jumped up and slammed his boot down on the flat of the man's blade, trapping it long enough to cause the Neddari to lose his balance when he tried to draw back. In that moment Therain cut upward in a two-handed swing. The point of Baleringol caught the helmless Neddari just under the chin and split most of his face in two.

Elmen was stabbed through the thigh by a broad-shouldered Neddari with a livid scar that wound down the right side of his face and into his scraggly beard. Elmen screamed and tried to thrust at the scarred man, but the Neddari blocked the blade with a small square shield of thick oak. The scarred man pulled his weapon free of the captain's leg and was about to drive it into Elmen's face when Therain slid the point of Baleringol behind his breastplate and into his heart. The man turned to look at him, his eyes widening with surprise before his life left him. He tumbled down the steps, leaving a wet trail of blood behind him.

Elmen was lying on the top step, clutching his wounded leg. The blade had run it through completely, and even to Therain's untrained eye it was apparent the injury was severe. Dark blood pumped from both sides of the wound. "We have to stop the bleeding," said Therain, crouching down over him. He pulled out his knife, cut a long strip from his cloak and tied it around Elmen's thigh above the wound. He stuck the handle of the knife beneath the strip of cloth and twisted it around twice to tighten the tourniquet. Donael helped him lift Elmen to his feet. "We have to get inside," the big lieutenant said. He gestured with his head toward the open yard before the keep. Other Khedeshians were falling back in their direction, overwhelmed by the forward surge of Neddari and drogasaars who had entered the castle in large numbers.

Agdenor has fallen, Therain realized. He found it hard to draw a breath. *We've lost the siege.* I've *lost it. Barely two days old and already it's gone.* He wanted to put his head in his hands and weep.

But he did not. He meant to live to avenge what had been done here. *Agdenor will be mine once again, I swear it by all the gods of heaven.*

They carried Elmen into the Thorn and closed and barred the doors behind them. He knew he was condemning the men in the yard to death, but if he left the doors open the Neddari would be within the keep in moments. The doors were thick and solid, forged of steel that would take the Neddari some time to break down.

They lowered Elmen to the floor. "Are Vaiseth and Lorel in your chambers?" Therain asked.

Hearing his wife's and his daughter's names, Elmen nodded, his teeth clenched in pain. His face had gone white. Blood still leaked from his wounds. *He'll bleed to death if we can't stop it,* Therain thought. He twisted the knife stuck into the tourniquet another half turn. Elmen stiffened and grunted in pain. "Can you get him to the dungeons?" Therain said to Donael. "There's a secret door—"

"I know about the door, my lord," said Donael. "Not to interrupt, begging your pardon, but I know where we're going and why, and I think it's best you go get Vaiseth and Lorel."

"Your wife's not here, is she?" Therain asked Donael.

"No, my lord. I sent her to Merrenthal with my mother. They left days ago."

Therain helped hoist Elmen to his feet and left him with Donael as the fighting outside drew closer to the Thorn.

Therain found Vaiseth and Lorel in their rooms on the fifth floor of the Thorn. They huddled near the windows, watching the battle below with a group of servants and chamberwomen. A few candles burned atop a granite mantel, but otherwise the room was dark. They did not hear him enter or cross the carpeted floor.

"The door should have been locked," he said. They all jumped at the sound of his voice; some of them screamed. When Vaiseth saw him, she clutched her heart. Her black hair was bound into twin braids whose ends were tied with ribbons of red silk, her daughter's chestnut hair braided in the same fashion. Vaiseth clutched Lorel's shoulder and pulled her close. "My lord, why are you here? Where is my husband?"

"He's wounded but alive, and waiting for us below. All of you, follow me."

"How goes the battle, my lord?" asked an old serving woman with gray hair tied up in a bun atop her head. Strands of it drooped about her face like the branches of a weeping willow. Her three daughters and five granddaughters were with her, huddled close by the window. "Have you any word of my sons and my daughters' husbands?"

"I won't lie to you, Mistress Semeth. The battle goes poorly. And I can tell you nothing of your sons or daughters' husbands. Come, we have to leave. The Neddari will be in the Thorn very soon now."

"Them bloody savages in the keep itself?" said Mistress Semeth, her eyes wide with horror.

As he led them down a torchlit stair, one of Semeth's granddaughters, a girl no more than seven, asked him, "My lord, where are you taking us?" She held her mother's hand tightly as they made their way down.

"We must escape the castle." They saw no one else, but the sounds of fighting reached them from seemingly every direction, echoing up and down the stairwell. "We'll never reach the postern doors or the gate, and even if we could, they are more than likely guarded now by the Neddari."

"Then how will we get out?" asked the girl.

"There are other ways out of the castle," he said, trying to sound reassuring. "Secret ways that the Neddari will not be watching. Now be quiet for a time. Our voices will carry, and I do not want others to know we are here."

On the ground floor they followed a long corridor past the kitchens to a heavy steel door painted black and set in a deep recess in the wall. Beyond the door, a wide stair led down into darkness. Therain heard some of the girls behind him begin to cry and whisper that they were frightened. Their mothers shushed them and said the prince would protect them.

The stair ended in a dank brick corridor with locked cells spaced evenly throughout its length. A flickering light was visible at one end, where the corridor turned to the right; less than ten feet farther it ended abruptly at a blank stone wall.

The light was coming from a torch on the floor. Donael and Elmen were there. The captain was on the floor with his legs stretched out before him. He was leaning against the lieutenant, who in turn had his back against the wall.

"Daddy!" cried Lorel. She dashed forward and threw her arms around her father's neck. Vaiseth crouched down and hugged them both. Elmen put his arm around their shoulders—Therain could see at once how weak he was, and the growing pool of blood beneath his wounded leg.

Donael saw where he was looking. "The movement to get him down here started his bleeding again, my lord. I turned the knife more, but it won't stop."

We need Master Evernyes. He would know what to do. If they had the time—and a needle and thread—they could stitch the wound closed, but Therain knew that even with the wound sewn shut Elmen could still bleed to death. But they had nothing with which to make a poultice, not even wine to clean it with. Tending to the wound would have to wait until they crossed the river.

"We need to get moving," he said. "There's still a long way to go. Donael, help him to his feet."

Therain handed his torch to Mistress Semeth and went to the end of the short passage and felt along the right-hand corner. He'd been shown this passage only once, by Velarien, after he'd arrived in the castle. *And where is Velarien now? And Wilfros? And Master Evernyes? Dead like so many other good men?*

He fumbled along the wall, searching for the hidden latch. He felt panic begin to rise in his throat. What if he couldn't find it? He knew it was here, but there was always a chance that they would be—

Then his fingers found the narrow gap between the stones. He jammed them in deeper until he felt the latch, curled the tips of his fingers around it and squeezed. He heard the counterweights move and grind, and suddenly the wall in front of him swung inward on its hidden hinges. Some of the women gasped and one of the girls was going to scream, but her mother clamped her hand over her daughter's mouth.

"This leads down through the heart of Henly's Hill," said Therain. He picked up the torch from the floor stepped through the hidden door. He gestured for Mistress Semeth to lead the way. "Follow the stair to its end. I will close the door after everyone is through."

Semeth trembled with fear. "Wh-Where does this lead, m'lord?"

"At the bottom is a cavern, with a door to one side that leads to the Angle. The door is well hidden and can't be seen or opened from the outside."

"The Angle? But how will we cross the rivers?"

"There are boats hidden in the cavern. No more questions. Go!"

She jumped at his words and started down the stair. Donael heaved Elmen to his feet and helped him through. Vaiseth tried to help her husband as well but the stair was too narrow and she had to fall back and follow them with her daughter. When everyone had passed, Therain pulled the lever on the inside of the passage that closed the door. The thick stone moved on its tracks across the floor as the counterweights fell and the pulleys turned. It closed with a solid thud.

The stairway was cut from the rock and had no rail. The steps were slick with lichen. He almost slipped twice, and had to brace himself against the rough stone wall. Some of those ahead of him also slipped, and one of Mistress Semeth's daughters fell on her backside before her sister caught her to prevent her from sliding farther. The air in the passage was close and stale. *I am the first lord of Agdenor to use this escape,* he thought bitterly. For over three hundred years the castle had remained strong, and though it had been besieged before, had never fallen. *I will be a nice entry for the historians. The first lord in all its long history to lose the castle, in two days.*

Then he was at the bottom, passing through a ragged arch

into a large black space. The cavern was long and narrow, the ceiling no more than fifteen feet high at its peak. The center length of the cavern's ceiling and floor had more than a score of stone stumps where the natural columns had been cleared away. "There are boats here, at the far end," said Therain. Once a year they were inspected by the castellan and repairs made if necessary. A single man performed the work: he was sworn to secrecy under pain of death before he was led, blindfolded, down the secret stairway to the cavern. "They're hidden to the sides," he said. "We'll have to drag them out."

They found them easily enough. Six boats were hidden in the cave. They would need two to get them across, seven in each. He and Donael would take the oars of the boats; Elmen was in no condition to row. Because of the rains, the rivers were high and their currents swift. He would have preferred to have a single man on each oar—the boats were broad and shallow—but that was not possible.

Elmen's leg had begun to bleed steadily again on the descent to the cavern. Donael had torn a large strip from his cloak and tied it around his leg across the wound, but it was already soaked through with blood. He was feverish and trembling. "Be strong, my love," Vaiseth said. She stroked his face and kissed his forehead. Donael set him down with his head in his wife's lap so he and Therain could drag the boats to the entrance to the cavern. The prince hoisted the thick rope attached to the bow of the boat and dragged it along the floor. It was terribly heavy, and he was sweating when he reached the end of the cavern where the door was hidden.

The cavern narrowed to a section of wall about a dozen feet around. In the center of the wall, two wide doors were cut from the rock, thick iron handles sunken into the center of each. Donael and Therain took a handle and pushed. After a moment the doors began to grind open, spilling dust and a few pebbles on their heads. A cold wind gusted into the cavern. Mistress Semeth squeaked and tried to protect her torch from the wind. "Put the torches out and leave them," said Therain. "We don't want to be seen crossing the river."

The doors opened behind a ragged line of scrub pines and a few oak trees. Therain and Donael dragged the boats out of the cave, then Therain went back to close the doors, which vanished into the granite face of the cliff. He turned to study the terrain, which was dark, the stars and newly risen moon hidden behind a thick veil of clouds, but his eyes soon adjusted and he saw some light on the far sides of the rivers from campfires and torches.

"I smell smoke," said one of Mistress Semeth's granddaughters.

"Hush, child," her mother replied. She pulled her daughter close. "It's nothing to worry about."

She does not want to tell her that the castle is burning, Therain thought. *That her home has been put to the torch.* He could smell the smoke as well. He craned his neck and stared up the long face of the cliff. The castle wall was an impenetrable blackness at its summit, visible only in contrast with the dim red glow the fires cast upon the bellies of the low-hanging clouds. It was strangely quiet on the Angle. He could hear the wind and the close sound of the rivers, the constant rush of water, but no hint of battle reached his ears.

Elmen groaned and sagged against Donael. "My lord . . ." said the lieutenant.

"Yes, I know. I'm coming."

Vaiseth and Mistress Semeth supported Elmen so Donael could move one boat as Therain moved the other, and the two of them dragged the boats across the stony field toward the Samaro River. The captain groaned again and began to shiver uncontrollably. "We need blankets," said Mistress Semeth.

"We have none," said Therain. "Now be silent, everyone."

The lines of trees along the riverbank, mostly oaks and a few willows, leaned out across the water as if frozen in the motion of falling. The rains had swelled the rivers, which were nearly above their banks, the roots and lower trunks of many of the trees now underwater, the swift current flowing around them trapping all manner of debris against the bark.

Therain and Donael dragged the boats to a narrow gap between the trees where they could easily shove off. He assigned the lieutenant, Elmen, Vaiseth, Lorel, two of Mistress Semeth's daughters and one of her granddaughters to one boat; the rest would go with him. Therain helped get Elmen settled in the boat—the captain was feverish and barely conscious—and then the women. "Get him across as fast as you can," he whispered to Donael. "You're stronger than I am and probably a better rower. As soon as you get across, get him to the camp and find a physician. Don't wait for us if we fall behind."

"Yes, my lord." Donael pushed the boat into the swift current. He slipped smoothly over the boat's side, slid the oars into the oarlocks, then began to row with a strong, steady pace. Though he tried to row straight across, he was quickly carried downstream. Therain cursed silently, knowing he'd be a half mile beyond the camp before he reached the other side.

Quietly, Therain said, "Come on now, in you go." He helped each of the women step into the boat, which rocked back and forth in the current. When they were all in and seated, he gripped the side and pushed the grounded stern the rest of the way into the water. He waded in up to his thighs—the water was icy cold—before hoisting himself into the boat's shallow bottom. Shivering and with his teeth chattering, he locked the oars in place and began to row.

The boat was at once carried eastward with the current. He tried to angle it back into a more direct course across the river but had little success. His shoulders began to burn as he pulled the oars through the water. Distant voices reached them across the surface of the river. He could not see the faces of the women in the boat with him; they were nothing more than dark shapes huddled together against the darker background of the receding bank. One of the young girls was whimpering and had buried her face against her mother's side.

He could not see the other boat from his position. "Where are the others?" he whispered to Mistress Semeth.

"Nearly to the other side, my lord," she said quietly. "We should come aground quite close to them."

As they moved across the river, he had a better view of the castle. There was a pulsing red glow and columns of churning smoke coming from the top of Henly's Hill, as if an ancient volcano were stirring to life there. Several of the towers stood out as stark silhouettes against the glow. Therain clenched his jaw and looked away. How many of his people were dying there while he fled?

Several leafless branches appeared suddenly high overhead. He was almost to the bank, he realized. He glanced over his shoulder to get his bearings and saw he was no more than a dozen feet from a sharp upthrust of bare rock. The momentum of the boat and the current would carry them the rest of the way. He folded the oars and jumped over the side when they were about six feet away and was startled when his feet did not touch bottom and his head nearly went under. He kicked his feet and held tightly to the side, cursing. The bow of the boat smacked into the rock and slid across it with a harsh scraping noise, catching him between the boat and the rock: he reached out with his left hand, grasped a spur of stone and held on tight. His shoulders were wrenched when the current tried to carry the boat farther downstream. He kept his grip and tried to angle the boat in toward the bank.

"Mistress Semeth, get out and hold onto the rope until I can get there!" he urged her. She clamored out of the boat, coming dangerously close to falling into the river when she stepped too close to the side, and asked one of her daughters to throw her the rope. Therain let go of the side and scrambled up the rocky outcrop. He was soaked and freezing, and the wind cut through his wet clothes and set him shivering. He took the rope from Semeth, coiled it around his arm, and braced one foot against a twisted oak tree. "Quickly, help them out." She extended her hands and one by one helped her daughters and granddaughters to the bank.

Once they were out of the boat, Therain dragged it up onto the stony shore. When it was safely out of the water he threw down the rope and sagged to his knees, exhausted. But he could not rest. Not yet. They had to find the others and then make their way to the camp. He got to his feet and turned to face upriver. "Mistress Semeth, you said the other boat landed this way?"

"Yes, m'lord. The last I could see of them they was coming into shore by those trees." She pointed to a black smudge in the dark night.

"Then let's go find them. Follow me and stay close."

There were small woods and copses along the northern bank of the river, with bits of open land between them. Therain could no longer see the fires from Urthailes's camp ahead of him; there were too many trees in the way. He wondered if they were seen crossing and Khedeshian soldiers sent to intercept them. He kept a watchful eye out for any approach from upriver. It would do them no good to be killed by Khedeshians believing them to be Neddari before he could identify himself. And if disaster had truly struck and the camp was held by the enemy, he wanted to be ready for any attack that might come. *Not that I'd stand much of a chance, with six women to protect.*

Therain made his way into a stand of pine trees. It was so dark within the trees he had to find his way mostly by feel. He was startled when a bristly branch brushed along his cheek. "Stay close to one another and hold hands if you must. I don't want anyone getting lost in here."

He could hear the river ahead of him, the rush of the rain-swollen current. He was debating whether to call out to Donael when a scream shattered the night.

It came from the river. "Stay here!" he said to Mistress Semeth, and dashed ahead, his sword drawn, crashing through branches as his boots crunched across the needle-covered ground.

Then he was free of the pines and on a narrow rocky patch of ground that stretched ahead of him for a dozen yards before sloping down to the water. He heard a woman weeping behind a ragged ledge of dirt-crusted granite. On the other side of the ledge he found Donael.

The clouds had broken a little and faint glimmers of moonlight shone down upon the river. Donael was kneeling by the boat, which he had dragged completely out of the water. Elmen was on the ground, his head in Vaiseth's lap. She was weeping and stroking her husband's face. Lorel lay with her arms around her father, her face buried against his chest. She was sobbing hysterically. "Daddy, Daddy, Daddy . . ."

Therain lowered his sword. His limbs felt leaden. Behind him Mistress Semeth and the other women clamored over the ledge of granite. "Ah, the gods preserve us," he heard Semeth mutter.

"I'm sorry, my lord," said Donael. His voice was faint and dejected. "The captain is dead."

36

Baron Eljon Sheridel spluttered awake when icy water splashed into his face. "Wake up, now," he heard a gruff voice say. "You'll be gettin' visitors soon, and I was tol' to get you awake."

Eljon shook his head to clear the water from his eyes and immediately regretted it. He groaned as pain shot up his neck and into his skull. His arms were secured above his head: his shoulders burned and his wrists ached from the ropes that bound them. At least his feet were flat on the floor.

He opened his eyes. His vision took a moment to focus. He could see fires burning in the night and shadowy shapes moving through the darkness. He blinked several times to clear the water from his lashes, careful not to shake his head too much. As best he could tell, he was in the bailey of the castle, somewhere to the north of the gate. He did not know Agdenor well and his view was mostly blocked by two buildings that stood between him and the outer wall of the castle. *It doesn't matter. I am where I am, and where I will most likely die.*

A Neddari stepped in front of him. He seemed almost as broad as he was tall, with a fat stomach hanging over his thick leather belt. The man's nose had been broken more than once and was now a crooked jumble in the center of his wide face, like a road that had been shattered in a violent upheaval of earth. His head was shaved and either war paint or blood—or perhaps a sweaty mixture of both—was smeared down the left side of his face and across his neck.

The Neddari slapped Eljon across the face. His teeth clacked together and he groaned as hot liquid pain filled his head. He squeezed his eyes shut and tried not to throw up as he remembered what had happened. The Neddari had breached the walls and were overrunning the castle. It was clear the battle was lost, that Agdenor would soon fall. There was nothing to do but survive and hope for revenge. He'd been with Elbran and a dozen other soldiers, making their way toward one of the postern doors with a group of women servants who'd fled from their quarters near the Thorn. The women were hysterical, weeping and screaming in terror, huddled together in the center of the ring formed by the men, when a group of Neddari appeared from inside a building they were passing. He remembered hacking through the neck of one man and ramming the point of his sword through the eye of another, and then . . . nothing. *Someone must have hit me from behind.*

He prayed to Telros that Elbran and Collem had gotten safely away. *Please, send them to their mothers. Let them live to avenge whatever will be done to me here.* He had little hope that he would live to see the dawn. He was not a coward and did not fear to die in battle, but he did not want to be tortured. If they tortured him, he would try to take his own life, to cause them to make some misstep that would kill him before they were finished. *If only I could get a knife to my throat.*

He opened his eyes once more. He saw bodies littering the sward ahead of him but could not tell if his son and nephew were among the dead.

He was watching a Neddari drag away a Khedeshian corpse by his heels—boots, armor, and weapons had already been stripped from the body—when three of the Red Robes appeared before him, materializing out of the air itself, forming from what looked like a sudden swirl of dark smoke.

Fear chilled his blood and made his teeth chatter. He'd seen these beings help their grim master create the tornado that devastated the gate of the castle, and later use their own powers to destroy the temporary barrier that had been erected across the ruins of the gate tunnel. Their strange blue fire had demolished stone as easily as a hammer-fall shattered pottery. He had no idea what they were—demonic servants of Shayphim, for all he knew—but they terrified him. How could you fight such beings, when weapons passed through them as if they did not exist? They were nightmares made manifest, dark and terrible dreams that had somehow found a way to walk the earth.

And now they were here, staring at him with their over-large eyes as if he were a filthy, unclean rodent, somehow an affront to their very existence.

"You will tell us the true name of the summoner," said the Red Robe. It spoke with a strange inflection—Eljon did not think of it as a "he"—and stepped so close that he could have leaned forward and touched the Red Robe's forehead with his own. He had to fight hard not to recoil from it. "And where the Horn of Summoning may be found."

"Shayphim take you," said Eljon. He steeled himself for a blow from the bull-necked Neddari, who had stepped to one side when the Red Robes appeared, but no blow fell. "I'll tell you nothing."

"You will tell us everything. What you will not give, we will take."

It reached out and touched the tip of its staff to his forehead. Eljon tried to pull away, but the Neddari grabbed his head and held it firmly in place.

He felt only the slightest pressure from the staff on his head. Then the Red Robe began to speak in a strange tongue, its eyes staring into the depths of his own.

Eljon felt a coldness slide into his skull from the staff. The Red Robe continued to speak. Memories long-forgotten appeared in his thoughts. *The gods save me, please, please, what is happening to me?* He realized that the Red Robe was reading his mind, shuffling through his memories, searching for the knowledge it felt was hidden there. *I have to fight it!* But the more he tried to not think of Lord Gerin, the more he did think of him. His name, his face, his castle, the fact that he was heir to the throne of the kingdom, what Lord Therain had told him about Gerin's wizardry, how he had used a horn of magic to try to call King Naragenth from the grave . . . it all flashed through his mind before he could help himself. He tried to think of something else, anything else. He pictured the faces of his wife and son, tried to think of the bawdy songs he and Tevethur would sing together when drunk, imagined himself walking through his castle on crisp autumn evenings; he tried to see everything in as much detail as he could to occupy every moment of his thoughts—

The staff was withdrawn from his head. "I said you would tell us everything we need to know." The red robe turned away and joined his companions.

"Holy Ones, what should I do with him?" asked the Neddari.

The Red Robe did not even bother to turn. "Whatever you will." They vanished together, disappearing in the same manner in which they had arrived.

My prince, forgive me, I did not mean to betray you. Eljon wanted to weep. What would come of his betrayal now that the Red Robes knew Gerin's name? *I'm sorry, I'm sorry.* But what could he have done? How could he defend himself against a creature that could take his very thoughts from him?

He felt the Neddari's huge hand grip his hair and raise his head. He began a prayer to Telros to take his soul and to watch over his wife and son and keep them safe. He had not finished it before the long knife cut deeply into his throat.

May the gods preserve us all, thought Gerin as he read Therain's account of the twister created by the Storm King.

I fear he will send another whirlwind at us soon, his brother wrote. *We cannot withstand another attack like the first. Please, I implore you, come at once with all haste. I hope you have some means of countering this with your wizardry. I need your men, but I need your magic more.*

Therain's letter stunned him, in no small part because he had no clear idea of how he—or any of the wizards—could counter the Storm King's devastating powers.

The letter had arrived the night before, but Master Aslon had not noticed the pigeon in his tower's loft until earlier this evening. It was at least two days since the siege began.

He was about to rise from his chair when he was enveloped once more in a gray mist with the sounds of battle clanging all around him. The sounds were very close this time; he heard an arrow streak by, followed by a clash of steel right next to him, though there was nothing there for him to see. The grayness was uniform and unbroken.

The pull to the west was strong. *I have to understand this.* Each time he'd had his visions, he'd fought to get out of it, to force it to end. But this time he willed himself into a state of calm and tried to penetrate the gray haze and see what, if anything, lay beyond it. *There is something here, something I need to know.*

He ignored the sounds of battle and tried to follow the western pull he sensed so strongly. He could not tell if he were moving, but the western pull became much stronger at one point, so he halted his effort. The battle drifted away now, receding until the disparate sounds melded together into a low, steady rush of faint noise. Ahead of him the grayness was unchanged, but the pull was undeniably stronger.

The grayness abruptly darkened, as if whatever mysterious light fell upon it had died. Then he saw a landscape appear ahead of him. It was dim and indistinct, little more than a jumble of blurred shapes, as if he were looking at it in a predawn gloom; but it soon brightened and grew clear.

There were wooded hills, with long narrow lakes filling the valleys between the slopes like ragged fingers of water. Beyond the hills he could see an immense cliff more than two thousand feet high. It stretched from horizon to horizon in a long curve that receded from him at its edges, diminishing until it was lost in the hazy blue distance. His gaze was drawn to the top of the cliff, where its face had shattered into fractured sheets of rock that leaned against one another like chipped and broken teeth. In some places the fractures between the stone had widened to create dark fissures penetrating deep into the rock; in other areas, parts of the cliff had fallen away to create bowl-shaped valleys. To the right he could see the bright slender spray of a waterfall as it cascaded downward in a sparkling haze of vapor. Though it was too small for him to see, he knew that Dian's Stair was somewhere to the left of the great falls.

This is the Sundering, he thought. *That is where I have to go.*

"Come to this place, Summoner." The voice of the Storm King thundered from the sky. The very earth shook with the power of its sound, but Gerin could not see anyone, not even the haunted apparition that had spoken to him in a dream. *"You must finish the summoning you began. Here is where it will be done. I command it."* The pull to the west, toward the Sundering, intensified until it was like a white-hot nail in his skull—

The vision ended. He was back in his study, slumped in his chair. *Was I sitting here with my eyes wide open?* The pain in his head was quickly fading, but the pull to the west remained, a gentle but steady tug that he could not ignore.

Gerin rubbed his eyes. The vision had been stronger than ever before, and the sight of the Sundering something completely new.

What will I do once I get there? What does Asankaru want from me? And what can I do to defeat him? The last question was the only one that mattered. He prayed that Reshel returned soon with news.

He read Therain's message once more. *Come at once with all haste.* He decided he could not wait for his father to arrive. He would march his army to Agdenor.

Pendrel Yevan Hirgrolei sat in the Lord's chair in the Great Hall of the Thorn, savoring his victory. The unbelievers had fallen before the might of the God Who Has Returned. The dead were being burned, the survivors being herded together to become clan-slaves. Their necks would be banded with slave-collars and they would be forced to swear oaths to the Slain God and renounce their allegiance to Khedesh and its false gods. Those who refused to swear would be killed. Those who swore and were shown to be false would be killed. *How can they deny the God Who Has Returned after what they have seen? Where were the gods of Khedesh? Why did they not appear to save their people? That is what we will ask them, and they will have no answer because there is no answer. Their gods are false. We have shown that with our victory. And we will show it again and again as we conquer more and more of the unbelievers.* There would be a vast Neddari nation with himself as its earthly king—greater than even the greatest clan Chieftain—answerable only to the Slain God.

Odan Iktoret Perochan had indeed seen the wisdom of Hirgrolei's idea that the clan Chieftain help the *kamichi* make decisions pertaining to warriors and battle. "I will give you all the honor you are due," Hirgrolei had said. "Serve me well, and the God Who Has Returned will know of your efforts on His behalf. You will be richly rewarded." He was presently out with his commanders, securing the castle and searching the surrounding lands for Khedeshian stragglers or spies.

The Slain God appeared in the center of the room. Hirgrolei was still not used to seeing the God and His servants appear out of the air, and he wondered if he would ever grow used to it.

He stood at once and stepped away from the chair, then knelt, as did Guso. "Great One, I am yours to command."

The Slain God looked around the room, examining the columns and arches, the windows high on one wall and the mosaic in the floor. He scowled. "There is no art here, no beauty in these forms," he said. Hirgrolei was not certain if the God were speaking to him. It sounded as if He might be speaking His thoughts aloud for Hirgrolei's benefit. He decided to remain silent and listen. "They have cut and polished this stone until its true form has been lost. Stone should not be so abused. It can be carved and shaped in ways that do not destroy the beauty of what it was. This is little more than butchery."

Hirgrolei was not sure he understood what the Slain God was saying, but did not want to admit his ignorance. "The Khedeshian armies beyond the rivers have mostly withdrawn, Great One. They flee before Your might and splendor."

The God Who Has Returned made a dismissive gesture. "They mean nothing to me. Do with this stone travesty what you will. I took it only to find the summoner and horn, but they are not here."

Hirgrolei felt stricken. "But Great One, we have only begun our conquests! We must vanquish all the unbelievers and make them deny their false gods. There is so much more we need to do . . ."

He faltered when he saw the Slain God's face. He had turned his head slightly, as if listening, though Hirgrolei himself could hear nothing that would interest the God.

Guso came to Hirgrolei's side and whispered, "Is something wrong, Master?"

"I don't know. Be silent."

An expression of rapture, of *triumph,* filled the Slain God's face. He spoke in the God-tongue that He and His war priests used among themselves; seconds later the priests appeared in the room, all of them together, in a line before Asankaru. They bowed their heads to Him, and He spoke to them in His holy speech. Though Hirgrolei could not understand a word of it, he could sense the excitement in the Slain God's voice. *He has discovered something, just now, here with me in this room.* His hands shook with the honor that had been bestowed upon him.

The God Who Has Returned faced him. "I require your fastest riders. I have sensed the presence of the horn to the north. It is not far—a few days if your men are swift."

"You shall have them, Great One. They will set out at once. Do you know where the horn is? Do the Khedeshians have it in another castle?"

"I can sense that it is moving. It is a strong source. Much stronger than the summoner himself."

"But would not such an important thing be well guarded?"

"I will send my war priests to guide your men to it. They can sense it through me. They will take it, but your men are needed to bring it here."

Hirgrolei bowed his head. "It shall be done, Great One."

37

Reshel and the wizards had ridden hard toward Ailethon. It seemed to her that she'd been gone forever. *So much could have happened by now,* she thought. Had Gerin managed to put an end to the killing? What was the Neddari army doing? Was Therain all right? She could not wait to speak to her brother.

Another day, two at most, and I'll be home. She had loved her time at Hethnost despite the urgent reason for her being there, but now she wanted to be home, to help Gerin and Therain and then, perhaps, marry Balandrick and have children. She did not know what her father would think of that, but the more she pondered it, the more determined she was to marry him. Let Gerin and Claressa and Therain be married for political gain. They did not seem to mind the prospect of an arranged marriage. She wanted to choose her own path. Her wizardry set her apart. Balandrick, at least, accepted that. He was kind and caring—qualities she found surprising in a soldier—and adored her, though she still didn't understand why. But he did, which was all that mattered.

She frowned as she stared into the fire as more pressing problems pushed aside her thoughts of Balandrick. *Asankaru.* More specifically, the problem of how to force him back into the realm of the dead and seal the doorway that was the cause of the deaths that had plagued southern

Osseria. She, Kirin, Hollin, and the Warden of the Archives had spent every night of their journey poring through the books and scrolls that Aelos Eridon had decided they should bring, searching for a means of Compulsion other than the one devised by the Baryashin Order. So far they had failed. Oh, they'd found one or two that might work to trap a spirit, but Warden Eridon doubted they could hold one as powerful as Asankaru for long, even with the strength of an amber wizard behind them. "And there is no mechanism in any of these spells to force him out of this world," he'd grumbled one night after they talked themselves hoarse. "The Baryashins devised their own spell for a reason: apparently there has never been anything else like it."

But still they kept looking. They all felt that they were running out of time, that if they did not find an answer soon they would never find one.

Now they were almost to Ailethon, with no solution for Gerin. What would they do? What *could* they do? Her brother would never sacrifice an innocent life, even if the wizards could condone it.

She stretched her back and yawned, then returned to the book she'd been reading. After reading the same sentence for the third time and still not having any notion of what she'd read, she decided it was time to get some sleep. She could barely keep her eyes open. She turned to say good-night to Hollin—

—and saw seven beings appear from nowhere, forming a circle around their fire. It was so incomprehensible that at first she could not make sense of it. But her confusion lasted the barest of moments. She knew they were in terrible danger. She jumped to her feet. "Intruders! Intruders in the camp!"

She knew at once what they were. The Red Robes that Therain had described, the servants of Asankaru. *How did they find us?* she wondered as she opened herself to magic.

Four arrows struck the Red Robes, shot from the soldiers of the Sunrise Guard, but they passed harmlessly through the immaterial bodies. Reshel heard the guards at the edge of the camp shout, but then everything was lost when she sent a stream of white-hot magic from her hand at the closest Red Robe. Mortal weapons might not have any effect on them, but they might not be immune to the effects of magic.

Her lance of fire struck the Red Robe and pushed it backward, causing its form to ripple a little before the magic passed cleanly through. It looked up at her with a feral grin on its face even as her magic pierced its body. *What is it made of?* she wondered. How could it assume a physical form that she could see but her magic could not harm? She did not understand it.

A soldier rushed forward with his sword raised high, ready to bring it down upon an intruder's head with enough force to split a man's skull down to his throat. But before he could swing his weapon, the Red Robe jabbed its staff at him. Blue fire rippled down its length and shot from the end, striking the man in the chest and spreading around him like a cloak of light before vanishing a second later. It took Reshel a moment to realize the soldier had been frozen solid, his body turned into a single block of bluish ice that tumbled to the ground. Two more suffered the fate of the first as they tried to attack the invaders. One of them fell against an outcropping of stone with such force that his frozen body cracked in two just above his waist. No blood spilled from the broken halves, just flakes of ice and a sludgy, blue-white liquid that might have once been his blood.

One of the Red Robes aimed its staff at Kirin. The wizard created a Warding just before the freezing power of the Red Robe shot from the dark twisted wood of its staff, but even that was almost not enough. Reshel was at once fascinated and horrified to see a ten-foot-tall disk of ice appear in the air where the magic of the Red Robe collided with Kirin's defenses. *It's frozen the Warding!* she thought in disbelief. The vertical disk of ice—hovering in the air with no visible means of support—thickened and widened as the Red Robe pressed its attack. The edge of the disk kept shattering as it grew, throwing off slivers of ice and snow that sprinkled the

ground. She could see the strain on Kirin's face as he poured
more power into the Warding. She desperately wanted to
help him, but there was a Red Robe advancing on her and
she was using all her power and concentration to build a
Warding of her own.

Another soldier of the Sunrise Guard got close enough to
hack down through the neck of the Red Robe attacking
Kirin. The blade passed harmlessly through the creature's
body, but there was a sudden flash of blinding light when the
steel of the weapon intersected the Red Robe's staff. The
soldier was hurled backward through the air and landed on
one of the cookfires. Reshel could not tell if he was unconscious or dead. His comrades dragged him off the logs and
smacked out the flames that had sprung up in his hair and the
worn edge of his leather jerkin. His sword had fallen to the
ground, its blade twisted and blackened.

The Red Robe staggered. The blue fire on its staff had
gone out. The frozen Warding exploded outward as the power
Kirin had been pouring into it suddenly met no resistance.

Just as Kirin's Warding exploded, Warden Eridon waved
his hand at the campfire around which they'd been sitting.
The fire blazed thirty feet into the air, roaring like some
crazed beast. As Reshel stepped backward, her heel caught
in a tree root. She pinwheeled her arms but landed hard on
her backside and jammed one of her wrists against another
section of the root. Barely feeling the pain, she jumped back
up to her feet just as the campfire fell back to its normal
height. It then dwindled to little more than coal-red embers,
its fuel consumed by the Warden's spell.

She heard more shouts from behind her and glanced over
her shoulder. The men of the Sunrise Guard were turning
away from the wizards to meet a new threat—Neddari horsemen charging down on them. She saw three men cut down,
two with their heads completely severed, before she turned
back to see what the Red Robes were doing. *The soldiers
will have to deal with the Neddari. We can't let the Red
Robes take the horn.*

Out of the corner of her eye she saw a Wizard leap upon one of the horses. The Red Robes were startled by the sudden fire and their attack had faltered, but now they turned to the wizards once more. She realized that it was Warden Eridon who was galloping away on the horse. The sight stunned her. She would not have thought him a coward to flee for his life when there was so very much at stake.

Then she saw that the box containing the horn and the spellbook were gone. The Warden had created the huge fire as a diversion so he could take the box and flee. He had wasted no time in taking the prize the Red Robes sought away from them. Shame welled hotly in her.

But there was no time for remorse or reflection. The Sunrise Guards had managed to regroup and were now holding their own. The Neddari, sensing that their surprise attack had failed to grant them a swift, easy victory, faltered in their advance, unsure how to coordinate their numbers against foes who had suddenly organized themselves into small, well-armed groups rapidly firing arrows at them.

Reshel took all of this in with a single glance, then turned and sprinted for her own horse. "Wizards! Scatter! Draw them away!" she shouted as she undid the picket and leaped onto Dari's back. The animal was terrified of the raging battle— her gray mare was no war horse—and she spoke a quick spell to calm it before charging off into the night after the Warden.

She thought Warden Eridon had ridden off to the northeast, away from the road. She had not gone far through the clusters of wind-bent oaks that crowned the steep, tree-covered ridge like mangy clumps of hair when she caught sight of him. He was ahead of her—she had chosen the right direction after all—on the far side of the slope, away from their camp. He was working his way down the ridge in a narrow steep-sided gully. She could just barely make out his head as it bobbed up and down above the gully's rough lip.

She spurred Dari ahead at a breakneck pace. She could hear the sounds of battle in the distance behind her but did not dare turn to look. By the time she reached the top of the gully the Warden was nearly to the bottom, but she did not call out to him for fear of the Red Robes hearing her.

The gully made for a treacherous descent. Its floor was narrow and piled with fallen rocks and branches; leaves had blanketed the floor in the autumn and decayed during the winter, leaving a slick residue that made Dari's footing unsure. She wanted to push the horse to go faster, to will her to catch up to Eridon, who had just reached the foot of the ridge, but she could not for fear of endangering both herself and the horse. She feared, though, that if she did not catch him soon she would lose him again in the dense, dark woods that filled the shallow valley below.

Then a bit of luck. The Warden turned to look back up the slope, searching for signs of pursuit, when he saw her coming down. At first she wondered if he could see her clearly enough to make out who she was—she did not want him to begin hurling death spells at her, thinking her one of the Neddari. But he did not attack her. He paused at the bottom, moving his horse to a more concealed place behind a moss-covered boulder.

When she reached the bottom, Warden Eridon appeared beside her. "Why are you here?" he asked in a harsh whisper. "What's happened to the others?"

"I told them to scatter to confuse the Red Robes. I was hoping they wouldn't realize who'd taken the horn."

"I don't think it matters what they saw. They have some means of sensing where it is. I can think of no other explanation for how they found us. We cannot tarry here. I've placed a spell upon the box I hope will keep it hidden from them, but who can say if it will work? The powers of these beings are strange to me."

Her breath caught in her throat when three of the Red Robes appeared around them. Eridon cursed and spurred his horse forward. One of the Red Robes pointed its staff at him and released its deadly blue energy. Even with his defenses in place, the impact was still strong enough to nearly knock the Warden from his horse. The animal staggered and fell. One of its legs snapped beneath its weight. Warden Eridon tossed the box containing the horn to Reshel as he tumbled from his saddle. "Run, girl!"

She caught the box without thinking. She was already moving before she had a sure grip on it. She held it tightly to her stomach with her left hand. Dari leaped over a fallen tree; there was a small depression on the other side that she had not seen, a bowl-shaped hollow ringed with trees. Dari neighed in fright, then sat back on her haunches with her front legs extended to keep from falling in an out-of-control tumble down the side of the hollow. The weight of the horse ripped through the brush and brambles that covered the slope. Reshel held the box as if it contained her soul.

When they reached the bottom, Reshel urged Dari on and ran her down the length of the hollow. The side at the far end was lower and had a shallower slope; four or five long strides and they would be up and out. She did not yet know how she would lose the Red Robes, but she knew she had to. Too much was at stake.

They reached the end. She kicked her heels into Dari's sides and lowered her head so the box was folded into her body, as protected as she could make it.

They were nearly to the top when the Red Robes appeared in front of her. A cry of despair escaped her lips. Their staffs were pointed right at her. She flung up her hand and invoked a simple shield—she was not yet experienced enough to create a Warding so quickly. She charged forward anyway; there was nothing else she could do.

Crackling blue fire filled her vision. She screamed as the power of the Red Robes cut through her shield and slammed into Dari. She felt the horse freeze beneath her. Dari's flesh was suddenly as immobile as granite, colder than the coldest ice. Reshel threw herself from the saddle before the power froze her as well. She flung her arms out to break her fall but lost her hold on the box.

She'd thrown herself from Dari with too much force. A tree loomed before her, and she curled up to protect herself from the impact. Her shoulder slammed into the trunk, hard; her head snapped forward and cracked against a branch, opening a deep gash in her scalp. She tumbled to the ground and landed on her side on a thick tree root. The impact drove the air from her lungs. Gasping for air, she rolled down the slope. Just before she reached the bottom, her head struck a blunt outcropping of stone and everything went black.

"She's alive." Gentle fingers probed the wound on her scalp, then lifted her head to examine the growing lump on her skull. Reshel groaned and licked her lips.

"How bad is she hurt?" It sounded like one of the soldiers of the Sunrise Guard—Tammel Kean? Was that his name?—but she wasn't sure.

She heard Kirin invoke a spell of Sight. She felt its power move through her, searching out the extent of her injuries. "She has no serious wounds. Leave me to tend to her. You see to Warden Eridon."

"Kirin . . ." she murmured.

"Don't try to speak yet. Let me tend to your injuries first. Keep your eyes closed. You took a nasty crack on the head."

"The horn . . . Where . . ."

"Gone." There was anger in his voice. "The Red Robes have it. I suppose in their ephemeral state they can't actually carry the thing themselves, which is why they brought the Neddari. As soon as they had it, they disappeared. Hollin and some of the soldiers are pursuing them, but I don't hold much hope that they'll recover it."

She managed to open her eyes. Her vision was blurred. Kirin's pale face was a murky shape floating in the darkness, like the moon behind a veil of clouds. "The Warden—"

"Enough. I told you not to speak. Your questions will wait." He spoke once more in Osirin. She felt the healing spells in her body, bright spots of warmth around her ribs and upon her head that glided over and then into her flesh. Her eyes fluttered closed and she slipped once more into dreamless sleep.

38

"My lord," said a male servant who had appeared in the doorway of the Sunlight Hall, "your brother has arrived."

Gerin and five of his vassals were in his study, examining maps one last time before they marched forth with their army. Mid-morning had come and gone. He'd hoped to set out by noon, but he would be lucky now if the van took to the road before the mid-afternoon bells sounded.

"Prince Therain is here?" asked Nuven Kelais, the Earl of Carmethos. Gerin despised the earl, a hot-tempered braggart who was rumored to have slain three mistresses who displeased him in some trivial way. But he had brought the largest contingent of men, so his demands for a high seat on the war council could not easily be refused. His small dark eyes were set close together; his upturned nose gave Gerin the impression of looking at a boar's snout. "In person?"

"Where is he now?" Gerin said.

"Right here," said Therain, entering the room. A large hulking soldier came in behind him. "I thought it best that you hear what I have to tell you right away."

Gerin was shocked by his brother's appearance. He was even thinner and more worn than the last time he'd seen him. The stockiness that had always been a part of his physical presence was all but gone.

"You looked exhausted, my lord," said Baron Patren Yescariel.

"I've ridden without stop for two days," he said. "One of our horses died on the way. We had to get fresh mounts in Paxtan."

Nuven opened his mouth to ask a question; Gerin cut him off with a sharp wave of his hand. "Tell us why you're here. I fear the worst."

"As well you should." Therain sat in an empty chair. He leaned his head back and stared at the ceiling, taking several deep breaths before looking at them once more. "Agdenor has fallen. The castle is in the hands of the Neddari and their thrice-damned Storm King."

"Outrageous!" said Nuven, slapping his hand against the table. "How could it have fallen so quickly?"

Gerin glared at Nuven. He did not like the earl's accusatory tone. *He'd best watch his tongue. That soldier with Therain looks like he'd break the jaw of anyone who speaks disparagingly of my brother, no matter what their station or rank.* "Therain, tell us what happened. *Without* further interruptions."

"The Storm King has convinced the Neddari that he's a god returned from their past. The Neddari think they're on some kind of holy war to convert unbelievers to the worship of Asankaru. He's playing them for fools. I don't think he cares at all about his status as a 'god.' Before the siege began they demanded that we hand you over to him. They didn't know your name; they wanted the 'god-summoner.' That is Asankaru's true purpose, though the Neddari don't understand that. He's using them because he needs their warriors to help him find you and the horn."

"Please, my lord, tell us of the fall of your castle," said Patren.

Therain turned to his brother. "Did you receive my message about the twister?"

"Yes."

"Then I'll tell you what happened after that. No use recounting what you already know."

He spared them no details. Some of the lords asked questions as he spoke, but after a while they just let him talk. They learned that the soldier with him was Donael Rundgar, the last surviving member of Therain's personal guard. Rundgar scowled across the room, his gaze lingering in a dangerous way on the pug nose of Earl Kelais. It looked to Gerin like Rundgar would gladly take off the head of anyone in the room, himself included, who so much as looked at Therain askance. *He's done well at Agdenor—in some ways at least—if he's inspiring this kind of loyalty in his men.*

Therain recounted that after they'd learned that Captain Hiremar was dead, they left his body by the river and made their way to Urthailes's camp. Urthailes himself had led the attack across the river when the Neddari stormed the castle, and had not returned by the time Therain and the others arrived.

Therain had ordered the army to fall back to Cregael-Thelakor and sent messengers to Lord Stehlwen's army to do the same. "I sent men to retrieve Elmen's body, then Donael and I took horses and left. That was two days ago."

Patren said to Gerin, "My lord, can your powers counter those of the Storm King? I don't see how we can defeat Asankaru even if we emptied the Naege itself and sent every man of arms-bearing age against him. What can men do against the might of a cyclone?"

"I know of no spell that can stand against a twister, but as I'm still very much an apprentice, I can't say that such a spell does not exist. Until the Lady Reshel returns from Hethnost—with Hollin, I hope—I'm afraid I have no idea if magic can help us."

"Have you had word from your sister?" asked Nuven.

"No. Nothing from her so far."

"What are we to do then?" asked Patren. "We were hours from marching our army to the defense of Agdenor. Do we now march to take it back from the Neddari even in the face of the Storm King's power?"

"We should wait for the king," said Nuven. "The forces

we've gathered here, even if we combine them with what remains of Lord Therain's men at Cregael-Thelakor, are not enough to retake a castle as fortified as Agdenor with a large army protecting it."

"I think we should remain until the Lady Reshel returns or sends word," said Patren.

Gerin folded his hands, considering his options. "We'll wait for my father before marching. And pray that Reshel returns before then. I'll command Lord Stehlwen to remain at Cregael-Thelakor and gather any survivors to him."

"We need to send scouts back to Agdenor," said his brother. "The Neddari may not remain there long, since you aren't there. They may march again soon and leave just a token force to hold the castle."

"I want you to go to Cregael-Thelakor and assume command," Gerin said to Therain. "I'll leave the scouts to your discretion. If the Neddari begin to move, I want to know at once."

Gerin then sent word to his field captains to cancel their preparations for the march. They were not going anywhere just yet.

39

W hen Ailethon at last came into view, Reshel nearly wept. Even surrounded by thousands upon thousands of soldiers, their many-colored tents and banners forming neat rows that extended from Ailethon's walls down Ireon's Hill and into the rolling lands beyond like some mystical woods that had sprung magically from the earth, it still seemed to be calling her home. She felt she would be safe once she got there, that within its old, strong walls the horrible things that had happened to her would be reduced to little more than bad dreams.

But they're not bad dreams, she thought wearily as they neared Padesh. *They're real, they happened, and they can't be undone.*

When she'd awoken after the attack by the Red Robes, dawn was just arriving, like a red omen growing to the east. Kirin was sitting close to her. A bright fire blazed nearby, but there was no warmth or cheer in it. She could tell from Kirin's expression that her foggy memory of the events of the previous night were not the product of a fever-dream: they had been attacked by the Neddari and the Red Robes, and the horn was lost.

She had propped herself up on her elbows. She felt terribly weak, and her head spun the moment she lifted it from the ground. She closed her eyes and tried to steady herself. The dizziness passed and she opened her eyes once more.

Kirin stared into the fire. "How are you feeling?" he asked, only glancing her way before turning his gaze back to the flames.

"Weak, and my head hurts. Where is Hollin? And Warden Eridon?"

Kirin looked at her, and this time did not turn away. Even before he spoke, she knew what he was going to say.

"Warden Eridon is dead." His voice was flat, hollow. She could see the pain of the loss in his eyes. "They froze him with their power. I tried to thaw him, but he . . . he cracked . . ." He clenched his hands into fists. "When I gave him to the Releasing Fire, he disintegrated in seconds."

She sat up and touched his arm. "Kirin, where's Hollin? I think I remember you saying he'd gone after the horn." She held her grief for Warden Eridon in check for the moment. She needed to know exactly what was going on, the full extent of this disaster.

"Yes, he pursued them. He hasn't yet returned, and in my heart I fear the worst."

He gave Reshel some bread to eat while he checked on the wounded Sunrise Guards. Six of them had been killed and nine others wounded. Most of the wounds were not serious— cuts or burns that Kirin could easily heal—but one man had lost his arm below the elbow and another had had most of his left ear taken off by an arrow. Both of them were still unconscious, lying near another fire while other soldiers finished the graves for the fallen.

When Kirin returned to the fire, she asked, "How long will we wait for Hollin? I don't think we should linger here. He knows where we're headed. If he retrieves it and finds us gone, he'll follow on the road."

Kirin nodded. "And if he does not find it, the same is true. And if he is dead, then there is, again, no point in waiting."

"I didn't mean that."

"I know you didn't, but it's still a possibility. We'll go as soon as they're done with the burial. The wounded men can ride with others if need be."

Hollin and the soldiers arrived back at the camp just as the last clumps of dirt were being shoveled onto the graves. Reshel's heart leaped when she saw him, hoping that he had somehow managed to wrest the horn from the Red Robes. But the look on his face when he halted at their fire said otherwise.

"They've escaped," he announced flatly as he swung down from his horse. He was angrier than Reshel had ever seen him.

"Is anyone injured?" asked Kirin, surveying the men who were with him.

"No. We're fine. We never got close to them. We were following them in the dark. The path the Neddari made was easy to see—they certainly weren't trying to move in secret. I made a Farseeing and found them a few miles ahead, so I gave all of our horses a little nudge of speed to help us close the gap. We'd gone maybe a mile or so farther when a fog rose up out of the ground, all at once, though there weren't any marshes or ponds nearby that could have caused it. It had to be the Red Robes. It grew so thick I couldn't see the man next to me, and when I called out to the soldiers, all I heard was my own voice echoing back at me from every direction. I created another Farseeing, but my power was blocked from going beyond the mist. We tried to continue on but got lost. It was as if there was something in the mist designed to confuse the senses." He paused and clenched his jaw, the anger and frustration he felt at being thwarted by the Red Robes rising in him once more. "The mist cleared only a little while ago. The men and I were scattered across a plain between two lines of hills. I gathered everyone, then tried a Farseeing again so we could take up the chase. I couldn't find them anywhere."

That was yesterday morning. Now, finally, she was nearly home.

* * *

They were met by Gerin's vassal soldiers several miles from the castle itself. A young lieutenant who scowled when he demanded that they halt so he could ask them questions— Reshel thought he scowled in an ill-fated attempt to look older or more authoritative, or perhaps both—was caught completely by surprise when she snapped at him, "I am the Lady Reshel Atreyano, sister of your lord, and if you do not let my companions and me pass *this very instant,* you will regret it for the rest of your life, which you will find is not as long as you might have believed."

The young lieutenant stumbled back, stammering, his scowl all but gone. "My lady, forgive me, I had no idea . . . we are to stop all travelers and make sure—"

"Yes, that is all well and good, but I must get to my brother as quickly as possible. You were given instructions regarding my return, were you not?"

"Y-Yes, my lady. I was told that you would be arriving from the west. And that you were to give me a password, since I regret to inform Her Ladyship that neither myself nor any of my men know you by sight."

She leaned down toward him and gestured for him to move closer. When he did, she whispered in his ear, "Varsae Estrikavis."

When they at last reached the castle, she scarcely recognized it as her home. The baileys and keep were jammed with soldiers, servants, attendants, horses, mules, weapons, forges, tents, wagons, carts, barrels, crates, and many other things. From a distance the camp seemed well-ordered and quiet; up close it was a different story altogether. Men practiced with their weapons, played dice on planks of wood, sharpened swords and spears, polished their armor, and drank. Other soldiers brought women into their tents after flashing a bit of gold or silver. *Whores on Ireon's Hill!* she thought in wonder.

She would see Gerin soon. *Without the horn of Tireon, without a way of defeating the Storm King, without Warden Eridon, without . . . anything.* She sighed and slumped in her saddle. So much had gone wrong. So very, very much. *And there is no way I can see of setting it right.*

Reshel and the wizards were waiting for Gerin in the Sunlight Hall, along with Matren. "It's good to have you back!" Gerin swept her into his arms and spun her around. "I hope you have good news for me. A lot's happened while you were gone."

"We have news," she said. "I don't know that I can call any of it good."

Gerin's face fell. "I can't say that what I have to tell you will be any better. Did you hear anything on your way here? Did the soldiers tell you what happened?"

"No. We spoke to no one but the men guarding the road, and then just enough for them to allow us to pass. We did not tarry to talk."

His face grew even more somber. "Reshel, Agdenor has fallen."

She stiffened and put her hand to her chest. "Fallen? How? Therain . . . ?"

"Therain is alive. He left here yesterday to take command of the remains of his army at Cregael-Thelakor." He told her and the wizards of the Storm King's attack. "The Neddari army is still encamped around the castle. Father has sent word that he's on his way here. Unless the Neddari move and force my hand, I plan to wait until he arrives and join our forces together before trying to drive them out."

"The Neddari are incidental to all of this," said Hollin.

"An army tens of thousands strong that has invaded Khedesh and captured one of our strongholds is *not* incidental!" fumed Matren. "They've killed hundreds of our people and sent hundreds more fleeing their homes in terror. They're only a few days from this very castle. There is nothing incidental about any of that!"

Hollin held up his hands. "Forgive me, Matren. I spoke poorly. I did not mean to belittle the suffering of your people or the very real threat this army poses to your kingdom. I do understand the enormity of the situation. But that army is nothing more than a tool that Asankaru is using to get to his true goal."

"Then you've discovered what he plans? This summoning he wants me to complete?" asked Gerin.

"Perhaps. We can speak of little with any certainty. But we do think we've learned who he truly is." Hollin told them what they had discovered of Asankaru's history as the last leader of the vanished race of Eletheros, his desire to truly live in the flesh again, and of the spell of compulsion that was the only means they had found of sending him back to the world of the dead.

"That is a dreadful thing you speak of," said Matren after Hollin had described the compulsion. "Who would create something that feeds on the death of an innocent?" He shook his head in disgust, his mouth drawn down in a deep frown.

"Evil wizards created it, wizards who were hunted down and destroyed long ago," said Hollin. "But their evil remains. There is no other way we have found to do what needs to be done. Asankaru *must* be forced out of this world, or the imbalance will eventually destroy us all. The Neddari are not incidental, but the true stakes are so much higher. Many others besides Khedeshians will suffer and die if the Storm King is not stopped."

"So you're saying I'll have to perform this compulsion in order to defeat Asankaru?" The thought of having to make a human sacrifice made Gerin sick to his stomach. *How can they possibly expect me to do such a thing?* He realized that his failure to do so could very well mean the death of everyone in Osseria, but the possible deaths of so many seemed somehow remote, unreal; faceless people he did not and never would know. But to have to kill someone himself to perform a *spell*? That was altogether different, a more personal and ghastly kind of death. How would they choose a sacrifice, if that is what it came to? Would they ask for a volunteer, an innocent willing to pay the ultimate price to save so many more innocents? Who would ever agree to it?

"Gerin, are you all right?" asked Reshel.

He shook his head once. "Give me a moment, please. What you just said is too horrifying for words."

"There is more for us to tell," said Hollin. "You need to hear us out."

Gerin breathed deeply and opened his eyes. "Go on."

"We were coming here with the horn and the spellbook of the Baryashins," said Reshel. "We were attacked on the road by the Neddari and the Red Robes. Warden Eridon was killed and the horn was taken."

Gerin was speechless. *First Agdenor falls, now this.* He was beset by disasters at every turn. "So we now have *no* way to combat the Storm King?"

"We have the compulsion," said Kirin, raising his head and speaking for the first time. "That is all. With or without the horn, that is all we ever had. Any of us can teach it to you, but without the horn it is useless."

"But the horn is useless to Asankaru without Gerin to complete the summoning," said Hollin. "It appears we are at an impasse."

"Do you know that for sure?" asked Matren. "Do you know that the Storm King can do nothing with the horn? If it is useless to him, why did he take it?"

"As I said before, there is little we know for certain," said Hollin. "But by Gerin's own account, Asankaru has been searching for him specifically to complete the summoning."

"He can't use it without me," said Gerin. "I'm sure of it." He told them of the vision in which he saw the Sundering and heard the voice of Asankaru command him to come there to finish the summoning. "He needs the horn, but he also needs me."

"He has half of what he needs already," said Matren. "We must make sure he does not get the other."

"But that is exactly what we *cannot* do," said Hollin. "If we're to defeat Asankaru, our only hope is for Gerin to undo what he's done, and to do that, he'll need the horn."

Matren was about to protest, but Gerin cut him off. "The

only way you've said I can defeat him with the horn is to perform a human sacrifice. I won't do it. There has to be another way. You can't ask me to kill someone."

Hollin's expression grew stern, as if the bones beneath his pale skin had shifted and settled into a granite hardness. "We have looked for other ways but have found none. The power of death that is moving through Osseria has already killed many. More will die the longer the doorway between the worlds remains open." His voice was cold, harsh, glazed with anger; the voice of someone who would not be argued with. "If this spell is the only means to stop the deaths, then it is what you will do. The choice is not yours or mine to make."

Kirin spoke, his tone gentler and more forgiving. "Yes, it is a terrible spell, and what it asks is dreadful. But there is no other way. I'll study the problem more, but I don't hold much hope that we'll find another means to compel Asankaru. You must learn this spell and be prepared to use it."

Gerin's face grew hot. He clenched his jaws but said nothing. He felt an almost superstitious fear of performing the spell. He was the son of a king, a man who would one day be king himself. He had already condemned men to death. *But this is not the execution of the guilty. This is a sacrifice. The sacrifice of someone who* must *be an innocent if the spell is to work.* He felt that if he performed this spell, he would be damned.

Kirin and Hollin were led off by Matren, who had the unfortunate task of finding rooms for them somewhere in the already overcrowded keep. Reshel went to her own chambers to change her clothes and wash, then was to meet Gerin and teach him the Baryashin compulsion.

Gerin paced the halls of the keep for a while, his stomach fluttering with guilt and a bubbling sense of panic that threatened to boil over at any moment. He hated the thought of even learning the spell; he felt he would be tainted if he committed it to memory, stained forever by its dark knowledge.

The spell I used to call Naragenth was nothing like this, he told himself as he made his way to his study to meet Reshel. He cursed the *kamichi* for placing such a terrible burden on him, then sat down and prayed to Telros for strength and guidance. *Show me what I should do.* He prayed to the divine being who had appeared to him on the road to Hethnost, but that entity did not appear to him again, and no answers came to his mind or heart.

He wondered if Asankaru were the Adversary of which the divine being spoke. But then he remembered he was told the Adversary had existed before the beginning of the world and had the power to oppose a god. Asankaru, if the wizards were right, could not be the Adversary. He had once been a being of flesh and blood who died many ages ago. He was powerful, yes, but his power was not divine.

What could be worse than Asankaru? Worse than the possible destruction of Osseria? If we survive this, what will we face when the Adversary rises?

He stared out the narrow window at the darkening sky. *What will Father say when he learns of this?* For the first time in his life he was glad his mother was not alive. She would be appalled and horrified by what was happening, and the single remedy open to them.

He was still staring out the window when the darkness beyond the frosty glass reached forward like a black hand and enveloped him. The darkness changed, becoming the now-familiar gray mist. In a few moments the clashing sounds of battle and the horrid cries of the dying filled the void. He knew what was happening; once again he calmed himself and allowed the vision to play out before him. It was easier to do so than to consider the spell he would have to learn.

The sound of the battle swept past him, then once more the mist cleared and he saw the Sundering in a gauzy, early morning light. He felt himself drawn toward the summit of the cliff; he began to move toward the great scooped-out hollows, sliding through the air silently as if he were a feather borne upon the wind.

I know your name, Summoner, boomed the voice of the Storm King. *You are Gerin Atreyano. You are the one who has freed me from death, but only to a half-life. I will be whole once more. I have the calling horn. You must come to this place to finish what you have begun. I command it.*

The pull toward the summit of the cliff was overpowering; he could almost see an unbreakable tether drawing him to it.

Do not think to defy me. Come here, or your people will die.

He was back in his study, but the sense of a connection to the west remained. His head ached with a dull throb. He leaned his elbows on his desk and rubbed his temples. *I have to go. I have to face Asankaru.* And he would have to do it alone. He could not ask anyone else to go with him. The Storm King would not be defeated by force of arms; one could not kill something that was only partially alive to begin with.

But I can kill someone who is fully alive.

The thought came to him with sudden, startling clarity. Would it be possible for him to do as Asankaru asked and revive him bodily, then kill him? Could he kill the Storm King without having to perform the Baryashin compulsion? *There must be something wrong with this. I'm sure Hollin and the others could not have overlooked something so obvious.* But he still held out hope.

Reshel arrived. "What's wrong?" she asked. "You look as if your head's going to burst."

"I just had an idea." He explained his thought about killing Asankaru after he'd been restored to life.

"We didn't get a chance to explain everything to you. If Asankaru is completely revived, it may open the doorway between the worlds to such a degree that it *can't* be closed. If you kill him after that, even if it's within moments, it may not make a difference. It could already be too late."

"But you don't—"

Reshel held up her hand. "Let me finish. The Wardens are not sure of the process by which Asankaru would regain his life if the spell is completed. It's possible that if you were to complete the spell, Asankaru's current incarnation would somehow transform itself into flesh and blood. But they did not think that was likely. The Baryashin's spell called for their displaced spirits to take possession of another living body, preferably an infant or child, which would be more easily controlled by the hostile spirit. It may be that Asankaru will need a body to house his spirit when you perform the spell. *But he probably does not know this since he does not have the book of spells.* If his spirit discovered it did indeed require a living host, he would search for a body to possess. It might be a Neddari if there are any present. But it could also be you.

"Think about it. He knows you want him dead. He might deduce that you would attempt what you just told me—to kill him once he was fully alive. The best way for him to thwart that is to take possession of *your* body. He would be alive once more, out of danger from you, *and* control the powers of an amber wizard."

"I wouldn't be easy to possess. You said the Baryashins wanted to use children because they would be easier to control. I'm certainly not a child."

"And Asankaru, even now, is far stronger than any of the Baryashin Order ever was. His disembodied spirit can hurl storms at Agdenor. If anyone has the strength to overcome you in a battle of possession, it is Asankaru."

"But you don't know that. You and the Wardens are just making guesses. You've never used the Baryashin's spells or dealt with a spirit like the Storm King before. You don't know what will happen if he's resurrected."

"True. But it's conjecture based on studies of the horn and the spells of the Baryashins. They're not just guesses pulled from thin air."

"But the point is you don't *know*. He *could* be brought to life and then killed, and that might fix everything."

She looked at him long and hard. "Gerin, I know you don't want to have to perform the compulsion. I can sense how much you dread it. I understand that. But it's the best hope we have of defeating Asankaru and fixing the imbalance between worlds. The sacrifice—" She closed her eyes and drew a breath, as if she needed to summon strength even to speak of it. "The sacrifice of an innocent person is a *terrible* thing. I can only guess what the thought of it is doing to you. *But you must learn the compulsion.* If for no other reason than as a final, desperate resort if everything else fails. You have to be prepared, even for the worst. And this, I suppose, is the worst."

The western sky beyond the window was now fully dark and the first stars were starting to awaken in its velvety depths. Gerin could still feel the commanding call of the Storm King, tugging him toward the Sundering.

"He called me again, you know. A little while before you got here. He knows my name now. He must have learned it from someone they captured at Agdenor. He called me by name and commanded me to go to the Sundering. It was a very powerful vision. He said if I didn't, he would destroy Khedesh. There's some power he's using to try to force me to obey him—I can still feel it."

"That sounds terrible. Were you asleep? I thought he appeared only in dreams."

"No, I was awake. I was awake the last time as well. He knew I was the summoner but didn't know my name. Now he knows *who* I am as well as *what* I am. He can probably find me through my tie to the horn."

"And you can feel his power even now? Calling to you?"

"Yes. To the west. For some reason he wants me to go to the Sundering. I don't know why, or what might be there."

She held out her hands to form a circle in the air and invoked a spell. A luminous golden mist appeared within the confines of her hands.

"I can't sense it," she said. "His powers are so unlike ours that they're invisible to us, though I may not know the proper spell to use. Hollin or Kirin might know of something better suited." She started to get up from her chair.

"Sit down," he said. Startled, she did as he said. "It doesn't matter if you can sense it or not. It's there. I know it. Whether you can see it or not won't change anything."

"Yes, but there is—"

"Teach me," he said. "Teach me that damned compulsion of the Baryashins. You're right, I have to be prepared. And right now that's what's most important." *I will learn it,* he thought. *But I will not use it. Not unless all else fails.*

Long after midnight, Reshel made her way back to her rooms. She wanted to find Balandrick, to see his face and hear his voice and just be in his presence for a while. But she hadn't found him earlier and now it was far too late. He would either be sleeping or, if awake at this hour, involved in something too important to interrupt. *I'll see him tomorrow,* she thought. *I'll find him first thing, before we both get caught up in other duties.*

Even this late at night the keep was full of an almost living energy. Servants glided quietly through corridors like tangible ghosts, keeping to the walls with their eyes downcast, trying as much as possible to keep out of the way, while lieutenants and adjutants ran errands or carried messages to and from their commanders. Fires and lamps still burned in many rooms and in the yards of the castle. *Armies never fully sleep,* she thought as she glanced out a stairwell window at the soldiers keeping watch on the battlements. Hundreds of men were on the walls, awake and alert, with hundreds more keeping guard in the camps on the hill and beyond while their fellow soldiers slept.

She reached her rooms and fell on her bed. She was tired but did not think sleep would come just yet. The session with Gerin had been long. He now knew the Baryashin compulsion as well as any of them did.

Something nagged at her about her brother's behavior. Was it simply his insistence that the compulsion was not the only answer to their dilemma? He'd wanted so badly for there to be another way that he seemed to have already planned a strategy.

Asankaru had commanded him again in a vision this very night. Gerin himself had admitted that the command was powerful and hard for him to ignore. *Just how strong is it?* she wondered. He had been called to the Sundering. What was it he'd said to her just before she'd left?

It's time for me to act. Therain bore the Neddari assault while you gathered the knowledge I needed from the wizards. Now it's my turn. Force of arms can't beat him. We saw that at Agdenor. And even if it could, even if all of the wizards of Hethnost marched against him, it doesn't solve the larger problem of forcing him from this world. Everything we know points to me. I complete the Summoning and kill him, or I use the compulsion to send him back to the world of the dead. Either way, it all falls to me, and only me, to finish.

She'd been so tired at the time, she'd hardly heard what he'd said. *It falls to me, and only me, to finish.* What exactly had he been trying to say? Would he actually go to the Sundering without telling anyone? He'd given her an uncharacteristically warm embrace when she left his rooms, and there had been a strange look on his face—a look of determined resignation, perhaps. Of inevitability. *Damn me for being so tired! I should have noticed all this at the time.*

She roused herself from her bed. She might as well check on him now. She wouldn't sleep otherwise. *I hope I find him snoring like a baby,* she thought as she shuffled down the hallway.

The number of people in the corridors of the keep had thinned since she'd first returned to her rooms. A hushed stillness had fallen across the building. It seemed to her that the keep had become something quite different in the dead of the night from what it was during the day. Now it was a place of silence and secrets and darkness. *My tired mind is getting carried away. Next I'll be seeing ghosts.* Then she remembered that Asankaru was himself a kind of ghost, and she frowned as a shiver ran down her back.

She checked Gerin's study first to make sure he wasn't still there, but the door was locked and no one answered her knock. She created a Sensing, but there was no one within the room, asleep or awake.

There was a guard stationed at the head of the hallway to Gerin's rooms. "Has Prince Gerin come this way tonight?"

"Yes, my lady. The prince was by a little while ago, but left again soon after."

Her heart skipped. "Did he say where he was going?"

"No, my lady. He'd changed into warmer clothes and had his cloak with him. I thought he was going to talk to one of his captains."

She ran back down the stairs. How could he possibly do something so stupid? How could he think he could just walk out of Ailethon with an army—*his* army—camped in and around it? She didn't know if she should be angry or worried. She prayed that she was wrong, that he *was* going to see one of his captains, or survey his men, or whatever it was commanders did with their armies in the dead of night, but in her heart she felt certain he was going off to the Sundering.

Guards in the main hall had seen him leave the keep. Outside, she headed for the stables and found his horse gone. "The prince didn't tell us where 'e was goin'," said Elchael, an old man with only five or six yellowed teeth poking up from black gums. He smelled of sour sweat and horse manure. "After tellin' us to get 'is 'orse ready, 'e went off to get supplies from them soldiers there." He pointed to a group of men standing around a tall fire. Their banners were the hill and river of Castle Merlaimen; the men wore the distinctive blue and red helms over a cowl of chain mail. Reshel remembered seeing them with Baron Styros at her father's feasts.

A quick questioning of the men told her that Gerin had indeed taken two packs of provisions from them before returning to the stables. "He rode off not too long ago, less than an hour, I'm sure," said one of the men. He gave her a hard, appraising stare. "And who might you be, lass?"

Reshel tried to draw herself up straighter. "I am the Lady Reshel Atreyano, the sister of the crown prince."

The man's eyes widened and he bowed his head. "I beg your pardon, my lady!"

"Your apology is accepted. Do you know where the prince was going?"

"He didn't say, my lady, and I did not feel it my place to ask."

A check of the castle gates revealed that Gerin had left by the western postern door. He was gone.

40

He has less than an hour's head start, Reshel thought as she stood at the postern door, trying to determine what course of action to take. Should she rouse the guards to go after him? Wake the wizards? But what if she were wrong about his destination? What if he actually were going to visit one of the lords at the edge of his army's encampment? *In the dead of night, with enough provisions to last a fortnight? And no escort?* No, he was definitely going to the Sundering to confront Asankaru. That was the only reasonable explanation.

But what to do? If she called his own men to go after him, she risked not only humiliating him but creating the impression that he was fleeing out of cowardice or some other base reason. She knew that word would spread through the camp, and with each telling it would be worse for Gerin. *What will they think if he succeeds in getting away and awake to find their commander and prince has deserted them? Had Gerin even considered that?*

She decided it would be best if she could find him herself and convince him to return with her. No one else need know about his foolishness. But she had to go quickly. To the stables to have them prepare her horse, then back to the keep to change into riding clothes.

Within a quarter of an hour she was on her horse and

heading for the postern door. He would not have been able to avoid sentries until he was beyond the edge of the army. They would be able to tell her which road he followed, though she knew the general direction well enough: west, toward the Sundering, just as Asankaru had commanded.

As soon as Reshel left his study earlier that night, Gerin had written two brief letters: one to Matren, telling him what he was doing and why, who should be placed in command of the army until the king arrived, and several other commands; and one to his father. The letter to his father had been harder to write. He wanted very much to come back alive, but doubted that he would survive his confrontation with Asankaru.

He sealed the letters and them gave to an adjutant with strict orders that they not be delivered until noon that day.

He kept his pace slow while threading his way through the camp. He pulled his hood low over his face and only identified himself when challenged by sentries. When he was forced to reveal who he was, he explained in hushed tones that he was making a quiet survey of the men and did not want others to know he was there. "I didn't want fanfare or an honor guard," he told them, as if letting them in on a secret. "The men will act differently if they know their prince has come among them." Mercifully, no one asked him what he thought he would see or whom he would talk to at this hour of the night. He asked the sentries to keep his presence secret until morning, but doubted it would hold that long. Soldiers liked to talk.

He passed through Padesh and followed the Agdenor Road to the southwest. The road made a wide curve as it skirted the Halbern Hills on its way to Thorn Hill. When he reached the outlying edge of the army, he created an Unseeing and slipped off the road. He had not made one earlier because there were too many men around for it to do him much good, but he did not want to be observed actually leaving the confines of the camp. He moved quickly across an empty field once the Unseeing was in place, toward a hunting track that led into a dense wood on the road's southern side. *Wouldn't do me much good to have someone see me and think the crown prince was deserting them, or that I was a spy trying to return to the Neddari.* Though how his absence would be explained by Matren, even with the help of his letter, remained to be seen. He would probably be cursed as a coward by many of the men, but that could not be helped. In the end it would be worse—and his name held in far greater contempt, if anyone were left alive to remember it—if he did not act. There was simply no other choice.

His passage through the woods was slow. Even with his wizard's sight it was fiercely dark beneath the trees, and there was no moon in the sky to cast its pale light down through the tangle of bare limbs.

Leaving the woods, he found himself a few hundred yards to the east of the road. He had passed beyond the rim of his army's encampment—beyond the last of the sentries and watchmen—and decided it would be safe to travel on the road again.

He was nearing the south gate at Thorn Hill when he heard someone on the road behind him, riding at a full gallop.

A moment later the rider appeared, and he realized it was a woman. *Reshel!*

"What are you doing here?" he demanded when she reined her horse to a halt. She was wrapped in a deep blue hooded cloak clasped with a golden brooch shaped into the Hand of Venegreh. Her hands were covered by black leather gloves trimmed in rabbit fur. He recognized them as the gloves their father had given her on her last birthday.

"I might ask you the same thing."

"Did the wizards send you? Or was it Matren?" He assumed the soldier had delivered his letters early.

"Don't be a fool. No one sent me. I figured out what you were doing, and when I found you gone I decided to come after you myself. I could have told Matren or the wizards or sent half your bloody army to find you, but I thought it would be in your best interest to keep it quiet."

"What do you mean, you figured it out? How could you do that? Did you find my letters?"

"I have no idea what letters you're talking about. I thought about our talk and realized you might try something like this. I just wish I'd seen it sooner so I could have prevented you from leaving in the first place instead of chasing you across the countryside in the dead of night."

He was confused. "Do you have any idea what I'm trying to do?"

"Yes! You're going off on your own to try to kill Asankaru. You practically admitted it to me."

"If you know that, why are you trying to stop me? This is the only choice we have. I have to answer Asankaru's summons. I have to finish this. No one else can do it."

"Yes, but why do it alone? And why in secret? At least you had the forethought to prepare letters. I thought you'd just vanished in the middle of the night."

"Reshel, you and the other wizards are the ones who said I'm the only one who can finish this. Why *wouldn't* I go alone? Asankaru's not going to harm me. He needs me to get what he wants. But that wouldn't be true of anyone else who goes with me. Not only would they be in needless danger, but if he captured them, he could use them as hostages."

He could see her thinking about what he'd just said. "But still, why go in secret in the dead of night?"

"Because if I told everyone I was going to go, I'd have people like you telling me what a bad idea it was and insisting I take a small army with me. Do you think Matren or my vassals would agree to let me go off by myself? They'd risk my wrath and probably rouse the entire army to keep me in the castle, and then what would I do? Fight my way *out* of Ailethon?"

He could see her scowling beneath the hood of her cloak. *She knows I'm right and doesn't like it one bit.* "You make some good points, I'll give you that," she said. "It seems you thought this out more than I did."

"Good. I'm glad you see it my way. Now I have to go. Go

back to the castle and do whatever you can to make sure they don't send anyone after me."

"I said you made *some* good points. I didn't say all of them were good. I agree you have to do this, though I hate to admit it. And I agree that taking soldiers along would be useless. But I'm going with you. I can help protect you while you do . . . whatever you have to. I know the Baryashin spell. I studied their works while I was at Hethnost. There may be something I can help you with. The last time you worked the Baryashin spell you were left near death. You're going to need someone to guard you. Someone with enough power to protect you. Soldiers and steel won't be much good for that. But I will."

"Absolutely not. It's too dangerous."

"It's far too dangerous *not* to have me along, and you know it. I know you don't want to take me because I'm your sister, but if I was some other wizard, you'd take me without a second thought. I know you would, because it makes sense."

"Reshel, I will not—"

"We're wasting precious time, dear brother. I am going with you. It's not open to debate, so we might as well get going."

"You're right that it's not open to debate, but you're not going with me."

"And just what are you going to do about it? If you ride, I'll follow. If you try to use your magic to stop me, I'll fight you. Won't that be a pretty sight? Two wizards locked in battle near a sleeping army. You can beat me, but I'll make enough noise to rouse every one of your soldiers and the wizards as well. They'll come flying here. Do you still think you could slip away by yourself after that?"

She really would fight me, too. He could hear the resolve in her voice. And deep in his heart he knew it would help him to have her along, if only because he would feel better with her at his side.

He thought about his father's letter admonishing him to keep Reshel away from the fighting. *Telros save me, he'll flay me alive for this,* he thought. "You're not being fair, you know."

"No, I'm not. But life's not fair, either. Come on, let's get moving."

"Gone? What do you mean, gone?" Hollin said to Matren. Hollin had been summoned to Matren's study, a small room with a view of the inner courtyard of the keep. Balandrick was with him, his back turned to the room, staring out the tall narrow window.

"It is a simple enough word. They are gone. Not in the castle. Gerin left this for me, to be delivered at the sounding of the noon bells." Matren handed the wizard a sheet of paper with a few brief sentences scrawled upon it.

Hollin read it in disbelief. Gerin had gone off on his own to face the Storm King? "This says nothing of Reshel. You say she is missing, too?" Balandrick tensed at the mention of Reshel's name and turned around, looking both angry and afraid.

Matren nodded. "It appears she somehow deduced what he was planning to do. I have reports of her taking her horse and following him through the camp. No one is quite sure how they got past the perimeter of the encampment."

"It would be nothing for a wizard to slip past your guards." Hollin read the letter again and rubbed absently at his jaw. They'd been looking for Gerin for several hours. They knew he'd taken a horse and left the castle during the night, but no one seemed to know where he'd gone. They'd assumed he'd gone to see one of his commanders, but messengers sent to all of them had returned with word that Gerin was not with them and had not visited during the night.

"What are we to do?" asked Balandrick.

Hollin came to an immediate decision. "Kirin and I will go after them. We'll take the Sunrise Guards with us. Will you send word to have them prepare? We've already lost half a day at least. I want to leave as soon as possible."

"I'll see to it, and make certain you're well-provisioned."

"I'm going with you," said Balandrick. "I'm the captain of Gerin's personal guard. And Reshel and I have a special bond. I'm not going to remain here."

Hollin nodded. "All right. You may join us."

Reshel had brought no provisions for herself. She had expected to bring him back to Ailethon, not accompany him to the Sundering. Fortunately, the stores Gerin had taken from Lord Styros's men would be enough for them both.

They'd left the road behind early in the day, afraid of encountering outriders searching for them or messengers traveling between Ailethon and Cregael-Thelakor or one of the other manned strongholds. After leaving the road, they passed through the empty lands of Lores Darethil and entered the rugged, woody terrain that marked the edge of Trelheton. They stopped for the night among some ash and dogwoods that covered a gradual downward fold of the land toward a small lake. The still black water reflected the blazing stars above; it seemed to Gerin that a piece of the night had been torn from the sky and flung to the earth to settle into the round hollow among the hills. The ruins of a small walled manor that had once contained a tower of some unknown height sat upon a hillock near the edge of the lake. The broken remains of the tower jutted upward from the crown of the hill, its glassless windows gaping like empty eyes, its sides crawling with ivy.

They sat with their backs against two trees, facing each other. Wary of pursuers or other watchful eyes, they lit no fire.

"Do you have a weapon with you?" he asked quietly.

"No."

He unclasped his knife from his belt and handed it to her. "Take this."

She eyed it for a moment, then drew the dagger from its sheath and examined it. "Did Father give this to you?"

"Yes. Therain has one just like it."

"Then I'll be sure to take care of it." They were silent awhile, then Reshel said, "Are we going to climb Dian's Stair?"

"I don't know. It depends on where Asankaru is. That . . . pull, call, summons, whatever it is, drew me toward the top of the Sundering when I saw it in my vision. But if he's waiting at the bottom . . . "

Reshel took another bite of salted pork and chewed. "Are you scared?"

He scowled. *Why does she always ask absurd questions like this?*

"I'm afraid of dying, if that's what you're asking. Only fools and madmen aren't afraid to die. And maybe holy men, but some might argue that there's a bit of madness in them as well. I'm not afraid of what I have to do, or afraid of Asankaru, but I don't want to die. I want to marry someday and have children, and I want to watch them grow up. I want to know them and I want them to know me. But if my life is the price I have to pay to rid the world of Asankaru, I'll pay it. Not gladly, and not without regrets. But I'll do it because there's no other way."

Because this is my fault, and it's up to me to end it. He saw Nandis's dead face once more, cold and white, like an image of the barren moon. He tried to wish it away, but it would not leave his mind. *So many are dead because of me,* he thought. Even if he succeeded in driving Asankaru from the world and managed by some miracle to remain alive himself, was success alone enough to make amends for those who had died? What would the mothers and fathers, husbands and wives, brothers and sisters and children of all those who died have to say to him? He did not want to know. He did not think there was anything in this world that could ever truly heal the horror he had unleashed.

A deep sadness welled up within him, a sense that nothing could ever be made right again. "Is that what you wanted to hear? For me to admit that I'm afraid?"

She moved across the short patch of ground separating them and kissed his cheek. "That's not why I asked. But if you weren't afraid, I'd be more frightened than I already am. And you're afraid for all the right reasons." She patted his arm. "Good night." She went back to her spot beneath the tree and curled up in her cloak.

They continued through Trelheton, avoiding any roads or trails whenever they happened upon them. The land grew more rugged the farther west they traveled—the hills steep-sided and forested with leafless trees, the valleys between them narrow and filled with deep shadows and trickling streams, many glazed with a thin sheen of ice that glinted like mirrors in the sun. They passed the ruins of a Pasthi village, little more than foundation stones overgrown with weeds. They ventured by solitary keeps and towers built upon the higher hills, and one castle that looked abandoned. "That is Craigievel," Gerin told Reshel when they saw the old castle upon its motte. "Baeleg Teldremes is lord there. He's a vassal of Therain's. It's not deserted, but most of the men would have gone to the defense of Agdenor."

They'd been heading almost directly to the west after leaving the road. On the morning of the second day, Gerin bent their trail a little to the south. After the first vision of the Sundering, he'd studied maps of the area and learned that Dian, the maker of the great Stair, had also built a bridge across the Samaro above a narrow gorge, which was how he planned to cross the river to reach the base of the Stair.

"What if the bridge isn't there anymore?" Reshel asked when he told her about it. They were riding around the base of a grassy round-topped hill. "I didn't think there was any-one living in those lands, even when Dian built the Stair."

"There isn't anyone there, at least as far as I know," he said. "Dian made his Stair where he did because . . . well, because the Sundering was there. The Stair doesn't go any-where. There's nothing at its foot and nothing at its summit. He made it to be a marvel. I think one of the reasons he built it where he did was *because* there wasn't anything there. For people to see it they'd have to travel out of their way, to a place where the Stair itself was the only destination."

Reshel smiled. "I'll have to learn more about Dian when we get back to Ailethon."

"All the accounts I read said he was almost completely crazy," said Gerin. "Maybe that's why he was able to build the amazing things he did."

Their shadows had grown long behind them when Gerin again had a vision. It was the same as the others, with the gray void and the sounds of approaching battle, then a shift to a view of the Sundering and the disembodied voice of the Storm King commanding him to come.

As soon as the vision ended, Reshel said in a pained voice, "What in the name of the gods was that?"

Gerin halted his horse and steadied himself in his saddle; he had slipped to the side while in the vision and was in danger of toppling off. "Are you telling me you felt that?"

She was rubbing her temple with one hand. "I felt *something*. I have no idea what it was. Gods above us, my head hurts."

"I just had another vision from Asankaru."

She looked up, startled, then stretched her hand toward him and spoke in Osirin.

"The world has thinned again," she said. "And it seems it is *still* thinned, as if a layer of reality has been peeled away."

"Are you saying the power of the vision hasn't completely gone?"

"I'm not sure." She thought for a while, then performed another spell. "Our world is definitely not what it was. I'm not certain how to explain it. Here, you do it." She told him how to create the spell, which Hollin had taught her after they'd learned the worlds of the living and the dead were growing closer.

When Gerin invoked the spell, he could see that there was indeed *something else* inhabiting their plane of existence, an indefinable sheen of *otherness* atop everything he could see. "What is it? Do you have any idea?"

Her brows furrowed. "It might be the world of the dead,

being pulled closer to our own world. Maybe just the fact that you're nearing the horn is increasing its power. No one knows how all of this works. There's no way to tell what might happen as we get closer."

"Are you saying that just getting closer to the horn could cause a catastrophe?"

"I'm saying I don't know. But it's possible."

"Nothing you're saying is making me feel any better, Reshel."

"If it's any consolation, it's not making me feel any better, either. If it continues to worsen, we may not even *be* in this world when we reach Asankaru."

41

They reached the Samaro River early the next morning. The hilly country ended in an abrupt line a mile or so from the northern bank to form a flood plain of tall grasses and wind-bent trees. The river plain narrowed until the hills to their right loomed above them, sloping down toward the water in long narrow ridges. The Samaro itself was wide and deep, the current fast and muddy from a brief but strong rain that had fallen during the night.

The fourth day came and passed. The hills bent away from the river once more, leaving a swath of forested earth between the water's edge and the rise of the land to the north.

Dawn of the fifth day arrived, cold but bright. They spoke little; they were close now to the Sundering, and there was nothing more to say until they found the bridge or its ruins.

They'd only been traveling a short while when a ridge rose across their path. It was divided in two by a deep cleft, like a dam with its center cut away. The river flowed through the cleft with thunderous force. "That's the Neck of the Samaro," said Gerin. "I remember it from the maps." The water in the Neck itself was a mass of churning white foam that battered the rocky sides of the cleft. They could hear the roar of it from far away, a faint growl echoing among the hills.

They had to climb the ridge through which the Neck was

cut; there was no way around it. When they reached the peak of the ridge, they stopped to rest.

"It's even bigger than I imagined," Reshel muttered as they caught their first glimpse of the Sundering.

Gerin gazed at it in wonder. The vision had been impressive, but nothing like seeing it for real. He looked toward the high summit of the cliff, wondering if he would see some sign that Asankaru waited for him there, but saw nothing.

The Sundering itself had no foothills or skirts; it rose straight from the earth in a vertical precipice for several hundred feet before its face angled back as it climbed toward the summit high above. Deep fissures and long cracks scarred the vast expanse of rock like old wounds. Eagles circled the air, riding the currents that rose and fell along the wall.

The Falls of Samaro burst from the top of the Belsend Plateau between two jutting horns of stone. The great weight of the water fell into a long narrow lake at the foot of the Sundering. A cloud of spray hung above the lake where the water crashed into it, sparkling and flashing with misty light. The water flowed out from a deep rounded lip in the lake's eastern end and down a sloping channel into the bed of the river, where it continued on to the east.

The cliff receded from them in a great curve to the north and south like a tightly drawn bow. The ground at the base of the Sundering was sprinkled with copses and thin woods, though there were long sections where the trees yielded to scree or patches of bare earth.

"I can't believe someone actually built a *stairway* up that," said Reshel. She shielded her eyes with her hand and peered at the cliff. "Is that little line there the Stair?"

"Yes." Gerin had never seen the Stair in person, and in his vision he had seen the Sundering from a much different perspective, but he was certain that the threadlike line zigzagging up the cliff was Dian's great Stair. He could feel the pull of the Storm King's summons draw his gaze toward the top of the cliff where the stone face was scooped out in parts, forming ragged hollows like great bowls filled with mist and shadows. Asankaru was there somewhere; he could sense him calling even now.

"At least the bridge is still standing," said Reshel. West of the Neck, where the river's channel was still narrow but the current not as violent, they could see a narrow bridge across the water. It looked strangely out of place. There was no road leading to either end, and no towns or villages nearby whose people would use it for travel and trade.

They made their way down the ridge toward the shallow valley below. After that it did not take them long to reach the bridge. It was about thirty feet wide with thick curbs along the edges, interspersed with decorative stone pillars. There had once been carvings upon the pillars, but nearly all of them had been obliterated over time. Two of the pillars had been sheared off just above the level of the curb; the rest were cracked and pitted, with large pieces missing. But the bridge surface itself and its supporting arches were nevertheless solid and strong, though worn and crumbling in parts.

The Stair was clearly visible now. The treads were cut at right angles to the cliff face and seemed to follow natural contours as much as possible. There were landings at every point where the Stair reversed direction, and it appeared that it had been made with parapets along its outer edge. "Thank the gods for that," said Reshel when she saw the railing. "I wasn't sure I'd be able to climb without something on the edge to keep me from falling."

"You won't fall." But he, too, was glad there was a parapet. He craned his neck. *That's going to take us hours to climb.* He wondered what the wind would be like higher up.

Closer to the Sundering, they saw two rows of tall columns whose capitals had once been connected by arches. The columns flanked the remains of a road. The paving stones, though cracked and broken, were still visible, with grass and weeds growing up through what was left of their broken surfaces. There were no buildings or shelters of any kind that they could see. *Built only for visitors to the Stair,* he thought. *Like a marker or sign pointing the way. Maybe that's the point. No shelter, no place to tarry or linger. Either climb or leave. If you want to stay you'll have to find your own shelter. Dian certainly wasn't going to make it for you.*

From the base of the cliff the height of the Sundering was daunting. The summit seemed lost in the cloudy heights above them. "Are you sure we have to get to the top?" asked Reshel.

"As sure as I can be of anything that came in a vision from a long-dead spirit."

"I've followed you this far, I guess I shouldn't start to question things now." She got down from her horse. "The world is even thinner. I feel like everything here is close to becoming insubstantial, that with one step I could just slip right through to . . . somewhere else."

Gerin did not like the sound of that, but he could sense it as well. "Let's hope we don't get that feeling when we're halfway up the Stair."

The large rectangular landing at the base of the Stair had once been covered with colored tiles in an intricate mosaic, but now many of the tiles were gone. The empty squares were filled with dirt or gravel or other bits of debris that had blown across the landing or tumbled down from the cliff.

Carved into the rock face in bas-relief on either side of the landing were gigantic images of two men more than three hundred feet tall. To Gerin they looked frozen in the process of stepping out of the face of the cliff. They wore flowing robes over shirts of chain mail and strange helms upon their heads that might have been crowns, but were carved in such a way that Gerin could not be entirely sure. Their hands rested on the pommels of sheathed swords whose points rested on the ground. There were runic inscriptions upon the sheaths, but Gerin did not recognize the language. *Were these Dian's patrons, or the kings he served? Is one of them Dian himself?*

* * *

"The steps are wider than I thought," said Reshel.

They were seven or eight feet across at the base, though it seemed to Gerin that the width varied at different sections along the cliff. *We'll know soon enough.*

They crossed the landing and began to climb.

At first, it was not a hard climb. The parapet had crumbled away in some places, but more often than not it remained standing and was still strong, though neither of them felt the need to test it. They hugged the cliff as they climbed, keeping as far from the edge as they could. As they neared the head of the leftmost bas-relief statue, Gerin could see birds' nests in the crevices of the shoulder and neck and small fissures through the rock of the helm. The height was already dizzying, and they were not quite a third of the way to the top yet.

The muscles in Gerin's legs began to ache once they'd reached the second landing, and a while later a deep burn kindled in his legs. He could feel the muscles and tendons tightening. He stopped to massage them before they cramped. Reshel, too, was in pain—probably worse pain than he was, judging from the grimace on her face—and was thankful for the respite.

They climbed for hours, stopping at each landing to rest for a few minutes and drink a little to keep up their strength. The view from the Stair was incredible. They could see for miles and miles until the horizon faded where distant hazy clouds seemed to merge with the earth. The wind blew steadily but only gusted a few times with enough strength to frighten them. One gust was so bad that Reshel dropped to her knees and Gerin pressed himself so tightly against the cliff face that he was surprised he did not leave an impression of his body against the stone.

They could both sense that the thinning of the world was growing stronger the higher they climbed. Gerin commented on it at their fourth stop. "How much stronger can it get?" he asked. "What if the two worlds become equally present? Will we be able to pass from one to the other? What if the other world becomes stronger than our own?"

"I don't even want to think about that." She shivered. He did not think it was entirely from the cold.

Afternoon was waning when they finally reached the summit. In places the Stair had been forced to follow odd curves and angles in the cliff. Three times it had tunneled into the rock to bypass deep, sharp-edged fissures that opened in the face of the Sundering. The longest tunnel went on for at least a hundred yards before emerging at the ninth landing.

The Stair ended at a thick shelf of granite. The ruins of a domed building greeted them a short distance away. There was little left of the structure; the dome itself was completely gone except for a few jagged pieces rising from the circular wall. They took shelter inside the ruined building, sitting on the weathered remains of a stone bench.

"Where to now?" asked Reshel. "Asankaru isn't here."

"I didn't think he would be waiting at the top," he said. "He's somewhere south of here. I don't know why, or what exactly is there, but I can feel his power pulling me."

They rested for a while before leaving the structure. The edge of the Sundering was fractured and broken, with deep crevices yawning up from the ground. The soil was thin and dry, barely concealing the hard stone beneath it. They remained a good distance from the edge of the cliff, worried that the ground near the edge might suddenly shift and give way beneath them.

They soon saw a fog ahead of them. It glowed softly, as if a strong light were contained deep within it.

"That's not a natural mist," said Reshel. "There's magic behind it. It may be Asankaru's power, or it could be caused by the thinning. Can you feel it, how strong it's become? Or rather, how fragile our own world has grown?"

"I feel it. There was a fog when I blew the horn at Hethnost."

It was apparent now that the mist glowed of its own accord, imbued with some innate power. Once they entered it they could see thirty feet or so ahead, but as they continued it quickly grew thicker, until they could scarcely see where their next step would fall. Reshel threaded her hand through Gerin's arm. "Make sure you don't lead us off the cliff," she said.

"I'll try not to."

Then the fog vanished. Suddenly they were in clear air once more. Reshel created a spark of magefire to illuminate their view. They looked back and saw that the fog ended as abruptly as a wall, as if it were contained by a shield or Warding. *But whatever power is holding the fog back allowed us to pass,* he thought.

"I'm not certain we're in our world anymore," said Reshel.

They stood near the lip of a huge hollow, a deep bowl-shaped scoop in the cliff face a mile across and several hundred feet deep.

"So the Atalari have come again."

They both wheeled around, calling their magic. The voice had come from behind them and sounded very close.

The tall being standing there looked like a man, but Gerin realized almost at once that there were subtle differences that showed him to be other than human. Impossibly large eyes, an elongated and oddly shaped skull, limbs longer and more slender than any man's would have been. The light from Reshel's magefire cast an eerie, shifting illumination upon the being.

It looked directly at Gerin. "You are the summoner. The one who has called us from our unjust graves. I have been waiting for you."

42

Pendrel Yevan Hirgrolei was troubled. The Slain God had vanished from the castle. He had appeared before Hirgrolei in the Great Hall and said, "I go to complete the summoning. I will return when I am whole once more." Then he'd vanished before Hirgrolei could even open his mouth to voice a question. Was he to take the war to the unbelievers or wait for them to attack? Now he was left to guess what the Slain God wanted and risk the God's displeasure if his guess were wrong.

The Slain God's war priests had not returned from their journey to recover the horn; neither had any of the warriors Hirgrolei sent with them, handpicked by Odan Iktoret Perochan himself. He could only assume they had succeeded, otherwise why would the God have left them? Hirgrolei longed to have but a tenth part of the Slain God's powers. What a wonder it would be to know, in an instant, what had happened many miles away!

When he gained more of the Slain God's trust and confidence, after showing his worth by conquering the kingdoms of the unbelievers, he planned to ask the God if He would elevate him to the status of a war priest and grant him the powers they enjoyed. The war priests were dismissive of the Neddari—even him—and regarded everyone else with open contempt. But even so, Hirgrolei had learned something of their nature through carefully worded questions to both the priests themselves and the Slain God. Most often they did not answer, but they deigned to speak with him enough that he understood they were not born with their powers—the powers had been bestowed upon them by secret rituals performed to honor the Slain God, rituals that called upon hitherto unknown entities who created a unique bond between the war priests and the God Who Has Returned. If that were indeed the case, then it was reasonable that others could undergo the rituals once the summoning was complete and the Slain God had regained His lost essence.

Hirgrolei intended to be the first to be made a new war priest of the Slain God. He would be patient; if he made his request before he proved his importance, the Slain God would dismiss it out of hand, and rightly so—such powers could not be granted to the unworthy. Each of the war priests had in some fashion shown their value to the Slain God, which was why Hirgrolei showed them only courtesy and respect even when they displayed their contempt. They had accomplished something he had not.

But I will be one of them some day, he vowed to himself. *I will be both war priest and* tevi *of the Neddari. My power will be even greater than theirs; I will rise above them in the eyes of the Slain God, becoming His most valued servant.* His heart soared when he thought of it. An honor unlike anything a Neddari had received in the long and glorious history of their people. Far greater than becoming a *kamichi* or being named warlord.

But he had other matters to consider first. The Khedeshians had not yet moved against them. *They fear our might, and the might of our God.* But he also believed that they would not allow him to remain in this castle unmolested. His riders had spied Khedeshian scouts but were unable to capture or kill any of them. Three groups of his riders had vanished, killed or taken by their enemy.

He was in his sitting room, wrapped in his thoughts, when word came that the riders who had gone with the war priests had returned. He commanded that they be brought to him at once in the Great Hall.

"Tevi Hirgrolei," said Tordet Eglurezi Mydin, the captain of the riders. Mydin bowed his head and saluted his warlord with his right fist curled to his shoulder. "We have returned in triumph."

"Where is the horn?"

"With the war priests, Tevi Hirgrolei. The day after we took it from the unbelievers, they commanded that five of our riders follow them to the west. They did not tell us where. The rest were commanded to return here."

"When the God's servants told you to return, did they give you any other commands? Did they say what the warriors here are to do?"

"No, Tevi Hirgrolei. I've told you all that they said."

He dismissed Mydin and called for Guso.

"Yes, Master?" said his *nirgromu*. "What is your command?"

"Bring Perochan to me at once. I need his counsel."

"Yes, Master." Guso bowed and hurried from the room.

The Slain God has left matters for me to decide. Perhaps He is testing me to see what I will do without His guidance. To see if I am worthy. Perhaps the God was already considering him as a new war priest. He would not disappoint Him. It was time for boldness, for strength. He would plan with Perochan how best to proceed, but he'd already decided what course of action to take; he needed only to work out the details. He was going to take the war to the unbelievers.

Therain did not know whether to feel angry, confused, or both. He'd just received word from Matren that both Gerin and Reshel had secretly left Ailethon the previous night. Apparently they were on their way to confront the Storm King. *The two of them? Against a being that can summon twisters from thin air?* He shook his head. They were both mad.

So once more he was in charge. He could not command Ailethon from here, of course. Gerin had named Patren

Yescariel to take command of his vassals and their forces, though by law Therain had nominal control over all of the assembled troops. Gerin certainly had not made it easy by slipping off without word to anyone, leaving only a written record of his wishes, one that the bolder and impetuous lords were certain to challenge. He was glad he was here and not there. He did not think he would have the patience to listen to nobles whining over station and rank. *I'd end up throwing the whole lot of them in the dungeons, and wouldn't that just make a mess of things? Father wouldn't be too pleased with that.* But the king was not here; the king had not had to flee from his castle like a thief in the night and leave the corpse of his friend lying on the bank of a river. And his latest reports indicated that the king and his army were still four or five days away. He wondered what even three armies could do against the Storm King's power, other than to get crushed beneath it. And if the wizards were right that Asankaru would grow even stronger if he regained his flesh and truly lived once more, then the gods save them all.

Cregael-Thelakor was in fact two castles side by side on adjacent hills that flanked the Agdenor Road. The western and larger castle was Cregael, built upon the high flat-topped mound Laikari Reás, one of the few Pashti place-names remaining in Khedesh. It was the older of the two castles, an ancient fortress built in the first years after Khedesh had come to these lands. The original timber structure had long since been replaced by stone, and had been greatly expanded over the centuries, until it sprawled across the entire hilltop. Thelakor had been constructed much later on the Argáos, the easternmost hill of the Corlagos Heights, a short east-west line of rocky peaks that rose from the surrounding lowlands like a tree-capped wall of flint. A narrow valley ran between the two castles, and it was through this valley that the road passed. A curtain wall of ashlar thirty feet high named Sarod's High Fence joined the two castles, cutting across the heart of the valley like a dam. A massive fortified tower, the

Kynsleri, stood across the road in the center of the Fence, with heavy gates on both the northern and southern sides and an iron portcullis between them.

The castle was home to Earl Stenwek Hedresien, a proud old man and vassal to Agdenor. Therain had been duke for less than a week when Stenwek himself arrived to demand a reduction in the "ridiculous" amount of tax he had to pay. Therain flatly refused to grant his request. The earl had grumbled ever since.

But when Therain had arrived to assume control of the remains of his army, Earl Stenwek ceded command of the troops without complaint and gave him fine quarters near the earl's own in Eglimond, the keep of Cregael. Therain had heard whispers that the sight of Asankaru's whirlwind had completely unnerved the earl, who had since formed a grudging respect for the young duke who'd stood fast in the face of the Storm King's dreadful power.

The army was camped on the northern side of the Fence, where the valley widened before it spilled out into the lowlands of Hodremenien. The castles themselves were packed with as many men as they could hold; the walk of the Fence was never wanting for soldiers to man it.

Gerin, I pray you know what you're doing. The relief he felt that Reshel had gone with his brother surprised him, though it was tempered with concern for her safety. Still, he trusted Reshel's cooler thinking to make sure Gerin did not do something stupid.

Word arrived the next morning that the Neddari were massing their men on the northern side of the Samaro. The scouts had seen no signs of Asankaru or his Red Robes, but that meant little. "At the rate they were preparing, they'll be marching by midday," said the messenger.

Therain fervently hoped that Gerin and Reshel had the full attention of the Storm King and Red Robes and could keep them from joining the battle that would be fought here. *If we can keep magic out of this fight, we might just have a chance to win.*

43

Gerin prepared a death spell but did not release it. The being before them was alone and unarmed and had not yet made any threatening moves or gestures. He regarded them curiously, with a slight tilt of his head, his large silvery eyes reflecting the light of Reshel's magefire.

"I've come, Asankaru," said Gerin. "But if you think—"

The being threw back his head and laughed. The sound was strange—harsh and shrill, like the cawing of some wild bird. "You know nothing, Summoner. I am not Asankaru."

Gerin faltered. "How can you *not* be Asankaru?"

"Because I am his brother, Teluko. Fear not, I mean you no harm."

"How is it that you know our speech?" asked Reshel. "Your race died out thousands of years before Kelarin was fashioned."

"I speak your tongue because I drew knowledge of it from those you name the Neddari. The power to touch the minds of others is one shared by all of the People of Theros. It allowed us to know other races, to learn not only their languages but also their customs and the *ways* in which they thought. It was our greatest gift, said to have been given to Theros himself by one of the Great Spirits, yet it was another reason the Atalari despised and hated us. It was a power they did not have, nor could we teach it to them. Their beings were wholly different than our own; they could not learn our powers, nor we theirs. They were envious of us and feared us because we had abilities they did not. They were a petty, jealous race, always distrustful of outsiders, always ready to destroy those who threatened their self-righteous superiority."

"That's not true!" cried Reshel. "The Atalari feared you because you worshipped dark gods and sacrificed your enemies upon your altars."

"The People of Theros did not worship gods of darkness, nor did we sacrifice enemies. Those were lies told by the Atalari to justify their hatred of us. I do not ask that you accept my word. I will show you the truth of it soon enough."

"Why are you here?" asked Gerin. "In this world? How did you pass through the doorway I opened? Were you drawn here with Asankaru, like his Red Robes?"

"The bonds my brother and I share are deep in ways you would not understand, deeper than even his ties to his war priests. That is why I was drawn here from my restless sleep. When my brother returned to the world of the living, I too was brought back, though he did not know it at first. But surely you realize that we are not truly in your world any longer? That we are standing on the edge of two worlds, where one bleeds into the next?"

"Yes, we know," said Gerin.

"Where is your brother?" asked Reshel.

"Close. I have concealed your presence so that he does not yet know you are here. There is something I must show you first, so you will understand the madness that consumes him."

"What do you want us to see?" asked Gerin.

"I will say no more until you follow. Time is growing short." He walked past them toward the edge of the cliff. Gerin and Reshel exchanged a glance, then fell in behind him.

Teluko led them on a sloping path that ran like a ramp down the rim of the scooped-out section of the cliff. The curved inner face of the bowl-shaped depression contained dozens of cantilevered terraces at differing heights, like tongues protruding from the rock. Some of the terraces had broken away and fallen long ago, though the rough stumps of stone that marked where they had been were clearly visible.

Gerin stumbled to a halt as the world shifted around him. He seemed to be in two places at once. The rocky trail was still visible to him, though dim and transparent, as if he were seeing a reflection in a night-darkened window. At the same time, he could see a majestic road occupying the same space as the path, paved with patterned tiles that gleamed with their own inner radiance. He blinked, and suddenly there were hundreds of tall men on the path, soldiers with long spears and strange armor made of overlapping plates that shimmered with the multicolored light of rainbows. He could hear the sounds of battle—

And then it was gone. Reshel had stopped beside him. A dozen feet ahead, Teluko turned back to face them.

"My power is waxing," he said. "You can see it before you even now. Come. Soon you will understand."

The path led them to one of the terraces, an expanse more than fifty feet wide where it joined the cliff that narrowed like the prow of a ship as it thrust outward. Gerin did not see how it could have formed naturally, though there were no obvious signs that the stone had been cut or shaped—he saw no seams, no indications that anything was formed of smaller blocks of stone. If the terrace were indeed not a natural formation, its makers had somehow contrived to create it from what seemed a single unbroken slab of rock, as if it had been coaxed into *growing* from the face of the cliff.

Gerin noticed a high arched opening where the terrace joined the cliff wall. It looked as if once, long ago, it had opened to a tunnel or passage leading deep into the rock, though the roof of the arch had long ago collapsed and filled most of the opening with debris. A few scraggly weeds and shrubs grew where enough soil had gathered for them to take root, lonely things struggling to live among so much cold, lifeless stone.

"When you summoned us from death, you called more

than just these phantom forms that house our spirits—you called part of the past as well, when our people were exterminated by the blood lust of the Atalari."

"That's a lie!" said Reshel. "You invaded the lands of the Atalari, which they defended, as was their right. Your brother was driven back and defeated, and it was only later that your people died out. The Atalari did not destroy them."

"It is your history that is a lie." There was no anger or vehemence in his voice, only a deep, somber regret. "The past is alive in this place. That is why I have brought you here. I have the power to bring it forth from its fitful slumber so you can witness the crimes of your ancestors."

He closed his eyes, clenched his long-fingered hands into fists, and began what sounded to Gerin like an incantation, though in a language he did not know. *The dead language of the People of Theros.* He wondered how long it had been since it was spoken in Osseria before Asankaru's release.

A glowing mist once more formed around them, swirling through the air on currents the wizards could not feel. Once or twice Gerin thought he saw intricate designs form in the mist, only to have them vanish moments after taking shape. *There are patterns of power here,* he thought. *That's what's making the mist move in this still air. It's like a spell unlocking . . . what? What is he going to show us?*

The fog thickened until it seemed almost a solid thing. It completely obscured Teluko's form. Once more they could hear the sounds of battle all around them, the clang of metal and cries of men and women. It was loud and terribly real. Gerin found himself flinching at the sounds, ducking as arrows whisked by or turning suddenly when he heard the sharp ringing of swords behind him; he drew Glaros and slipped into a battle stance, prepared for whatever was about to happen.

"The past cannot harm you." Teluko's voice was faint, distant, as if it had become something less than real; it was the sound of a true ghost, a spirit speaking across the vast gulf that separated the living from the dead.

A sudden wind blew the fog away. Gerin drew a sharp breath, stunned by what he saw.

The terrace was wholly transformed. It was no longer an ancient, crumbling ruin. Its floor was smooth stone with delicate patterns traced through it like seams in marble, though these pulsed and throbbed, resembling the veins of a living thing driven by some unimaginably vast heart deeply buried in the earth. There was a garden in the center of the terrace, filled with strange bright flowers and small trees that formed a ring at the base of a round, symmetrical mound. A tree larger than the others grew at the peak of the mound, its trunk slender and smooth, with no knots or openings or cracks. Its bark was silver-gray, as if sheathed in pewter. All of the slender branches were clustered near the top of the tree and projected outward from the trunk at nearly right angles, drooping near the ends to form a flattened canopy like the cap of a mushroom.

The edge of the terrace was guarded by a high parapet of stone. The balusters twined upward in a strangely fluid shape, reminding Gerin again of something that had been grown rather than cut. Lamps of delicate crystal shone with a pale silver radiance. He could clearly see that the arched opening into the cliff face was in fact a gate, its doors thrown open to reveal a long tunnel sunken deep into the cliff. He saw columned galleries and side tunnels branching off the main passage, all lit by crystal lamps on tall stands or hanging from the high ceiling on slender chains. Some of the walls were paneled in wood; others were covered by bright wall hangings; and in some places he could see bare, unfinished stone.

People were everywhere. Or rather, Eletheros were everywhere. Men, women, and children, old and young. There were dozens on the terrace, and he could see hundreds more in the passage that delved into the cliff. They walked right past him and paid him no heed. One young woman walked through him from behind, emerging suddenly in front of him; apparently in this place he could not be seen, even though his body was still visible to himself. *They are ghosts,* he thought. *They can't see me because all of this happened thousands of years ago. They are only a memory of what was.*

He realized he was looking at a city, a place that could hold many thousands of people. The other terraces also had been made whole. Some were connected by ramplike paths cut into the side of the bowl-shaped hollow, similar to the one he and Reshel had descended; others, which were closer together, were joined by bridges that arched delicately through the air.

He heard Teluko speak again in the Eletheros tongue. Wind blew once more, bringing with it the shimmering mist, as thick and opaque as a wall.

It did not remain long. The wind paused only a moment, as if something huge and invisible were catching its breath, then blew once more.

Gerin heard Reshel groan at what they saw.

The entire city of the Eletheros was now a battlefield. The floor of the terrace was awash in blood. Bodies lay everywhere, many of them hacked to pieces. The tall warriors in shimmering rainbow armor he'd glimpsed earlier swarmed over the stone, the narrow triangular heads of their spears drenched in blood and gore. The garden was burning; the tree upon the mound was a torch, its branches already withered in the flames. The rainbow warriors were hacking the heads from old men and throwing them into the burning garden. Gerin watched helplessly as a woman's arm was chopped off at the shoulder. She screamed and clutched at the bleeding stump, but before she could even sink to her knees, the soldier whirled his spear into her waist from the side, cutting all the way to her spine.

These were Atalari warriors, Gerin realized. His ancestors at the height of their powers, when the nation under the Matriarch still ruled in the North. He could sense the power in each of the soldiers—a power similar to yet somehow different from that of a wizard. Their magic was certainly present, protecting them and killing their enemies. Their spears channeled power from them, yet they were not magical weapons in the way Gerin thought of it. These beings had no need to open themselves to their magic or create spells; their powers were completely at one with them, as natural to them as breathing or clenching a fist.

"Where are the defenders?" Reshel's shout had a distant, dreamy quality to it. *"Why isn't anyone fighting them?"*

"We were already dead," said Teluko. *"Slain in the last battle of my brother's doomed war. Once we had perished, nothing stood between the blood-crazed Atalari and Tanshe-Arat. Our wives and children were here, and men too old or infirm to go to war. This is the truth of your history."*

"We have to help them!"

"You cannot change what happened so long ago. The past is immutable. Watch, and understand."

There were fires on all of the terraces now, and more deeper in the cliff, infernos that raced through the tunnels and caverns, burning everything, consuming the air of those trapped deeper within the city. Gerin could see Atalari soldiers moving methodically through the galleries and halls visible through the gate in the cliffside. They killed anything that moved. One warrior on a gallery grabbed an infant from its mother and dashed it to the tunnel floor twenty feet below. The woman screamed and tried to claw at the soldier, who ran his spear through her chest.

The Atalari retreated from the tunnel. Some of the soldiers hurled fire from their hands—raw, unformed magic that set even naked stone ablaze. He saw three children run from the tunnel onto the terrace, only to be set afire by a soldier behind them who shot a lance of flame from his spear. They stumbled for a few more feet, screaming until their lungs withered within them. Other children had been impaled on spikes set into the terrace floors. Some screamed and others hung limp, all hope gone as their lives slowly drained out of them.

The Atalari soldiers were using their powers to tear the very stone apart, collapsing walkways and ripping the terraces from the side of the cliff. Gerin saw one of the terraces shudder and then break free with a thunderous roar, flinging dust and debris into the night. Dozens of people scrambled for something to hold onto. Others leaped off, screaming, too terrified to remain where they were, plunging to certain death.

A group of women were being raped near the parapet of Gerin's terrace. The women who had collapsed after multiple rapes or who resisted too much were hurled into the yawning darkness below. A few of the soldiers slit their throats before throwing them from the edge. Some of the women were limp when they fell, either dead or nearly so; others clutched at their opened throats in a vain attempt to stanch the spray of blood and vanished over the parapet with red hands on their necks, their eyes mad with terror, unable to scream because of their terrible wounds.

Two young children, a boy and girl perhaps five years old, ran down from the clifftop hand in hand, following the same path Gerin and Reshel had taken, fleeing more soldiers coming down from above. An Atalari stepped in front of them, but in their terror they did not see him. Gerin shouted to them and tried to use his weapon against the warrior, but in vain. He was the ghost here, a silent witness to this long-dead horror. There was nothing he could do but watch.

The boy turned and saw the soldier just as the warrior's spear rammed through his chest. Blood gushed from his wound and open mouth; he let go of the girl's hand as his arms spasmed; she turned and screamed when she saw what had happened. The soldier levered the spear upward, raised the boy into the air, and with great strength flung him forward. The boy flew from the spear and crashed against the cliff with bone-crushing force. His body left a bloody smear on the stone as it slid down to the terrace, where it lay in a heap.

The soldier, his spear and armor coated in blood, grinned down at the little girl. It was one of the most horrible things Gerin had ever seen. The unbridled hatred in it, the sheer malevolence, chilled his very soul. How could someone have so much hate for a child, even the child of an enemy?

"So, little one?" said the soldier. He spoke in Osirin. A very ancient form of it, with strange intonations and accents, but Gerin could understand him well enough. "Should I stab you through the heart or cut off your head?" He laughed and jabbed his spear at her.

The girl turned and ran to the edge of the terrace. She jumped onto the parapet and propelled herself out into the darkness. Her scream somehow stood out against the other screams and wails, an echo that Gerin did not think would ever leave his ears.

The wind blew one last time, bringing with it the swirling wall of mist. This time when it cleared, the terrace was as it had first been: the long-forgotten ruins of a murdered race.

44

Reshel collapsed to her hands and knees, weeping uncontrollably. She vomited on the stone, then retched dryly after her stomach had emptied itself. Gerin knelt and held her head, gently pulling her hair back from her face.

"That is the crime you have forgotten," said Teluko. His face was terrible to see, grim and sad and accusing all at once. "That is why my brother is maddened with thoughts of revenge. He knows what was done here, how our people—the mothers and wives and children we had left behind—were butchered until none were left. Though he perished at the last battle, as did I, his spirit returned to this place. It is the way of my people. At death our spirits return to our families to watch them and at times guide them, if the spirit is strong enough to make itself known. But we could do nothing, since our race was killed. Only watch as you now did, with impotent, helpless rage."

Reshel was still crying. "How could anyone be so cruel?"

"War is always cruel," said Teluko. "And we committed our own cruelties; I will not say that we were wholly innocent. But our race did not deserve to perish. My brother had hurt the Atalari badly at the final battle between our armies, when they thought there was little resistance left in us. Perhaps they thought we would surrender, or that their victory would come at little cost to themselves. But my brother rose from near death and was able to summon the most powerful storms he had ever created. We wounded them, but in the end even Asankaru's strength failed and we were overrun and destroyed.

"It crazed them. They hacked our bodies upon the battle-field and placed our heads on their spears as banners. They did not take prisoners that day; anyone they found alive was impaled upon a stake and left for the wolves. In their blood lust they came here, to our home, and made their way up the Gray Wall through the inner passages we ourselves had made that spiraled down within the rock and emptied out into the land below through many hidden gates. Though the gates were closed and barred, they forced their way through. They would not be stopped until the last of us were dead."

"I believe what you have shown us," said Gerin. It was a hard thing to admit, but he would not flinch from the truth, no matter how difficult it was to face. "What was done here was an unspeakable crime. But I cannot undo it. I have borne witness to it, as you wanted, and I will see that the truth is made known to those for whom it will have meaning. But that does not change the fact that your brother cannot be allowed to use the Horn of Tireon. He cannot live again."

Teluko's expression shifted once more; he grew resigned and weary, as if the cares and worries of many years had fallen upon him all at once. "I know the truth of what you say. When I was alive I had the power to see the future in visions that would come to me in dreams. I foresaw the disastrous end of my brother's war and told him of it, but he would not listen. It seems this power has not completely left me. I have had visions of what will happen if my brother uses the horn. I have seen the terrible damage that will be inflicted upon the people who now live in the world, the millions of pointless deaths."

"Then you can convince him he must not use it?" asked Reshel.

"Even if he believed me, he would not care. He might

even welcome it. He is consumed with hatred for what was done to us. It is his goal to destroy any being who is not of the People of Theros. If he is told his resurrection alone might accomplish this, so much the better."

"Then he would be alone in Osseria, with only you and his servants," said Reshel. "Even *he* might not survive it. Is that truly what he wants?"

"You still do not understand what Asankaru plans to do. It is not simply himself he hungers to revive. His desire is to bring *all* of our people back to life. When he has restored our people to life, he will wage a war of extermination against your race so that no one will remain who can harm us again. I know his thoughts, his plans. He has learned that the horn cannot make his phantom body real. He will have to possess the body of a living being to complete his resurrection. Once that is done, he will use the Neddari to resurrect all of the People of Theros; the spirits of our race will possess *their* bodies. He will be unstoppable. The Atalari, it seems, are nearing their own extinction. It is plain that you do not have the powers your ancestors had, and from what we have learned from the Neddari, there are no other races with strength to oppose my brother. He will destroy you utterly, and then the last of his enemies will be gone."

Gerin was shocked by the magnitude and audacity of Asankaru's plan. "Why are you telling us this?" he asked. "Do you defy your brother?"

"My brother and I were often at odds when we were alive. It does not surprise me that things have not changed, even in death. I have said that I have foreseen the future—a *possible* future—if my brother does indeed carry out his wish to be resurrected. It is terrible. I have tried to tell Asankaru that the time of our people has long passed, that our tragic and unjust end cannot be undone. But as always, he will not listen to what he does not want to hear."

"I don't know how you could have seen a future in which he was revived," said Gerin. "Only I can bring that about, and I will never help him."

"When the time comes," said Teluko, "you will not have a choice. My brother—"

Asankaru and his Red Robes appeared in a circle around them, striding confidently toward them with haughty, arrogant expressions. One moment the space was empty, the next they were there. Gerin instinctively raised his sword. He heard the sound of feet upon the path descending from the top of the cliff and saw Neddari warriors approaching the terrace. One of them carried the chest that contained the Horn of Tireon.

"Etuv'aqa m'neruq uvë'olovi na'qi nen Teluko?" said Asankaru. *"Vendre'lashë enurqa averil b'mortä uvë geth-rel'menduvos?"*

"I have betrayed nothing," said Teluko, using Kelarin. "I've sworn no oath to you. I have used my own powers to show the summoner the crime that happened here to our people, nothing more."

"Avro'sheret enduvö menkav'irada esen—"

"Speak to me in their tongue," said Teluko with a dismissive wave of his hand. "There are no more secrets to be kept."

Asankaru took several steps toward his brother. Gerin watched him closely. The Storm King, despite sharing the same strange shape of Teluko's form, was nevertheless a figure of regal beauty; his bearing and demeanor were those of a king. Gerin could sense the tremendous will within him, the fire that burned in his heart.

"You are my younger brother," said Asankaru. "By all our laws you must defer to me and do as I command."

"Our people and our laws are long dead. *We* are dead. I will do as I see fit, since you are too blinded by your hate and your pride to see that you are once more on a road to ruin."

"Always the naysayer," said Asankaru. "Always the first to concede defeat, or to say it cannot or should not be done."

"I say what is the truth, which you have never wanted to hear if it displeases you. Did I not warn you that if you waged war against the Atalari it would doom us all?"

Asankaru grew enraged. "We failed because you and

those you led were not strong enough! Victory was within our grasp—"

"Victory was never ours to be had." Teluko faced his brother's anger calmly. *If he ever feared Asankaru in life, he does not now,* thought Gerin. "My visions showed what would happen, but you chose to ignore them. The failure was yours, Asankaru, and yours alone. I told you on that day so very long ago that I should have killed you before you could begin your war. It was my failure that I did not."

One of the war priests stepped forward and leveled his staff at Teluko. He looked as angry as his master. "You speak treason!"

"It is no more than the truth, Tageluron. And treason to what? Our people are vanquished, our nation destroyed. To whom am I being a traitor? To my brother's folly? He is not our people."

"Enough of your jabbering," said Asankaru. "I am weary of your protests. I will show you that I have the strength and courage to carry out my plan. I will prove to you the error of your ways."

"As you proved me in error when you warred with the Atalari?"

Asankaru ignored him and turned his attention to Gerin. "So you are the summoner. You are different from the Atalari of old. How far the mighty have fallen." He glanced at Glaros. "Your weapon cannot harm me or my war priests. Come. It is time for you to complete the summoning."

"I never intended to summon you," Gerin replied. "I do not fully understand how you entered this world, but I will not do as you say. I know that the horn's power is tied to me alone. You cannot use it without me."

"That you are here is enough. I do not need your consent."

Four of the Red Robes pointed their staffs at Gerin and spoke in their alien tongue. Blue fire rippled up and down the black wood. Gerin's body froze, as if he had been encased in unbreakable adamant. He saw Reshel begin to cast a spell, but then she, too, froze in place.

Though he fought against the power holding him, he could not break it. His magic still flowed into him, but he no longer had the ability to shape it to his will, to direct its energy or mold it into spells.

Asankaru spoke to one of the Red Robes. It gestured with its staff, and Gerin, against his will, dropped his sword. He was little more than a puppet. He wanted to scream in frustration but could not open his mouth.

At a gesture from the Storm King, the Neddari holding the Baryashin box came forward. The horn was the gleaming instrument of gold Gerin had first seen, not the obscene horror of fangs and yellowed bone that had later appeared.

"Give it to him," commanded Asankaru.

The Neddari did not hesitate. He placed the horn in Gerin's hands.

Gerin felt his fingers tighten around it, as if drawn by a winch. The Red Robes were all fiercely intent in their concentration. Gerin wondered how close he might be to breaking free of their power. How much longer could they hold him if he continued to fight? If only he could—

He did not have time to finish the thought. Asankaru spoke to his Red Robes once more. They gestured with their staffs, drawing some unknown symbol in the air. Suddenly, Gerin was raising the horn to his lips. He fought against it with such strength that it seemed his very bones would crack and shatter from the strain. But his body was no longer his own. He could no more stop his hands from moving than stop the sunrise. He prayed to Telros and all the gods of Khedesh to strike down Asankaru and his servants, but they did not come or answer.

He was filled with terror and revulsion as the horn reached his mouth. He drew air into his lungs, held it a moment, pressed his lips to the mouthpiece, and then sounded a single, clear note that rang through the night.

45

"Where is the thrice-bloody Storm King or his bloody Red Robes?" asked Baron Velton Reiches, staring down from the summit of the Tower of Cregael, which straddled the castle's curtain wall and anchored Sarod's High Fence into the western castle with its Tower of Thelakor. The baron was a vassal of Gerin's, the lord of Castle Vallaser. He had not yet witnessed the power of Asankaru or his servants but had heard plenty about them from those who had retreated from Agdenor. Baron Velton was a natural skeptic and eager to see these "spirits" for himself.

"I don't know where they are," said Therain. "If my brother has drawn their attention, we can consider ourselves lucky."

Velton snorted. "Spirits who can call twisters," he muttered, half to himself. "Sounds a lot of rubbish to me."

"I assure you it's not," said Therain. The baron jumped a little; apparently he had not expected to be heard above the din of battle. "I can easily show you the ruins of Agdenor's gates when the opportunity presents itself."

"Forgive me, my lord," said Velton, bowing his head so fast he looked like a bird pecking for seeds. "I meant no offense. It just that the stories I've heard, they all sound so fantastic . . ."

"I can tell you with the greatest confidence that the stories you've been told cannot hope to do justice to the truth of the matter. The Storm King's power is something that must be seen to be truly understood, and trust me, Baron, it is not something you want to see up close."

Below them a battle raged on the rocky slopes south of the Fence. The Neddari army had arrived earlier in the day and once again halted their forward lines just out of range of the Khedeshian longbows. The survivors of Agdenor waited tensely for the Storm King to appear and again hurl a whirlwind at them, but so far neither Asankaru nor the Red Robes had shown themselves. Tired of being on the defensive, Therain decided to take the battle to the enemy. His captains had advised him against such an attack, said it would be too costly and of little real value, but he overruled them. *Better to bloody them first this time,* he thought. *The men will take heart from a quick victory, no matter how small.* He ordered the cavalry hidden in the Carlagos Hills to the west of Cregael to sweep down on the Neddari western flank at nightfall and inflict as much damage as they could, then make a hasty retreat. When the attention of the Neddari turned toward the west, more cavalry and foot soldiers would sally forth from the Fence and castles.

That battle was now going on below them. The Khedeshians were falling back after setting fire to parts of the enemy camp. The Neddari had not been as surprised as Therain had hoped, but it still had gone well. The Khedeshians were retreating up the road toward the Kynsleri; the Neddari were pursuing them hotly, but were now close enough for the bowmen on the walls to punish them fiercely for each step they advanced. Once he was certain his own men were inside the minimum throwing distance, Therain ordered the trebuchets upon the Fence to release their missiles. Those few Neddari who managed to stay close enough to the retreating Khedeshians to avoid the rain of rocks and fire were surrounded and killed just outside the Kynsleri. The rest of the Neddari withdrew to their camp to lick their wounds and take stock of the damage that had been done to them.

Not too much damage, thought Therain. *Mostly to their pride, and I hope to their sense of invulnerability.*

The men upon the Fence and the castle's battlements cheered and shouted. Therain smiled at the sound, though he knew this small victory meant little. They had won similar skirmishes at Agdenor, and look what had happened there.

"A bold plan, my lord," said Captain Rundgar. Therain did not think Donael completely approved of the attack, but knew his captain would rather chew off his own arm than contradict or question one of his decisions. "Do you have a plan for the morrow?"

"As a matter of fact, yes. We will do what they will least expect. Attack them again, hard. We ride at dawn."

Therain looked out into the darkness. He had slept only a few hours but was wide awake and filled with a strange calm. He felt at peace with himself, as if his decision to take part in the attack this morning had relieved him of all other duties and cares. *Is this how someone feels on the day of their death? Am I having a premonition of what is to come?*

Despite the crackling fire in the room, the air was damp and cold. Therain wondered if spring would ever come again.

Dorlem Hedresien, the eldest son of Earl Stenwek, entered the chamber dressed in full battle gear. "They are digging trenches and making palisades," he said. The future earl was in his late thirties and had a long graying beard that reached his collarbone; his brown eyes were so deeply set they seemed to regard Therain from the center of the man's head. "But they're far from complete."

"Is everything prepared? Are the men ready?"

"Yes, my lord. We await your command."

"Has a fog risen?"

"No. The air is clear. We won't be able to take them by surprise."

Therain cursed to himself. The fog at Agdenor had worked well for them in their attack, but they would have no such luck now. He wished one of the wizards were here. Maybe they could have conjured a fog for him. Was there something they could throw into the swamp to cause a fog to rise? *Too late for that now*. They would have to make do with the weather they had.

"How is that, my lord?" asked Hurother as he buckled the last strap.

"It's fine." The strange sense of calmness had not left him. He wondered again what, if anything, it meant. "It's fine."

"Dig, you dogs!" bellowed Tero Hamman Chendret, the master builder of Clan Kendritíchun. He'd been commanded to build a defensive palisade near the border of the foul-smelling marsh. He had no idea why he'd been told to do such a ludicrous thing—why would the unbelievers attack them from the bog when their castles held the high ground?—but Tero was not one to question orders. He would do what he was told. "I want this ditch eight feet deep and six wide before midmorning!" He swung around to face a knot of men hacking away at freshly cut timbers. "And get those stakes finished or I'll have the lot of you whipped!" The few trees along the edge of the marsh were small and stunted; most of them had already been cleared. His men were now hauling in wood from a forest more than a mile to the south. It slowed things considerably, but he would not allow that to become an excuse for failing to meet his deadlines. He *would* meet them, or by the Slain God Himself, his men would feel the bite of his lash.

Tero turned to look up at the eastern castle. It loomed above them in the dark, blotting out the stars, crouched upon its hill like some great beast with a hundred glowing eyes burning upon its walls. As a builder, he could not help but be impressed with the place. It felt strong to him, like an old tree with deep roots. *But trees can be cut down and uprooted. We will do the same to this place. We will take it in the name of the God Who Has Returned, may His name be revered forever.*

He heard shouts and saw the men of Clan Brekélawan running toward the front of the camp. Tero could not make out what they were saying, but he did not need to hear their words to know what was happening: they were under attack.

His men were drawing their weapons and retreating behind

the defensive works they'd completed so far. Tero leaped across a narrow section of the ditch and drew his own sword, waiting for the captain to issue a command. He was in charge of building—no one built better than he—but when it came to battle, he let the warriors lead.

He looked up at the castle, waiting to see some sign of advance from the Khedeshians, but saw no movement upon the hill. Were they attacking only at the center? Testing their defenses, perhaps, or trying to wreak havoc with their construction? *If that's what they're doing, we should let them advance and then drive in from the sides. We'll crush them between us.* He wondered if that would be the command the captain would give. He was not a strategist—he did not have a head for such things—but the idea made sense to him. They could keep a line of defenders between themselves and the hill in case the Khedeshians sallied from the castle.

Shouts erupted all around him. He looked and saw hundreds of horsemen charging down the hill toward them. They were moving fast and suddenly seemed very close.

The captain give the order for the archers to fire. Tero heard the dull thud of dozens of arrows being released. A few of the horses fell, but the charge did not falter. The men and horses were both well armored, and the soldiers carried tall shields of gleaming steel.

One of the Khedeshians shouted a hoarse command. Riders with torches touched them to buckets or casks at the end of chains that were carried by a group of horsemen just behind the leading edge of the charge. The men began to swing the chains over their heads, the flaming casks making circles of fire in the air.

The Neddari archers fired a second volley of arrows but took down less than ten of the enemy. Then arrows began to strike Tero's men; a digger next to Tero fell backward with an arrow in his face.

The horsemen swinging the chains released them, the fiery casks hurled toward Tero and his men with their chains trailing behind them like dark metal tails.

They crashed into the palisade and exploded with fire far larger than Tero would have expected from their size. He was stunned. He squinted his eyes as gouts of flame erupted around him. The contents of the casks were filled with what he could only think of as liquid fire. *It's what they used at the walls of the castle.* The fire that could not be put out. He had not seen it for himself—he'd been much farther back in the camp at the time—but heard men tell of the unquenchable fires hurled from the battlements of the castle. Tero had seen one man whose arm was burned off just below the elbow.

The palisade was burning in a dozen places. He shouted for men to get water even though he knew that water could not extinguish the substance; the command came from instinct.

A second group of Khedeshians released more of the fire-filled casks. He saw one break on the back of a mule and set the beast blazing from head to tail. It shrieked and dashed about madly, trampling two men as it tried in vain to put out the fire consuming its flesh to the bones.

"In the name of the God Who Has Risen, repel the unbelievers!" shouted Tero. The Khedeshians were upon them. They leaped across the unfinished ditch and crashed through the burning stakes, thrusting with their swords and lances. Men fell, pierced in the throat or face, or with arms or heads severed. Tero raised his sword and jumped into battle, praying to the Slain God to give him strength. He'd only gone a few steps when a Khedeshian and his horse leaped the ditch and slammed into the ground in front of him. Tero thrust the tip of his sword at the rider's belly, hoping to drive it up under the man's armpit. The rider knocked his weapon away with the flat of his own sword, which he then drew back and drove into Tero's unprotected chest. Tero looked down in horror at the steel protruding between his ribs. Then it was gone as the rider pulled it free and spurred his horse away.

Tero slumped to the ground. He was very cold, though there was a fire in his chest where the sword had penetrated. He put his hand over the wound and then held it up in front of his face; it was covered with blood. He knew he had to stop the bleeding, but he was suddenly so very tired. *I'm going to die.* It did not matter, he realized. When they were victorious, the God Who Has Returned would revive him, as the God Himself had awakened from the dead. There was nothing to fear. He believed, and that would save him. He closed his eyes. *So very cold. So very tired.* The blood seeping from his wound slowed, and then Tero drew his final breath.

Therain was well-protected by his guards and other soldiers as they pierced the forward defenses of the enemy that lay across the Agdenor Road. Fierel's Fire had worked well. It had thrown the Neddari into enough confusion that he and his men could make their long approach down the open road with relatively little resistance. There were fires all across the leading edge of the camp. Their attack and the damage they were causing was still on a relatively small scale; they were certainly not going to deal the Neddari a fatal blow, or even cripple them. This was about demoralizing them, taking them by surprise and making them feel vulnerable. And about giving his own men something to cheer about after the disaster at Agdenor. His plan was to do whatever he could to hurt them while the Storm King and his Red Robes were elsewhere, presumably dealing with Gerin and Reshel and unable to bring their powers to bear on the castles.

They had fought their way past the palisade and were wreaking havoc within the camp. Therain had grabbed a torch from a free-standing brace and set a row of tents on fire. The Neddari were too busy scrambling to repel the attack to fight the fires blossoming all around them.

Reining his horse to a halt, Therain looked about. It was time to go back, before the Neddari could close in behind them and cut off their escape. He shouted, "Fall back! Return to the Fence!" He heard soldiers relay the message to others farther out. He wheeled his horse around and galloped back up the road with Donael to his right and an older but hale fighter named Olmar Reiseleng on his left. The other members of his personal guard were behind them.

Several clouds of shimmering light appeared in their path, floating head-high above the ground. *Elementals!* he realized. *Kamichi* were somewhere close by, but so far he had not seen them.

Before he could shout an order for them to ride around the elementals, the glowing entities raced at them with incredible speed.

One of them attacked Therain. He threw his arms up as the sparkling cloud enveloped his head and chest. The air seemed to vanish from his lungs; he felt his armor grow suddenly hot and his flesh begin to burn. He thought he heard Donael shout, but could not see his captain; the cloud of light blocked his vision almost completely. Panicked, he threw himself from his horse, hoping he would not be trampled by it or any of the other riders.

He slammed hard into the ground, the impact driving what little air remained out of his lungs, but the elemental seemed to have vanished. He gasped for air and tried to stand. He'd dropped his sword when the elemental attacked but saw it close by and staggered to it. The skin of his face still burned painfully. He looked about for the elemental, but it was nowhere to be seen.

His horse had ridden off. Neddari were shouting and charging toward him. He saw his personal guards on the road a short distance away, locked in battle with Neddari and more of the elementals. Two of his guards and their horses lay dead on the ground, their flesh burned away by the caustic power of the spirits. He spied a *kamichi* by one of the burning tents, an arrow protruding from his belly. He wondered if that had been the man controlling the spirit that had attacked him, and if his death was the reason he was still alive, rather than his tumble from the saddle. He'd been told that once an elemental latched onto a man, he was as good as dead.

But he did not have time to dwell on such questions. He ran toward his guards, limping from the force of his fall. Another of the elementals vanished as the *kamichi* controlling it died.

Donael killed the foot soldier he was fighting with a
quick jab of his sword into the man's face, then turned and
saw Therain. "My lord!" he cried, then spurred his horse
toward him.

A Neddari reached Therain first. The man thrust at him
with a short, broad-bladed sword. Therain swept it aside
and lunged, but the other man danced away too quickly and
avoided Baleringol's point. Therain leaped forward and
feigned a high strike, and when the man moved to counter it,
he lowered his blade and drove it through the man's thigh. The
Neddari screamed. The sound ended abruptly when Donael's
sword cut off most of the back of his head.

"My lord, I believe it's past time we leave." He held out
his hand and helped Therain swing up on his horse.

He saw another of his guards go limp within the glowing
form of an elemental, his flesh blackened and smoking. One
of his archers released an arrow that killed a *kamichi* lurking
near the flaming wreckage of one of the tents. The *kamichi*
fell back into the fire, the shaft protruding from his chest,
and did not get up. The last of the elementals attacking them
vanished, but more Neddari were closing fast.

Donael galloped back up the road toward the castle.
Therain jabbed his sword at two Neddari who tried to pull
them down. One stayed out of the range of his weapon; the
other felt its bite just below his collarbone.

A few more Khedeshians joined them. The remaining
members of the raiding party waited for them on the far side
of the palisade. The archers were on their flanks and provided cover fire for Therain and his companions.

They had almost reached the road when Therain felt a
sharp, biting pain in his side. Something had hit him, and the
force knocked him sideways in the saddle. He had to hold
onto Donael to keep from falling off. He looked down and
saw an arrow protruding from his side. It had slipped in just
under the edge of his armor. When he drew a breath he
nearly screamed. He clenched his teeth and tried to keep his
breathing shallow. Blood was seeping down his leg. The

jarring motion of the horse flared into white-hot agony. "Donael, hurry . . ."

The captain glanced over his shoulder and muttered a curse when he saw the arrow. "Hold on, my lord. We'll be back at the castle soon."

They reached the rest of the men, who formed a protective line behind Therain, and they raced toward the Fence with Neddari arrows falling around them.

Therain slipped in and out of consciousness as they neared the gate in the Kynsleri. He could distantly hear the men cheering on the walls. Donael spoke to him, but he could not make sense of the words. The arrow in his side burned as if it were made of molten lead. He banged it once with his arm by accident, nearly passed out from the pain, and wondered vaguely if it were poisoned.

Arms were all around him, helping him down from the saddle. He was so weary he could barely lift his head. His vision was blurred and dim. Donael's face was above his, very close. "Be strong, my lord," he said. "They will heal you." Someone poured a hot liquid down his throat. He coughed some of it out and nearly choked, but most of it went down. It did little to dull the pain, but the warmth of it was comforting as it seeped through his body.

He was carried to another room and placed on a table. A voice spoke in his ear. "Brace yourself, my lord. We must remove the arrow." He was too tired to open his eyes to see who it was. His face still burned from the elemental's attack. Someone stuffed a cloth in his mouth. "For you to bite on, my lord," said the voice. Hands pinned down his arms and shoulders and legs.

It seemed that in the distance he heard the sound of horns or trumpets blowing. Somewhere above him, men began to shout and cheer. He heard a commotion somewhere close by: the sound of heavy boots pounding down stairs and through a hall. He heard a door open and someone rush inside. "The king has come! The king has come!"

The hands holding him released their pressure a little.

"Where is he?" It might have been Donael. "Here in the castle?"

"No, but soon! He sent messengers to tell us that he comes with thirty thousand men! Ten thousand are Taeratens of the Naege!"

The sound of the trumpets grew louder. Once more the men cheered. Therain still could not open his eyes, but he tried to speak. He spit the cloth from his mouth and drew several ragged breaths. "I must talk to . . . my father . . ."

The voice returned to his ear. "You will, my lord. But he is not yet here, and we must remove this arrow and dress your wound. Now be still." The cloth was placed back in his mouth and the hands braced him one more. He stiffened and grimaced when someone grabbed the arrow in his side. He thought he could feel it grind against one of his ribs. "Hold him," said the voice. Then the arrow was wrenched free. He bit down hard into the cloth and screamed. He heard the trumpets once more—it seemed the sound of triumph, of victory—and then blacked out.

46

The sound of the horn echoed across the face of the cliff, a sad, mournful note that lingered long past the point where it should have faded. At the foot of the Sundering, where Dian's Stair began its long climb, Hollin, Kirin, and Balandrick looked up in alarm. "Venegreh preserve us," whispered Hollin. He bounded onto the Stair. Kirin, Balandrick, and the soldiers of the Sunrise Guard followed.

"Can we still stop it?" asked Balandrick.

"It will take hours to reach the summit," said Hollin. "I fear that whatever is happening with Gerin will be finished long before we can reach him."

His heart black with despair, Balandrick followed. *Stay safe, Reshel. Whatever happens, stay safe until I get there.*

Gerin still held the horn to his mouth. The Red Robes had not commanded him to lower it, and he was powerless to move otherwise. He continued to struggle, but the only sign of it was a sheen of sweat that sprang from his forehead.

Asankaru spoke to the only Red Robe not holding Gerin and Reshel captive. The Red Robe bowed his head and then vanished from the terrace.

One of the Red Robes began to chant in its native tongue. The very air of the terrace became charged with the energy released by the horn. Gerin could feel it against his skin, a warmth that caused the hair on his arms to stand on end. The darkness seemed to grow deeper, as if some power were draining or occluding the light from the torches the Neddari carried.

Asankaru stepped closer to Gerin as the spell grew in intensity. Though Gerin did not understand the words, he could feel their effect. Asankaru was bending the unleashed power of the horn to his will. The landscape around him became dreamy, indistinct. The Neddari standing behind the Red Robes faded almost completely, as if their torches had begun to radiate darkness instead of light.

But Asankaru and the Red Robes had grown intensely bright, as though an inner fire had risen to the surface of their flesh. Only the blue fire of the Red Robes' staffs remained unchanged.

Gerin realized what was happening. He had crossed over into the realm of the dead.

Reshel, too, realized that the worlds had thinned to the point where there was no longer a meaningful distinction between them. It terrified her to know that she was no longer in Osseria, or only partly in it, but mostly someplace . . . else. She fought against the power binding her but could not break free.

The power unleashed by the horn was so vast it took her breath away. It felt as if an ocean of energy had swallowed the clifftop whole. This was far greater than what Gerin had done at Hethnost. *Because the doorway between worlds is already open. And Asankaru and his Red Robes are trying to open it even further*. She could sense them molding the immense force, shaping it into a spell of possession as the Baryashins had intended.

Asankaru stepped closer to Gerin. Her heart turned to ice. The Storm King was going to take her brother's body.

The power formed a translucent vortex around Asankaru, a whirling shimmer in the air that partially obscured his form. The power of the spell was focusing on him, drawn to his will.

She blinked, and then her vision changed with such abruptness that she would have staggered had she been able to move. She saw Almaris from a great height, as if she were a gull circling high on the ocean winds. She fell closer to the city at an impossible speed, then halted a few hundred feet above the streets and drifted slowly above the rooftops.

The city was lifeless. There were bodies everywhere—soldiers and merchants, servants and nobles, craftsmen and guildsmen, women and children, horses, sheep, cattle, birds. Dead fish had washed upon the beach by the hundreds. Even the trees and grass were dried and withered as if they'd been consumed by fire.

She could not tell how the people had died. There was no sign of war. The walls and gates of the city were intact. There was no blood or wounds upon the bodies, no weapons lying about, no sense that the city had been invaded. It seemed they had all just fallen over dead during the course of a normal day, their lives abruptly snuffed out.

Her view shifted again, to a point high above Ailethon. It, too, was dead. She hovered above the castle a few moments before the scene changed once more, to a city on the edge of a cold, stormy sea. She did not recognize it. It was a city of unburied dead, thousands upon thousands of them. The view moved again, and then again, to cities and towns on plains and in the shadows of bleak mountains and on the banks of great rivers, where she saw no living thing, only corpses. It seemed all of Osseria had been turned into a graveyard.

She felt with an unshakable conviction that what she was seeing was somehow true. *It's a vision of the future.* She was overcome by a sense of utter despair. *It's what will happen if Asankaru succeeds. Our worst nightmares will come true. He will destroy Osseria completely.*

The vision before her shattered with the violence of a stone hurled through a pane of glass. She was back upon the cliff, immersed in the tide of the horn's power, caught somewhere between the worlds of the living and the dead. She tumbled forward to her knees. It took her a moment to realize that her

sudden fall meant that she had somehow been freed from the
binding power of the Red Robes. She looked up and tried to
understand what she was seeing.

All of the Eletheros glowed with a diamondlike radiance.
Their brightness seemed even greater in contrast to the
dense darkness around them, as if the air itself had become
dusty and opaque.

Asankaru stepped closer to Gerin and reached toward him
with his long-fingered hand. He paid no heed to Reshel or
the fact that she had somehow been freed. Gerin lowered the
horn with the slow, precise movements of a sleepwalker,
then froze once more in place.

She saw what had freed her. Teluko had attacked one of the
Red Robes and thrown his staff to the ground. He held the
Red Robe's wrists and was forcing him away from the others.
But it was more than a physical struggle—though she wondered what *physical* could truly mean to spirits of the dead.
*But we are in their world now, or the worlds are so mixed that
it makes no difference.* A sullen red glow, like the light thrown
off by heated iron, radiated from the places where Teluko and
the Red Robe touched.

"Tuso'leri aves hía, Asankaru!" shouted Teluko. The
Storm King did not take his eyes from Gerin. If he heard his
brother's cry, he gave no sign of it. The other Red Robes
were focused on Gerin and either had not noticed that she
was free or were expending so much power to control her
brother that they could not divert their attention to her.

Teluko appeared to be losing his struggle with the Red
Robe, who was slowly forcing him back toward the fallen
staff. If he regained it and trapped her once again . . .

She knew what she had to do. She straightened and tried
to calm herself, but could not stop her hands from shaking.
Her eyes filled with tears, which she wiped hastily away
with the heel of her palm. With her right hand she drew from
her belt the knife Gerin had given her. She looked at the long
blade in the darkness and thought of Balandrick, the husband she would never have, the children she would never

bear. She thought of her father and Therain and Claressa, and of Hethnost and the wizards there. She would never see any of them again. *But if I don't do this, I will never see them anyway.* Tears filled her eyes again; she blinked several times to clear them, and two spilled down her cheeks. *I am my father's daughter. I must be strong.*

She steadied herself, drew a deep breath, and began to speak the Spell of Compulsion.

Gerin saw Teluko attack the Red Robe and disrupt the power binding Reshel. He wanted her to run, to flee and save herself, but she did not move. He thought he saw her draw her knife, but then Asankaru's hand was on his face and the insubstantial fingers slipped beneath his flesh.

The possession was about to start. Asankaru's essence bled into him like a trickle of cold water. He could sense in a dim way the spirit's thoughts, the bone-deep anger and hatred that compelled him to do what he did as surely as the *kamichi* had compelled him.

Reshel began to speak. Gerin realized in horror that she was invoking the spell of the Baryashin Order. The spell that could force Asankaru back to the world of the dead and seal the rift between them.

The spell that required an innocent sacrifice to complete it.

The building power of her magic disrupted Asankaru's attempt at possession. He stepped back from Gerin, a look of fury on his face, and turned to see who dared interfere.

The magic gathering around Reshel broke the concentration of the Red Robes. The crackling blue fire spluttered and vanished from two of the staffs as the conflicting energies collided on the terrace. Gerin suddenly found himself free. His magic surged through him with incredible force, as if a dam had just broken to release the fury of a pent-up ocean. Amber fire exploded from his body and destroyed the last of the Red Robes' power.

Reshel completed the first part of the spell. She looked at him with tears on her face. "Gerin!" she shouted. "You must finish it!" The words caught in her throat, but she forced them out. "Tell Balandrick I love him! And tell Father I'm sorry!"

She raised her knife and in one swift motion drew it across her throat.

"Reshel, no!" A second later Gerin was knocked to his knees by the force of the magic that erupted from her slumped body. Blood gushed from the terrible wound. She lay on her side, pale and limp, while the power of the spell overwhelmed the fading energy that had been called by the horn. The horn's power ended, and the world around them changed. They were once more in the realm of the living. Balance had been restored, but not completely.

He knew what she had done. She had sacrificed herself to release the power he needed to compel Asankaru. It was the only hope they had of defeating him. Gerin had felt the world itself tremble when Asankaru touched him, as if a fracture had opened through the whole of creation. If Asankaru had finished his possession, Osseria itself might not survive it. He could not revive Asankaru and then kill his physical body. Reshel must have realized that.

He could not let her sacrifice be in vain.

He continued the spell. Rage filled him; he could not calm himself to help the flow of magic, but there was already so much power in him—and so much power released by Reshel's sacrifice—that it did not matter. He spoke the words and felt the magic bend to him, obedient to his will, supple and pliant, waiting to be shaped.

Gerin focused all of his concentration on the completion of the spell. He could feel its magic gathering around him, waiting for him to direct it.

Teluko had released the Red Robe and knelt by Reshel's side.

The Storm King backed away from Gerin and raised his arms toward the sky. The Red Robes had recovered from the shock of the compulsion and pointed their staffs at their master. Asankaru began to chant. Gerin knew that Asankaru was going to summon a twister to stop him, but he did not falter as a blustery wind began to whip across the terrace.

A cloud of darkness formed near him. It looked like a ragged hole floating in the air, its edges blurred and indistinct, its center utterly black. He knew this was the rift that had opened between the worlds of the living and the dead, held open by Asankaru's presence in Osseria.

He completed the spell. There was a flash of white light, and then its power settled over him like a mantle upon his shoulders.

"Go to your rest, Asankaru," he said. He tried to hate the creature before him, but after witnessing what had happened to his people, the pointless and terrible slaughter, he could feel only sadness and regret. He was furious with the Storm King for what he had done, but he did not hate him. It was too easy to understand what had driven Asankaru, the bitter needs that burned in his heart, the desire to right such a horrible wrong. He would not hate him.

But he would defeat him.

The glow of Asankaru's body dimmed as the magic devised by the Baryashin Order bound him in its unbreakable power. The Storm King fumed and raged in the grip of the compulsion but could not break free. His Red Robes shot lances of blue fire at the power holding their lord, but the fire was consumed by the compulsion, swallowed as if it had never existed.

"The time of your people has passed," said Gerin. "I cannot bring them back or undo the terrible crime that happened here, but neither can you. You cannot live again. Go to your rest, and find what peace you can."

The circle of blackness moved closer to Asankaru. "Stop! *Stop!*" He struggled against the confines of the compulsion. Gerin felt the magic under his command flex and bend as the Storm King fought back, but as powerful as he was, Asankaru did not have nearly enough strength to undo the spell.

The Storm King's form became even dimmer as the circle neared him. He bellowed for Gerin to halt what he was doing, and his Red Robes turned their diminishing power on Gerin once more. But Gerin had erected Wardings that repelled their attempts to control him. A Neddari soldier fired two arrows at him, but they broke against his magical barriers.

The circle of blackness touched Asankaru. His body drained of color and grew transparent, all of its essence and vitality leeched from it. He screamed once more, but the sound was swallowed by the blackness as the Storm King's body was pulled into the black void and disappeared.

Teluko and the Red Robes faded and vanished from view, drawn by their connections to Asankaru back through the rift between worlds. Within moments they were gone. Then the circle of darkness itself evaporated into the air. No trace of it remained. Balance had been restored.

Gerin did not lower his Wardings. With his aura flaming around him, he faced the Neddari. "Your God is gone and will not be coming back. If you value your lives, leave now. Otherwise I will kill you where you stand." He was tired of killing, tired of death, but he would do as he said if they did not leave.

Fortunately for them, they listened and hurried away.

An enormous pool of blood had spread from Reshel's neck. The sight of the deep wound—like a wide lipless mouth—was ghastly. He went to her and sat by her body. He let his aura go out once the Neddari were out of his sight. He created a spark of magefire and then gently lifted her head and cradled it in his lap. "Oh, Reshel . . ." he sobbed. "What am I going to tell Father?" He should have protected her. His little sister.

He began to cry. Once it started he could not stop. Tears poured down his face. "Oh, Reshel . . ." He spoke her name over and over, as if it were a sacred word.

He was still holding her when Balandrick and the wizards finally arrived.

47

In the autumn of that year, eight months after the fall of the Storm King, Gerin returned to Almaris. There was to be an Assembly of Lords to discuss Gerin's involvement in the Neddari War, as well as his wizardry. His role in the release of Asankaru had become widely known, and though it was explained that he had not acted of his own free will but from the influence of a spell placed upon him by the Neddari, there was nevertheless a great deal of grumbling among the nobles for explanations and remunerations. The Council of Barons had finally demanded that the king call an Assembly for their concerns and grievances to be aired. After mobilizing so many of his vassals to engage the Neddari, Abran was left with little choice but to agree.

Gerin sat on the balcony of his rooms in the Tirthaig, drinking wine and watching the shadows lengthen.

It had taken months to drive the last of the Neddari out of Khedesh, but the invaders had lost the moment the Storm King was cast from the world. Gerin was pleased that Hollin and Kirin had allowed the Neddari who were fleeing from the summit to pass them unhindered. "They looked frightened out of their wits," Hollin told him later. "They did not even draw their weapons when they saw us. They were just running for their lives. I saw no need to kill them." And so they had lived to return to their army and tell the story of the fall of their Slain God. The Khedeshians later learned from Neddari prisoners that the clan chiefs already suspected that something had gone wrong. The Red Robe that had vanished after the blowing of the horn apparently returned to the Neddari army, on Asankaru's command, to see how they were faring. The clan chiefs were terrified when the Red Robe shrieked in horror and vanished before their eyes, dragged back to the world of the dead along with his master. The Neddari did not yet know what had happened, but it was apparent that something was terribly wrong. Almost at once the clan leaders began fighting among themselves. Two of the Chieftains and the newly appointed Warlord—apparently the same *kamichi* who had placed the spell on Gerin to set the wheels of the conflict in motion—were killed in a bitter argument that occurred that very night, which threw the entire army into chaos.

The king's army, with the Taeratens in the van, had poured out of Cregael-Thelakor into the ranks of the Neddari the morning after their arrival at the twin castles. The Red Robe had disappeared the previous night, and the encampment was unprepared for a sudden, overwhelming assault. Therain was still in a feverish sleep, recovering from the arrow wound he'd taken.

The battle had raged for days. The Neddari army began to splinter, and finally broke completely when their soldiers returned from the Sundering with word of what had happened to the Storm King. Many clans had retreated to Neddar as fast as they could. They were driven back to Agdenor, which was besieged once more, this time by the Khedeshians. The castle was abandoned by the Neddari eleven days later and reclaimed by Captain Melfistan in the name of Duke Therain.

But there had been a cost. More than eight hundred of the Taeratens had died during the campaign, and many more were seriously injured. The king had already issued a summons for more men to fill the depleted ranks of the Naege, but it would be years before the elite fighting school had fully recovered.

"What do you think will happen in the Assembly?" asked Therain as he stepped onto the balcony, rousing Gerin from his thoughts.

Gerin looked out at the darkening sea. "I think there will be hard questions about my wizardry, but they will all be questions I can answer. There's plenty of evidence that this was started by the Neddari. Nothing can be blamed on me or Father. In the end, I don't think anything will change."

"I've heard the treasury's been sorely depleted by the war. Jaros Waklan is worried that we won't be able to meet the demands of the nobles with the garrons on hand."

"The nobles can demand all they want. That doesn't mean Father has to meet them."

"They *could* force Father to name me as his heir instead of you." He said it with a grin to show he was not serious. "They might want to keep a pesky, troublesome wizard off the throne who's shown he's not terribly reliable. Wouldn't that be something? King Therain. I rather like the sound of that."

Gerin took a sip of wine. "Only in your dreams, brother. Only in your dreams."

The three barons chosen to sit as Advocates in the assembly interrogated Gerin vigorously. There were a great many questions about the attack by the Neddari and the nature of the compulsion placed in Gerin by the *kamichi*. Gerin recounted for them how the spell had forbidden him to let anyone know what he was doing, even when he felt a desire to confess his actions to his sister or one of the wizards. Hollin, who had accompanied Gerin to Almaris, confirmed the nature of the spell and that even the most knowledgeable wizards of Hethnost had been unable to discern its true purpose or remove it.

The Advocates next demanded to know whether his status

as a wizard compromised his ability to rule one day. "How do we know you will not be a slave of this foreign power, subject to the same kinds of compulsions you have just described?" asked Baron Kaffir Styros, the Chief Advocate, as he stroked his beard and scowled in indignation.

"The wizards of Hethnost have no interest in the affairs of Khedesh, or any other nation," said Gerin. "That is one of the reasons they live where the do, in lands among the Red-horn Hills unclaimed by any sovereign nation and subject to no rule but their own. They have set themselves apart from the mortal world in many ways and have only limited contact with it."

"Yet a wizard now lives with you at Ailethon," said Baron Drommid en'Ukaredis, a wisp of a man with thinning black hair and a deeply cleft chin, gesturing toward Hollin.

"He is there to complete my training as a wizard, *against* the traditions they have long held. Wizards are usually taken to Hethnost to learn the ways of magic, but I cannot be gone from the realm for so long. They made an exception and are allowing me to be trained here in Khedesh, but it is an accommodation that, to the best of my knowledge, they have never made before."

Hollin spoke next. "Prince Gerin is correct. You need not fear influence on the internal policies of Khedesh from the wizards of Hethnost. We have no agenda, no interest other than the preservation of our kind. It matters little to us what you do within your own borders, or to your neighbors, as long as we are left alone." He asked the barons to provide a single instance when wizards had interfered with any kingdom of Osseria. On this the Advocates were silent.

Gerin's father talked to them of the reparations that would be made to the houses that played significant roles in the war against the Neddari, but he cautioned that the crown would not be nearly so generous if they censured his son. "You did your duties as vassals and in truth should expect nothing more from the coffers of the treasury," said Abran. "Think hard on this offer before you cast your vote."

They left the hall while the lords cast their votes. Gerin tried not to worry, but he could not prevent a nervous, nauseous flutter from growing more severe as the hours passed by. Hollin told him not to be concerned, but a few minutes later they heard raised voices coming through the closed doors, and Gerin's nausea increased to the point where he thought he might be sick. *How can their shouting at one another be good?* he wondered as he strained to make out what they were saying. But the walls and doors were too thick, the voices too distant, even for his sensitive ears to understand.

Five hours later they were summoned back to the hall to hear the outcome of the vote.

"It is the will of this assembly of the nobility of Khedesh," intoned Baron Styros gravely, his gaze leveled on Gerin, "that Prince Gerin is hereby reaffirmed as the heir to the Sapphire Throne. No action or censure of any kind will be taken against him. We have concluded after a careful deliberation of the evidence that the Neddari bear the responsibility for the release of the Storm King and the subsequent war, and that it was through the efforts of Prince Gerin and the sacrifice of the Lady Reshel that the realm was preserved. This assembly is concluded. May Telros watch over us and bless us all."

Hollin clapped him on the shoulder and offered his congratulations. Abran, who'd stood stiffly next to his son during the judgment by the baron, his hands clasped behind his back, turned and left the room without saying a word.

But Gerin scarcely noticed. It was finally over. He could stop worrying. At last his life could go on.

He would, one day, become king.

The evening following the assembly, Abran asked that Gerin come to his chambers, alone.

"You asked to see me, Father?" he said as he entered the study. The king was seated in a large chair cushioned with velvet, staring out the window toward the sea. Gerin could hear the distant cry of gulls flying above the waters of the Cleave.

"Yes." There was a dull, hollow quality to his father's voice. *He still hasn't gotten over her death,* thought Gerin. He recalled vividly that terrible meeting at Cregael-Thelakor when he had told his father what happened upon the Sundering. Gerin had wept as he spoke of his sister's sacrifice, how brave and true she had been. "She saved all of us," he'd said, sniffling like a boy. "Without her, I would have failed, and all of us would have died."

He told Abran her last words. "And tell Father I'm sorry!"

The king had listened with a haunted look on his face as he stared down at his daughter's corpse. They had washed her and covered the wound in her throat with a strip of white silk, and Hollin had placed several preservation spells on her to slow the decay of her body, but the violence of her death was unmistakable. When Gerin finished speaking, his father placed his hand gently upon her head. "Leave me with her for a while."

The two had spoken little since then, even during the preparation for the assembly. Her death had created a rift between them that Gerin was unsure how to bridge.

Now, his father turned to look at him. Gerin wanted to run and hide from that gaze, the terrible accusation in it, the flinty coldness, the utter lack of forgiveness. "I stood by you in the assembly because you are my son and heir," his father said. "It is not for the nobles to question such matters, though they have the legal right to do so in circumstances such as this. I am ultimately the protector of our family and the succession, and if there is to be a change in that, then it will be *my* decision and mine alone."

"I understand, Father." His stomach trembled with the same churning fear he'd felt as a nine-year-old after he accidentally wounded his father's favorite hunting dog while playing with a knife he was not supposed to have.

"When I agreed to allow Reshel to be trained as a wizard with you, I told you I had reservations and worries. And I asked that you do one thing: watch out for her and keep her safe. I also sent you a letter specifically commanding you to keep her out of the conflict." His father's expression hardened even more; the line of his mouth grew tight, and his brows furrowed over his eyes even as the lower lids filled with unspilled tears.

The mingled look of grief for his lost daughter, and his disdain—if not outright contempt—for Gerin, cut him to the bone, and despite his attempt to remain calm, a sob escaped his lips.

"You failed in that, Gerin. Failed completely. And my daughter, your sister, is dead because of it. I rue the day that this cursed wizardry entered our lives. No good has come of it, and no good that may come can ever make up for the harm it has done. I despise it, and do not want it spoken of in my presence.

"You are my son and my heir. One day I hope I can forgive you. But that day is not today."

He turned away from Gerin and dismissed him with a wave of his hand. Gerin fled the room, miserable and heartbroken.

A servant summoned Gerin to dinner with Therain and Claressa an hour later. The servant was a young Pashti boy, perhaps eleven years old. He said nothing to Gerin as they made their way through the hallways of the Tirthaig. As Gerin followed the boy, he remembered Nandis's dead face and his father's words, spoken to him many years ago: *Better if Khedesh had killed them all when he conquered these unworthy wretches.*

No, it would not have been better. He'd seen firsthand the destruction of a people; it was not something he would wish upon anyone, even the Neddari. No people, no race, deserved such a terrible fate. He could better understand now the resentment the Pashti must feel for their Khedeshian overlords, even after so many centuries had passed. What was once theirs had been taken away. They would see the Khedeshians as conquerors, not benefactors or bringers of a greater civilization.

But what could be done about it after so much time had

passed? Certainly the kingdom of Khedesh could not be given back to them. But then what? Was there anything that could be done to mend the age-old wounds inflicted upon the Pashti?

It was not a question he could answer. But he would think about it long and hard, so that perhaps, when he became king, something could at last be done. *It has to begin somewhere,* he thought. *It might as well be with me.* He knew it was something his father would not ever understand. He'd not witnessed the horror of the end of the Eletheros. He did not think it was something that could be explained; it had to be *seen,* the indelible, visceral carnage they'd been shown atop the Sundering. A memory that could never be forgotten.

Reshel would understand, but she, too, was gone.

The young boy opened the door for him. Gerin looked at him and smiled, but the boy quickly averted his gaze, as if fearing to offend someone of such high rank. "Thank you," Gerin said, making sure that the pain he felt in his heart did not appear in his voice.

The boy nodded but did not reply or look up. Gerin resisted an urge to place his hand upon the boy's shoulder, then entered the room.

After the meal, they retired to a terrace where they sat at a table surrounded by torches flickering in the ocean wind. Balandrick and Hollin joined them a short time later.

They all sat in silence for a time. Gerin lost himself in thought. So much had been destroyed, so many had died, because of his desire to find the Varsae Estrikavis, and still he did not know its location. The royal archivists in the Tirthaig had been searching for references to the Chamber of the Moon, but so far they'd found nothing.

I will find it someday, I swear by all that is holy, but not for my own glory to or to make my mark in history. I'll find it for Reshel, for the memory of what she did for us.

The messenger of the divine presence had not appeared to him since that day on the road to Hethnost. It seemed it had happened a long time ago, a thing almost a dream; he had to remind himself that it had been real, that a divine being *had* appeared to him and marked him for a purpose he did not fully understand. He could never forget that. It was too dangerous to pretend otherwise.

He'd thought once that the messenger's words, *Even a prophet may not fully understand what he is shown,* had referred to Stefon Malarik's vision regarding him, but events with the Storm King had proved him wrong. Malarik had been released from the dungeon at Ailethon, though he was watched carefully by the castle guard and constables of Padesh in case he felt the need to act on another one of his visions. Gerin saw no need to have him executed since the events he'd seen in his vision, a possible but not inevitable future, had not come to pass. Matren protested hotly, arguing that Malarik's life was forfeit for attempting to kill Gerin and that the reason for the attempt was irrelevant, but Gerin overruled him.

Now he did not know what to think about the messenger's words. He would be mindful for signs of an Adversary, or a prophet, but other than that he was unsure of what, if anything, he should do, or could do.

Therain said, "I miss her. More than I would have ever dreamed." His eyes glistened in the candlelight. "I still can't believe what she did. How brave she was . . ."

Gerin nodded. He did not trust himself to speak. Grief and guilt filled him anew. Next to him, Balandrick wiped at his eyes and looked down at the table. He'd been crushed by her death, his hope for a life with her irrevocably lost in that dark night upon the Sundering. He'd been the one who had cleaned and bandaged her wound before her body had been brought back to Cregael-Thelakor, and he'd walked beside her every step of the journey, clutching her hand, weeping quietly in the darkness. Gerin did not know if Balandrick blamed him for her death; they had not spoken of it. It was simply too painful for both of them.

Balandrick had wept when she was placed in her tomb next to her mother, the image of her face freshly cut into the stone door of her crypt, her name etched beneath: RESHEL ATREYANO, BELOVED DAUGHTER, WHO DIED THAT HER PEOPLE MIGHT LIVE.

Tears fell openly from Claressa's eyes. "Who would have thought," she said, "that she was the strongest of us all?"

Glossary and Pronunciation Guide

The pronunciation guide included in this glossary is in no way intended to be absolute, especially where Kelarin is concerned, which was a language of diverse regional dialects, accents, and vocabulary. The pronunciations of Kelarin words given here reflect the speech of central Khedesh, where in later years these accounts were compiled. For reasons of clarity and brevity, alternative pronunciations, even when they are known, are not included.

Osirin poses less of a difficulty, since by Gerin's time it had long been a "dead" language and therefore mostly immune to the kinds of changes in vocabulary and pronunciation that affect a language used in everyday speech. The forms of Osirin had been fixed for centuries, and they changed little since the time of the Empire, when its widespread use ceased. Osirin became a largely ceremonial language, used by wizards in their rituals and spellmaking but for little else, not even record-keeping—at least not consistently—and even in Hethnost centuries had passed since it had been used for daily intercourse.

An apostrophe *after* a syllable indicates stress (*af'ter*).

Abran Atreyano (*Ah'bran At-ray-ahn'-oh*): King of Khedesh, son of Bessel.

Ailethon (*Ay'-leth-on*): Castle of the Crown Prince of Khedesh.

Aisa Néhos (*Ay'-sa Nay'-hose*): "Red Water," a stream flowing out of the Redhorn Hills that feeds the Tivar Lhasaril.

Akhalosserë (*Ahk'-hal-oh-sayr'-ee*): "Land of Eternal Light" in Osirin, the name that the Atalari Emunial gave to the region that later became Osseria.

Alkaneiros (*Alk'-ah-nare'-ohs*): Ruby ring of Demos Thelar, worn by the Archmage of Hethnost.

Almaris (*Al-mare'-is*): Capital city of Khedesh.

amber wizard: The most powerful kind of wizard. There have only been two: Naragenth ul-Darhel and Gerin Atreyano.

Ammon Ekril (*Ah-mon' Ek'ril*): Diamond set into a circlet of braided gold that signifies the rank of Archmage. The circlet and diamond together are also referred to as the Ammon Ekril.

andraleirazi (*an'-drah-lay-rah'-zee*): Magical powder that can be used to create the Binding Rings of Barados to imprison beings of spirit.

Aneldromari (*Ah-nel'-dro-mar'-ee*):   "Shadow-earth-people," Osirin name given to the Eletheros by the Atalari.

Angle: Triangle of land at the foot of Henly's Hill, at the confluence of the Samaro and Azren Rivers.

Archmage: The elected ruler of the wizards of Hethnost.

Argáos (*Ar-gay'-ohs*): The easternmost hill of the Corlagos Heights. The eastern half of Cregael-Thelakor is built upon it.

Arkenland: Region of Khedesh.

Ashlynne Woods: Woods located just north of Ailethon.

Assembly of Lords: Gathering of Khedeshian nobles.

Atalari (*At-ah-lahr'-ee*): Race of beings infused with magical powers who came to Osseria in the distant past.

awaenjir (*Ah-wain-jeer'*): Device of magic used to Awaken a wizard's dormant powers.

Balandrick Vaules (*Bah-lan'-drick Vole'-es*): Youngest of the four sons of Earl Herenne Vaules of Carengil, and the captain of Gerin's personal guard.

Baryashin Order (*Bar'-yah-sheen*): A secret order of wizards who secretly committed murders in an attempt to grant themselves eternal life. They originated within Hethnost, but fled when they were discovered and were later destroyed.

Bellon (*Bel'on*): The Khedeshian god of the dead, who dwells in the mansions of Velyol.

Belsend Plateau (*Bel'-send*): Expanse of land atop the Sundering.

Binding Rings of Barados (*Bah-rad'-ohs*): Wards of power formed with *andraleirazi,* designed to imprison beings of spirit.

Blackstone Keep: The keep of Ailethon, named for the black stone forming the arch and keystone of the keep's main doors. It is said the stone was made from the remains of a falling star.

Brekélawan (*breh-kel'-ah-wan*): One of the Neddari clans.

Brithkee (*brith'-kee*): A village in Calad-Ethil, near the Neddari border.

Calad-Ethil (*Kal'-ad Eth'-il*): Region of southern Khedesh.

Chamber of the Moon: The secret location of the Varsae Estrikavis.

City Watch: Military order charged with enforcing the king's law in Almaris.

Claressa Atreyano (*Kla-res'-ah At-ray-ahn'-oh*): Princess of Khedesh, twin to Therain.

Cleave: Deepwater harbor bisecting part of Almaris.

Commanding Stone: Device of power used by an Atalarin to control the Nahalreng to wage the Doomwar.

Common Age: Era in which Gerin is born. The eras of the world are: the Forgotten Years, the Dark Age, the Dawn Age, the Imperial Age, and the Common Age.

compulsion: Powerful magic that can force a person to act against his will.

conclave: A formal gathering of wizards during which unique knowledge is shared.

Council of Barons: Group empowered to sit in judgment over certain matters of law in Khedesh.

Cregael-Thelakor (*Kre-gay'il Thel'-ah-kor*): Twin castles located between Agdenor and Ailethon.

Death of a Son: Statue in Hethnost showing a father carrying his son's corpse.

Delgo Nerat Igrulun (*Del'-go Nair'-at Ig'-roo-loon*): A Neddari, Chieftain of Clan Térutheg and Overchieftan and Warlord of the army of the God Who Has Returned.

Demos Thelar (*Dem'-ohs Thay'-lar*): Wizard who created the *methlenel* and *awaenjir,* and devised the Rituals of Discovery and Awakenings, among other accomplishments. Considered one of the greatest wizards who ever lived.

dera (*dare'-ah*): Khedeshian silver coin.

Derasdi Tower (*Der-ahz'-dee*): A tower within Hethnost.

Dian's Stair (*Dee'-in*): A stairway carved into the face of the Sundering, south of the Falls of the Samaro.

Doomwar: Vast conflict that ended the Age of the Atalari. It was begun by an Atalarin who used the Commanding Stone to wage war against the Atalari nation and Gendalos kingdoms. It raged for years and ended in the Last Battle.

drogasaar (*droh'-gah-sar*): Creatures indigenous to Neddar and Hunzar that can be taught to speak and understand basic commands. They often use two scimitars at once when in battle. They have powerful legs that propel them at great speeds and enable them to make long leaps. They have bat-shaped heads, and their bodies are covered in a coarse fur.

Eglimond (*Eg'-lih-mond*): The keep of Cregael.

Ekalé Lavaraelios (*Ee'-ka-lay Lava-ray'-lee-ohs*): "The Book of Creation." Khedeshian holy book that recounts the creation of the gods, world, and men.

elementals: Beings of spirit that can be summoned by *kamichis* for brief periods of time. The touch of an elemental is caustic and usually fatal. They cannot be harmed by mortal weapons.

Eletheros (*El-eh-thair'-ohs*): the People of Theros, a race who warred with the Atalari in the distant past.

Emunial (*Em-yoo-nigh'-al*): Female Atalari, leader of the first tribes to enter Osseria.

Eredhel Anyakul (*Air'-ed-hel An'-yah-kool*): Wizard who sculpted *Death of a Son.*

Evrosúlar (*Ev-roh-soo'-lar*): A Neddari clan.

Farseeing: A spell that allows a wizard to see across large distances.

Field of Nenweil (*Nen'-way-il*): Large gathering field outside of the Okoro Gate.

Fierel's Fire (*Fee-air'-il*): Resinous compound composed of sulfur, quicklime, naphtha, and several other substances.

First Siege: One of the rulers of Hethnost, second-in-command behind the Archmage.

Flestos (*Fles'-tohs*): The war horn of Miendrel.

Forbidding: A powerful magical shield.

Foretelling: A wizard's dream or vision of the future. Foretellings are not spells that can be worked by any wizard—through the ages, the ability has been rare. It is thought that Foretellings show what may occur, rather than what will occur.

garron (*gare'-on*): Khedeshian gold coin.

Gate of the Gray Woman: The main gate of Ailethon, named for the figure of a hooded woman set into the steel.

Gendalos (*gen-dah'-lohs*): "Short-lived." Osirin word, somewhat pejorative, for races that do not possess magic.

Genshel Gate (*Gen'-shel*): Gate into the inner bailey of Ailethon.

Gerin Atreyano (*Gare'-in At-ray-ahn'-oh*): Crown Prince of Khedesh, eldest child of Abran Atreyano.

Ghesevaras (*Ges-eh-var'-as*): Unclaimed region of southern Osseria extending from the western border of Khedesh to the Gap of Ellohar.

Glamour: Magic that can create the illusion of an altered appearance.

Glaros (*Glar'-ohs*): Gerin's sword.

Gray Wall: Neddari name for the Sundering.

Hakán (*Ha-kahn'*): Language of the Neddari, now used mostly by the *kamichis* in their ceremonies.

Hammdras (*Hahm'-dras*): Wall enclosing the Valley of Wizards.

Helca (*Hel'-ka*): The Conqueror. King of Melnon (later Helcarea) who launched the Wars of Unification and created an empire that controlled nearly all of Osseria.

Henly's Hill (*Hen'-lee*): Hill upon which Castle Agdenor is built.

Heralds of Truth: Those sworn to the service of the Storm King.

Hethnost (*Heth'-nost*): Fortress-city in the Redhorn Hills, home of most of the remaining wizards in Osseria.

Hodetten (*Ho-det'-ten*): The language of Khedesh before the Imperial Age. Hodetten is rarely spoken anymore, though many of its words have been incorporated into Kelarin.

Hollin Lotheg (*Hol'-lin Loh'-theg*): Wizard of Hethnost.

Holly Bridge: Bridge crossing the Samaro River near Castle Agdenor.

Horn of Calling: Red Robes' name for the Horn of Tireon.

Horn of Tireon (*Teer'-ee-on*): A device of magic designed to weaken the barrier between the worlds of the living and the dead.

hronu (*hron'-oo*): "Aura" in Osirin, describing the radiance of fire that engulfs a wizard if enough magic flows through his body.

Hurother (*Hew-row'-ther*): Therain's squire.

Ireon's Hill (*Eer'-ee-on*): Hill upon which Castle Ailethon is built.

kahladen (*kah'-lah-den*): Type of tree held sacred by wizards. Drops of water that sometimes form on the trunk are called Wizard's Tears and are believed by some to be the source of powerful love potions.

Kalabrendis Dhosa (*Kal-ah-bren'-dis Doh'-sah*): The great meeting hall in Hethnost, where conclaves are held.

Kalóros (*Kal-or'-ohs*): Pine woods located in Neddar.

kamichi (*ka-mee'-chee*): A Neddari sorcerer-priest.

Kelarin (*Kel-ar'-in*): Common speech of Osseria, adopted by Helca in the Imperial Age to help unify his empire.

Khedesh: Kingdom of southern Osseria. Also the name of the founder of the kingdom.

Kilnathé River (*Kil-nath'-ee*): Small river flowing past Ailethon.

King Olam's Road (*Oh'-lam*): Long east-west road stretching from Ailethon to Almaris. Originally a trade route, it was enlarged during the reign of the Helcarean Empire to better accommodate troop movements.

kisurwa (*kih-sur'-wah*): Mystical tattoos given to Neddari *nigromus* upon their first successful return from the World That Is Above.

Kotireon Guards (*Koh-teer'-ee-on*): Elite soldiers charged with protecting members of the royal family.

Kynsleri (*Kin-slair'-ee*): A massive fortified tower set in th[...] of Sarod's High Fence.

Laikari Reás (*Lay-ih-kar'-ee Ree'-as*): The high, flat-topped hill upon which the western half of Cregael-Thelakor is built.

Last Battle: The final engagement of the Doomwar, in which the Atalari unleashed a power called the Unmaking to destroy the Nahalreng and their master.

Lokuras (*Loh-kyur'-as*): A Neddari god, twin of Panndri. Together they rule the Long Night, a void of eternal darkness that the *kamichis* believe is the source of their powers. The Twins are the spirit masters of the *kamichi*.

Lores Darethil (*Lore'-es Dar'-eh-thil*): A region of Khedesh.

magefire: Unformed magic that can be used to create light, either as a naked flame or contained within a crystal lamp.

Maratheon's Hill (*Mar-ah-thee'-on*): Tallest hill on the eastern side of the Valley of Wizards.

Marren's Ferry (*Mar'-ren*): A town near Ailethon.

Merel (*Mare'-el*): One of the Twins, gods of Khedesh. Her brother is Volraneth, and together they are charged with lighting the stars each night and keeping the sun and moon on their courses.

Merrenthal (*Mare'-ren-thal*): Fortified town east of Castle Agdenor.

methlenel (*meth'-leh-nel*): "Truth's Light," device of magic used by wizards in the Ritual of Discovery to locate potential wizards.

Miendrel (*My'-en-drel*): The Khedeshian god of war. When he sounds his horn Flestos, it means many will die.

Mirdan ne'Cuimaras (Meer'-dan neh Kyoo-ih-mar'-as): "Tower of the Clouds," a hilltop guard tower flanking the entrance to the Valley of Wizards.

Mirdan ne'Keleth (*Meer'-dan neh Kel'-eth*): "Tower of Wind," a hilltop guard tower flanking the entrance to the Valley of Wizards.

Molok (*Mol'-ok*): One of the Hounds of Shayphim.

Naege (*Nayg*): Massive ringed fortress in Almaris where Taeratens are trained.

Naevos (*Nay'-vohs*): City on the western border of Khedesh.

nahalreng (*nah'-hal-reng*): "Fire-beasts" in Osirin, great winged beasts from beyond the southern borders of Osseria who were controlled by the Commanding Stone during the Doomwar. In Kelarin they are remembered as dragons.

Nanjelkir (*Nan'-jel-keer*): Asankaru's chief war priest.

Naragenth ul-Darhel (*Nare'ah-genth ool-Dar'-hel*): The first amber wizard, killed during the Wars of Unification.

Neck of the Samaro (*Sah-mar'-oh*): Section of the river where it flows through a narrow gorge, a short distance east of the falls.

Neddari (*Ned-dar'-ee*): Warrior society ruled by various clan chieftains.

Neldemarien (*Nel-de-mare'-ee-en*): Region of Khedesh famous for its wool.

Niélas (*Ny'-eh-las*): The wife of Paérendras, to whom sailors pray during storms to calm the anger of her husband.

nirgromu (*neér-groh'-moo*): An apprentice of a *kamichi* who has ventured into the spirit realm known as the World That Is Above.

Okoro Gate (*Oh-kor'-oh*): Large western gate in the wall around Almaris.

Olassa (*Oh-las'-sah*): Spouse of Telros, the goddess of spring and all growing things.

Olgren-na-Pugúlo (*Ol'-gren na Poo-gyoo'-loh*): Lake in Neddar.

Order of Laonn (*Lay'-on*): Group of philosophers and teachers whose chapter house is in Almaris. Many of their members are sent out to teach the sons and daughters of the nobleborn.

Osirin (*Oh-seer'-in*): The language of magic. It was once the native tongue of the Atalari.

Ossland Plains (*Os'-land*): Region of Khedesh.

pacca trees (*pak'-ah*): Slender, smooth-barked trees that in Khedesh are planted as memorials to the dead.

Padesh (*Pah'-desh*): Walled town near Ailethon.

Paérendras (*Pay-air'-en-dras*): The sea god of Khedesh.

Paladin's Tower (*Pal'-ah-din*): Tallest tower in Ailethon. An observatory was once housed in its summit.

Panndri (*Pan'-dree*): A Neddari god, twin of Lokuras. Together they rule the Long Night, a void of eternal darkness that the *kamichis* believe is the source of their powers. The Twins are the spirit masters of the *kamichi*.

Parglati Qesh (*Par-glah'-tee Kesh*): High hill upon which Ziren-Billek is built.

paru'enthred (*par'-oo en'-thred*): "Inner eye" in Osirin, describing the ability of wizards to focus and shape the flow of magic through their bodies.

Pashti (*Pash'-tee*): Indigenous people of southern Osseria, conquered by Khedesh and his Raimen when they came to the southlands. They are now mostly a servant-class in the kingdom.

Pelkland (*Pelk'-land*): Island kingdom in the Maurelian Sea, off the coast of Khedesh.

People of Theros (*Thair'-ohs*): The Eletheros.

plansa **wood** (*plahn'-sah*): Trees from the far south of Neddar with roots so deep they are said to reach to the center of the world. They are used in many *kamichi* rituals and considered to be sacred.

Red Robes: Khedeshian name for Asankaru's war priests.

Redhorn Hills: Line of hills running east from the Graymantle Mountains. Hethnost is built in a valley on the hills' southern side.

Releasing Fire: Spell used by wizards to cremate the bodies of their dead.

Rengel (*Ren'-gel*): A town near Castle Agdenor.

Reshel Atreyano (*Re-shel' At-ray-ahn'-oh*): Princess of Khedesh, youngest child of Abran Atreyano.

Sarod's High Fence (*Sar'-od*): A curtain wall that joins the two castles that comprise Cregael-Thelakor.

Shatani Zahamburrik (*Shan-tahn'-ee Za-ham-bur'-ik*): An Archmage of Hethnost who planted one of the *kahladen* trees within the fortress.

Shayphim (*Shay'-fim*): Demonic figure of evil who is said to roam the southlands of Osseria with his Hounds Venga and Molok. He searches for wayward men and women whose spirits he captures and deposits in the Cauldron of Souls, where they are trapped forever, cut off from the light of the gods and unable to enter Velyol. The saying, "To Shayphim with him!" or "Shayphim take him!" is a curse that the dead will be denied the afterlife with the gods.

sheffain (*shef'-fayn*): A spirit being that can be summoned to this world by wizards. They are extremely dangerous and must be confined within powerful Wards.

Sherenna (*Sheh-ren'-nah*): The wife of Bellon. She greets the dead when they enter through Velyol's gates.

Shining Nation: Name of the Atalari's kingdom.

Slain God: A Neddari deity who was believed to have died long ago in battle against the Dark Ones. The *kamichi* teach that he will one day return to lead the Neddari to victory over their enemies.

Storm King: One of Asankaru's titles.

Sundering: Massive cliff extending in a long bow-shaped curve from southern Ghesevaras into Neddar. The Samaro River creates a waterfall at the cliff's midpoint.

Sunlight Hall: Large audience hall in Ailethon, with tall stained-glass windows along one wall.

Sunrise Guard: The mortal soldiers who guard Hethnost.

Suvendis (*Soo-ven'-dis*): Prince Teluko's chief war priest.

Taeraten (*Tare'-ah-ten*): Elite fighter of Khedesh, marked with circle-within-a-circle tattoos on the backs of their hands. They are trained in the fortress of the Naege in Almaris.

Tageluron (*Tah-gel'-yoor-on*): One of Asankaru's war priests.

Tanshe-Arat (*Tan'-shee Air'-at*): The Home-in-Exile of the Eletheros. A city built after they were driven from the north of Osseria by the Atalari.

Telir Osáran (*Tel-eer' Oh-sar'-ran*): "Valley of Wizards," Osirin name for the valley in which Hethnost is located.

Telros (*Tel'-rohs*): Chief god of the Khedeshian pantheon.

Teluko (*Tel-oo'-koh*): Younger brother of Asankaru.

Terokesh (*Ter'-oh-kesh*): Region of Khedesh inhabited by many Pashti.

Térutheg (*Tare'-oo-theg*): One of the Neddari clans.

tevi (*tev'-ee*): Neddari title for their warlord.

Therain Atreyano (*The-rain' At-ray-ahn'-oh*) : Prince of Khedesh, twin to Claressa.

Theros (*Thair'-ohs*): the Lord Father of the People of Theros. He united the Nine Clans of the Prenvi earth-dwellers and forged a single kingdom from them.

Thorn: The keep of Castle Agdenor.

Thorn Hill: A town near Castle Ailethon.

Threndish (*Thren'-dish*): The people of Threndellen, a kingdom to the north of Khedesh.

Tikomei Ruwan (*Tee'-koh-mee-ih Roo'-wan*): A region of Neddar near the border of Khedesh.

Tireon al-Vashkiril (*Teer'-ee-on al Vash-keer'-il*): A member of the Baryashin Order and maker of the Horn of Tireon.

Tivar Lhasaril (*Tee'-var Las'-ah-ril*): "Lake of Dreaming," a lake within the Hammdras of Hethnost. Also the name of a secret underground lake that can give prophetic dreams.

Tower of Cregael (*Kre-gay'il*): Tower into which the western end of Sarod's High Fence is anchored.

Tower of Thelakor (*Thel'-ah-kor*): Tower into which the eastern end of Sarod's High Fence is anchored.

Trelheton (*Trel-het'-on*): A rugged, woody region of Khedesh.

Unmaking: A singular power unleashed by the Atalari during the Last Battle of the Doomwar to destroy the Nahalreng and their master. The Unmaking was so powerful that it destroyed the Atalari as well.

Unseeing: A spell that negates the ability of an observer to take note of someone or something encased within it.

Urgden Zeya Maldrúlu (*Urg'-den Zee'-ya Mal-droo'-loo*): A Neddari *kamichi* who discovered the World That Is Above.

Vacarandi (*Vak-ah-rahn'dee*): Capital of the Atalari Shining Nation, rumored to have been the most beautiful city in the world.

Vanya Atreyano (*Vahn'-yah At-ray-ahn'-oh*): Gerin's mother, who died of a wasting disease.

Varsae Estrikavis (*Var'-say Es-trih-ka'-vis*): Legendary Library of Naragenth, whose location was lost when Naragenth was killed during the Wars of Unification.

Varsae Sandrova (*Var'-say San-droh'-vah*): The library of Hethnost.

Veilos Tirban: Mortal man who designed and oversaw the construction of Hethnost.

Velarien Harres: The castellan of Castle Agdenor.

Vendel Atreyano (*Ven'-del At-ray-ahn'-oh*): Founder of the Atreyano royal line.

Venegreh (*Ven'-eh-grey*): Wizard who founded Hethnost.

Venga (*Ven'-ga*): One of the Hounds of Shayphim.

vesai (*ves-eye'*): Honorific for wizards, no longer used outside of Hethnost.

Volraneth (*Vol-ran'-eth*): One of the Twin gods of Khedesh. His sister is Merel, and together they are charged with lighting the stars each night and keeping the sun and moon on their courses.

Ward: A magical shield.

weirstones (*weer'-stones*): Magical artifacts designed to contain a spirit summoned from the world of the dead.

witchwood: Enchanted wood used by the Eletheros war priests to channel their powers.

World That Is Above: A spirit world that can be accessed by Neddari *kamichis,* from which they draw elementals into this world.

yavas (*yahv'-as*): "Taint" or "stain" in Osirin.

Ziren-Bellek (*Zeer'-en Bel'-ek*): Large wooden hall in Neddar where clans meet to resolve issues between them.